Hot Mess

summer in the city

JULIE KRAUT & SHALLON LESTER

Hot Mess

summer in the city

Delacorte Press

Published by Delacorte Press
an imprint of Random House Children's Books
a division of Random House, Inc.
New York

Visit us on the Web! www.randomhouse.com/teens

Educators and librarians, for a variety of teaching tools, visit us at
www.randomhouse.com/teachers

Library of Congress Cataloging-in-Publication Data
Kraut, Julie.
Hot mess : summer in the city / Julie Kraut & Shallon Lester. — 1st ed.
p. cm.
Summary: To escape a bad breakup in Bridgefield, New York, almost-eighteen-
year-old Emma takes a summer internship in New York City where she, her best
friend, and their rich, sophisticated landlady face a series of dating disasters.
ISBN 978-0-385-73506-3 (hardcover) — ISBN 978-0-385-90499-5
(Gibraltar lib. bdg.)
[1. Dating (Social customs)—Fiction. 2. Internship programs—Fiction. 3. Best
friends—Fiction. 4. Friendship—Fiction. 5. New York (N.Y.)—Fiction.]
I. Lester, Shallon. II. Title.
PZ7.K8753Hot 2008
[Fic]—dc22
2007034793

The text of this book is set in 11-point Goudy.

Book design by Angela Carlino

Printed in the United States of America

10 9 8 7 6 5 4 3 2 1

First Edition

To my parents for always being totally supportive and totally embarrassing. I love you guys.   —J.K.

To Mama, the hero down the hall. To Gigi, the late bloomer. And to all the girls who trust their dreams more than they doubt them—be brave, fortune favors the bold.   —S.L.

One

Rachel, Kyle, and I rocked up to El Shack del Tacos straight from seventh period. My boyfriend, Brian, and his posse had been there for hours. This was their last day of high school *ever*, and they'd commemorated it by ditching, which didn't make sense to me. Because then yesterday was their last day. Whatever, I always tried to be fun, cool girlfriend and not logical, naggy girlfriend, so I didn't mention it.

Brian's posse was really tight. They were all a year older than Rachel, Kyle, and me, and always reminding us of it. They call themselves "The Hombres." I know—eye-roll central.

I was sitting next to Bri, who was dressed in the typical Hombre uniform: khakis and a lame slogan tee. Today's read "I Like Girls Who Like Girls." What can I say? That's my boy! Captain Classy. We'd been together for nine months officially and, I guess unofficially, ten and a half, and I couldn't believe he was leaving at the end of the summer. Sure, he'd only be two hours away in Albany, but I knew things were going to be different between us. The *official* plan was to stay together. My plan was to savor this summer and hope for the best when he packed up and headed off to college in the fall.

Luckily, we were both going to be lifeguarding at the swim club this summer, so we'd be able to hang out between adult swim and kids crapping the pool. My parents were really pushing this "summer internship in New York" idea for a while. One of Mom's "Golf Gals!"—that's what they call themselves. Yes, with the exclamation point. And no, not to be funny, either—said that she could set me up with some kind of internship at a branch of her company in New York. And I have to admit, a summer of pink drinks and high heels in Manhattan would have been pretty awesome, but I decided to stick with my chlorine-and-flip-flops summer here in Bridgefield. New York was always going to be New York, and I could go there another summer. But who knew with Brian? I kind of wanted to carpe diem while the diem was good with him. Pathetic or romantic? I couldn't decide.

I looked over at Rachel, who was all up on Warren, her apparent crush of the moment, sitting on his lap and feeding him taquitos. And poor Mister Sister Kyle, as always, was just kind of lingering around the periphery of The Hombre bunch, twisting his kabbalah bracelet uncomfortably. I knew he didn't like Brian or The Hombres—they didn't exactly follow Perez Hilton the way he did—but he sometimes pretended to for my sake. Not today, though. I heard him sigh loudly and then mumble something to Rachel about asphyxiating on all the testosterone. She looked at me and twirled her finger around in the air. I nodded back and reached for my bag. The finger twirl was our code that it was time to leave. Rachel's uncle taught it to her. It was some military sign that meant start up the choppers . . . or missiles are coming or something. Whatever—it worked. Surprisingly, Bri took a last gulp from his soda and announced that he was going to leave with us.

"Rach, you think you're gonna have enough room for me?" Brian asked between belches. "I ate an extra taco. I'm feeling a little bigger than usual."

We all laughed at the thought of Rachel's battleship-sized car. The girl drove a bona fide mom-mobile station wagon, complete with a "Bridgefield Elementary Super Speller" bumper sticker. The thing was so huge, it pretty much had its own zip code. I was jealous that she had a car at all, but it wasn't exactly the Nissan Z she was hoping for on her Sweet Sixteen.

Kyle hopped in front with Rachel and I scooted next to my still-belching bf in the back. As she turned the key to start up the bus, "Ring of Fire" blared from her speakers and we sped off, going at least twenty miles above the speed limit, as usual. Rachel tried to compensate for the fact that she drove a covered wagon by going 120 miles per hour on Ridgeline Drive.

"Lady, it's two-forty-five *p.m.*, not a.m. We're not late for curfew or anything. Slow down before we turn into a driver's ed cautionary tale."

3

"Fine, Emma," Rachel snapped at me, and rolled her eyes, slowing down by about four miles per hour. I still felt like I was on the Bezerker.

"Honey, will you do something about this music, *puhleeze*." Even Kyle's whines were sassy. "I need to be celebrating the last day of junior year. This shit would make my Latin oral exam sound like music. I need to work this out, bitch!" He did his signature body wave. It totally didn't go with the Johnny Cash blasting out of the speakers.

Rachel slapped his hand as he reached down to find another song on her playlist. "Don't you dare, Ky. Johnny Cash stays on. I'm doing research."

"On what, Professor Wolfe? How long it takes before country music will make a brother's ears bleed?" Unless Kyle was talking to one of his siblings, he surely was not a brother. Yes, he was darker than Rachel and I were, but that had more to do with self-tanner than minority status. And Lancôme Flash Bronzer does not a black man make.

"According to Danny's MySpace page, Johnny Cash is now his favorite artist," she said matter-of-factly. "By the time we're on the bus up to camp together, I'll be a total expert." She turned up "Folsom Prison Blues" and pretended to sing along, but I'm pretty sure "Get this party started" isn't part of the lyrics.

She was what some would fondly call "boy crazy" and others would not-so-fondly call "stone cold psycho." Either way, Rachel Wolfe was a seventeen-year-old on a mission to find a boyfriend. And "tall, dark, and handsome" were not on the checklist for her ideal mate. "Funny, intelligent, and rich" were missing, too. But "bar mitzvahed, circumcised, and from a nice family?" Check, check, and check!

4

She was on the warpath to find a nice Jewish boy and she'd already exhausted all of the Semitic studs in Bridgefield. Well, to be fair, there was only one barely popular-enough Jewish male in our class, Josh Kleinman. After two weeks of dating him last year, she was already talking about marriage and the theme of their kids' bar and bat mitzvahs—*Casino Royale* for a boy and *Hollywood Lights* for a girl. Needless to say, he dumped her. She totally didn't get what scared him off.

Anyway, Jewish summer camp was where my girl really shined. For eight weeks each summer, my best friend abandoned me in Boringsville suburbia and hauled her bugsprayed butt over to the Pocono Mountains to be a counselor at Camp Oakmere. There, she basked in sunshine, Popsiclestick crafts, and the groping hands of nice Jewish boys. And that's where Danny Steinberg, the boy she was researching/stalking, was waiting for her.

"Why don't you stalk him in some quieter way? Like something that wouldn't subject your best friends to this god-awful country music? I mean, is this off the *Red Neck Funeral Favorites* album or something? Read his favorite book, for God sakes!" Whine on, Ky, whine on.

"He doesn't have any books listed," she said, like there was no shame in Internet stalking. Then again, maybe there wasn't.

"Stop being such a little bitch about this," Brian yelled way too harshly at Kyle. "It's a classic."

"Thank you, Brian!" a vindicated Rachel said, smiling at him in the rearview mirror.

So we listened to the symphony of Johnny Cash and Kyle's wails of agony all the way to Brian's place.

"So, what's up for tomorrow?" Rachel asked as we pulled into his driveway. Brian climbed out of the car and bounded up to the house to give us—and Kyle—time to chick-chat.

I leaned forward between the massive seats. "Well, I'm going to wake up early and say goodbye to Brian. He's going to that freshman orientation thing in the morning. So I'll be free later. Want to lie out in my backyard?"

Rachel nodded. "I'm so there. I need to get rid of these tan lines before camp."

"What? Did Danny list tan lines under turnoffs on Facebook?" Kyle has more sass than Pete Wentz has eyeliner.

I rolled my eyes and hopped out of the car, closing the door on Rachel hissing, "Shut up! He actually has 'bitchy men who wear too much foundation' under turnoffs!" and hustled up the driveway and into Bri's. Neither of them noticed when I turned to wave goodbye.

Brian's door was unlocked, as usual. That's what a Snoozeville this town is. No crime, even when we're asking for it.

"Brian?" I said as I stepped into the empty foyer.

"Yo, I'm up here."

I followed his voice up the stairs and found him lying on his bed, shuffling through his iTunes. I nestled myself next to him and he closed his laptop. As he was putting the computer on his nightstand, my arms found their way around him. This was my favorite way to be with Brian: one hand on his six-pack, the other smooshed between the arch of his back and the bed, enjoying the electric seconds just before a long kiss.

"Emmy babe, I love you."

It was moments like this when I didn't know how I was

going to make it without him every day. I loved him. Well, I was like ninety-four percent sure it was love. And yeah, I was pretty sure that he wasn't The One. I mean, I knew he'd never grow beyond a *Superbad*-quoting, *Madden*-obsessed, *high school* boyfriend. But to throw away ten and a half months? That was longer than most Hollywood marriages. I couldn't imagine life without him. Who'd take me home from parties when I turned into a pukey, weepy mess next year? Who'd be my date to homecoming? And who'd act like he had a secret to tell and then when I came in close, burp in my face?

"I love you, too," I said back to him.

As I craned my neck up to kiss him, we felt the rumble of the garage door opening.

"Crap," he growled.

His mother was home from work. We quickly positioned ourselves in our typical "We're not having teenaged sex under your roof" pose—sitting on opposite sides of the bed staring at a textbook. It was only after Mrs. McSwain had already poked her head in to say hello that I realized how stupid we looked.

"Happy summer, guys! Oh, my big guy is all grown up," she sing-songed. "How was the last day?"

In unison, "Good."

"Well, that's nice. Whatcha up to now?"

"Nothing, Mom, just studying," he said automatically. Oh, nice one, Bri. Studying on the first day of summer? "Fending off alien attacks" would have been more believable.

Mrs. McSwain either didn't care or just chose to ignore it. "You staying for dinner, Em? I'm going to try and do something fun with the ziti from last night."

"Um, sure, Geri Anne. Thanks." I always felt weird calling Brian's mom by her first name, but after months of her insisting, I finally gave in. Maybe I wouldn't feel so weird if her name weren't Geri Anne.

Once the door closed behind her, he pulled me close again and I rested my head on his chest.

"Em, it's going to be so sweet in a few months when I have my own place and we don't have to worry about parents and shit." Brian flashed that open-mouth smile that kind of made him look like a mouth breather. But a totally cute mouth breather.

"Your own place? Didn't you sign up to live with a roommate?"

"Well, yeah. But in college, you just hang a sock on the door and boom—sexapalooza!"

"Real romantic, babe." I laughed and he pulled me in for a noogie.

Two

"Em, hand me the tanning oil, will you?"

I groped around without opening my eyes until I found the bottle under my lounge chair. I passed it Rachel's way.

"Uck, I had no idea I was this pale, Emma, seriously. I look like a piece of paper. Someone's going to try to write an essay on my— *Ahh! Omigod omigod!*"

I ripped my sunglasses off to see Rachel flapping her arms hysterically, covered in blood.

"Omigod, Rachel, you're bleeding!" I mentally ran through how to do CPR. I'd taken a class for the lifeguard job, but I couldn't remember any of it right now. Not like it would help with bleeding appendages, though.

"I'm not bleeding, you idiot. I'm covered in fucking taco sauce!"

I'd accidentally handed her the bottle of picante we'd poured over our midafternoon nachos. I laughed with relief as she kicked and screeched for help.

"Will you please do something? I don't want to ruin my towel. It's the only one that matches this suit!"

"Well," I said, passing her my used napkin, "I could get Ajax out here to lick it off! Jaxy! C'mere, boy!"

My half-ton Newfoundland came loping into the backyard, leaving a trail of slobber in his wake.

"Gross! I'm not Jenna freaking Jameson!" she yelped with disgust as she dabbed herself off.

I put my earphones back in, waiting for her to calm down. Normally she's really mellow, but every once in a while Rachel has a shit fit that makes Naomi Campbell look like a Sunday school teacher. I think it's because she's an only child. Everyone says people without siblings are selfish, but that's not true. Rachel is the most generous person. She'd give her Chihuahua a kidney if it needed it.

"Hey, have you heard from Brian yet?" she asked, after she finished desaucifying herself. "How's the orientation going?"

I realized with a stab of alarm that no, I hadn't. "Uh, no. Not really." I bit my lip nervously, and then quickly added, "But he's probably just busy." What could he possibly be doing? "He'll call by dinnertime, right?" He *said* he'd call me as soon as he got to campus. That must have been six hours ago. I felt one of my nausea-inducing panic waves hit me.

"Em, don't stress. He so will." She sounded like she meant it, but I couldn't really see her eyes. She was still wearing her faux Diors, even though the sun was pretty much gone. The shades were a purchase made at the Boca flea market while visiting her grandparents in their retirement community. Ky and I call them the Velveteen Sunglasses because she acted like if she loved them enough, one day they just might turn into real live Diors.

"Really, stop the freak-out," Rachel commanded. "Let's think about something way more important, okay? You only have a few more days until you're the big one-eight! We still haven't planned anything. We're not leaving these lounges until we figure it out."

"Uck, I don't know. I don't even want to think about it." My birthdays were never something I was happy about. Wait, no—I was always amped for them, but then they always turned into a disaster. Like in second grade, when I had the bowling party and little Rachel dropped nine pounds of bowling ball on her foot, broke all her metatarsals, and had to go to the hospital. Even back then, a party just wasn't a party without my bestie, and I was miserable for the last eight frames. I saved her all of the butter cream flowers from my birthday cake, and we spent the rest of my birthday together dipping fingers into frosting roses in the ER while her cast set. And then there was my first boy-girl party in sixth grade, where I caught Paul Wechter—my boyfriend at the time—making out with Lexi Brown in the laundry room, and we hadn't even made out yet. Totally traumatic at the time, but I guess it doesn't matter now because Lexi got sent away to boarding school and Paul turned into one of those weird goth kids that draws red tears on his face with a Sharpie and smokes in front of Burger King at lunch. They're even at Burger King every day during the summer, puffing away and partaking in group misery. Anyway, the point is that I normally build up my birthday so much and it turns out to be the worst day of the year. But I *was* turning eighteen this year, so despite a lackluster track record, I had to do something cool.

"Oooh! I know, get everyone to go to Wild Waters and have a big pool party. They just put in that new slide, too. It's supposed to be sick."

I wrinkled my nose. "A water park? Rachel, I'm becoming an adult, I don't want to be in a urine-y wave pool surrounded by thirteen-year-old boys. Besides, didn't someone break their nose there last summer on that twisty slide thing? That's the last thing I need: 'Welcome to adulthood, here's a nose job!' We could go dancing?"

I knew that was a stupid idea as soon as I said it. I danced like a donkey on Rollerblades and Rachel was even worse. The only thing she knew about rhythm was based on Dance Dance Revolution. And a girl who danced in a perfect square faster and faster just made everyone uncomfortable.

"Um." Rachel absentmindedly rubbed on more SPF 4. "Oh! We'll make Jackie take her dad's party boat out on the lake and have a booze cruise! No parents, we'll just float around all day and tan and get drunk."

The idea of cutting loose and splashing around with my friends for eight hours was definitely appealing but . . .

"Isn't that illegal? Like, that's considered drunk driving. I really don't need a DUI on my permanent record the very day I become a legal adult. Besides, my parents would so not dig that, and I doubt that we'd even be able to get alcohol. I feel like everyone with fakes is going to be away the entire summer."

The two of us sat there, reapplying tanning oil and stressing over my birthday until all the good sunlight was gone.

"Hey, wanna stay for dinner?" I asked Rachel as she examined the spot on her hip where she was going to get a tattoo—wings or a bat or something lame—the second she turned eighteen. "Kyle's coming over."

"Sure, let me just call the mom. Dammit, I never get the sides of my body tan. I look like an Oreo."

We retied our tops, balled up our towels, and trekked across the lawn. Between the grease of the tanning oil and balancing the dirty plates and Nalgenes we were carrying, opening the sliding door that led to the kitchen was going to be a Herculean feat.

"Yo, Beyoncé, put that booty to use." I motioned with my head to the door. The technical term for Rach's body was "smokin'." She had 34Ds and a perfectly curvy size 6 bottom to match. She complained that she couldn't run without her tatas giving her black eyes, but I'd totally trade my entire soccer career to get rid of my chest of rib bones.

"The preferred nomenclature is *ba-dunk-a-dunk*," she said as she shook her hips.

"Hips don't lie!" I laughed and tried a shake of my own, but just looked like I was having a seizure.

Still balancing her nacho plate, towel, and water bottle, she gingerly hoisted her butt up to the door handle and pushed it open.

We slammed our dishes into the washer and tossed our towels over the banister to dry.

"First shower!" she hollered, bounding up the stairs. I glared at her for calling dibs in my house. "What? I'm covered in a sweat-and-hot-sauce compote. Give me a break."

"Fine, go." Actually, I was glad to be alone for a sec. I reached for my cell and speed-dialed "My Guy Bri." Sometimes I even can lame-out myself. Five rings and then voicemail.

"Hey, baby doll! It's Emma, your girlfriend, remember me? Just in case you don't, I'm that girl back in Bridgefield with big blond hair, boobs like watermelons, tramp-stamp tattoo, and legs longer than *The Shawshank Redemption*. Or green eyes, brown hair, and legs, two of them. Anyway, just wondering how you're doing with your first taste of college. I miss you. Call me, 'kay?"

Was I being screened by my own bf? I brushed away the thought. It was probably too loud at dorm orientation or whatever and he couldn't hear his phone. So I did what any sort-of-crazy girlfriend would do. I sent him a text.

Hope ur having fun, Mr. College. Miss n luv u. Call when u can.

There, I'd be hearing back from him in nanoseconds.

Just then, Rachel came dripping into my room. "It's all yours. Oh, and I kind of used the last of your leave-in."

Sometimes I wished she weren't quite so comfortable with me.

"Whatever," I sighed, and jumped up. "Watch my phone. Bri's probably going to call. Pick up if he does, 'kay? I'll just be a hot minute in the shower."

"Okay, I'm borrowing some stuff." Rachel was already pawing through my underwear selection.

It was the fastest shower of my life, helped a little by the fact that I had no more conditioner, thank you very much, Rachel. I rushed back into my room still sopping. "Did Brian call?"

"What?" She was dressed in my favorite velours with her hair in a high wet knot, engrossed in whatever website she was looking at.

"Brian, did he call?"

"Oh, no. Come here. Is this girl a squirrel-faced slutbag or what?" She was pointing to the most recent comment on Danny Steinberg's MySpace page.

"How do you know that's not his sister or something?"

"Would a sister post about how awesome his profile song is? I mean, it's him trying to play "The Black Parade" on guitar and singing like a dying cat. Listen to this shit." She cranked up the volume on my crappy laptop speakers and it sounded like a prepubescent deaf Gerard Way singing in falsetto.

I shot Rachel a look of pain. "Yeah, total slut."

I heard knocks on the door and Kyle's screech. "It's me!"

"Come in," Rachel yelled. I was still in my towel, but it was just Kyle. While Rachel toured him through the highlights of Danny's newest MySpace updates, I texted Brian again.

Helloooo! Where are you?

I got dressed in matching sweats and kissed our testosterone sister on the cheek as he weighed in on the squirrel-faced slutbag. "Yeah, she's a sea donkey. Telling him that screamo shit is good? She's totally trying to get some boo-tay."

"Ladies." I interrupted their MyStalking, standing hands on hips in the middle of my room. "Brian was supposed to call me hours ago. I just called him and texted him twice and he still hasn't called me back. What the hell is he doing?"

"Girl, you know *what* he's doing. You just don't know with whom!" Kyle sassed. Normally, I loved his honesty—he steered me away from the gaucho pants trend and from trying to pop-n-lock at homecoming—but sometimes I needed some sugarcoating.

"Kyle!" Rachel snapped. "Don't say that to her! He's probably just busy, honey. You know, picking classes and stuff."

Visions of Gamma Phi Whatevers with paddles and beer bongs and no curfews danced in my head. "That's it. I'm calling him again."

Rachel and Kyle lunged for my cell but I beat them to it and bolted into the hallway while I dialed. They didn't need to hear the whiney girlfriend hissy I was going to throw when Brian picked up.

"Hell-oooooo?" a girl chirped. I froze.

"Brian," I eventually croaked out. "Is Brian there?"

"Oh, he's . . ." She giggled. "Well, let's just say he's 'tied up' at the moment." And she erupted into peals of drunken laughter. "Who is this anyway? His sister?"

"This is his girlfriend!" I hissed through clenched teeth.

"Oh yeah. I think Brian mentioned you. He called you his *current* girlfriend?"

"Excuse me?"

"Oh, Brian, you're so naughty." I heard her set the phone down as her voice drifted away. "Someone's a bad little pre-frosh. Naughty, naughty boy!"

I lowered the phone, every part of me pulsing with rage. I marched back into my room, slamming the door behind me. "Rachel, Kyle, start looking on craigslist. I need a new summer job. Lifeguarding with Brian is no longer an option."

Three

"Wait, what?" a very stunned Rachel asked.

Kyle looked up from Danny's MySpace page and whipped his head around, almost poking out an eye on the popped collar of his Lacoste. "Yeah, what's this crazy talk? What's up with Mr. Bri-Bri." He sang "Bri-Bri" in the same mocking tone first graders use when they sing the K-I-S-S-I-N-G song. It made me want to puke.

"Um, hello! Did you hear what just happened?" I whimpered, tears leaking out.

"No. You left the room. Did you think we were pressing up to the door like two Veronica Marses?" Even though he didn't quite qualify as a real guy, Kyle could still be a huge dick.

"I just can't believe it. Not even twelve hours after leaving and he's Big Man-Whore on Campus." I knocked my ancient Bratz collection off the shelf, still on display from when they were the It in elementary school.

The toppling of overpriced hoochie dolls triggered a best friend alarm in Rachel. She rushed over to me for a hug. "Em, what happened?"

Just then, my mom hollered, "Guys, dinner's ready!"

I rolled my eyes and wiped my cheeks. Perfect timing. "Nothing. Nothing's wrong right now. I'll tell you later, okay? I'm fine." Such a lie. I was as close to spontaneously combusting as you can get without being in the Fantastic Four.

Kyle and Rachel stared at their "fine" friend.

"Hey, Em. Are you guys coming?" Mom bellowed again.

"Yeah, Mom," I shouted back as I charged downstairs, stomping on every step. I could feel Rachel and Kyle following me, way quieter than normal. I turned around and stopped when I got to the bottom of the stairs. "Don't mention anything at dinner," I demanded. "I don't want to talk to them about it yet." They nodded silently.

We sat down to heaping plates of pasta and red sauce, pretty much exactly what I had for dinner last night at Brian's house. I hate that, how you can be so mad at somebody and just want them out of your life completely, but everything reminds you of them. I nearly cried into the carbs.

Normally at family dinners when friends are over, I try to bridge the awkward gap that's always there between teenagers and parents. Like, I'd bring up something that everyone could talk about—Kyle's controversial casting as Yenta in the school's production of *Fiddler on the Roof* or Rachel's new Chihuahua, Jennifer Aniston. But not tonight. I let them flounder, reaching for conversation topics while I sat silently, shoveling pasta down my throat, barely even chewing. I've never been one of those girls who can't eat when she's upset.

After a few minutes where the only sound was the squishing of forks twirling noodles, Dad cleared his throat. "So, Kyle, what are you up to this summer? Hanging around Bridgefield, I'm assuming. Apparently, *everyone*'s going to be here," he said, still needling me about turning down the resume-building, chance-for-real-growth, this-will-look-so-good-on-your-college-applications internship thing in New York. "And that reason's compelling enough for *some* people to turn down the opportunity of a lifetime for just another summer of bronzing and bumming around."

How is it parents know *exactly* when you don't need to be hassled about certain things and then go straight for it? It's like when they have kids they magically gain an instant sense of inappropriate nagging.

Kyle, also trying to ignore Dad's totally obnoxious fatherly behavior, told the table that he was working at El Shack del Tacos as a cook for the summer.

Before my father could say something horrible about how he was wrong, I actually *could* have made a worse choice than staying home to lifeguard, I cut in with "Yeah, Kyle wants to be a chef. So this is a great first step for him." And that's only half true, he does want to be a chef, but this job wouldn't be his first step in that direction. His very first step was watching the Food Network. He's normally glued to the tube with the zeal other homosexuals reserve for Kylie Minogue. He yells "Bam" along with Emeril's studio audience and mouths "EVOO, Extra-Virgin Olive Oil" while Rachael Ray giggles the words.

With Kyle at the taco shack, I was planning on free chimichangas during adult swim all summer long. Even though now the pool gig with Brian seemed totally unappealing, I was still pumped for Kyle's job because it meant that now he could spit in Vile Brian's quesadillas. Ugh, I tensed at the thought of sitting around a pool, stewing in sweaty awkwardness with Brian every day. No way could I spend my summer like that. Not even the world's best tan would be worth that kind of stress.

"And Rachel dear, what about you?" Mom asked, trying to get some sort of conversation flowing.

"Um, well . . ." She hesitated, knowing that my kaiser of a father would be jumping down her throat in point five seconds. "I'm going back to Oakmere to be a counselor."

"And your parents are happy with this? With your father's connections, I'm assuming you're doing this instead of pursuing a valuable internship as well. I never had the kinds of opportunities that you kids have. . . ." For once, I found myself paying attention to Dad's diatribe of overbearing crazy talk. Maybe New York *was* my opportunity. I mean, not for, like, career stuff or whatever the eff he was blabbing about, but just a chance to get away from my ex. God, Brian was my *ex*? Just like that. It sounded so awful.

"You know, Dad, minds can change at the last second. Maybe we *will* pursue those opportunities you've laid at our feet like Ajax lays dead squirrels."

Everyone at the table shot me question-mark looks and then went back to silent eating, trying to pretend that I hadn't just compared my father to the family pet.

Kyle, still obviously uncomfortable, wolfed down his spaghetti and then made up some excuse to my parents about

20

needing to be home immediately for his weekly mother-son *So You Think You Can Dance* viewing. Rachel stayed and helped me clear the table and load the dishwasher. After we sponged down the table, we headed up to my room.

Both of us plopped down on my bed. "So, what the hell happened with Brian? I haven't seen you this upset since Davey Borney made fun of you for wearing those suspenders to my bat mitzvah."

Despite my current tragedy, I smiled at the memory. I had these clear plastic suspenders that I thought were totally awesome and wore them to Rachel's bat mitzvah. Apparently, Davey did not think they were so hot and called me Emma Urkleman all night. I couldn't take them off, because my skirt would have fallen down. So I just hid in the handicapped stall until Rachel came looking for me when I wasn't there for her candle-lighting ceremony. Then, after I told her about being compared to Jaleel White, she marched right up to Davey and asked him very loudly, "Hey, Davey. Do you poop your pants all the time or just have butt cheek chafing?" She let a dramatic pause pass. "I mean, it's got to be one or the other, right? Why else would you waddle around like a Teletubby?" She was loud enough for all the parents to hear. Davey hobbled off to the corner and stayed there through the entire Village People medley. And no one commented on my suspenders for the rest of the night.

"No, this is way worse than suspenders." I curled up on my bed and hugged my pillow. I told her about the phone call and the girl and him not even calling yet to apologize.

"*Current* girlfriend? Who does this bitch think she is? I bet she's some dork peer advisor who's way too lame for anyone in her own class to date, so she gets with incoming freshmen who don't even know how foul and untouchable she is yet."

My haze of misery lifted a little. But not much.

"Anyway, so now it's like, why am I even staying in Dork City, USA, all summer?" I said, my voice sounding very shaky.

"So what are you going to do instead?"

"What about going to New York like my dad wants?" I asked.

"Wow. You just decided that you're going to do the New York thing? Like live by yourself and stuff?" She looked at me wide-eyed.

"Well, no, I was thinking *we* could do the New York thing."

"You mean, *skip camp?*" The incredulousness in her voice and the anguish on her face would have been funny if I didn't love her so much.

"Well, no," I said quickly. "Forget it. You've been going to camp since before you were in a training bra."

"And I was an early bloomer." She stared wistfully off into space. "It's been a long, long time."

"Yeah, I'm sorry, what was I thinking? Those eight weeks are your favorite of the whole year. And then you spend the other forty-four wearing your friendship bracelets, listening to granola folk rock, and reliving 'one time at summer camp' stories. Totally forget it."

There was a moment of silence, very rare when the two of us were together. I could tell Rachel was thinking hard. I thought she was searching for a new conversation topic. But she wasn't.

"Screw camp. I'm in." She beamed from her side of my bed.

"What? What about Danny Steinberg?" I was flabbergasted.

"Hello! Why would I spend another summer making out with Danny Steinberg in poison ivy patches when I could spend it in the big city with, like, a million and a half way cuter guys? New York is like boy-toy Mecca for a Jewish girl, right?" I nodded, struck speechless by what an awesome best friend I had. "Plus, I'm getting too old for summer flings, I need to get serious. My cousin just got married and she's twenty-four. That's only seven years away."

I laughed, thankful that I had a BFF who was obsessed with settling down.

"And this'll be awesome practice for dating in the big city when I get into Columbia." Rachel was third-generation Columbia legacy. And while her GPA and SATs might not have seemed like they were the golden key to the Ivy League, her last name and granddaddy's checkbook opened doors at that school automatically.

I scootched over and hugged her. "This is going to be so fun! I think I need to get away from here and everything that reminds me of him."

"Totally," Rachel agreed. "And let's take all that shit down." She pointed to the Brian shrine on my nightstand, once what I loved to look at right before falling asleep. Now it was more painful than naked pictures of pregnant celebrities.

"It's just going to upset you," she added.

I sighed heavily and rolled over to the side of my bed with the nightstand.

As we switched out pictures of Brian and me—most of us looking uncomfortable in dress-up clothes for school dances—for pictures of my family and friends and Zac Efron, we planned out our metropolitan adventure.

"So, like do you know anyone in the Big Apple?" Rachel asked, positioning a close-up of herself in a frame that used to hold a corsage-pinning picture from homecoming.

"No one calls it 'the Big Apple.' Real New Yorkers call it 'the city,' and no, not really. Just my cousin Jacob. I haven't seen him in years, since three Thanksgivings ago or something. But he's really nerdy. I remember him being super into World of Warcraft and having more acne than the Olsens have hobo bags."

"Uck, then what are we going to do there?"

"We can't spend our whole lives only going places where we know people. If we did that, then we'd never get any farther than the outlet malls two exits away. Plus, as long as we're together, we'll never get lonely."

She looked at me with a way cheesy grin. "Aww! It's like we're on *The Gilmore Girls* or something. But you're right, we won't be alone if we're together."

Once the Brian display was dismantled, Rachel wanted to rush home and tell her folks about our change of summer plans. I walked her to my front door.

"Bye, babe," I hollered after her.

About halfway down the walkway, she turned around and bellowed, horribly off-key, "*If I can make it there, I'll make it—Ba! Ba!—anywhere. It's up to you, New York, Neeeew Yorrrrrk!*" As she hit the first "New York, " she thrashed her legs into wonky high kicks, looking not unlike a giraffe having a seizure. It was a bizarre mélange of a Rockette routine with the self-defense moves we'd learned in last semester's rape awareness class. She finished the routine by yelling "I Heart N-Y" at the top of her lungs and shimmying her fingers jazz-hands style. Across the street, the neighbor's baby started to cry.

I almost choked I was laughing so hard. "That city's never going to know what hit it once we show up."

"We're so taking it by storm! It'll be like *Sex and the City*, only we're young and wear cheap shoes!" She high-kicked the rest of the way to her wagon, and as she pulled out of my driveway, she shouted through the passenger's side window, "I'll call you as soon as I tell them, okay? We'll make more plans for the move tomorrow."

And just like that, my summer changed completely.

My parents were ecstatic when I told them. I didn't mention the Brian sitch at all. I played it off like out of the blue I just realized they were right—it was time to start thinking like an adult and lifeguarding was going to get me nowhere. But all the networking and schmoozing I could do at an internship would totally get me into the college of my choice, launch me into a solid career, yada, yada, yada.

Mom was on the phone with Golf Gal! Eileen in two seconds and I sat at the kitchen table and eavesdropped, trying to decipher from my mom's side of the conversation—consisting mostly of "yep's" and "uh-huh's"—whether I was going to get an internship or not. Wouldn't that be suckerrific—finally deciding to go to New York and then not be able to because I was too late for the internship? When their conversation segued into this week's golf plan, I gave Mom a "what gives" look and she smiled, gave a thumbs-up, and continued to plan her game with Eileen. Woo hoo! Plan Summer Fabulous was in gear. I was so psyched for living in New York City by myself. I mean, with Rachel, yeah, but totally on our own. No supervision for an entire summer. It was going to be unreal. Totally the makings for an MTV reality show, except for without the

LC/Heidi drama . . . mostly because neither of us had boy-friends. Sigh.

I snapped out of my mini-melodrama moment in time to hear Mom wrapping things up with Eileen.

"Yeppers, nine a.m. on Sunday. I'll be there and I'll bring a thermos of coffee for all of the Golf Gals! Talk to ya then and thanks for this, Eileen."

I could barely wait for her to put down the phone. "So, I'm set for the internship, right?"

My mom smiled and sat down at the table with me. "Eileen said that there'd still be openings left for interns. You can interview when you get to the city and are all set-tled in down there."

"That's great!" I was so stoked for the burb evacuation that I didn't even bother to ask what kind of internship it was. As long as it wasn't at the Bridgefield Swim Club, it would be perfect.

"Have you given any thought to where you are going to live, hon?" Mom asked.

Actually, not at all. "Um, maybe I could call Jacob and we could crash on his couch for a while?"

"*Both* of you on a sofa bed? In a young man's apartment?" my dad scoffed as he waltzed into the kitchen, not at all em-barrassed that he'd obviously been eavesdropping on our en-tire conversation. "That's what we call a recipe for disaster."

"First of all, I'm not one hundred percent sure what you mean by that, but still, gross. Let me remind you, he's my cousin." I shuddered. "Do you have a better plan?"

"Well, I'll talk to Rachel's parents and we'll pitch in some money for you girls to get a hotel for your first few nights in the city. I'm sure that with Jacob's help and a little hard looking, you ladies will have a place in no time." Money and words of encouragement? This was the most un-Dad I'd ever seen Dad. I was completely speechless.

"And I'll help you pack tomorrow, Em," my mother offered.

Who knew parents were so nice when you did exactly what they wanted? Maybe I should try this more often.

Just then the phone rang and the caller ID read Mark Wolfe—it was Rachel. I flew upstairs to my room to talk in privacy. With a breathless hello I answered the phone, so excited to tell her all the details.

"Em, my parents are stoked," she squealed. "My dad said he'd probably be able to hook me up with a sweet internship, too. We're going to be working girls in the big city! I'm already practicing wearing my hair in a sensible low bun."

"Right, once you get your hair-did figured out, we have to think about where we're going to live." Jaxy bounded into my room with the grace of a sumo wrestler on ice and hauled his slobbery self onto my bed. Finding New York digs would be like the first adult thing I'd ever done, and I was already getting nervous. I didn't even know where to start.

"No worries. I'm thinking we'll just find something off craigslist."

"Okay, we can give craigslist a shot," I said, petting my pet. "But we can't just walk off the Amtrak and into an apartment. There's going to be time right when we get to New York where we're going to be looking for a few days. We need somewhere to stay. Are you sitting down? My dad told me that he'd toss in some cash for a hotel if your dad did. Weirdly generous of him, right?"

"Sweet! Let me see if I can get more." I heard her holler

across her house, "Dad, I need five hundred dollars for that New York thing I was telling you about. No, on top of my allowance. *No, not for clothes!* For a hotel. I'll pay you back when I'm picking out your nursing home in like fifty years." Then there were a few beats while I'm pretty sure I heard Mr. Wolfe groan and then reluctantly agree. "Cool, thanks, Dad." And then she started talking back into the phone. "Cool, so we have five hundred bucks for a hotel plus whatever your folks are putting in. That should totally cover us for like a while, right?"

"Def. And that'll probably buy us some room service, too. Do you think they card with room service? 'Cause we should totally celebrate our first night in the city with champagne!"

My New York summer was totally coming together and I was buzzed on the thought of it. I don't know if the buzz came from being nervous or excited, but either way, I said my goodbyes to Rachel and hung up feeling like a rock star. A *boyfriendless* rock star, though. But didn't Carrie Bradshaw always call the city her boyfriend? So, it could be mine, too. I guess that makes New York a polygamist. Whatever.

Four

Brian didn't call until he got back from his *whor*ientation.

I saw his name flash on my cell's screen and I almost threw my phone out the window. I'd been expecting him to call for days and now that he did, I barely wanted to pick up. I decided to answer and give him a real-life example of hell hathin' no fury.

"Hey, babe," he said as I flipped open my phone.

" 'Hey, babe'? Did you just 'hey babe' me like I am the kind of girlfriend who would be okay with you frolicking with state school skanks and forgetting about me for three whole days? So. Not. Me."

"What are you talking about, Em? What's wrong?"

"Seriously, Brian? You don't think that anything's wrong

here?" I screeched. "You go away to your college weekend, don't call me for three days, and let drunken college sorority sluts answer your phone? So much is wrong with that, I don't even know where to begin." I tried unsuccessfully to sound like I'd been doing something besides cry on and off for the last seventy-two hours.

Brian pretty much stuck to his guns. "I mean, *jeez*, what else do you want me to say?"

"I don't know. But, uh, not that."

"Sorry, I can't control who answers my phone," he said.

"Of course you can! And you don't sound very sorry. Just so you know, you can forget about our summer together." I was in total ice queen mode, now that I'd cried out all of the water in my body. "In twenty-four hours, I am getting on a train, and I am getting away from here and away from you. Have fun frenching it with college girls. I hope they liked your lizard-tongue-down-the-throat move as much as I did! I can't believe I ever even liked someone as lame as you."

I slammed my phone shut and cried into my pillow for the millionth time since he'd left for that stupid orientation. I realized that I *really* couldn't believe that I'd liked him, maybe even loved him. How could I have been so wrong about him for so long? Does that mean that I was wrong about other things? Should I have really got those wide-leg AG jeans last week? Wide-leg might not even catch on. But more importantly, what about my completely spontaneous New York summer plan? Was that a huge mistake, too?

I could totally feel a grade-A freak-out coming on, and even though I was about ninety-nine percent packed and ready to go, I called Rachel and made flimsy excuses to back out.

"Rach, are you having second thoughts about this New York thing? Why are we acting like this is the best thing that ever happened to us? Don't you think that we'd have a good time even if we stayed in Bridgefield and just got really into a hobby, like karate or yoga or something?"

"So, let me get this straight," Rachel said testily on the other end. "You want to cancel New York so we can stay here and take a jujitsu class?"

"Um, yeah," I floundered. "I mean, why go aaaaalllll the way to New York and eat pizza all summer and get fat, when we can stay here and have a six-pack by fall?"

"Emma," she said sternly. "You can fool your mom when you come home buzzed. You can fool your teacher when you cheated through the bio midterm. But you cannot fool your best friend. I know you're having second thoughts about the Brian breakup and that totally makes sense. But I'm not letting you screw up both our summers so you can stay here and text him a hundred times a day and look psycho."

"First of all, that wasn't cheating. I just studied off a copy of last year's midterm, okay? But I know, you're right. I just feel like maybe I'm being too hasty. Like, don't you think it's weird that I broke up with him over one weekend of Bad Brian when I had like ten months with Good Brian? Well, like Medium-to-Good Brian?"

"Have you ever seen *Moonstruck*?" she asked.

"I—what? Yeah. Why?" I really wasn't in the mood for a subject change.

"You know how Nicolas Cage is that tormented bread guy whose hand got chopped off? Cher told him that he did it to himself on purpose to get away from his fiancée. Like a wolf chewing off its own foot to escape."

I didn't get it. "If this is leading up to you wanting to go for pizza, I'm going to be pissed, Rachel."

"No! Look, you are the Nick Cage, here. You are gnawing your way out of a trap. If you really, really loved Brian, you'd try to work it out. But I think deep down you're happy that this happened, because now you finally have an excuse to leave. Well, for two months, at least."

Tears welled up in my eyes. "You're totally right. I did need a way to get out."

"So, will you turn off the freaking Gavin DeGraw? Gav is clearly too much right now. Take a chill pill and get some sleep," she commanded.

"Okay, fine. I'm just going to go cut myself to feel and flip through my copy of *He's Just Not That Into You.*"

"That's not funny. I didn't want to resort to this but . . . *when the pimp's in the crib, Ma.*"

I knew this was my cue. "Drop It Like It's Hot" was our happy song. You just can't sing it out loud and be bummed at the same time. It's pretty much mathematically impossible.

"Drop it like it's hawt, drop it like it's hawt," I dutifully responded to each of her rapped-out calls until she ended with,

"We got the rollies on our arm and we're pouring Chandon, and we're movin' to New York cause we got it goin' on!"

I hung up still smiling and cracked open my journal, which I'd been ignoring for the last few days. I was avoiding writing about the Brian meltdown. Sometimes I felt like writing about something made it more real. But I finally put pen to paper, documenting Brian's douchiness. And, yeah, I teared up again. How I wasn't dying of dehydration from all of this crying, I don't know.

But then I moved on to the impending New York summer and how effing excited slash nervous I was for it. I didn't think I'd ever spent two nights in a row without my parents, so how was I going to do this alone? What if I forgot to eat or shower or sleep or breathe or something else important? At least Rachel and I would be together. I was lucky to have her in my life. I thought it was kind of lame how eighty-five percent of all *Sex and the City* episodes ended with the ladies announcing that they were each other's soul mates. But maybe they were right.

Five

The train doors opened into the sweltering heat of New York City. We dragged our luggage out and stood on the platform.

"Here we are! The Big Ap—I mean, the city!" Rachel said, gesturing around the dank train station grandiosely, almost hitting a guy in a business suit.

"Watch it, lady," he barked at her.

"Did you hear that? He called me 'lady,' not 'girl'! I feel grown up already!" she exclaimed, completely oblivious to the fact that he didn't mean it as a compliment.

I giggled and hoisted my luggage into rolling position. "Okay, *lady*, let's follow the crowd and hope that takes us to a place where we can find a taxi."

We made our way slowly through the station, stopping every five seconds to shift our laptop bags and purses.

"Hey," Rachel whispered to me, "do you feel like there's a weirdly large number of people napping here? Is that, like, a New York trend or something?" She tried to be inconspicuous as she pointed to a guy sprawled out on a sleeping bag.

"Yo, Toto, we're not in Kansas anymore. That's not a trend. Those people are homeless." I shook my head at her and plugged on.

"When were we ever in Kansas? That road trip with your parents three spring breaks ago?" Rachel asked as she trailed behind me.

We followed the signs to the taxi stand and stood in line, marinating in our own sweat. Since when did taxis have lines? Didn't you just flap your arm out and holler and they came to you? Finally we made it to the front and piled our luggage into the trunk. I uncrumpled the piece of paper with the hotel address that Rachel and I (and my father) had Pricelined for the next two nights and yelled it through the plastic window at the driver.

As we drove through Manhattan, we pressed our faces against the windows and guessed what buildings were which. Rachel tried to say that most everything was the Chrysler Building and even called one skyscraper the Sears Tower.

"That's in Chicago, Rach."

Our cab pulled up to our new digs for the time being, a Best Western near Tenth Avenue. It wasn't the Ritz, but it was cheap. Besides, it would only be a few days, probably less. I was sure we'd find a place in no time.

"Hmm, that's weird," Rachel said as I unpacked some of my stuff. "I don't see a room service menu."

35

"Rach, come on." I bent down to the dingy rug near my bed and picked up a hair ball the size of Pam Anderson's left boob. "It looks like they don't even have a vacuum in this joint, let alone a working kitchen." I flicked the triple-D's worth of hair and fuzz at her.

"Ew! Gross me out, Emma! Uck, do you think this room is clean enough? I mean, remember on *Dateline* when they turned a black light on inside a hotel room and you could see, like, blood and jizz stains everywhere, even on the ceiling? I'm sleeping above the covers. God knows it's hot enough."

"Do you think we should do some exploring of the city?" I asked, ignoring her whining.

"It's stinky hot out there. Let's hang out in the AC for a little bit longer," Rachel moaned as she dramatically fell back on her bed. "Actually, I'm going to take a quick nap before we head out and paint this town glittery!"

"A little bit longer" really meant all night. Rachel's nap turned into a coma kind of sleep. Even when I shook her and demanded that we at least leave the room and get some authentic New York deli food for dinner, she just mumbled and rolled over. And there was no way I was heading out into the New York night solo. I'd probably end up lost and sleeping over with one of Rachel's trendsetters in the train station.

So I sat on my bed and ate all six of the granola bars my mom had packed for train snacks and felt very un–New York. Carrie Bradshaw would so never binge-eat Quaker Chewies in a Best Western. Convincing myself that this was no indication for the rest of the summer, I unpacked my computer onto one of the particle-board nightstands and set up shop for the craigslist hunt.

Where was Rockaway? Wasn't that where Jay-Z was from? I glanced over at Rachel, fast asleep in her "Princess" eye mask, and decided Brooklyn or Queens wasn't exactly our taste. After hours of scouring the postings, I e-mailed six people about their summer sublets and made us a list of which places to visit first.

I finally closed the laptop and laid down in my probably-bodily-fluid-stained bed, listening to the sounds of the city. At one-thirty a.m., exhausted from a trip, a move, and the worst—fine, only—breakup of my life, the restless city was still too tantalizing for me to sleep. I was high off the energy and what tomorrow might bring. This was New York City! We could see Andy Samberg on the subway, sign a lease on a cute two-bedroom walk-up, and buy some imposter Chloé hobos all before noon! With all that bouncing around my head, it took me forever and a half to fall asleep.

We got up early and planned out our subway routes in advance so we wouldn't look like head-scratching tourists in public. The first apartment was in TriBeCa. The place sounded really cool—big windows, huge rooms, washer and dryer, pretty inexpensive. And it was a loft. I loved that word. *Loft.* It was so Olsen-chic.

We walked up to the door of the building and punched in the intercom number the woman from the craigslist ad had mentioned in her reply e-mail. Something garbled and staticky came from the intercom, and then there was a buzzing sound.

"Shit, is that the fire alarm or something?" Rachel asked, face scrunched in concern at the sound.

"I don't know what that was," I answered, confused and

waiting for a mass of people to come fleeing from the building, some of them on fire.

And then a voice, barely audible through the static, came from the intercom: "Are you guys coming up or not?" Even the static could not camouflage this woman's bitchy-ass tone.

The horrible buzzing sound came again and this time we didn't try to stop, drop, and roll. Instead we pushed open the front door and headed up in an elevator.

"Woah! This place is awesome," Rachel exclaimed as we walked off the elevator and directly into the apartment. Yes, that's right, the elevator opened right into the apartment, and the place took up the entire floor.

"Awesome" totally was the word. The place was as big as my house, with hardwood floors and a sick view of . . . some pretty tall important-looking building. It even had a baby grand piano and several pieces of, I guess, modern art.

We bopped around the place, squealing and clapping our hands.

"See, people are so wrong when they say rent is expensive in New York," Rachel said. "I mean, eight hundred dollars each for all of this is totally not that bad from what I hear."

After a lot of whining and several parent conferences, the foursome had given us a couple thousand dollars for the summer. We did the math and spending eight hundred bucks a month on rent would leave us plenty of leftover shopping money. So far New York really didn't seem that expensive. The hot dogs on the street were only one dollar!

"Oh, sorry," said the girl who was moving out. "I forgot to put the one in front of the rent on craigslist."

"Oh, no. We got it. Each *one* of us is going to have to pay eight hundred. That's completely reasonable," I responded.

"No, you don't *got it*. I don't know where you girls are from, but eight hundred dollars for this place is obscenely ridiculous." She rolled her eyes so far back, I think she could see her frontal lobe. "I mean the number one in front of eight hundred. As in eighteen hundred dollars."

"Wait, eighteen hundred dollars? Each?" Rachel asked. My mouth was so open in shock, I'm sure my chin was resting on the padding in my bra.

"Uh, obviously!" she sniffed. "You didn't really think a loft in TriBeCa was eight hundred dollars a person, did you? David Bowie used to live here."

Our hearts sank and we exchanged brokenhearted glances.

"Um, thanks for your time," I said quickly and pulled Rachel out of there.

We were completely deflated as we slumped into opposite sides of the elevator and watched the numbers decrease as we went down.

"What the crap?" Rachel screeched, breaking the silence as we stepped out of the front door and onto the sidewalk. "What shade of moron do you have to be to not proofread your posts? Didn't we learn to double-check our work in, like, the third grade? And who cares that David Bowie lived there? He's not even that famous."

"Yes, he is, Rachel."

"Okay fine, so maybe he is. But still, that's just not cool. And if that place was a thousand dollars over our budget, does that mean we're going to end up in a place that's a thousand times less cool?"

I shrugged lamely, too hot to reassure her or correct her

algebra skills. Even though we were really only two hours away, I swear, the city felt like the tropics compared to Bridgefield. I could feel the end of my ponytail sticking to my neck sweat. I was totally grossing myself out.

After sweating through only a two-block walk, we decided we needed something refreshing. We stopped into a deli to get some iced tea.

"Sorry, miss, no iced tea," said the cashier man without looking up from his paper.

Rachel threw up her hands in disgust. "Oh, that's great. Just perfect! We're going to spend our summer drinking Mountain Dew in a shoebox."

"Relax! We'll find a cool place. That was only the first one. We have a million more to see. I mean, what are the chances that *all* of them are going to be heinous?"

"Fine. What's next?" Rachel said, devoid of enthusiasm.

I handed her my Diet Mountain Dew to hold and pulled out my list of potential apartments. "A place in the West Village."

Rach perked up. "That's like celeb central. I think SJP lives there!"

"That's the New York spirit, Rach!"

"Here, let me see the map. I'll take the lead on this one, since you did the rest of the legwork," she offered as we shuffled back to the subway station.

With Rachel at the helm, we MTA-ed uptown a bit and then, of course, got mind-bogglingly lost.

"Is it me or is every street called Greenwich here?" Rachel asked as she looked for street signs. "I can't tell if we're *on* Greenwich Avenue or *intersecting* it—that sign is on a weird diagonal."

We asked about eleven people to point us in the direction of Christopher Street. I couldn't tell if we were walking around in circles or if the West Village had a sushi place, an ironic T-shirt shop, and a nail salon on every single block. Just as I was about to ask a twelfth person for directions, we stumbled onto Christopher.

"Finally!" Rachel exclaimed. "We just need to walk west a little bit now. Did you see anyone famous when we were lost? I was too busy looking at the street signs. Jake Gyllenhaal could have walked right past me or something." She was scanning the block with the intensity of a Secret Service agent.

"Celebrities probably don't come out when it's this freaking hot. Humidity does not mix with glam."

Finally, finally, finally, we found the right building and were buzzed up by a man's voice.

"That's weird. The ad was for female students only. I just assumed it was going to be a girl."

"Well, you know what assuming does? It makes an ass out of the both of us." Rachel looked at me with all sincerity, adorably unaware of her fumbled joke. This one was getting into the Ivy League next year. I shook my head in disbelief.

We walked into an elegant lobby. I pointed to the brown leather comfy chair in the waiting area. "Me likey," I said.

Rachel nodded and we hopped into a classy elevator that was dark wood and expensive looking. The elevator doors opened and a man was waiting for us in the hallway. He guided us two doors down into his place. As he turned to open the door and let us in, I surveyed his graying sideburns and leathery skin. This guy was about a jillion years too old to be a student. Rachel was too consumed by the grown-up awesomeness of the place to be concerned with our possibly forty-year-old roommate. "This is better than the last one," she whispered to me.

I had to agree, the place was swanked out. "So, you're still at the six-hundred-fifty-a-person offering price?" I asked, trying to sound businessy and older than almost eighteen.

"Yep," he said, eyes glued to Rachel's boobs. "But you would have to do your share of the housekeeping." I couldn't put my finger on exactly why, but he was totally giving me the yucks.

Rachel was examining some black-and-white photos of the New York skyline and she turned around. "Totally. I can do dishes or whatever." She went back to checking out the apartment, dragging her finger along the windowsill and checking it for dust. I think she thought that made her look official. "I'm also not a big sprinkler when I tinkle, so no problems there."

"Maybe I wasn't clear. I assumed that you would have understood this from the ad. I expect you to perform these housekeeping tasks in the nude." He said it with condescension, like we were idiots for not assuming he was a total perv.

I almost choked on my revulsion.

"What?" It came out of my mouth as a screech. I stuttered, trying to form a coherent reaction. I turned to Rachel, looking for some kind of help, and she bypassed her "let's go" finger and gave the guy the middle finger instead. We ran out of there faster than Nicole Richie from a Vegas buffet and headed for the AC of the closest Starbucks. There was one right across the street, so we didn't have to go far, but the creep-induced fight-or-flight adrenaline could have carried me to the Bronx and back. We collected ourselves at a table by the door, hoping the Birkenstocked college guy behind the counter wouldn't notice we weren't buying overpriced mochachocalattadadas.

"Ew! That was freaking scary, Em. I think I need a shower to wash off his creepiness. I swear I can feel it on me. It's like a wet suit of perv. And what the hell is wrong with you? What exactly did his ad say, Emma?"

I scowled and looked away. "Uh, just that he was looking for 'open-minded' and 'sexually liberated young women.'"

As the words hit the air I realized how absolutely stupid I was for not getting the meaning. I scrunched my face and waited for Hurricane Rachel to unleash its fury.

"For Christ's sweet sake, Emma! Even *I* could've seen through that! Just please tell me that the other places on our list didn't include the words 'sucky sucky' or 'friends with benefits.'"

"No!" I said indignantly, and grabbed a honey packet from the sugar station and sucked it down. Maybe if Rachel had bothered to do some of the work in finding an apartment, she'd have room to get pissed. But her passing out and sleep-talking about Jared Leto didn't qualify as "doing your part" in my book. I stayed silent, though, not wanting Rachel to blow up full throttle.

After a while, the icy AC air cooled my temper and I decided we should hit the pavement once again.

"Okay, quiet time's over. Do you want to see any more apartments today or should we call it quits?" I looked at my watch. "We could probably make it back to the hotel in time for *The Tyra Banks Show*."

"I say we keep going. We can't let that be the last taste in our mouth for the day. Let's just hope this next apartment is the Listerine to that one's gingivitis." We both laughed at her total nonsense.

"Okay, let's see," I said, looking at our dwindling list. "A place in Hell's Kitchen. Eight hundred dollars each. The lady sounded really nice."

"Oh my God! Hell's Kitchen? Emma, I don't want to end up in the river with my throat cut or sold into white slavery."

"Hell's Kitchen isn't a bad neighborhood. My cousin Jacob lives there. He says it's full of gay guys and vegan restaurants. And it might be cool to live near Times Square. We could totally stalk the cast of *Rent* if we were that close!"

"Really? Near Broadway? I think Fantasia is in *The Color Purple*, so famous people are definitely around there, too."

After forty-five sweaty minutes spent asking homeless people for directions, we trotted up to an adorable brownstone with a white marble hallway, supercute doorman, and best of all, central air.

Rachel let out a loud sigh as we were buzzed through the front door and started up the stairs. "Central air? Who cares if this place is a Tic Tac box and our roommate is a legless taxidermy collector? Feel that air? I'll take it!"

"Hi, girls!" an older lady chirped as she showed us in. "Come in and have a look around."

It wasn't a million-dollar loft in TriBeCa, but it was definitely cute. There was just one problem.

"Uh, I only see one bedroom."

"Well," she said slowly, "technically there's only one bedroom, but you two would share this."

She rounded the corner into the living room with two La-Z-Boy recliners and a clothing rack on wheels.

"Share what?" Rachel exclaimed. "The remote control? Are we seriously supposed to sleep in easy chairs?"

"They pull out so that they're almost flat. And you can use this as a nightstand." She pointed to the card table. "Travis is really nice, too."

"Travis? I thought you were going to be our roommate."

"Oh, no, no. This place is Travis's. I just show it because he's, well, not really what you'd call a people person. Well, actually not even a person. He's my Pomeranian."

"Hold up. You want us to live here over the summer, with a dog as a roommate. *And* give the mutt the bedroom?" Rachel said flatly. "I see. Do we at least get to use the toilet or do we have to pee in the sink?"

The New York real estate scene was starting to frighten me. I felt like every subletter we'd met could have had their own act in a carni freak show. We bolted again.

Back on the street, we decided to cool off with some Italian ices and give ourselves a pep talk.

"Our dream apartment is totally just a click away on craigslist. We've just got to keep on trucking," I tried to convince Rachel . . . and myself.

"Yeah, this is the big city. It's not supposed to be easy," Rachel agreed. "If living here were easy, ugly people could do it. And who wants the most fabulous city in the world filled with fugs?"

But as the heat of the day peaked, our hopes wilted along with our ponytails. Things went from bad to worse. The apartments got smaller and smellier, and the parade of potential roommates started to resemble a *Surreal Life* highlight reel.

"I have my Wiccan sisterhood meetings here every full moon. That's why I have this goat."

"I have this lower intestine issue and I use a lot of toilet paper, but I barely use paper towels. So it evens out."

"I cook with curry."

Finally, as the sun started setting, we made it back to hotel, sweet hotel. We flopped down on our beds, exhausted and stressed.

"How long do you think we can stay in this hotel and then still have money for subletting an apartment?" I asked, starting to get stressed that we might be homeless at some point in the not-so-distant future.

"I don't know, Em. We've already paid for tonight in this shithole, so let's not think about it. I really want to hit the minibar, okay? Our parents would totally never know and it's just sitting there, begging for us to drink some stuff." She could reach the minifridge from her bed—that's how small our room was. She started pawing through the mini-bottle selection.

"You go for it, Rach. I'm going to hit craigslist again and see if there are any serial killers, dominatrixes, or part-time mimes that are looking for summer roommates." I tried to sound like I was joking, but seriously, I was starting to think that we should ditch the apartment hunt and just find us a couple nice refrigerator boxes and set them up next to some place that had free wireless.

But I continued to point-and-click my way through the posts, this time trying to be a bit more discriminating and avoid any overt pedophiles. By the time Rachel had downed her third mini-Malibu, I'd found three new apartment possibilities.

Six

I woke up at seven a.m. to the sound of Rachel heaving her mini-Malibus into the toilet. I could have predicted the hurling from the second she opened the minibar. That girl knows her limits about as well as Britney knows her underwear. She limped out of the bathroom, almost folded in half she was clutching her stomach so tightly, and crumbled onto the bed.

"Put me out of my misery, Emma. Just do it. *Old Yeller* style. Do it 'cause you love me." Her whiney voice, normally shrill, was husky with dehydration.

"Rach, I was just thinking back to that *Dateline* special—you know, the black-light one? Didn't they say that the toilet was like the dirtiest thing in the whole room? Like, way worse than the ceiling."

"If I had any energy right now, I'd come over there and smother you with your diseased pillow." Then she went back to moaning and I rolled over and went back to sleep.

Three hours of slamming-bathroom-door-and-muffled-retching-interrupted sleep later, I was up for good. Rachel looked a little less green, kind of a washed-out taupe. But I was not going to let her self-induced ailments ruin my second day in New York.

"You know what you need?" I said way too cheerfully.

She shook her head and pulled the covers over her face, shielding herself from the light I knew was giving her a headache.

"Some ibuprofen and a greasy brunch." She ignored me, still wrapped in her bedding cocoon. Having little sympathy for Little Miss I'm Going to Get Me Drunk and Not Surf Craigslist, I leaped over to her bed and started jumping up and down. "Greasy brunch! Greasy brunch!" I chanted over and over, bouncing her near-lifeless body up and down.

"Fucking, fuck you," said a voice from under the blankets.

I stopped jumping for a second and pulled the comforter away from her face.

I got nose-to-nose with her and gave her my best puppy dog eyes and yelled, "Greasy brunch!" There was no way she was sleeping through the day and sending me out into the New York freakfest alone.

"Fine, fine." Rachel got out of bed rather nimbly for the hangover she was nursing. That girl can be such a drama queen.

"Yes! Sweet!" I pumped my fist and felt like a fifth grader who just won the annual magazine sale. I tossed her some ibuprofens and a half bottle of Diet Sunkist I'd had since we boarded the train in Bridgefield.

We got dressed and headed out down Tenth Avenue. Turned out that finding a place that looked dirty enough to have a solid grease-laden brunch was not that challenging in this 'hood. Within half a block, we were in deep-fry heaven.

Over plates of scrambled eggs, fried potatoes, and pancakes, we discussed our options.

"So," I asked seriously, "out of the crap shacks we saw yesterday, which one do you think is the least rank?"

"I will not even dignify that with an answer." Rachel wouldn't even look up from pouring syrup all over her pancakes. "Seriously, I cannot live in any of those dumps. We could stay in homeless shelters and live in that kind of squalor for free. At least then we'd get free soup and toiletries. And probably even get felt up nightly."

"I know," I conceded. But I really did want to know if anything we saw yesterday was an option at all in her mind. Today might pan out to be the same, so we did need some backup. "What about that last one? That wasn't so bad, was it?"

"Are you out of your mind? That was a prison cell. Literally, it was eight-by-eight and had no windows. And what? Were we both going to sleep in that twin bed? Dude, not going to happen." A syrupy forkful went into her mouth.

I sighed heavily. Why was I doing all the work here? Like, yeah, I'd *kind of* talked Rachel into this, but now we were both here and if she was going to be so damn persnickety, she could stay up all night looking for apartments instead of getting wasted on rum like a pirate.

"Well, fine then," I said testily. "What are we going to do? We only had two nights at the hotel, which are over. We can totally extend our stay there—I think—but we need to set aside some money for the rent that we will hopefully eventually be paying. I'm no math genius here, but that only leaves us with enough of the parents' money for just a couple more nights in our shit-ass hotel. We have to find something fast." Rachel nodded in silent agreement. One night in our rank room at full price cost just about as much as what I would have made in a week lifeguarding. Despite the one-dollar hot dogs, cash goes fast in this town.

I heaved a big sigh. "If I were home right now, I'd be lifeguarding with Brian." Just because I was a little sad and a little hopeless and a little homesick, I let it slip out. I didn't even really mean it. Or at least, I don't think I did.

Rachel leaned forward out of her side of the vinyl booth and pursed her lips in a "Mama gonna set you straight, girl" kind of way. "Emma, seriously? If you were home right now, you'd be miserable. You'd still be fighting with Brian and crying about it to me until I left for camp. And then, once I was gone, you'd be crying alone, listening to Paramore and giving yourself some hideous emo haircut one night and I just don't know if I could be friends with you if you looked like that."

I smiled in spite of myself. She was right, I wouldn't be thinking about Brian if this apartment hunt were going even just a smidge better. A few silent seconds of egg eating went by. "Well, I e-mailed three people last night while you were Malibu-ing yourself into a coma."

"Don't ever mention Malibu ever again. Ever." And she really did go a little greener at the mention of it. "Not even if you're in California and talking about the place, okay?"

The girl may not have a sense of her limits, but she at least has a sense of humor.

"Whatever, Pukey Brewster. Let's go back to our penthouse suite and see if anyone wrote back. Then we'll map out Mission: Apartment Hunt Part Deux."

While Rachel showered off the hangover icks, I checked my Gmail. I'd gotten two answers out of the three messages I'd sent the night before. One was for a two-bedroom in Queens. In a moment of—I don't know if it was weakness or reality—I broke down and boroughed it out. I'd come to realize that our limited cash flow was not going to get us anything close to livable on the island of Manhattan.

My plan was to take Rachel to the Manhattan rental first and it was sure to be a dump. I wanted to have how stinky and tiny it was fresh in her mind, and then take her to see the Queens apartment and hopefully wow her with cleanliness and space we could actually afford over there. The Manhattan craphole was a three-bedroom right on Union Square. The woman was renting the other two bedrooms for $750 each. After yesterday, I'd learned that if it sounds too good to be true, it certainly is. So when I clicked open the response e-mail about the place, I was expecting to see an embedded image of her with dozens of gerbils or a baby pool filled with ranch dressing or maybe an e-mail explaining that by "roommate" she actually meant "babysitter/housekeeper/Scientology scholar." But that totally wasn't the case . . . at least as far as I could tell. As I clicked open the message from GlamnGlitterGrl@gmail.com, I found no bestiality jpegs, no condiment ponds, and no mention of indentured servitude. She was twenty-one, a student at NYU, and looking for some chill roommates.

"We're so chill!" I screamed into my computer screen.

In the e-mail, the landlady said she'd be home between twelve and three and we should just drop by. She gave her cell number just in case, which seemed pretty friendly to me. Jeez, how could my positivity be rebounding after yesterday?

Rach was sopping when she came out of the bathroom. "There's a hand towel the size of a maxi pad for me to dry my entire body." She wrung out her hair onto the floor. "This place blows."

"Get dressed, babe. I have a good feeling about this apartment."

"Didn't you say that about the pedophile guy?" she asked, squishing gel into her curls.

"Okay, so we just hop on the blue one and go to Fourteenth Street and then transfer to the gray one. We'll get off at Union Square and be right at her doorstep." I finger-traced our route on the MTA map, which was nearly destroyed though we'd only had it for a day and a half. Rachel nodded as we stepped into the subway car. We got two seats next to each other in a really well air-conditioned car. Could this be going any better? Maybe today was going to be totally different from yesterday's horrendousness. I was actually getting pumped about the Manhattan place, and I started building up the apartment. "It's a real three-bedroom and two bathrooms. Meaning we'd have our own bathroom for you to puke in." She gave me a fake glare. "Plus, Union Square's supposed to be awesome. Jacob listed it as a cool place to go out when I e-mailed him."

"I thought he was, like, captain of the geek squad. How would he know where to go out?"

"Well, yeah, he is." I shrugged. "But, geek machine or

not, he's our only gauge as to what's cool in the city and that's what he said." I couldn't let my cousin's dweeb-o rep wreck day two's apartment search before we'd even seen a place. I continued with my virtual tour of the craigslist ad highlights. "And apparently the place was just renovated. So there's, like, a new kitchen and everything. Which I know we won't use for more than heating up Lean Pockets, but still. How awesome, right?"

"Nice! I likey!"

I started to go over the questions about utilities and whatnot that we needed to ask the landlady if we were going to love the place as much as I hoped, when Rachel interrupted. "Hey, you think Kyle's doing okay at home? I mean, who is he hanging out with if we're here?"

We rode along for a while debating the possibility of Kyle's happiness sans our company. Rachel thought it was impossible but I thought that he would be fine without us. I went through every possible social outlet in Bridgefield where he could make friends.

"Ky's not looking to meet divorced women who are too clumsy to scrapbook on their own," she responded to my suggestion that he would take a crafting class at the Y to make new friends.

Valid point. I realized then that I hadn't been paying much attention to the subway stops and we'd been on for a while. "Um, Rach, do you know what stop we just passed?"

"I thought you were Magellaning this expedition. I'm concentrating on not barfing in public."

Not puking? Not really what I'd classify as teamwork in my book.

Just then we pulled into the 190th Street station. And I

54

may not have gotten a 5 on my AP Calc test, but I know enough math to tell you that's nowhere near Fourteenth Street. "Shit! Get out!" I yelled, maybe a little too frantically. Everyone in the car turned to see if I was having some kind of emergency. Aside from dying of embarrassment, I wasn't really in critical condition, so I just looked at the floor and tried to be invisible until the doors opened and we shuffled out.

As we stood on the platform, trying to figure out how to get back downtown, I looked down at my watch—two-thirty.

"We're never going to make it to this apartment by three," I sighed.

"Should we skip this one and just move on down your list? We're probably close to Queens already," Rachel offered.

Actually, we were probably close to Kuwait, we were so far away from where we needed to be.

"I dunno, we could just skip it, but I have such a good feeling about this one."

"Okay, well, then let's head aboveground for some cell service so you can call and ask this chick if it's okay that we're late." Rachel was being uncharacteristically flexible. Maybe I should get her hungover more often.

We climbed the stairs up to daylight and I dialed the number GlamnGlitterGrl had e-mailed me.

"Talk to me, babes," came from the other end of the phone.

"Uh, hello? Is this Mrs. St. Clare?"

"Well, I'm Ms. Jayla St. Clare."

"Oh, this is Emma. Freeman. And Rachel. We met on

the Internet. Well, that sounds creepy. I just mean that we e-mailed, you know?" Why had I built this place up so that I was more nervous than I was on my first date with Brian? "Anyway, we're on our way to see your place and I know you said to be there by three, but we're superlost and are probably going to be late."

"No worries, I'm actually still on my way back from the Hamptons, but I'll be home in twenty."

"Oh, right, the Hamptons!" I said, having only sort of heard about it on an episode of VH1's *Fabulous Life of*. . . . "Um, hey, could you give us directions to your place from 190th Street?"

"Are you kidding? I didn't know the streets go up that high. Call a car service, honey."

"Oh yeah. Car service. Maybe we will. Okay, see you later, then. Bye."

Rachel and I looked in our wallets. We hadn't restocked on the cash this morning and only had twelve dollars between the two of us. "That's only going to get us to like 189th Street in a cab," I complained. So we turned around and headed back down into the sticky heat of the subway entrance to continue the voyage.

An hour later, with our bra linings totally soaked in sweat, we announced ourselves to Jayla's doorman. Marble or mirrors covered every surface of the lobby.

"Ugh. I look like someone dumped a bucket of sopping wet ugly on me," Rach said, checking herself out in one of the mirrored walls. I tried to avoid my reflection. There was no way I looked any better.

The doorman pointed us toward the elevators and

mouthed "Thirty B" after a few seconds on the phone with Jayla. The elevators matched the lobby in their marbly mirrored–ness, and I couldn't help but catch myself in the mirror. Waterfalls of sweat and cheap makeup was a less than flattering pairing—I looked like the love child of a marathon runner and a raccoon. I pushed the frizz back into my pony, using my sweat as makeshift hair gel.

Finally the elevator doors opened and my reflection thankfully disappeared. We moseyed around the tasteful but pretty plain white hallway, until we found Apartment 30B. Rachel rang the bell, we heard a "Come in" through the door, and Rachel pushed it open. All I could see from the doorway was insanely blonde hair. So icy pale and shiny, when it caught the light, I was temporarily blinded. I focused on the person attached to the hair and saw who I assumed was our landlady. She was gorgeous, and as I walked closer, I realized that her skin was so perfect, I swear she didn't even have pores. She barely noticed us, she was so transfixed by the episode of *My Super Sweet Sixteen* she was watching.

"I wish they would have had this show on when I turned sixteen. I could have blown this skank party all the way back to dirty Jersey where it belongs," she said as I guess some sort of greeting. It was the episode where the girl arrived at her party by helicopter. "Anyway, welcome. And I'm Jayla. Take a look around," she motioned with a perfectly polished hand. "Those two over there would be your rooms and that's the bathroom."

The apartment was museum clean and decorated in that kind of nothing-matches-but-everything's-expensive-so-it-looks-good-together kind of way. We tiptoed around looking

57

into the rooms, which were huge, and not just by New York standards. Not only that, fully furnished with queen beds, chests of drawers, and nightstands. "Have I died and gone to sublet heaven?" Rachel whispered to me as we stepped into the bathroom. The bathroom that had a tub with jets. I was pretty much thinking the same thing as Rachel: *This is too perfect*. I wondered what the catch was. Did we have to sleep in the bathtub together or donate an organ or be a part of some horribly embarrassing weight loss reality show where they would focus in on my butt fat?

"Um, we're so interested, Jayla," I called out, my voice echoing off the hardwood floors and high ceilings. "Anything more we should know about this place? Or the details of the lease or anything?" I didn't want to insult her, but come on. There had to be something wrong with this place.

"Oh, utilities are included and I think that's it. I've never really done this landlord thing before, so I don't know. I have the sublease papers right there." She was pointing to the counter in the kitchen and checking her texts at the same time. "Just sign them. And you have checks with you, right?"

"Well, yeah." Could it be that easy? I looked down at the sublet form. The header read *St. Clare Realty*. "So, do you own this whole building?" I tried to sound casual, but damn, this girl must be loaded. And judging from the size of her diamond earrings, she probably owned more than just this building.

"Yeah. I mean, no. Not me." Done, or maybe just bored, with her four-hundred-dollar cell phone, she got up to come talk to us in the kitchen. Even on this lazy Saturday afternoon, she was wearing a gorgeous wrap dress that I would

58

drool over if I ever saw it in a store window. "My dad. This is his thing." She gracefully plopped herself on a barstool at the kitchen island and inspected her flawless mani. "Like, he thinks that I'm irresponsible with money and shit. There was this one credit card thing, well, in his words a 'fiasco,' with a last-minute trip to Sundance this winter. So he's *completely lost trust in me,*" she said, mimicking a gruff parental scold.

"This apartment is my big test for the summer. Like, if I don't burn this place down by Labor Day, I can have unlimited access to my—*his*—credit card when I'm abroad next semester. If this doesn't work out, I guess I'm going to be slumming it on a measly allowance."

For sure, even her measly allowance was more than what my dad made in a decade. Actually, probably both my and Rachel's parents combined. She continued her spiel. "I'm looking for tenants who won't break anything, because I'm not exactly handy with big tools." She paused before adding, "Well, any tools. And," she continued, looking sheepish now, "we kind of don't have a budget for repairs anymore. But if you need five bottles of Grey Goose and the name of a great masseuse, I'm your girl!"

"Why do you keep geese in a bott—" Rachel started to ask, and then abruptly shut up as I kicked her in the shin with my flip-flop. We'd totally just found the deal of a lifetime, and I didn't want to screw it up with our suburban high school dorkiness.

"The repair stuff is no problem," I said, trying to look useful. "I have a cousin in the city who could probably help us out with any handyman stuff."

Before Jayla could even respond, Rachel and I were

unfolding the signed checks our parents had given us and filling them out for Jayla.

"Fab, fab," she said, taking the checks and casually throwing them on the kitchen counter. "So now that I have your checks and stuff, you guys can move in whenever."

We made plans to move in first thing the next day, and I totally wanted to hug her, but refrained. My sweat would probably eat through her skin or something.

"I'm so glad this worked out! The thought of talking to sweaty strangers all week long was making me ill," Jayla said. As soon as she closed the door behind us, Rachel and I did a silent celebration dance in the hall. The dancing kind of made us look like epileptic crabs, but who cared? We were so close to being glamorous New Yorkers, I could almost smell the party invites and designer bags!

We got back to our room without getting lost once. The hotel looked more like a dungeon than ever now that we'd seen the splendor that was to be our summer home. Rachel and I jumped back and forth from bed to bed like ten-year-olds.

"That place is so awesome! It's like where they stay on *America's Next Top Model,* but those skinny bitches have to share rooms and we don't have to look at Tyra's face every time we turn a corner!"

"Totes. And Jayla's prettier than Tyra anyway. She's totally going to be our hook-up for all of the cool stuff that happens in the city. She probably has a ton of friends from going to NYU."

Rachel leaped from her bed to mine and I noticed what she was wearing, actually what we both were wearing: khaki shorts and colored tank tops. God! Compared to Jayla we looked like bums. She probably thought we were modeling L.L. Bean's new line of suburban lesbian wear. I made a mental note to wear something trendier to move in the next day. Would kitten heels be trying too hard?

We went back to the diner down the street for a celebratory dinner. Not the glam champagne-soaked night I would have liked. But twelve dollars doesn't get you too far in the city that never sleeps. We congratulated ourselves with grilled cheese, onion rings, and an ice water toast.

I e-mailed Jacob about our new digs when we got back, bragging about our sweet Union Square location. He insisted on helping us move in. Each of us only had a rolling duffle and our laptop cases, so there wasn't much to help with. But a totally nice gesture, I guess.

Jacob was meeting us in the hotel lobby at noon. Rachel and I stood at the reception desk at about 11:58, checking out and hissing at each other.

"Your minibar binge wound up costing us thirty-two dollars!" I growled.

"How was I supposed to know that three ounces of rum cost nine-fifty? That's crazy!"

"You could have read the card thing they have laminated to the door of the minibar. That's how you were supposed to know!" I hushed my yelling because I thought we were scaring the receptionist. "Here's the thing, we've already blown through five hundred dollars on this hotel, eighty dollars each for the subway passes, and *at least* two hundred dollars eating every single meal out. We just need to be careful."

"Uh, thanks, Mama Freeman!" Her sarcasm was enough to drive me to violence before I'd had my a.m. caffeine.

Fortunately, I was distracted from best-friend-icide by Jacob walking through the door. He had totally shed his acne-ridden, D&D-playing exterior and actually looked pretty normal. If he weren't my cousin, he might even be cute. Well, that grow-on-you kind of cute, anyway.

"Long time, no see, little cuz," he said as he opened his arms for a bear hug.

After almost squeezing the life out of me, he turned to Rachel.

"Jake Freeman," he said with his hand stretched out.

As soon as he finished shaking Rachel's hand, he turned to pick up our suitcases. I mouthed to Rachel, "Not Jewish. Don't even think about it."

She rolled her eyes and silently faked puking, but I knew that if I hadn't put him off limits, Rachel would have been on full-throttle flirt-attack.

It didn't take long to heave our worldly possessions from curb to cab and from cab to apartment. Jake's mouth dropped open as we entered the apartment.

"Swank central. Right?" I asked.

"You are the luckiest two girls in the five boroughs. Seriously, this is unreal." He showed his true nerd colors as he caressed the entertainment center. "This screen is so sweet. Does she have a Wii?" He poked around for a bit and settled for watching *Curb Your Enthusiasm* On Demand while Rachel and I organized our clothing into our very own drawers. Then we joined him in the common room, ready to fully enjoy the AC and HBO. The combo of a clean place to live, air-conditioning, and premium cable was as close to heaven as I could get at the moment.

As we were soaking in the new digs, Jayla popped into the apartment. Aside from introducing herself to Jake, she barely seemed to notice we were there. She was a blond blur, running back and forth among all of the closets and the mirrors in the apartment. Jake was visibly smitten with her. When she walked by in just a towel, Jake's eyes practically popped out of his head. Just when I thought that she'd completely forgotten we were there, she paused for a second in front of us.

"Which?" she demanded holding two black dresses, both cut low enough to elicit a "Why buy the cow?" comment from any mother. She explained, "I have a date." Jake just sat there, muted by her frenzied beauty, nearly drooling. Before Rachel and I could answer, she was running back to her room, yelling at us, "Yeah, you're right. I saw Paris wearing the left one in the last issue of *Us Weekly*. I should probably burn it." Before Jake could regain his voice, she was throwing us air kisses as she left the apartment.

With no more real excitement guaranteed until her return, Jake took Rachel and me to a Chinese place around the corner for a Welcome to New York celebration dinner.

"We finally get to have our celebratory toast tonight. Is there Chinese champagne?" I asked.

"Hey, cousin, aren't you like twelve years old? You can't drink."

"Hello! Emma is almost eighteen and I myself am well past seventeen and a half," Rachel retorted, adorably pretending to have a valid point.

"Counting half years? Totally too young to drink." He may have gotten less weird looking over the years, but was still just as much of a square.

"Fine," I groaned as I lifted my water glass for a toast. At this rate, I was definitely on my way to becoming the most hydrated girl in the city limits.

"To one of my favorite Freemans, Emma, and her first big-city adventure! May you end up having more fun than Carly, Melissa, Samantha, and Charlie!"

Rachel and I exchanged puzzled looks.

"Uh . . . who are they?"

"Duh! The *Sex and the City* girls! Jesus, I thought you two knew what was up."

We laughed at his (kind of) endearing dorkiness and dug into our chow mein.

Seven

"Rach," I said while pouring my second glass of Jayla's organic orange juice, "do you realize we've been in this city for three whole days and I haven't called Brian once?" I was pretty impressed with myself.

"You haven't?" Her voice was laced with more than a little suspicion. "Wow, I just assumed that you'd been calling him in the middle of the night and hiding it from me. Like that time you hid the Clay Aiken CD and pretended it was your brother's when I found it."

Would she ever let me live that down? You didn't see me bringing up the fact that she had Ace of Base on her iTunes in a totally nonironic way. "I did *not* hide that CD! I just *forgot to mention it*. Anyway, no, I haven't called or even texted him. I don't know, I've barely even really wanted to, either. Now that we're here in this city and everything, it seems like there are so many more possibilities than Brian McSwain: Thirty-Second Keg Stand King."

Rachel smiled. "Well I'm glad to hear you say that. You totally don't need him, Emma. Let him catch the clap in college and come crying back."

"As my best friend, it is your duty to stop me from ever taking back a weeping man with VD. Hog-tie me and stow me in your station wagon till I come back to my senses. Or dress me in those homemade vests my mother made me wear all through middle school. That way, even a syph-ridden crybaby wouldn't want to date me."

We both giggled at the memory of those horrid vests I made every summer at Lil' Sew-n-Sews Summer Camp.

I put my glass in the dishwasher, and now that I was juiced up, I really wanted to start exploring the city and shopping so we could look the part of the New York glitterati we were so going to be by the end of the summer. "So, what should our plans be today? I say we head out to get fake Louis Vuittons in Chinatown. My guidebook says that's totally the place for knockoffs."

"Not me, babe." I was stunned that Rachel would turn down an opportunity for bargain shopping. "I have an interview at that dyke website, Sirlie.com, or whatever. And if we want a Louis, look no further," she said, gesturing toward Jayla's room. "That chick has more bags than Nicky Hilton. Her Chloé bag isn't even due out until September, how the hell did she get it?"

"Wait, what website?"

"I told you about it, right? My dad's cousin's cousin or whatever works there, it's some lesbian-power online magazine blog thing. I'm assuming I'd cover hard-hitting issues like which Birkenstocks go with which pair of overalls."

I was so busy looking for an apartment, I'd half forgotten, half just not wanted to think about a job. Mom was so amped on Golf Gal! Eileen's connection, but I was hoping to find something kick-ass on my own, maybe working for MTV. I could totally see myself holding the cue cards at *TRL* and beating the twelve-year-olds off Pete Wentz. "Are they hiring for more than one person? Could I work there, too?" I was really jealous that Rachel could spend her entire summer at a cool online magazine, especially one where she wouldn't have to shave her legs. She had absolutely no interest in journalism or writing at all. Why was she getting a cool writing internship? I was the one who kept a journal and was registered for AP English next year. I chewed a nail and avoided eye contact with her, hoping she wouldn't notice my envy.

"Em, don't be jealous, seriously," she said as she got up from the kitchen island and rinsed her cereal bowl in the sink. I hated how she could read my thoughts. "It's not like I'm writing stories or anything. I'll probably answer phones, get coffee, and fend off sexual advances from a woman named Spike. What's this place your mom wanted to set you up with?" she asked, leaning up against the counter.

"Uck, I don't know. Some boring office thing. What do you think, should I just do that or should I apply cooler places like maybe MTV?"

"You can try, but I don't know where else you're going to find something. Internships you'd actually want are all about connections and timing. Unless your dad is Carson Daly or something, you're so not getting anything at MTV. But who even cares what your job is? I mean, hello! I'm about to rock into Lesbo.org. Anything is a step up from life-guarding. I mean, you can't put 'Got tan, ate tacos' on your college apps."

God, my old summer plans sounded so lame now. Rachel was right. This office thing would be much better than station-wagoning around Bridgefield.

I was about to take another peak in the fridge to see if there was anything else of Jayla's I could snag for breakfast when I heard the front door open.

"Jayla!" Rachel chirped as our new roommate stumbled through the door.

"Where were you guys last night? I thought you wanted to come out," she said as she threw her clutch on the couch.

Rachel and I exchanged a quick glance, neither one of us wanting to fess up to what uncool freaks we were. It was true that we'd texted Jayla last night to see where she was, but totally not because we wanted to meet up. Rachel had burst into my room at two a.m. in a complete panic.

"Jayla isn't home and it's, like, really late," she whispered frantically as she shook me awake. "On *Law & Order*, it's always the roommate who reports her friend missing. Should we call the cops now? Do you think that she's dead or being tortured or something?"

Even though I was barely conscious, Rachel was lathering me into a worried frenzy. I mean, we didn't even know Jayla, but two a.m., come on, who stays out that late on a weeknight? As I slowly woke up, I was seriously thinking of dialing 911 but then realized we might try texting Jayla first, just to see if she would respond. I thought of her, lying in a car trunk or abandoned warehouse with her mouth taped as I punched into my cell, *Where R U? R U OK?*

"I'm going to call 911." Rachel was in extreme *SVU* mode. "Every second we wait is another second she suffers."

But, just as Rachel dialed 9, my phone buzzed with a text. *@ The Box. Come. Dress sexy!* Our relief quickly melted into feeling totally stupid about our Code Red terror alert, and Rachel shuffled back to her bedroom after promising that we would never admit to Jayla just what dorky suburban girls we were.

In the morning light, I felt even more idiotic. "Oh yeah. Um, we just decided to stay in last night," I lied. "You know, unpacking all of our stuff and getting organized." In reality, we each just had one suitcase that took all of an hour to unload, but Jayla didn't seem to care. She had gossip to spill.

She kicked off her heels and got more comfortable on the couch. "So, guess who I made out with last night."

"Who?" we gasped in unison.

She paused for effect before fake whispering, as if she weren't dying to tell us, "Adrian Grenier."

We shrieked in disbelief. Rach knocked over the box of Lucky Charms in a spastic lurch of excitement.

"Are you *freaking kidding me*? Omigod, Jayla, he's like *the hottest* thing ever. I have no idea what's going on in *Entourage*—I just watch it for him," Rachel squealed. "Where did all this happen? You kissed him at that boxing bar?"

Jayla looked horrified. "Not a bar, honey. A club. Bars are for uglies and fatties. And yeah, it started at the club." She rattled off more details, everything from denim brands to his drink choices, a memory to rival any *Jeopardy!* champ.

I could feel my face turn hot pink when she started to describe his boxer briefs. Rachel almost jumped Jayla when she said that they had exchanged numbers.

"Wait, so you have his number in your phone right now?" I hadn't seen Rachel this flabbergasted ever. "Let's send him a text right now. Ask him if he wants to come over today!" She was squealing louder than an entire stadium of girls at a JT concert.

"No! I just came from his place. That would be so weird. And I don't even know if I want to see him again. Anyway, I'm probably going to spend today doing my art stuff, you know," Jayla explained. I nodded, but the truth was I didn't know. The only paintbrushes in this apartment were attached to Jayla's NARS nail polish. Even through her hangover, she saw the confusion on my face. "Oh yeah, I want to be an artist and I'm trying to spend the summer developing my portfolio and whatever. I haven't gotten all that far, to be honest." She let out a huge yawn and stretched, then started her saunter over to her room. "You know, maybe I'll take a nap before I get started." She turned around in her doorway, sent air kisses our way, and then disappeared into her room.

Rachel looked at me with a question-mark face. "Art stuff?" She was apparently as shocked as I was.

"I know, as if." Even though I'd only known the girl a day and a half, I could predict her future like a crystal ball. "It'll probably be ten p.m. when she wakes up and the text messages are going to be rolling in. She'll Diane von Furstenberg herself out the door and not work at all on that stuff. 'Working' is so totally not her style."

"If I had her dad, it wouldn't be my style either," Rachel sighed. She glanced at Jayla's discarded Jimmy Choos lying by the door and then turned miserably to go print out Sirlie's homepage. "Seriously, Emma, as soon as I turn eighteen, I'm marrying for money."

As soon as Rachel headed off to her interview, I made a quick call to Mama Freeman. I was relieved to hear that she'd already talked to Golf Gal! Eileen and they'd arranged for me to interview at this company called MediaInc with their Senior Vice President of Marketing today. Thanks for telling me, gals!

I spent the morning trying to pull myself into some version of professional. I looped my hair into a low pony and tried to apply makeup that made me seem older and classy. But since I only had my everyday lip gloss and mascara to work with, I pretty much looked like the same high school Emma I always do. I tucked a collared shirt into my favorite black H&M pants and set off. By the time I'd taken the subway to Midtown, walked two blocks in the wrong direction, turned around, and ran until I found the place, I was so sweaty I looked like a bag of wilted lettuce.

I marched up to the reception desk, hoping the lobby AC would dry my sweat mustache by the time I spoke.

"Hi, I'm Emma Freeman, here to see, um . . ." I shuffled through my tatty Pokemon folder that contained the interview contact info and a hasty copy of my resume. "Margaret Pavese in Human Resources. I'm Emma Freeman. Oh shit, I already said that, sorry. Wait, did I just cuss? Oh damn, sorry about that. Omigod, I did it again, I'm—"

"Eleventh floor, suite two fifteen," the receptionist said curtly, and I scooped up my Japanimation Five Star and shuffled away, 100 percent mortified.

My sweat started to dry as I headed up in what had to be the world's nicest elevator. I surveyed the sleek LCD television that displayed breaking news and numbers that I guessed were stocks, though they could have been lotto numbers.

"Hello, I'm Emma Freeman. I need a reservation for ten tonight at your really expensive restaurant. Where do I work? Well, I'm typically not one to brag, but . . . the really big building with the TELEVISION in the elevator, maybe you've heard of it."

By the time the elevator binged open, I had daydreamed myself into a Fortune 500 CEO's life. A sharply dressed woman with long red nails was waiting for me when the doors opened.

"Hi!" I smiled. "You must be Mrs. Pavese. I'm Emma—"

"That's Ms. Pavese," she cut in curtly before I could finish. "Right this way, please."

I swallowed hard, feeling like I was tanking my very first interview before it had even really started, and trailed her to an enormous conference room where it looked like world wars were planned out.

"Resume?" she demanded and I passed her my best thrown-together-through-tears-over-Brian-and-too-many-reruns-of-*One Tree Hill* list of employment and skills. I'd had my mom look it over and she gave me the thumbs-up. But she'd been a sixth-grade Language Arts teacher for the past twenty years, when was the last time she'd even seen a resume?

I fiddled with my cuticles as she glanced at the ecru high-stock page.

"So you're in high school?" she said without looking up.

"Um, yes. I'll be a senior next year." I sat straighter in

72

my chair, hoping perfect posture would make up for the fact that I didn't even have a high school diploma yet. "I just got elected French Honor Society vice-president, and we're going to have a really awesome croissant sale fund-raiser this year. And I think our soccer team's county title is—"

She put up a hand to silence me. Had I even completed a single sentence since walking into this building?

"Can you type? Have you used Excel at all? PowerPoint? Internet?"

"Internet? Oh yes!" I decided to leave out my expertise in stalking people on Facebook. "I can type really fast and I use PowerPoint for all my school presentations and stuff. And I've only used Excel a little, but I'm sure I can pick it up."

She nodded silently, still scanning through my resume. I hoped everyone else at MediaInc wasn't this frosty. What if all the people were? What if *this* was New York? No, she's probably just *being professional*, I told myself. *This is how all grown-ups behave, New York or not.*

She folded my resume in half, looked at her watch, and rolled her eyes at me. "I'll show you to Mr. Dorfman's office. He's the one needing a summer intern." She was clearly bored with me and wanted to pawn me off on someone else.

She walked several paces ahead of me. I trailed her as she sprint-walked down a long hallway, not even looking back when I almost didn't make it into the elevator before the doors closed. We rode up several more floors in silence. When the doors opened this time, I stuck to her like glue. I wasn't going to lose an arm in a slamming door and show up to my very first real interview mangled. She opened a series of glass doors with her name badge and I was getting winded in the hustle to keep up with her. Finally I stepped inside Mr. Dorfman's office. It was like something out of a movie, a totally cliché big-shot office—huge windows overlooking the city, portable golf green in the corner, and a man in pleated-front khakis talking loudly into a headset. The only thing missing was the corner bar. But when I sat down in one of the huge leather chairs facing his desk, I could see a fully stocked one set up behind the door.

"Look, Takeru, we're going to close this deal with or without your involvement. Get it, sensei? I mean, I wanna pop open a Sapporo with you, too, but we gotta work out the details of this before anyone's bustin' out the *spricy* crunchy tuna rolls and *flied lice*."

Was he serious? I fiddled with my folder and decided that he was probably just kidding around with an old friend. Or maybe talking to no one and trying to joke with me?

"Hey, you must be Emma, c'mon in, have a seat," he said loudly, snapping off his headset, ignoring the continued squawking on the other end. "I'm Derek Dorfman, the head honcho around these parts." I smiled politely. "Some people call me the boss, the bossinator, bossman, bossmanerino. But *you* can call me Derek."

This was the Welcome Wagon for corporate America.

"So!" he clapped his hands loudly, making me jump. "Tell me about yourself."

I took a deep breath and tried to get comfortable, sliding myself back in the chair. My sweaty acrylic pants made a small fartlike squeak, and I blushed and rattled off my interests, hobbies, typing skills, and superhuman work ethic. I might have even included the words "move the needle"—something I'd once heard my dad's coworker say—to which Derek gave an appreciative nod.

"Let me tell you something, Em. Can I call you Em?" No pause for my response. "I'm pretty confident that you can type a letter and organize my filing system. I mean, I wouldn't be the boss here if I couldn't read people, you know what I'm sayin'?" He smiled self-importantly and paused, apparently so I could ooh and aah at his lofty status, which I dutifully did. "But I want to know more about Emma Freeman *the individual*. Are you compatible with MediaInc on a *mano y mano* level?"

I had *no* idea what he was talking about but I smiled sycophantically and enthused that I was.

"Like, Em baby," he pointed toward the "Personal Interests" section of my resume. "Tell me about this musical comedy troupe you're in." Crap. I may have exaggerated my fifth-grade starring role in *Stars, Stripes, 'n' Sharp Notes* into a full-blown extracurricular. "What skills have you learned from singing and performing that could be applied to a work environment?"

"Um . . . well, like now. The acting is helping."

Derek gave me an encouraging "Uh-huh."

"And, well, just watch this." I spread my fingers into jazz hands, shimmied them around, and sang, *"Ya dah dah dah dah, hire me!"* Then I struck a very Fosse finale pose. "You see, performing can apply to any situation."

What the flip was I doing? Bombing this interview, that's what. Did I *seriously* just do jazz hands? Good God. I started a mental list of the restaurants around Union Square where I could waitress this summer.

"That's great, Em." To my complete surprise, his tone wasn't sarcastic at all. "I used to do a little acting myself." He contorted his face into an exaggerated frown and then slowly moved his hand upward, over his face. When his hand crossed his mouth, he was grinning. "Pretty good, right? So, Em, what's your weakness?"

Before I could answer he shouted, *"Men! Okay, then, chillin', chillin', mindin' my business. . . ."*

He stopped mid-rap, leaning over his desk to hold an invisible mic in my face, and waited for me to take over. I shrugged my shoulders in complete confusion. Was he singing Salt-N-Pepa? For real? I think I was still a fetus when this song came out.

When I came up lyrically empty-handed, and more than a little horrified, he continued himself, proceeding to rap all four verses of "Shoop." I finally stopped him after *"I love you in your big jeans, you give me nice dreams, you make me wanna scream, 'Oooo, oooo, oooo!' "* and sputtered out a question regarding hours and lunch breaks.

"Oh, don't you worry about that. All that can be sorted out tomorrow."

"To—tomorrow?" I stammered. Did this mean I was hired? I hadn't expected to start so soon.

"Yeah, I'm going to need you to come back tomorrow around the same time for a second interview. Company policy, two interviews. But brush up on your hip-hop and rap, girlfriend. Tomorrow is Tupac Tuesday! Ha!" He laughed at his own joke for a good fifteen seconds before I awkwardly got up to leave.

Did all of that really happen or could I be hallucinating?

That night at home, Rach grilled me on the new/possible job.

"I don't know," I said, stirring the powdered sauce into my mac and cheese. "He's really funny and quirky but in a good way I think. I mean, who wants to work with someone who's uptight? Okay, so his jokes aren't really *that* funny, but he's old. Grown-ups are never funny, except for Jon Stewart."

I was trying to put a positive spin on things. Like it or not, this was my only option for a summer internship, and if I wanted the college resume builder and the guaranteed afternoon AC, I had to take it. Plus, there was no way Ma 'n' Pa Freeman were going to keep pumping the allowance money into my bank account if they knew I was just hanging out watching *Project Runway* marathons.

Through bites of mac, I told Rachel about my victimization via the white man cover of "Shoop." Even though it had been slightly unnerving when it happened, it was a pretty good story. She almost snarfed her Diet Dr Pepper, she was laughing so hard.

"Okay, what happened at your interview? Did you have to dance to TLC or something?" I asked.

She told me about her interview. It had gone wonderfully—she was offered the internship, the *paid* internship, and was going to start next Monday.

"But it's, like, barely enough to support my Claire's Accessories habit," she said in response to my jaw dropping at the word "paid." I didn't even know that interns could get paid. She could tell I was superjealous and didn't want to talk about it anymore. With a swift subject change, she asked what were the plans for my birthday the next day. "How about a fancy celebration dinner or something?" Then she turned and screamed toward Jayla's room, "Jay, is there an Outback in the city?"

A mud-masked Jayla popped her head out of the doorway. "What's an outback? Like a place with garden seating?"

"No, like the steakhouse. You know, where you go for Mother's Day and stuff," Rachel explained.

Ignoring how so not New York we were, Jayla asked, "Why don't we go to Gramercy Tavern? The maître d' loves me." She popped herself back into her room.

I had no idea what or where Gramercy Tavern was, but it sounded way better than any Bloomin' Onion. And I was amped that Jayla would want to come to celebrate my eighteenth birthday. She was twenty-one and glamorous and was by far going to be the most fabulous person I'd ever had at my birthday party.

In the kitchen, I turned to Rachel and mouthed a silent "Oh my God!" and she gave me a thumbs-up.

"Thanks, Jay. Really cool!" Then I realized that I might have a deal-breaker. I frowned a little. "Uhhh . . . but I kind of have to invite my cousin Jake. Is that cool?" I was yelling, hoping that she'd hear me over the running water she'd just turned on in her bathroom.

"The one who looks like a starfish?" she hollered back.

Rachel and I wrinkled our noses. "A *starfish*?"

With her mask only half washed off, she ducked her head back out. "Yeah, you know, like a starfish that's turned over—little tiny eyes and his round puckery mouth. And that mop of hair he's got is, like, the tentacles and stuff."

I hadn't taken bio since freshman year, but I was pretty sure that starfish didn't have tentacles. Though she was kind of right about the comparison. That was a pretty good description of him. Even so, I still felt the need to defend my cousin. "Oh, I think he's cute!"

"Cute for a crustacean," she murmured, and went back to her beauty routine.

The next day—my eighteenth birthday!—I trekked back over to MediaInc again to meet with Derek. And this time when I got out of the subway, I walked the right way. I'd like to say that was a sign of good things to come at the interview, but that would be a lie.

He was reclining back in his massive chair with his legs crossed on his desk when I entered his office. "Emmmmmmmmmmmmmahhhhh!" he yelled like a soccer commentator announcing a goal.

"Hi, Mr. Dorfman."

"Uh-oh! I didn't know my father was here," he said, laughing loudly at yet another unfunny joke. "Hey, let me ask you something, kid. Do you know anything about this MySpace craze that's just starting?"

MySpace was way beyond just starting, but like so many adults, he'd found one morsel of pop culture that his friends didn't know about and my guess was he tried to bring it up whenever he could. It was like when my mom first learned the word "blog." She used it to describe anything that ran on electricity. "This blender is broken. Em, why don't you go blog about it and see if you can get it fixed?"

Even though he didn't ask me to, I took a seat in the same chair I was in yesterday. I just felt too weird lurking in the doorway. "Uh, yeah, I've heard of it. It's really cool."

He informed me that he'd asked MediaInc's design engineers to spend a few days making a page for him.

"Well, you can make a page yourself in about ten minutes if you want to. You can just upload pictures and a song and—"

"Whoa, whoa, whoa! Upload? Okay, now you've lost me."

I suppressed a heavy sigh and said that I'd be happy to explain it all to him sometime.

"Can you just show me your page so I can get an idea of what it looks like?"

79

I broke into a cold sweat. It had been weeks since I'd updated my profile and I was almost positive that Kyle's most recent comment on my page said something about me being a slut for leaving him in the burbs all summer. I also really didn't need him to see my "You're Just Jealous, BITCH" avatar that sparkled pink. Rachel and I had put them on as a joke, but to a stranger I'd just look like a psychotic brat.

I squirmed in my chair, trying to think of an excuse to get out of this that didn't sound too shady. "Ooh yeah," I stalled. "My page is, um, broken. Yep, see that happens once in a while. You can only look at a page once a day, and I already did this morning, so we'd have to wait until tomorrow."

Talking to adults about technology was like discussing Santa Claus with younger cousins—you just make it up as you go along.

I leaned back in my chair—eliciting another fart-y sound from the leather—relieved that I'd managed to avoid showing him my page.

He grunted with disappointment and asked about "Facialbook."

"You mean *Facebook?*" I bit my lip, trying not to giggle. "It's mostly just students on that site."

"Well, I took a wine-tasting class at the Learning Tree last year, does that count?"

I dug my fingernails into my leg to keep from laughing out loud . . . or crying, I couldn't tell which. "Gee, Derek, I don't know. I'm going to say probably not."

He finally let it go and briefed me on the history of MediaInc, most of which I tuned out, thinking about what other avatars I needed to replace. Finally he stood up and extended his hand.

"Emma, I think you'll do really well here. But hopefully not better than me!" He paused, signaling this was the time for me to laugh, which I did. "Welcome aboard! You can start next Monday." He put his hand out for what I thought was going to be a congratulations shake, but turned out to be more of a congratulations phalanges crunch.

I was still shaking the pain out of my fingers when I pushed my way through the revolving doors. Out onto the street, I did a little skip and called my mom so she could gush about how proud of me she was.

"Well, I think it's going to be really cool," I said. "Derek is a little weird, but totally nice and I think he sees a lot of potential in me."

Yeah, he was lame and kind of unbalanced, but that's fun, right? Maybe he'd write me all these rad college letters and hire me on once I graduated from college. God, I was *totally* on the career path! I'd probably be CEO of the Empire State Building by the time I was twenty-one.

I was so excited that my trip home went by in a total blur. It was actually surprising that I managed to snap out of my desk-job daze in time to get out at Union Square. I rushed up to the apartment, slammed the door behind me, and jumped up and down squealing to my roommates.

"You can tell us everything over your birthday dinner," Rachel said as she and Jayla scooted me into the shower to get ready.

Jayla did my hair and makeup—I looked like Victoria Beckham, but I sort of liked it—and even let me borrow a

Marc Jacobs purse. "You can't walk into Gramercy Tavern looking like you just bought out the Ellen DeGeneres garage sale."

As I was deciding whether to tuck my newly straightened hair behind my ears or let it hang, I heard the buzzer, then Rachel letting Jake in. I grabbed my borrowed MJ and joined everyone in the living room, where Jake was in the process of making halfhearted small talk with Rachel while watching Jayla out of the corner of his eye. To my reluctant amusement, Jayla kept mouthing "Starfish" whenever he wasn't looking. I nearly peed my black H&Ms laughing.

Dinner was a lavish affair, with incredible plates of lobster and steaks, and even a bottle of red wine!

When we first sat down, Jayla asked, "Hey, how do you all feel about a cab?"

We had just sat down about five seconds before, so I was bummed that Jayla was already ready to leave my big one-eight celebration. "Oh, I just kind of assumed that we were going to walk back home. It's not that far." I glanced down at the menu, trying not to show how hurt I was.

Jayla and Jake looked at each other, confused, then started cracking up. "Cab, like *cabernet*," Jake explained, "it's a kind of wine. And you, my young cousin, are only allowed to have half a glass, okay?"

Was I on *Dork Factor* right now? Seriously, it was like Jake was trying to see just how geeky he could make me feel before I cracked.

Jayla insisted on paying because she said she wasn't creative enough to think of a proper birthday present. Which was a big Thank God! It would have taken Rachel and my entire summer allowance to pay for the meal.

Jake's contribution was sugar and calories. He'd brought along a banana cream cake from someplace called Magnolia. Jayla gasped when it was brought out and sighed that she loved Magnolia so much, she hoped she could be buried underneath it when she was dead.

"Well, you know," Jake said, puffing his chest and trying so hard to be smooth, "my friend is the bouncer there. I can get you in whenever you want."

Bakeries had bouncers? This town was insane. Jayla's eyes widened. Apparently, this was the one place in New York where the velvet ropes didn't part for her.

"Jake! That would be amazing," she said, touching his arm lightly. I'm pretty sure he swooned. Wait, can boys swoon?

We ate cake until we all felt sick and Rachel plopped a few presents on the table.

"Your family sent these down with me so you could open them on your real birthday. But here, open mine first."

Rachel got me a gift certificate to this jewelry store where you could put your name on a gold necklace, like the one Carrie Bradshaw wore.

"It can say 'Emma.' How chic will that be?" Rachel giggled.

" 'Emma'?" Jayla shook her head. "Oh no, no. You need a really sexy Manhattan alias. Everyone here has one. You can't be giving out your real name to randos at clubs."

"What's yours?" Jake asked.

"Jinx. It's a Bond girl. I always try to pick a Bond name for myself. Emma, I think yours should be . . ." She bit her glossy lips. "Domino!"

"Domino?" I laughed but then considered it. "Domino Freeman!"

"Oh *God* no, not 'Freeman'! How about 'Domino Frost'? That sounds so hot!"

"Domino Frost." I repeated it several times and Rachel demanded that she get a new name too.

"Okay, Rach, you need a hot socialite name. Something that says 'Hamptons.' You'd make a perfect . . . *Bitsy. Bitsy Onassis!*"

Rachel squealed with delight. Any comparison to a Kennedy, blood-related or not, was like being knighted. As I opened up a bottle of Curious perfume from my parents, Jayla christened Jake "Chip McAllister."

"He's a kid I went to Choate with. Dated him for a hot second," she said simply, as if that was a totally thorough explanation. Jake beamed at the idea of being named after someone who'd ever swapped spit with Jayla.

"Okay, last one." Rachel pushed a card from my grandparents toward me.

I tore open the familiar red Hallmark envelope. Oh, Nana and Pop Pop! This was about the third time they'd given me the same birthday card: *Granddaughter, you've grown into a fine young woman . . .*

"It's a subscription to *National Geographic!*" I laughed. "Domino Frost: Saver of Rain Forests! And I really thought this was the year they'd give me that trust fund I've been hinting at."

Rachel and Jake laughed but Jayla looked kind of confused. I don't think she got the joke.

After dinner Jake took a cab back to his place and the three of us waddled back to our apartment, my pants threatening to burst at any second. I was rarin' to check my e-mail and MySpace and see what kind of birthday wishes I'd received—fine, what kind of birthday wishes *from Brian* I'd received. And yes, technically, I was pretty much over him (kind of), but come on, a girl's got to obsess about something.

Two seconds after we walked through the door, Rachel was already on *my* computer.

"Sorry, my battery is dead," she said, already logging onto Gmail. "I can't find my charger."

Um, it was *my* birthday and that meant I got first dibs on everything, computer time included.

"That's fine, I just need to check my e-mail real quick," I said, trying to sound as casual as possible.

"Yeah, just let me reply to this."

"No! *Now!*" Smooth, Emma, real smooth.

"All right, 'roid rage, just take it easy there." Rachel slid the MacBook toward me. "You want to see if Brian wrote you anything, don't you?"

"Pffft, no!" I was a terrible liar, but as my best friend, it was Rachel's duty to ignore that and just be supportive.

"Take your time," she said, patting me on the head as she retreated to her room. "I'll just be in here jotting down the reasons why Brian McSwain will end up living in a trailer with only a farty dog to keep him company."

I clicked my way through the log-in page and quickly ran through my inbox. Wait, seriously? No message from Brian? On my *birthday*? He was never great at remembering that sort of stuff, but *hello!* We all know that birthday alerts come up. I bit back tears. I wasn't thinking about Bri all that much, but deep down, I had told myself that my birthday was the last chance for him to make things right again. If he sent me some big expensive bouquet of flowers or made some really heartfelt declaration over the phone or even just a freaking MySpace comment—I don't know if I'd totally take him back, but I'd totally *think* about totally taking him back. But not even a comment on my page? It was like a kick to the stomach. With a sad sigh, I officially changed my MySpace status to single and un–"It's Complicated" myself on Facebook. I climbed into bed and wiped away a few tears that slipped out. I fell asleep dreaming of the new New York–ified me that would sashay back into Bridgefield in September and blow everyone's, especially Brian's, stupid suburban minds.

Eight

I'd planned to spend my last jobless summer days tanning with Rachel on the roof deck and having my new stylist—Jayla—pick out fabulous working-girl ensembles. But it turned out that I kind of overestimated Jayla's enthusiasm for hanging out with us. For the next two nights in a row, she left the apartment in the evening, sparkly and fabulous, and came home early in the morning, raccoon-eyed and lethargic, without ever offering an invite to either of us. It was very clear that she lived on one side of the red velvet ropes and we of the underaged persuasion were definitely on the other.

So, without help from a real-life fashionista, I scoured

Glamour and *Cosmo*, hoping they would give me some guidance on outfits that went from office wear into nighttime gear when you lost the blazer and added some dangly earrings.

"Rach, this is totally what we need." I pointed to this nautical chic day-to-evening look. "Let's head out to H&M and see if we can find it for way cheaper. I can be ready in fifteen."

Rachel barely looked up from her laptop. "You go, I'm just going to stay here and take care of some things."

"Take care of some things? Are you suddenly a mother of three who has to juggle a career, parenting, and the housework? We have nothing to take care of here. We don't even have homework."

She was so busy with whatever Internet crap she was doing, she didn't even hear me.

"Yo, Wolferine. Snap out of it." I slammed her laptop closed. "Stop Googling yourself and come with."

"Hey, hey, hey! What are you doing?" She propped the screen back open and continued her cruise down the information superhighway.

"What are you doing?" I craned my neck around to find out what could possibly be more enticing than buying poorly made trendy clothing. And then to my horror, I saw what site she was surfing. It couldn't have been more shocking if it were a message board at IHeartSanjaya.com or more embarrassing than a "your shopping cart" page at LaneBryant.com.

I gasped, then choked, and flopped down beside her on the couch. "JDate? Rachel, you're seventeen! You don't need to resort to online dating. You're only going to meet those pervs that end up on *To Catch a Predator*!"

"So not true!" Jayla said, having awoken from her daily catnap and pranced into the common room. "One of my friends had free dinners this entire spring courtesy of Match. And she totally met her current boyfriend, who is way cute and in no way a middle-aged sexual predator." Rachel shot me a told-you-so look. "But, Rachel, you might want to re-think the JDate thing. My friend told me that all of the men on that site are short and nebbishy."

"Short and nebbishy?" Rachel swooned at the thought. "Exactly what a good Jewish girl should be looking for!" She could tell I was still way anti the online dating. "Em, I moved here to get some dating experience. I'm cool with going to college a virgin, but I don't have to be a raging virgin. A few dates would take the edge off."

Jayla nodded her approval of the strategy.

"The only thing is that I really need to lose ten pounds before I put my picture up." She grabbed the flab of tummy that even Kate Bosworth would have when sitting down. "So maybe I'll wait to start for another week or so."

I was about to give her the best-friend requisite you're-so-not-fat talk, but Jayla cut in before I could start.

"Hello! That's why God invented Photoshop!" She snatched the laptop from Rachel and plopped down on the other side of her. She cracked her knuckles and wiggled her fingers. "Okay, I'm ready. Let me see your pic."

By the time she'd finished, Rachel's body looked even hotter than it already was, the roots from her April Sun-In experiment were gone, and her vampirishly pale skin was as bronze as a third-place medal.

"Do me, do me!" I ran into my room and grabbed my laptop, shook it out of sleep mode, and found a pic of myself on Flickr to pass over to Jayla. I wasn't going to be online dating, but still, I wanted to experience the miraculous powers of Photoshop. Within ten minutes, my picture had blue eyes, a butt Jessica Biel would kill for, and cleavage that I couldn't get in real life with four Wonderbras.

"Make him look less like a starfish!" A giggling Rachel shoved her laptop back to Jayla with a close-up of Jake on the screen.

And that's pretty much how we spent the entire afternoon, doctoring photos and creating a JDate profile for Rachel. By five o'clock, she had two offers for dinner. She responded to the guy who had a Panic! quote in his profile and headed with Jayla to her room for wardrobe and makeup.

The two emerged from Jayla's House of Style an hour later and Jayla announced, "Ladies and, well, various houseplants, I'd like to introduce you to the newest hottie on the New York dating scene. She's a heartbreaker and tuchas shaker, Ms. Rachel "Chosen Men Choose Me" Wolfe!" Rach pranced through the door—and she looked cute! No, scratch that, *hot*! And the best thing was, she knew it. She stomped it out Tyra style around the living room for a while.

"And now for me," Jayla said, disappearing back into her room, starting her own beautification.

Rachel struck a final pose, complete with the ANTM pursed mouth and the sacred "fierce" eyes, then plopped next to me on the couch.

"Em." She turned to me with a superserious look. "I'm kind of freaking the freak out."

"About what? You look great!"

"No, of course I know that."

"Oh, sorry to state the obvious, Ms. Thang," I sassed.

But Rachel was in no mood for snark. "No, I mean, like, better than normal or whatever, but I'm actually getting really nervous. Like, for the date. This is going to be my first real date ever. Up until now, the longest time I've ever spent one-on-one with a boy was Seven Minutes in Heaven. And charming conversation wasn't exactly the main point there."

I smiled at the memory. It was in sixth grade and was the first real boy-girl party Rachel and I had ever been invited to. We were more nervous than Isaiah Washington at a gay pride parade. We had planned everything out for weeks: which UGGs we'd wear with which minis (ick, why was that look ever acceptable?), who to ask to slow dance, signals to give each other if we needed to be saved from Johnny Smigler's cheese breath, and timing for joint bathroom runs to check for food chunks in our braces. But when we got there, no one was dancing or even talking really. Everyone was sitting in a circle playing Seven-Minute Spin—pretty much spin the bottle, except for when you landed on someone, you didn't just kiss them, you went into the sports equipment closet with them for seven minutes. Being totally dorkified as I was (and, let's be honest, still am), I told everyone that I thought I was getting a cold and couldn't play. I ate French onion dip and baby carrots all evening while everyone else, including Rachel, pranced in and out of the closet in pairs.

I snapped out of the middle school memory and back into the sassy summer crisis. "Okay, calm down. There's no way I'm letting you have a panic attack and sweat off the bajillion dollars of makeup Jayla just applied, okay?" She took a deep breath as I continued, "Really, don't worry about this at all. You're going to be fine. Guys are just like girls, except for, you know, hairier and they pay for stuff. So just be normal, talk about what you normally talk about, and he'll totally love you, okay?"

She mumbled an "okay" but I could tell she was still a mega case of nerves. I squeezed her hand, careful not to mess her freshly touched-up nail polish. Jayla bounced out of her room, clad in a dress that ended right where her underwear started—if she was even wearing any, who knew with her?

"Let's hit it, babe. We have hearts to break!" Jayla grabbed Rachel and headed for the door, my best friend throwing me a look of wide-eyed panic over her shoulder.

"Have fun, sexies!" I called out after them as they headed to the elevator arm in arm. I gave Rachel a thumbs-up that I thought might be encouraging and then waved as I shut our apartment door.

An entire evening alone stretched out in front of me. I thought about doing something New York–y, like heading down to this pizza place in Brooklyn that *Let's Go* declared the best New York–style pizza. But Brooklyn? I would probably get crazy lost, never find the pizza, and have to call Jake to come rescue me. So I did what seemed like the next best thing—I ordered Chinese and burrowed myself into blankets on the couch for a night of TiVo.

"So?" I badgered Rach as soon as she walked out of her room, eyes still swollen with sleep and hair sticking out electrocution style. "One-to-ten it on the awkward scale." I was up way earlier than her from my wild-n-crazy night in and had already planted myself back on the couch.

She slumped into the armchair. "Well, when I walked up to him, it was like an eleven-point-five. I totally didn't know how we were going to say hi. Like, a hug, a kiss on the cheek, a handshake? So I kind of waited for some sort of cue from him and there, like, wasn't any. So I just went in for the hug. And, like, at that second, he put his hand out for a shake, so he pretty much punched me in the gut. And then I was like, well, that's as awkward as it can get, right? So it totally made me relax and after that, I was fine."

I laughed at the thought of my BFF taking a jab to the stomach.

"Well, I knew you'd be fine. How was he?"

"Oh, good on paper, but that's it."

I wrinkled my nose and took a sip of the über-expensive pomegranate juice Jayla kept in the fridge for Pomtinis. I was just borrowing it. I'd get her back when I went grocery shopping next—which would probably be never, but the thought was there. "What does that mean?"

"You know, like if I had seen his dating resume, I would have thought that he was perfect. Good family from New Jersey, wants to be a doctor, loves dogs, not wearing athletic sandals. Generally good in theory, you know? But in person— well, he talked about the summer chem class he was taking in excruciating detail. I thought about forking myself in the eye it was so boring. But then I remembered that I forgot to bring any extra contacts to New York, so I can't really fuck this pair up. Remind me to ask the parentals to send up more next time they call, 'kay? Whatever. I have another JDate tonight."

I couldn't believe this. Rachel, who normally wasn't even allowed to be out past nine-thirty on a weeknight, was now dating seven days a week.

She got up to fix herself some cereal as Jayla came in

through the front door. She slowly ambled into the apartment, teetering on her four inches of heel, and then patted her hips front to back. She looked like she'd lost her wallet or something. "Crappity crap. I lost another pair of La Perlas."

I shook my head and exchanged eye-rolls with Rachel. Who were these guys she was shacking up with? A rotation of the same ones or new dudes she picked up every night? I smiled, picturing a giant stable, but instead of horses in the stalls, there were bankers and lawyers and actors stamping their feet and tossing their hair around.

"How was dinner and, um, whatever else?" Rachel asked.

I had a feeling this was going to be a great story.

"Oh, good. You know, nothing special." She moved her hand to her jaw and massaged the joint. "I think I gave myself TMJ last night. But you know, when you've got a Nike shoe named after you, you have pretty good control over your own body." And with that, Jayla headed to her room for a nap that would last until date time tonight.

Rachel turned to me. "Is TMJ a designer I don't know about?"

"Uh . . . kind of." I changed the subject, not wanting to get into a full-blown health class. "So, shopping today? We still need our first-day-of-work outfits." I was getting a little stir-crazy from staying in the apartment for forty-eight hours straight. I needed out. And I needed something else to wear other than black polyblend H&M pants. It was nice I didn't have to iron them, but I could foresee some temperature issues—it was getting so humid outside, I could practically shower on the street corner.

But to my disappointment, I was dissed for the second time in twenty-four hours. "You go," Rachel sighed, then stood up and stretched. "I'm probably going to lounge around here for a while and maybe nap, too." Then she turned and headed back into her room as if choosing napping over shopping was totally acceptable.

Hello? What happened to "We'd never be lonely if we were together"? I was officially feeling lonely. Because I was the only one of us who slept normal hours, I was suddenly a social outcast. What was I supposed to do all day with those two sleeping? Frustrated, I threw a towel and some SPF 4 into my purse and decided to take a field trip to Central Park—alone. But as soon as I left the building, I realized that I'd been in such a huff I'd forgotten to take my map. Not wanting to head back upstairs to my snoozeville apartment, I headed across the street to the patch of green and brown that counted as a park in the middle of Union Square. Two hours later, after almost getting decapitated by a twelve-year-old on a skateboard, I'd gotten a wicked painful, can't-wear-a-bra-for-two-days burn on my back because neither of those bitches were there to help me lather up. Social skanks.

The next few days continued just like that. Jayla partied a ton, rubbing shoulders and other, unmentionable parts with New York's most fabulous resident models, Eurotrash, and rich older men. And Rachel was up to her pulkies in JDates that never panned out. Both girls kept their vampire schedules of sleeping during sunlight and only commenced socializing during twilight.

After two days of nursing a sunburn and pretty much memorizing every episode of *The Hills* (and fine, MyStalking Brian and just about every other person in Bridgefield), I decided to stop the pity party and take myself out on an adventure.

"I mean, that's what I'm here for, right?" I said to my

reflection as I pulled on the last of my clothes that qualified as "clean enough." I was sweating through clothes faster than Anna Wintour goes through assistants, and after barely a week, my entire duffle of clothing was stank-y. I def needed to get some laundry done. Jayla said something about washers in the basement, but from what I knew about New York—and by that I mean what I'd seen on *Law & Order: SVU*—104 percent of all crimes happened in basement laundry rooms. So I figured I'd avoid any potential underground-dwelling sociopaths and drop it off at the Laundromat on the corner—that's what Jayla did every Sunday. Apparently, people will just do your laundry for you. It sounded a lot like having a mom, but without the curfew. Why would I spend my last few days of jobless freedom messing with quarters and dryer sheets? I hadn't really thought about bringing a laundry bag to the city, so I'd been sort of shoving my dirty clothes in piles under my bed and hoping they'd magically clean themselves. I scooted past the dust bunnies and extracted my now really filthy clothes and stuffed them into the only thing I could find, a garbage bag. Looking like a hobo, I hauled an enormous Hefty down to the cleaners.

"Heavy!" the laundry lady shrieked. "You come back tonight!" I nodded dutifully. I tried to ask her how much it would be, but she just pointed to the giant scale behind the counter and shrugged. What the hell was she talking about? Did they weigh my laundry? Whatever. How much could a suitcase worth of clothes possibly cost to wash?

I had intended to head up to Macy's in Herald Square, but apparently ended up on an express train straight to the corner of Lost Avenue and Disoriented Lane.

I heard the subway conductor announce, "Next stop:

Seventh Avenue." Seventh Avenue? I was supposed to be going to Thirty-fourth *Street*. "Avenue" didn't sound right to me. I rushed over to the map and tried to finger-trace my path, but I was so flustered that I couldn't even find Union Square.

I turned to the fem man or manly woman—I couldn't really tell—sitting near the map. "Um . . . hi. How far is Seventh Avenue from Herald Square?" I tried not to sound too much like a frightened tourist, but that's exactly what I was.

S/he wrinkled her pierced nose. "Pretty far. First you'd have to get the train back to Manhattan and—"

"Wait." I stopped her/him. "*Back* to Manhattan? Where are we?"

"Park Slope."

I could feel a panicky fever spreading across my face, but it must have translated as blank confusion.

"Brooklyn," s/he said.

I suppressed a horrified gasp and I tried to pretend that I had fully intended on ending up in another borough.

"Oh yeah, Brooklyn," I said, waving casually with one hand while my other frantically pawed around my purse for my subway map, where I had highlighted the Union Square stop. "I'm totally here all the time. I just, you know, never hear people call it Park Slope anymore. My friends always say 'The PS' and stuff."

S/he gave me a weird look and went back to her/his iPod.

I fumbled with my map as inconspicuously as I could, but couldn't really figure out where I was. I leave the apartment one time in a week and end up in some park on the other end of the world that sounds like it's full of hills. I totally wouldn't have worn my platform flip-flops had I known today's adventure would involve a nature hike.

By now half the train had taken notice of the ridiculous lost girl, freaking out and sweating at the thought of leaving Manhattan. I swear even the homeless guy singing "Amazing Grace" for nickels was ridiculing me with his eyes. I should have probably stayed on and tried to find a stop that linked to a train that would take me back to Manhattan. But the thought of going any deeper into Brooklyn was terrifying. What if I ended up in Queens or something?

As soon as the subway doors opened at the next stop, I bolted, with no clue how I was going to get back to Manhattan. I followed the crowd as it ebbed toward the exit—I didn't see any signs for connecting trains and I was too embarrassed to ask anyone else for directions. Besides, everyone seemed to have a mullet and who would trust anyone with a carni-trash haircut? I took a deep breath and tried to pull myself together. I remembered reading in an article in *Cosmo* that Keira Knightley loved to go shopping in Brooklyn. So okay, I was lost, but maybe I could pick up some sweet outfits anyway? As Rachel always says, if life gives you lemons . . . stick them down your shirt and make your boobs look bigger! Too bad I might never make it back to Manhattan to show them off. "Them" meaning the clothes—I didn't think I was going to find boobs in Brooklyn.

I emerged from the wet heat of the subway to the even wetter heat of the street, and Park Slope didn't look much like a fashionista's paradise. There was a faint smell of garbage wafting through the air, and I think there was some gang warfare going on across the street. Well, fine, it was teen-aged boys in droopy pants hanging out on a sunny tree-lined block. But still, this was the closest thing to gang fighting I'd seen since the drama club put on *West Side Story* last fall.

I stood on the corner, trying to not make eye contact with strangers, studying my map. Out of the corner of my eye, I saw an old woman with a walker slowly making her way across the street and decided to ask her for directions. "Um, excuse me?" I said meekly. "Where is there good shopping?"

"What are you looking for, dear?" She stopped walking and turned her wrinkly face toward me.

"Uh, like, floaty tunics or something like that," I stammered.

"What? Tuna? Oh there's tuna over there at the Associated Supermarket." She gestured down the street and then started creeping away in her walker. "Canned or fresh. Whatever you want," she said as she passed me.

I thanked her quickly and scurried onward. I was frustrated, hot, thirsty, and embarrassed. Tears welled up in my eyes. Why did everything in this city have to be so damn hard? I couldn't even find a stupid department store without ending up on the dark side of the world, turning to a human prune for help. I took off down the street, no idea where I was headed. The smart thing to do would've been to go inside a bodega, get a Diet Coke, center myself, then head back to a subway and ask someone how to get back home. But instead I wandered around sketchy Brooklyn for forty-five minutes, getting hooted at by guys on bikes, trying not to picture the headline "Suburban Teen Dies at Hands of Marauding Bicycle Gang." I finally, finally came across a sort-of-cool vintage store and vowed to buy something to justify my totally failed retail-therapy adventure. Vintage stuff was never really my style, but I felt pretty good about my purchase of gray slouchy boots and a very J.Lo floppy hat.

My flip-flops had given me blisters, so I changed into the boots and threw the flops-o-pain in my bag. I put on my new hat, too, to complete my vintage-fab look. As I walked toward the subway—or at least what I was pretty sure was the subway—I checked myself out in store windows. Jayla and Rachel would probably freak when they saw my new makeover. They might even mistake me for a brunette Sienna Miller. Okay, maybe not. But still, I knew they'd totally be proud.

I sashayed down the streets of Brooklyn totally feeling like an old-school J.Lo video when I realized that the heel on one of my new boots was a little shaky. Eh, that's the beauty of vintage, right? But my hat still looked hot billowing in the wind.

I was pretty sure that I was retracing my steps back to the subway and things were starting to look more familiar, but then again, every bodega pretty much looks the same, so who knows? I could have been halfway to Coney Island. Just as I started to get the feeling that I should probably ask someone for directions, I heard, "Arrrggghhh!" from a guy hollering across the street and decided that relying on the kindness—or even sanity—of strangers was probably not the best idea. He continued his crazy rant with "Thar she blows, matey!"

What a perv. Who shouts to young girls about *blowing*? As I craned my neck to throw the guy a dirty look, my ankle twisted and I wobbled back and forth, teetering on the brink of eating the sidewalk. I won the tug-of-war with gravity and managed to stay upright, but when I looked down, I saw my heel lying pathetically on the sidewalk. As in, it was no longer connected to the bottom of my shoe.

Effing great. The thought of subjecting my already raw feet to more time in my torturous J.Crew flops was worse than limping around on a broken heel. So I kept the boots on and walked mostly on my toes, hoping no one would notice. I only had to hobble a block more before seeing an entrance to a subway, thank God. If I didn't think that I'd catch the herp, I would have kissed the grimy subway floor.

I swiped through the turnstile and just as I was stepping onto the Manhattan-bound platform, a train whisked into the station. I hustled in and sank into my seat, eager to get back to the safe TiVo-dom of my summer apartment.

"I wonder if she's got a peg leg, too!" a kid sitting across from me sniggered. I whipped around to see if they were talking about a homeless person smelly enough to require a car change, but everyone on the subway seemed home-full and deodorized.

Two wrong subways and three connections later, I was finally hobbling back to my apartment. As I made my way down Fourteenth Street, I remembered my laundry and stopped to pick it up. My feet were raw and my calves were burning from walking on my toes like an idiot for the past hour and a half. I dug around in my purse for my laundry receipt.

"Oh hell," I sighed with exasperation. "I'm sorry but I don't think I have my ticket."

"No ticket, no clothes!" said the old laundry lady firmly.

"But I see my stuff. It's right there!" I pointed to a cube of what I guessed were folded clothes with *FREEMAN* emblazoned across the attached pink receipt slip. "See? Freeman, Emma Freeman."

The laundry woman narrowed her eyes suspiciously.

"You have blood on pairs of underwear, yes?" she said much louder than necessary.

My face turned scarlet. Yeah, I'd had my period for about five years now, but for some reason, I still couldn't accurately predict when it was going to arrive. Crucify me!

"Yes!" I hissed, leaning in close and hoping the family folding their clothes didn't speak English. "It's mine, okay? The bloody undies are mine. Are you satisfied?"

She smiled somewhat smugly and slowly ambled over to the garbage bag full of my clothes. I pulled out my wallet, ready to pay my fifteen dollars or whatever, get the hell out of there, and just mellow out on the couch for a while. A new episode of *Sunset Tan* was starting in seven minutes and some quality time with the Olly Girls sounded like the perfect remedy for such a fiasco of a day.

"Forty-five dollar," said the old laundry lady.

"Huh? For what?" I looked incredulously at my bag of neatly folded clothes and wondered if they charged by the button or something.

"You drop off twenty pound laundry. Two dollar a pound! Plus folding, separate, softener."

Was anything simple in the town? Or cheap? I only had about twenty dollars in cash, and there wasn't an ATM in the Laundromat. I thought of my blistered feet, of the Olly Girls, and of my dad's "emergency" credit card sitting comfortably in my wallet. I scowled and plunked down the parental credit card, mentally noting to tell Dad about this and pay him back as soon as I got home in August.

As I lumbered back home with twenty pounds of clean clothes over my shoulder, I kept thinking about my expenses. How was an unpaid intern supposed to survive in this city? No, not just survive—*be fabulous*? How was I going to be fabulous in this city when I couldn't even afford clean clothes?

I was trying to calculate some sort of self-budget for the summer, but the thing about being unpaid was that you got paid nothing. And nothing divided by food and a new wardrobe and any partying I got around to doing was still nothing! I let myself into the apartment, scowling at how un-fab my finance situation was.

"Emma!" Jayla laughed as I walked in, sweaty and laundry-heaving in all my hat-and-boots glory. "Is that your booty, matey?"

"What?" I was honestly too sweaty and tired to care about how my butt looked.

"Yeah," Rachel chimed in, peeking out from her room. "Arrrrggghhh ya free Saturday night?"

What was going on Saturday? Considering my entire social circle in the metro area was sitting in that room, of course I was free. I really hoped that she wasn't expecting me to double with her and guys she met on MeetAFuture SexOffender.com. Then it dawned on me—the "Thar she blows, matey," the peg leg, the booty—I looked like a pirate, not Sienna Miller.

"You guys!" I stomped my heel-less foot. "I got these in Brooklyn! They're vintage! It's boho chic, not pirate!"

"Domino, Domino, Domino," Jayla sighed condescendingly, as if I was too idiotic to grasp the intricacies of dressing myself. "Boho is more like *no go*. There's a reason you can only find that shit at flea markets and not at real stores."

I started to say that it wasn't a flea market but didn't

want to subject myself to any more ridicule. I barged past Rachel into her room and flopped on her bed. Her computer was, of course, open to JDate, with some sexy Semitic single's page up. I was pretty much at my breaking point, and if Rachel left me alone again tonight, I might snap in a big way.

"Enough, Rachel. You can't go on a date tonight. Tomorrow's both of our first days at work. You're not going to be able to nap at work, you know. And seriously, what happened to the great Rachel and Emma New York adventure? If I'd known you were going to just come here and prowl for guys all summer like some desperate ho, I'd have just let you go to camp and come here by myself."

I knew as soon as the words hit the air that I'd crossed the line.

She rushed over to her bed and slammed shut her laptop, leaving Seth/Sam/Shlomo hanging. "Oh, really? That's a really interesting version of how things went down. Because as I remember it, you were snotting and bawling and having a nervous breakdown over Brian McHerpes and practically begging me to come to the city with you. And also"—she paused for effect and I cowered slightly, knowing I was really going to get it—"I haven't even kissed anyone here. You're my best friend and I don't need you of all people telling me I'm a ho."

She was so right. This was about my total lack of social interaction combined with a rotten afternoon in the depths of Brooklyn, not about her.

"You're right," I peeped. "I'm sorry. I'm just kind of overwhelmed with being here and underwhelmed with how little I have to do, you know? And I miss hanging out with you."

I could see her anger deflating. She sat next to me on her bed.

"No, I know. And I mean, I haven't really been that considerate with all this JDate stuff. I know you just broke up and me dating like crazy probably isn't helping you get over him."

I sighed, not wanting to admit that she was right. A moment of silence passed between us and suddenly she brightened.

"Okay, enough of this *Dr. Phil* special. Let's get some really professional-yet-cute day planners for our first day and then maybe a little sush to the bouche. Sound like a plan?"

Vague longing flashed across her face as her eyes darted briefly to her laptop, and I knew she'd rather be chatting it up online but, bless her heart, she was humoring me. Finally.

"So, like, what exactly is your internship, Em?" she asked, both of us diving into the mountain of edamame between us. We'd found a sushi place down the block that wasn't crazy expensive and didn't seem to be overrun with flies. As we sat munching our steamed soybeans, a waitress came by and slid a boat of sushi onto our table, which we attacked. We hadn't really celebrated getting internships yet, so that was the excuse for the sashimi dinner. And when my dad got the bill for it, I'd just tell him that I'd taken Jake out to thank him for helping me get situated in the big city. Totally valid reason that my dad would buy.

"It's media buying. The marketing department." I stuffed a soy-sauced piece of tuna into my mouth and licked my fingers loudly, not caring that the two immaculate gay men at the table next to us probably thought I looked like a competitive eater. I felt sophisticated saying "media." Who uses that word?

"Media?" Clearly, Rachel was wondering the same thing. "Media buying? Like, what does that mean?"

I realized, somewhat uneasily, that I had no idea. Like, none. I felt a stab of worry. I was so unprepared and I started tomorrow. But internships were about learning. If I already knew exactly what media buying was, they wouldn't have hired me as an intern, right?

"Is it picking which DVDs are at Target and stuff?" Rachel pressed.

"Umm . . ." That sounded logical enough. "Yes, kind of. Sure," I said with a mouth full of fish.

We finished up our sush and trekked back to the apartment. I didn't even partake in my typical Sunday evening *Law & Order: CI* marathon on Bravo because I wanted to be sure that I got a full night's rest. And watching an eighteen-year-old girl getting abducted on a block that could be right outside my building probably wouldn't make for the sweetest of dreams. But as I lay in my bed at nine p.m., I couldn't fall asleep. I had just woken up about ten hours earlier. So I pulled out my journal and started venting big-time. This was my first time cracking the journal open since landing in the city a week ago, so I started from the very beginning. As I scribbled about the skank hole hotel we stayed in and the deets of Jayla's celeb face-sucking, I felt myself getting super-nervous for the next day. I mean, I'd spent more time picking out my pink and brown faux Kate Spade planner than actually researching my position. And that was so not like me. I was always prepared—even for pop quizzes. I flashed to scenes from *The Hills*, which, aside from my interviews, was my only glimpse into the world of internships. I tried to calm down by comparing myself to LC. And I'm pretty sure that I have at least thirty IQ points on her. So if she could be an intern without getting fired on the spot, I'd be fine, too. Right? Well, I guess I'd find out soon enough. I placed my journal on the nightstand, closed my eyes, and tried my hardest to fall asleep. Trying to sleep never works, so of course I ended up flicking on the Bravo marathon and catching an episode of *Law & Order*. Thankfully, it wasn't an episode about a high school intern being abducted on her way to work, so I was nightmare free once I managed to fall asleep.

The next day, Rachel and I woke up early to get ready for our first day as interns. I buttoned up the same pink shirt I had worn to my first interview. I never did make it out for my planned working-girl shopping spree, so it was either that or the pirate outfit.

I slipped my day planner into my bag and popped my head into Rachel's room. She was tripping into a pair of tights and had some sort of cutoff shirt on. She looked at me with desperation. "I want to look funky but professional. I've tried on everything I have and nothing's working."

"R-Dubs, you need to start setting out your clothes the night before. Seriously, it saves like a million hours in the morning."

At the beginning of junior year, I made this weird resolution to always set out my clothes for the following day. That way I could just roll out of bed and into whatever jeans-and-sweater combo I'd picked out and devote my morning to more important decisions, like Frosted Flakes versus Pop-Tarts. I'd tried to get Rachel to do it about a thousand times, but she seemed to prefer racking up the tardy slips over just taking my advice. Being late for art history was one thing, but to cruise in ten minutes after everyone else at a *job* was really bad. I briefly thought about approving her outfit just to get her out of the house on time. But I couldn't, with a clear conscience, give her a thumbs-up looking like she just crawled out of a Mötley Crüe video.

"Well, that certainly looks . . . *funky*." I cringed. Sometimes you've got to be cruel to be kind.

"That bad?"

I nodded and she looked like she was going to cry. I wanted to help but I couldn't be late for my first day of media buying. I headed out the front door, calling over my shoulder, "Have a great first day, babe! I'll call you when it's over, and we can meet up for dinner or whatever."

Even though it was only eight-thirty in the morning, the heat of the day immediately enveloped me, and within the four-minute walk to the subway, the humidity had already managed to obliterate the twenty minutes I'd spent straightening my hair.

I hopped on the subway, smushed among all of the other work-bound commuters. Normally the subway was a stinky, unsanitary adventure that I loathed, but today I was excited. I felt like a grown-up, riding the train with all the business-people going to their very important, very adult jobs. It was weird to be among so many people and have it be so quiet. Not a single person was talking. I silently judged a lady who was wearing a full skirt suit with nylons and scrunch socks and sneakers. So ugs. I cranked up my iPod, held on to the pole, and tried not to inhale too deeply—someone nearby had definitely forgotten deodorant this morning. I wondered what it would be like to be an actual adult, instead of half-faking it for the summer. What would life be like without summer breaks or getting out before three p.m.? But then again, you're making money and you don't have anyone telling you to clean up your room and please put down a sheet of tinfoil when you make Bagel Bites in the toaster oven. Maybe I'd like it.

After we stopped at Times Square, I shoved my way toward the door, proud that I knew that my stop was next. But then I saw the sign for the Forty-ninth Street stop flash as we sped by. Dammit! What was going on? I broke out in a not-so-cold sweat, picturing me frantically calling Mr. Dorfman and telling them I'd gotten on the wrong train and was now in Hackensack, New Jersey, or wherever.

"Hey, how do I get this thing to stop? I wanted to get off there," I said, or actually probably yelled, because I still had my earphones in.

"Lady, this is an express. Don't stop at Forty-ninth," a man said, and then laughed to himself.

Oh, well, that's just great. I got off at the next stop, Fifty-seventh Street, and bounded up the grimy stairs into the humid world above. Sweating from stress, heat, and panic, I tried to run the ten blocks downtown to MediaInc as inconspicuously as possible, shuffle-skipping down the sidewalk. I nearly knocked over an old woman and stepped on a Chihuahua's paw, earning myself a nice "Fuck you!" from its owner. I wondered if all my makeup had sweated off and if my pink shirt was now dark red. Huffing into the front door of MediaInc, I realized that I had no idea what to expect from a first day at an internship. A welcome party? A nameplate for my desk? A company Treo? They'd want to be in touch with me at all times, right? There was no way to predict what I was in for.

The horrible ice queen from my interview turned out to be my greeter. I saw her waiting in the lobby for me and tried to kill her with kindness.

"Hi, Mrs.—I mean, Ms. Pavese. So good to see you again. Can you tell that I'm wearing the same outfit? Well, of course you can now that I've pointed it out. *Duh!*" I babbled, somehow sounding even more nervous than I actually was.

She held up her hand. "I haven't had my coffee yet today. Could you keep the chatter down to a minimum?" I nodded, feeling like a total tool, and followed her as she swiped me into the building and took me up in the elevator. Our first stop was the coffee machine, where she made a black cup with two Sweet'n Lows. Gross. What was the point of coffee if it wasn't a vessel for chocolate syrup or whipped cream?

I then trailed after her and followed her to her office, where she wordlessly sat down and checked her e-mail. I wandered around her office, checking out the books and family photos she had on display. Hmm, fat husband, bland-looking vacations, one vaguely cross-eyed child—it was non-stop glamour for Ms. Margaret Pavese. After a few minutes of silent snooping and vowing never to become such a suburban bore, I was sure that she'd forgotten about me and whatever first-day festivities she had planned. I coughed, trying to remind her of the future Intern of the Year's presence.

She snapped her head up from her keyboard. "Fine," she said as if I'd just verbally assaulted her instead of gently cleared my throat. "I'll drop you off at security, okay? I'll get more done when you're not skulking around my office anyway."

She led me down a few flights to a door with black lettering spelling "Security" and then turned on her sensible pumps and left me there. I knocked on the door, completely uncertain if that's what I was supposed to do.

"Um, hello in there," I yelled into the pine of the door between knocks. "I'm a new intern." The door opened and a small man in a blue uniform stood in the doorway, revealing a room with lots of screens that flashed from shots of hallways to offices and then to the inside of the elevators. I made a mental note to refrain from wedgie picking anywhere in the entire building.

"I'm Carl," the security guard said, and pointed to his name pin at the same time. "And you must be Emma Freeman." I nodded. "They told me you were coming today. We've just got a bit of a background check and some paperwork for you to fill out." He handed me a stack of paper that weighed more than the entire duffle I brought to New York. I got to work bubbling in Scantron-like forms and checking boxes affirming that I had never been convicted of any violent crimes as Carl photocopied my driver's license.

"Sheesh, Carl. This sure is a lot of security. This is MediaInc, right? I didn't get so lost on the subway this morning that I ended up at the CIA or something, right?" I kidded.

Carl didn't respond. So I giggled awkwardly at my own joke. I looked at my watch. Not even a full hour in and I was already counting down the minutes until the end of the summer.

He thumbed through my papers. I seemed to have

passed the security portion of the test, and moved on to the picture section, which I can say I failed miserably.

"Okay, one, two," Carl said from behind a digital camera.

"Wait, can I fix my—" Flash! Too late. The camera went off mid-sentence and I looked like I was mid-sneeze. And I was so greasy in the picture—leftover sheen from my humid subway-and-sprinting commute—that the pic ended up looking like a "before" shot from a Proactiv commercial. Carl ignored my pleas for a redo and gave me a laminated version of my heinous pic to wear on a lanyard. "Keep this on at all times in the building."

"At *all times?*" I asked brattily, annoyed that he hadn't let me take another picture.

He gave me a stern look and I felt a twinge of guilt for being such a bitch. Wearing my ugly mug-shot pendant, I waited outside the security room for Ms. Pavese to pick me up. Once she did—almost half an hour after Carl had phoned her to tell her I was done—she led me up to Derek's office and left me there without even a "Good luck." Honestly, I felt bad that so many trees had to be cut down to make a stick that big to go up her butt.

"Mr. Dor . . . I mean, Derek?" I stood in the threshold of his office, trying to get his attention.

"Emma baby, you're here!" He leaped up from his desk to greet me. *"Welcome to the jungle!"* He shrieked, Axl Rose style, and did the rocker's trademark crab dance. Then, with his hand on my back—which totally icked me out—he led me to my cubicle.

"Thar she blows!" He made a Vanna White gesture, displaying the three half-walls of the cube, and I inwardly cringed at the pirate joke. "Feel free to decorate it any way you like. You know, pictures of you and your little friends or even you and your boyfriend, if you've got one. You got a boyfriend, Emma?"

Wasn't this totally inappropriate first-day banter? None of my teachers had ever asked me that on the first day (or ever), and weren't bosses supposed to be über-professional or something? "Um, no." I don't know why, but I was almost going to explain my Brian situation. Thankfully, he interrupted me before I could even collect my thoughts.

"Hey, whaddya say I take you out to lunch?"

"Sure, I guess." I looked down at my watch—it was only eleven forty-five, which felt really early for lunch. But he was the boss, and if there's anything I've learned from sitcoms, it's that when bosses tell you to do bizarre things, you do them and you do them now.

I followed him out of the building and noticed that he was pretty much wearing the same pleated-front khaki Dockers and collared shirt that he'd worn to both my interviews. I didn't feel so bad about my recycled ensemble.

The place he chose for lunch was crazy expensive. With its cloth napkins and tuxedoed waiters, it felt more like a once-a-year-celebration place than a casual lunch spot. I looked over the options and realized I was screwed. I didn't want to order something way expensive and look greedy, but I couldn't order the cheapest thing on the menu without looking like a money freak either. Next to a cup of soup and a glass of water, the chipotle Caesar salad was the most reasonably priced thing on the menu at twenty dollars. As I overanalyzed how ordering the second-cheapest menu item would be interpreted, Derek made a huge deal of his selection.

"I've got a few questions to ask about your fish tacos. Exactly how fishy are they?" he asked our waitress.

He shot me "Get it?" looks and thought the whole thing was side-splittingly amusing. I started my fake oh-Derek-that's-so-funny laugh, but then I saw that the waitress had a look of restrained contempt on her face and I pictured her spitting in my soda. Trying to avoid a saliva special while still making a good first-day impression on Derek, I pretended to be really consumed with my salad selection, burying my face in the menu.

Realizing that the waitress was not going to give him a degree of fishiness, he said, "Fine. I'll have one order of those and a Michelob Ultra."

I ordered the salad and a soda, and when the waitress came back a few minutes later with his beer and my Diet Coke, I examined the glass to be sure that it was spittle free.

I slurped as he launched into a "back when I used to be fraternity president" rant that lasted all the way through the busboy clearing the plates. The check finally came, forcing Derek to stop talking about his 1987 keg stand record as he picked it up and looked over the tab.

"Em baby, looks like your share is going to be about thirty-five clams."

My heart stopped. I had to pay? I thought that first-day lunches were on the company. Where did I hear that? Maybe *Office Space*. I silently cursed Hollywood for feeding the youth overglamorized versions of reality and started to really panic. After my designer day-planner purchase—fine, *fake* designer day-planner purchase, but it still cost *real* money—I only had about fifteen bucks left in my wallet. Maybe I could work some sort of IOU out with Derek.

Derek must have been able to sense my budget break-down and he started chuckling. He pointed at me with finger guns and whooped, "Gotcha! Of course this is on me. That's the first thing you've got to know about me. The Dorf is a jokester, Em. But don't try to pull anything on me, girlie. No one can out-prank The Dorf!" He slid his AmEx into the check folder. "Like you could even pay for this. You're probably getting paid peanuts for this internship, right?"

My boss just punk'd me? There had to be a rule against that in some kind of company manual or corporate regula-tions video.

"Actually, Dorf, I'm not getting paid anything."

"Wow! That sucks! And it's *The* Dorf, Em. Not just Dorf. You got that, kiddo?"

I had to consciously try to keep my lunch down as he said "kiddo." It was going to be a long summer with this guy.

Once we were back on our floor, Derek led me through the maze of printers and cubicles to my little work area.

"Emma, you've got to get a computer log-in name and password," Derek told me. "Well, actually, I probably should have done that for you before you got here. But I didn't. So call the tech geeks and have them come up here and set you up." Then he disappeared into his office, slamming the door behind him.

"Okay, The Dorf. Thanks for lunch," I said to his closed door.

Derek gave me no clues as to how to get in touch with "the tech geeks," so I cracked open my cell and dialed Ms. Pavese. Her number was in my phone from the first interview, and even though she was the frostiest bitch I'd ever encountered, she really was the only person that could tell me how to get in touch with the company's tech team. And without some sort of MySpace or IM distraction, I could already tell that eight straight hours of The Dorf might kill me. Ms. Pavese was of course annoyed that I called, but she seemed more pissed that Derek hadn't asked for my computer to be set up. She said that she'd take care of it and that someone would be up soon to help me.

Hours with nothing to do but read my saved text messages went by before the tech guy actually showed up. By the time he had finally logged me in, it was pretty much the end of the day. All in all, it was a first day that did not bode well for the rest of my summer.

At 4:59, I said a loud goodbye to Derek's still-closed door and bolted out of the office. Rachel called at five o'clock exactly and we both decided that we were way too tired to do anything. Neither of us had been up before eleven a.m. since school ended two weeks ago. A 6:55 wake-up call was going to take some getting used to. We decided to meet at home and order in.

By the time I dragged myself through the front door, Rachel had already settled in on the couch and ordered for us, orange chicken, brown rice, and some egg rolls. Totally what I wanted. She was psychic—we were so Hilary and Haylie, except one of us wasn't busted and talentless.

I dropped onto the couch right next to her and asked her about her first day as we waited for the fried Chinese-y goodness to arrive.

I was expecting her to have a similar my-boss-is-a-freak-and-my-job-is-more-boring-than-a-coma day, but she was actually amped about her internship. "It was awesome. My boss, Jamie, is so cool. She's like twenty-three and has a nose ring. And it turns out that the website isn't a lesbian thing, it's a modern feminist blog. I always get lesbians and feminists confused. And it's like a good brand of feminism. It's more 'Yay, women' than 'Let's cut off all their dicks,' you know?"

I sat up from my slump in the couch. I was so excited for her. The Sirlie internship sounded amazing. But I couldn't stop myself from comparing it to my gig with Sergeant Psycho. What had I gotten myself into?

"I mean, there's going to be a lot of admin work, like I had to go to Starbucks to get coffees for this meeting. But then I got to sit in on the meeting, which was awesome! And by the end of the summer, Jamie said that I should be up to the level where I'd get to write some copy and maybe even edit some stuff."

"Did any girls hit on you?" Jayla asked as she came out of her room to join us in the living room.

"Nope! I was just telling Emma that it's feminists, not lesbians. They're really different. Well, kind of different."

But Jayla wasn't done with her lezzie rant. "You know what girl hit on me once? You'll never guess who."

"Who?" we both shrieked.

We scooted over and Jayla sat down. "Well, let's just say that I was feeling experimental, okay? And I'm not going to name names, but the evening involved a certain hard-partying, exhaustion-prone, A-list starlet, four bottles of Cristal, and some very naughty Sidekick pictures that ended up on Perez Hilton. Well, like only for a hot second. Daddy threatened to sue and he took them down pretty fast."

"That was you?" I squealed. "I totally remember those pics! Jayla!"

"I know, I know. But I'd just broken up with this guy, Carter, and . . ." She trailed off, her face darkening before she shook her head. "Anyway," she said with a sharp sigh, "I was on the rebound. Nothing really happened. Those pictures were way worse than reality. How was your internship, Em?"

I filled her in on my day with a little less enthusiasm than Rachel. "Today was so boring it made *March of the Penguins* look like a Jackie Chan film. And my boss is totally weirder than I thought. His name is Derek Dorfman but he wants me to call him The Dorf."

"Wait, he really said to call him The Dorf?" Jayla asked.

"I know, I wouldn't believe it if I were you either. But seriously, it happened." I kind of felt like I was telling a ghost story, except it was more frightening because it was really happening.

"Kind of like The Hoff?" she asked, still not believing that an adult could be this douchey.

"Yeah, just like that. Except The Dorf doesn't have the *Baywatch* six-pack. He's got one of those pregnant-man bellies going and he wears his khakis way down low, so that his entire gut sticks out over his belt." I didn't even mention that Derek had a beer at lunch and probably was an alky like The Hoff, too.

"That's hot!" Rachel said in a perfect Paris/Jayla impersonation. I laughed, but was still really bummed about how my internship had turned out.

The phone rang and Rachel told the doorman to send our delivery guy up. I went to the door to get the food and it was the same delivery guy who'd served me Chinese food for the four nights I was abandoned by Boy Crazy over there.

"You no call last night," he said, handing over our cartons.

Fabulous! I moved to the city hoping to meet socialites and Prince Charmings over fruity beverages and the only person I'd managed to make an impression on so far was the Chinese delivery guy.

Nine

Within a week on the job with The Dorf, I'd decided that working for him was some form of karmic punishment. For what, I'm not quite sure. It could have been for all the times I farted on the school bus and then blamed James Messaine. By fifth grade, he had transferred schools. Or maybe for the time I stole a lip gloss from the M.A.C. counter at the mall last spring and then gave it to Rachel as a birthday gift. I don't know. But really, I could have committed a felony and had a better summer than this. At least in jail I'd be working out.

On Friday morning, I got to MediaInc and sat down, preparing for another eight hours of Googling myself and everyone I knew.

"Yo, Em." I immediately tensed at the sound of Derek's voice. "You hungover today?" he bellowed loudly enough for the entire floor to hear.

What was he talking about? I hadn't had a drop to drink since the baby sip Jake let me sneak at my birthday celebration. "No, Derek. I'm not even old enough to drink."

"Really, Em? 'Cause you look mighty hungover."

Look hungover? I looked the exact same that I did every morning that week, tired and bored, but definitely not hungover.

He leaned into my cubicle, his gut cascading over the fabric-covered fiberglass wall that separated my cube from the mail cubbies. "Because I remember when I was your age. I used to party all the time." When he said "party," he kind of shimmied, which I assumed indicated that back in his day "partying" actually meant grotesquely fat men moving their shoulders.

"You partied last night. Don't think you can put anything past me, okay?" And then he did the two-finger point to his eyes and then to mine that I'd only seen pedophiles on *Law & Order* do. "I'm watching you, Em." I wanted to give him a swift kick in the gut but instead just avoided eye contact and went back to my self-Google session. He chuckled to himself and then marched off to find someone else on the floor to torment.

Eight hours of Derek was exhausting, but when I came home every night, Jayla and Rachel would insist that I relive the daily Dorf incident, and there always was one. I kind of hated that they thought my daily pain was so funny, but at least it meant that someone was getting something of worth out of my lame internship. I certainly wasn't.

That night, before I'd even shut the front door behind

me, the nightly Dorf recap ritual started. "How was work, babe?" Jayla asked, fully knowing that work was never anything but miserable.

I threw my purse on the floor and sank into the armchair. My clothes were sticky and clinging to me from another million-percent-humidity day. "Ugh. You guys are going to love what he did today."

I saw them both lean in closer, like this was story time at the public library. "So he calls me on the phone, even though I seriously sit six feet away from his door, and is all, 'Come into my office *stat*! I have a great opportunity for you.' I was all, Stat? Is this the ER, Dr. Doofus? So, I close the Fall Out Boy video I'm downloading before it's finished and hustle the three steps to his office. He's like, 'So, Em, wanna make some extra cash?' "

I rolled my eyes. Just reliving this was making me nauseous.

"He's going to start paying you?" Rachel squealed. God bless her.

Jayla joined the game of What Scent of Douche Was Derek Today? "He's pimping you out to one of his fogie friends?"

"No!" Sadly, though, I could totally see that happening. "Babysitting! He wants me to babysit his three kids. He's all, 'Five dollars and fifty cents an hour, tax free, Em. It's more than you're making here. Plus, there's probably some pizza in it for you.' " The shock on my roomies' faces was enough to know that I wasn't wrong in thinking that Derek was insane.

"Five fifty?" Jayla asked, stunned. "That has to be against labor laws, right? And would that even pay for the taxi ride to his dirty Jersey neighborhood?"

I nodded, surprised that Jayla had any concept of minimum wage. "I know. Re-dic. And then he was like, 'Get back to me. You know my door's always open.' And then, as soon as I turn around, he says, 'Em, could you close my door on your way out?' I swear, sometimes I think I'm on *Candid Camera* or something." And I really had looked around for hidden cameras that day.

The two of them laughed. "It's like you work in *The Office*!"

"Yeah, but it's not half an hour every week. Eight hours a day, every day—even with Steve Carell, that wouldn't be funny." I slouched down further in the chair, being as dramatic as possible, and turned on the TV.

Jayla interrupted my channel-flipping and came over to me. She petted my head like I was a lapdog. "Babe, why don't you just quit?" she asked sweetly. She really didn't get that not everybody can be a citizen of Jaylaville. Some people's parents expect more from them than not destroying a million-dollar apartment over a summer.

I hated to break her glittery illusion of my financial situation, but I couldn't help myself. "Oh yeah, good idea. I'll quit and then ride away on my unicorn made of gumdrops and puppy dogs. My parents would kill me if I quit. And worse, they'd cut off my allowance. So we'd all be shit out of luck, because that means no one would be paying my rent." Jayla nodded, feigning comprehension. But I was realizing that when it came to work or money, she totally didn't have the slightest sense of reality.

I let her continue to pat my head—it was kind of like a massage. If I took this internship one week at a time, maybe it wouldn't be that bad. I was ready to stop thinking about my job and start up some hardcore friend hang-out time. But just as I was going to ask the girls if they wanted to On Demand a movie, I noticed that Rachel was getting up.

"All right," Rachel said, rising from the couch. "I've gotta start getting ready. I'm meeting a JDate guy named Jason tonight. He described himself as a Jewish Tom Welling."

Another night alone? This was not happening.

Jayla cooed to Rachel, "Oh, JDate Jason, you are faster than a speeding bullet. More, more, more powerful than a locomotive. Mmmm."

"Shut up." Rachel chucked a throw pillow at her, and Jayla started fake making out with it and calling it Jason. "So not going to happen tonight. And I totally don't want tonight to crash and burn like last night."

"Wait, what happened last night?" I asked, realizing that I hadn't seen Rachel since before work yesterday. "You went on a date and didn't even e-mail me about it today?" Hello! I'm sitting in a cubicle prison all day watching Parkour videos on YouTube and she had real gossip that she didn't spill right away! What kind of best friend was she?

"Oh, sorry. I just didn't even want to talk about it. I was so grossed out. Like, it was a good date. We went to this concert at Irving Plaza because I had free tickets from work. And then we got Mister Softees and sat in Union Square Park. It was cute."

"So what was the problem?" Jayla asked from her side of the couch, putting down her pillow lover boy.

"Oh, well, he walked me home, which was good. But then he was all over me and totally wanted to come upstairs. And like, I'm looking for a boyfriend, so I can't just be a slut who makes out with every guy who buys me ice cream."

Jayla's eyes widened in shock at Rachel's definition of what constitutes sluttiness. I think her perfectly curled lashes actually touched her brows. I sat there shocked myself, but more because I still couldn't get over the fact that Rachel was dating and not letting me in on every single detail of it right away.

The two of them went to their respective rooms to pretty up for their evenings. I changed out of my black pants that were starting to get a little rank from daily wear and assumed my typical position on the couch. In sweats with my cell poised for takeout ordering, I waved to Rachel and Jayla as they left for their dates.

Once the door slammed shut, I sighed to myself. Another evening alone with my two new boyfriends, takeout and TiVo. I was starting to wonder just how different my summer would have been had I stayed in Bridgefield. My parents had DVR and my mom could whip up a mean stir-fry, so what was I experiencing here in the city that was new?

I pulled out my journal. I flipped through an entry I'd written in Bridgefield, back when Brian and I were still on. I couldn't believe that I was the same girl who had scrawled seven pages about Brian's prom. The lilac dress. The limo. The flask that we both sipped from. I hadn't let one little detail go by undocumented. Seven pages on one night! I'd actually referred to his prom as "the best, most glamorous night of my entire life!" Gross. Had I really called sharing a hotel room with five other couples and not being able to use the bathroom all night because Warren's date was puking glamorous?

After the trip down Emma and Brian lane, I put my pen to paper and began to detail more of my New York summer.

I started with my life flashing before my eyes when I was lost in Brooklyn and then moved on to venting about my days at the internship—mostly about Derek. Writing about the office horrors was even better than telling the roommates. Like, cathartic or something. I'd barely gotten through my terrible fish taco lunch with The Dorf and I already had eight pages. Wow, that was more than I wrote about "the best, most glamorous night of my entire life!" I guess that even the bad days in New York were more interesting than the most glam evenings back in Bridgefield.

The doorbell rang and my Chinese delivery friend was there with my order. After paying him, I settled back into my spot on the couch and pulled the carton of lo mein out of the I ♥ NY plastic bag. I glanced over what I'd just written and realized that even though I wasn't living the Carrie Bradshaw dream, this summer was still shaping up to be kind of kick-ass in its own way.

Ten

My internship was worse than seeing Nicole Richie naked, worse than your roommate eating all the chunks out of Toffee Heath Bar Crunch—*thankyouverymuch, Rachel*—even worse than muffin-topping in your favorite jeans. A typical day at work consisted of me refreshing my Gmail once every five minutes—if I could even wait that long—taking every single quiz on Seventeen.com, getting insulted/assaulted by Derek, and then making his lunch reservations. And—what an effing surprise!—today was no different.

"Em, you're not wearing any makeup today," he said as he poked his fat face in my cube.

"No, Derek. I am." Actually, that morning I had spent

an extra five minutes trying on some of Jayla's liquid liner. Not that I expected him or anyone else to notice, but still, no makeup? Way insulting.

"Wow, it doesn't look like it and I always notice the little things." He then slammed a pile of papers on my desk, thankfully changing the topic from how apparently busted I looked. "Here's a project for you, Em. Why don't you go ahead and make fifty copies of these? Have them on my desk in ten minutes."

Now, I'd only been a professional xeroxer for two weeks, but even I knew that barring a break in the space/time continuum, no copy machine could print out fifty copies of that one-hundred-page packet in under ten minutes. I rolled my eyes at the stack of paper and didn't even make a move to get started. Why even attempt the impossible? As soon as Derek strutted his fatness back into his office, I e-mailed Rachel to find out about whichever date she'd gone on the night before.

So, are you sending out save-the-dates for your wedding yet?????

Rach responded before I'd even clicked back into my inbox:

Ha ha. No, but this was the first really good date I've had. Really awesome. He's really funny! And not like I'm saying he's funny because he's hid-jus. He's funny *and* cute. He just texted me for a movie tonight. Should I go? Pretend not to be available? Act like I have another date to make him jealous? Wait for him to actually call? What? I'm clueless here.

As much as Jayla teased Rachel for being such a prudi-fied virgin, truth was that I didn't have much of a clue about dating either. Brian was so high school. In New York, there were different rules. I mean, there were no basements to have sloppy make-out sessions in, so my idea of a second date couldn't exist here. The closest thing I'd had to male atten-tion in this city was a wink from my Chinese delivery guy. But now that I think about it, he could have just had some-thing in his eye.

I wrote back:

AHHH! So exciting. I have no idea what you should do though. Ask our in-house love expert, Ms. Jayla St. Clare. Oh, and get more Ben & Jerry's, you greedy chunk picker!

Within minutes I got another message from Rachel. Jayla had texted her back that she should first say no, then five minutes later pretend that her plans had fallen through and agree to go. That way she wouldn't look too available.

My vicarious excitement for the day over, I trudged the one hundred pages of fun to the copy machine and then logged back on to MySpace, trying to think of yet another long-lost sandbox buddy I could search for.

The rest of my day trickled by, time moving slower than Jessica Simpson's reasoning capabilities. When four forty-five finally ticked around, I bolted, figuring that Derek would never notice the fifteen minutes and I might have over-loaded the Gmail server if I refreshed one more time. The apartment was empty when I got home. I knew Rachel was off with her Semitic stallion and figured that Jayla was prob-ably canoodling with someone named Fabian on a yacht.

Just as I was positioning myself into my now typical

Friday night couch-potato fetal position and thinking about how to start the day's journal writing, my phone rang. It was Kyle!

"Oh my God! Who have you been so busy frenching this summer that you couldn't return any of my calls?" I asked him, only half kidding. Really, where had he been these past three weeks?

Kyle filled me in on his summer. Busy at work. Hanging out with his B-list friends. Met a guy that he thought might be his summer flavor, but turned out he already had a boyfriend and was just a huge tease. He saw Mr. Harlevy, our pre-calc teacher, at the mall wearing shorts and he thought he was going to go blind from looking directly at the pasty flesh. Standard summer in the suburbs.

And then I filled him in on mine. I glossed over the daily boredom of the internship and nightly boredom at home with my journal to make my life seem more glamorous. I even walked around the apartment, opening and closing cabinet doors and clicking on and off my hair straightener, telling Kyle that I was getting ready for a big night out. I couldn't believe I was fibbing to one of my best friends.

"Well, Em, glad you're doing so well. I have some kind of shitty news for you and I wasn't sure if I should tell you. But because you sound stable enough to take it now . . ." I could hear Kyle's voice rise half an octave with nervousness. "So, you know Skylar Dichter?"

Of course I knew Skylar. Everyone in Bridgefield knew her. And let's just say that most of the Bridgefield boys would have an easier time recognizing her without her shirt on.

"That skank from St. Margaret's? Who has that plastic

surgeon dad who tucks every mom in Bridgefield? And The Hombres always ask her if her middle name is 'Everyone's' 'cause she's so slutty? Yes. I know her." When The Hombres pulled crap like that on Skylar, I didn't even do my typical "You guys, that's so not cool" routine. Because there was no defending her. She really had made out with most of the males between the ages of fourteen and thirty-two in the county.

I could hear him on the other line trying to build up the nerve to tell me whatever bad news it was. "Just tell me, poodle." I really couldn't care about anything having to do with Skylar Dichter. What was he so frothed up about?

"Okay, so, last week, Brian came into the taco shack with her." A beat of silence. "Like, *together* with her."

My stomach dropped.

"What?" I hissed almost inaudibly. My hands began to shake and I felt an awful prickly heat spread across my neck. Brian's replacing me with her? God, he couldn't have picked anyone more horrifying. I would be less hurt and shocked if he'd have come out and said that after dating me, he decided that he was actually into boys.

"Yeah. And Daddy definitely took his daughter to work one day this summer because she has a totally new rack. They were, like, poking my eyes out when she ordered. I mean, how is that even legal? And isn't that supergross, a dad fondling his daughter while she's unconscious? Even though I guess it is technically medical."

"Hello!" I shrieked, finding my voice—my hysterical, out-of-control voice. "Eyes on the crisis, Kyle! Skylar? I can't believe this. That Shasta McNasty and I are in the same club—The I-Know-What-Brian-McSwain's-Spit-Tastes-Like

131

Club. I mean, it was funny when you and Rach both hooked up with Greg Samkin last summer, but this is so not freaking funny."

I could feel myself starting to totally stop thinking rationally and lose it. The fact that I was living in New York, that Brian would have just held me back this summer, that I knew we would have broken up when he went to college—nothing logical mattered. Skylar had my Brian and I hated it. Tears welled up in my eyes. Kyle stammered some weak "You're too good for him's" before I croaked out that I had to go. The last thing I wanted was pity.

I could already hear everyone in Bridgefield talking about this.

"Oh! Did you hear about poor Emma? Yeah, Brian ditched her for Skylar. I guess he just couldn't resist her—ahem—personalities." And then they'd joke about how I was flatter than Kansas.

"For sure. Who could? I mean, Emma's smart and all but what is she? An A cup? B? Whatever, she just ain't no Skylar Dichter!"

And with that nauseating thought, all of the stress, loneliness, boredom, anxiety, and homesickness I'd been bottling up came bursting out with monster truck force.

"Baaaaahhh!" I wailed, only mildly consoled that Jayla and Rachel weren't there to see my nervous breakdown. "Mmmmhu-hu-hu-hu-hu!"

I let it all out, heaving the kind of sobs that make your chest hurt. I cried and cried, snorting and snotting all over myself, which only made me realize how disgustingly ugly I was, how Brian was right to get over me so quickly, and how I was unlovable and might as well buy a pack of Magic the Gathering cards and swear off boys forever. I rolled around the couch in indulgent agony for what seemed like hours, thinking of reason after reason why my entire life was worthless and beyond hope.

"I got a B-minus in honors chem," I whined to the furniture. "My dog doesn't really like me and I have cellulite on my thi-i-i-ghs. Ahhhh!"

But then something inside me whispered that maybe Kyle was wrong. I mean, sharing a taco combo basket didn't mean they were dating. They could just be friends. I knew that Skylar Dichter wasn't "just friends" with anybody, probably not even her grandfather. But still, this gave me a little hope. The geysers exploding out of my tear ducts slowed a little.

I pulled myself off the floor and crawled over to my laptop on the coffee table, yanking it down to me. I sat up, propping myself against the side of the couch, and cracked open the computer to do a little more investigating. I pulled down my Favorites menu and clicked on Brian's MySpace page, still bookmarked from when we were together. The heaving sobs came back as soon as his page loaded. I don't know when he changed his profile pic, I swear it wasn't like this earlier when I checked. His picture was now an image of him wearing the stupid T-shirt he'd picked up in Daytona Beach last spring. The top half of the shirt read "The Man" with an arrow pointing up, and the bottom had "The Legend" with an arrow pointing down. But that wasn't even close to the most offensive part of the picture. No. His right arm was raised, baring his pit stains with pride, and a very busty Skylar Dichter was in the crook of his elbow. There should have been another arrow on that T-shirt labeled "Herpes Machine 5000" pointing to her.

I dove into the freezer and found my emergency stash of

Cherry Garcia and brought it over to the couch for a good old-fashioned pity party. Even with nine and a half months of officially dating him, I was never in his profile pic. I spent the next hour sniffling in sweatpants, listening to Weezer, and giving myself ice cream headaches. Then, just as I was about to pick my laptop off the floor to write a comment on Brian's MySpace wall about his thirty-second keg stand not being the only thirty-second record to his name, Jayla pranced through the front door.

Eleven

"What the hell happened here?" she shrieked, surveying the mountains of Kleenex and empty pint carton—fine, fine, *two* pint cartons—of Ben & Jerry's that surrounded me on the couch. "Oh wait, did you try on my Jimmy Choos? Honey, it's not you. They're too small for even me. Everyone feels like Big Foot when they wear them. I don't know why I even keep them around."

The tears started afresh as I sniffled out the whole sordid tale, half of it obscured by my sobs and soggy nose-blows.

"Stop," she said, hands on her hips. "You mean to tell me that all of this is about that bro fag Brian? Seriously?"

"J-Jayla!" I groaned. "I 1-1-love him!"

"Oh, Emma. You do not. You love the idea of him."

I looked up, skeptical but intrigued.

"You love the fact that he fills in all of your blanks, like a Scantron. He's safe and comfortable and goes with everything in your life. He's a hoodie sweatshirt. And up until you arrived in this city, you were a hoodie also. But look at you," she said, beaming. "You're an Ella Moss cami! You're a Burberry trench! You're a Chanel suit! You still go with everything, only now you go with everything good!"

I looked at her with swollen eyes and nodded limply.

"All right," she said briskly, patting my knee and heading to the fridge. "Enough. I'm sorry, babe, but I can't have that in here."

I poked morosely at one of my empty ice cream containers. "Have what?"

"Sulking. It's just not allowed in this apartment. It was in really small print on the sublet form you signed. So stop." I tried to collect myself a bit. "Hot Child in the City" sang from her iPhone and all of her attention went to her convo. I listened miserably as she debated about whether the Meatpacking scene was too Murray Hill lately and then agreed to meet up with whoever was on the line.

I was still on the verge of a meltdown. I couldn't bear the idea of an entire night alone in the apartment. TiVo'd *Project Runway*s were definitely not going to be enough to distract me from the Bri and Sky development. Ugh, God. If I didn't hate them both so much, I'd think they sounded cute together. "Um, Jay," I asked as soon as she set down her phone, "do you think I could, like, come out with you? I know I'm not twenty-one or fancy or . . ." And then the Niagara Falls of tears kicked up again.

She looked over the kitchen counter, taking in my

complete patheticness. "Of course you can come." I couldn't tell if she really wanted me to come or just didn't want a night's worth of tears staining the leather couch. "And don't worry about being twenty-one or fancy enough. I'll handle everything, okay?" She turned back to the fridge, pulled out a pitcher and poured two huge glasses. "Let's start with this first. Drink up." I glanced at the tall glass and then back at her. "Jayla Juice." She smiled a perfect toothpaste-commercial smile and winked. "Try it."

I took a sip. Oh, Crystal Light and vodka, where have you been all my life? It went down like lemon cotton candy. After just a few sips, I could already feel the tingles I get right before a buzz.

"And put this on." I looked up just in time to have a gold sparkly tube top, still with the tags on, hit me in the face. Before I could even thank her for the loaner top, she was already texting my physical description to God knows who, arranging for a fake ID for me.

"Jay, a fake ID? How illegal is that?" Images of Paris's, Lindsay's, and Nicole's mug shots popped into my mind.

"Oh, you're just adorable, aren't you?" She came over and patted my head. "Don't worry about anything. People lie about their age all the time. My mother still says that she's thirty-five, which means that she was like fourteen when she had me. This is just a little fib like that, okay? What we *do* need to worry about is this situation." Her French-manicured fingers swirled around my face. "You're so puffy, you look like a prizefighter."

She led me into her room, sat me down on her bed, and flitted over to her vanity, which was packed with every high-end cosmetic on the market. She returned with a tube of . . . Preparation H?

"Look, Jayla, I like you and all and I do have a sense of adventure, but . . ."

"Relax! Pageant girls use this all the time under their eyes. And trust me, with all my late nights, it's the only thing that keeps me from looking like Gary Busey."

She patted the cream gently under my lower lashes and made me kill the rest of my Jayla Juice. Then she ran out to the kitchen and poured me another. I was already feeling the first one and totally needed to slow down. Normally I didn't worry about that so much, because Brian would be there to take care of me. But not anymore. I started to choke up again, realizing just how over Brian and I were. I fought hard to keep my tears back. I didn't want to be so pathetic that Jayla would change her mind about letting me tag along.

As I waited for my ointment to set in and deflate my face, I sat cross-legged on Jayla's bed and watched her get ready. Her beauty routine was astounding. She narrated each step with a soothing voice and effortless demonstration.

"Eyebrows are very important," she said seriously. "Invest in a good pencil. I recommend Chanel. You should create an arch that frames your face without overpowering it."

I nodded along dutifully, forcing myself to focus on Jayla's Cosmetics 101 class and not on being pathetic second string to slutty Skylar.

"Curling your eyelashes is a cheap, painless way to look instantly refreshed and doe-eyed. I like this little curler from Laura Mercier. Start at the base of the lashes and kind of walk the clamp out, curling it several times. If you curl just once, you'll look like Dolly Parton. Not hot."

"Okay," I said, trying to be a good student. But seeing how pretty Jayla was only reminded me of how ugly I felt

and how sexy that awful Skylar was and how she was probably hanging at the pool every day, flaunting her Pam
Anderson–ness to Brian and everyone who had a summer
member pass. This time I couldn't hold back.

"Oh, honey, no! No, don't cry. You'll take off all your
Preparation H." Jayla rushed over to me and dabbed at my
face. I had no idea she could be so maternal. It was weird.
But a good weird. Like that feeling you got when you watched
Mean Girls and realized that Lindsay Lohan could really act.

"Here, I'll do your makeup for you," Jayla offered. That
got my mind off Brian quickly. A chance to not only use all
of this crazy makeup, but to have a bona fide expert apply it
for me? I even started to get a little giddy, thinking that
maybe she could make me look as good in person as she did
with Photoshop.

After I was penciled and curled into a decent version of
hotness, she sent me off to get dressed. I shimmied into my
Paper Denims—my big birthday gift from last summer—and
the gold top and presented myself to Madam Jay.

"Oh, babe, you look . . . *ahh!*" she gasped, pointing at
my feet. I squealed and hopped around, thinking she'd seen
a mouse or cockroach. "Jesus Christ, Emma! What the fuck
are those shoes?"

"My shoes? Why, what's wrong with them?"

Barely able to get the words out, Jayla hissed, "Foam.
Flip. Flops. Honey, that's just not done here."

"But they're my fancy wedge ones. And they're all I
have. Plus, heels hurt too much." Not that these were amaz-
ingly comfortable or anything. They were the pair that
bloodied my feet during the Brooklyn fiasco. But I'd devel-
oped calluses since then.

"You're in Manhattan, not the Mall of America." She

turned around and stomped back into her room. She returned with a pair of strappy high-heels. "That shirt was made for these shoes, babe." She dangled a beautiful pair of glittery designer foot-binders in front of me and waited for me to slip them on.

"Don't worry, by the time we get to the club, you won't feel your feet anymore," she promised with a smile.

Twenty minutes later we skipped out onto the steamy streets and hailed a cab. Even though the sun was down, the heat and humidity were stifling. One more second sans air-conditioning and my hair would be Frizztown, USA.

With two Jayla Juices in me, I was just on this side of being a puketastic mess. I giggled as our cab sped across town, feeling like a real-deal heiress. "Thank you for bringing me out. So, where are we going?"

"First, we're going to Plumm."

I raised my eyebrows, impressed. I had no idea where or what Plumm was, but I was sure it was fabulous.

"Oh God, don't give me that look." I tried to protest but she cut me off. "I know Plumm is a little out but I think Mary-Kate is going to be there and I haven't seen her in ages."

"Mary-Kate *Olsen*?"

"No, Mary-Kate Letourneau," she teased.

"You mean the one who got pregnant by her thirteen-year-old student? I think her name's Mary *Kay*."

"Ew, the cosmetics lady? She screwed a sixth grader?"

We dissolved into laughter as the cab pulled up to an unassuming awning on Fourteenth Street.

"Keep the change, sir. Thank you," she said, handing

him a twenty-dollar bill. I hopped out of the cab quickly, not wanting to miss a second of Jayla in action.

"So, who are we meeting here?" I asked, trying to keep up with her leggy gait in the wobbly heels she made me wear.

"Chloe. Haven't you met her?"

I shook my head. I hadn't met any of her friends. For all Rachel and I knew, Jayla bayed at the moon all night or put on a cape and fought crime.

"Oh, two things. Chloe is kind of a spaz when she's drunk. So if you see her trying to call her boyfriend, take her phone. I'm not kidding. She'll start World War Three if she talks to him plastered." She looked at me gravely and I wished I had a notepad. "And secondly, my ex-boyfriend hangs out here a lot—totally not why we're here, btw—and he grosses me out. He's fat and horrible and looks like Shrek in Burberry. So if I give you this signal"—she tugged on her ear lobe—"that means Carter is coming and you need to pretend to get sick so we can both go to the bathroom, okay?"

"Uh, okay." I nodded. With the Jayla Juice churning in my stomach, I probably wasn't going to have to pretend to get sick. I followed behind her as she strolled past a mob of people waiting to get in. God, some of the girls who were getting turned away were a hundred times more pretty, not to mention a hundred times more twenty-one, than I was. What if I didn't get in?

Jayla sauntered right up to the bouncer, smiled, and watched the doors swing open for both of us. Jayla mouthed "Be cool!" as she slipped me back someone else's driver's license. Where it came from, I had no idea—it was like my roommate had turned into Criss Angel or something. The burly bouncer looked me up and down before waving me through. And like that, I was in! My first New York club! I flushed and felt like a twelve-year-old crashing prom.

And of course the first thing to come out of my mouth was, "Wow! A real club. I'm cool, daddio!"

Daddio? Uck, God.

Jayla clenched her jaw and pretended not to notice my *Grease* reenactment.

We rounded the corner and Plumm opened up before us, beautiful people and flashing lights everywhere.

"Snip to the snip snap, beeotch!" Jayla called as she spotted her friend. The two air-kissed and Jayla introduced me to Chloe, who looked me up and down, trying not to wrinkle her perfect twenty-thousand-dollar nose.

"If I have to pay for a drink in this place, I'm swallowing a whole bottle of Hydroxycut," Chloe moaned in a sophisticated British accent, flicking her glossy brown hair over a probably Miami-bronzed shoulder.

"I know," Jayla chimed in. "The last time I was here, no one was buying me drinks. I spent ninety bucks and that bitchy bathroom attendant thought I was puking in one of the stalls."

"You *were* puking. Remember?" Chloe said, rolling her eyes. "Then you went home with Max."

Jayla cocked her head, apparently not remembering a thing. I tried to look interested and laugh at all the right times.

"Wait, Max? Mafia Max? Mafia Max from Guesthouse who wanted to fly me to Rome? Ew, Chlo! Why did you let me go home with him?"

Now was my chance to say something clever!

"Wow, he has a guesthouse? That's pretty neat. Did he make you pasta like Tony Soprano?"

Silence. I could actually see the confusion and judgment radiating off their bodies.

Jayla finally broke the unbearable tension by laughing. "Oh, honey, Guesthouse is a club and Mafia Max probably only eats at Nobu. You're so cute." I tried to think of something to say to prove that I wasn't totally out of the know, but I couldn't think of a thing. Chloe ambled off to find cocktail buyers and Jayla snapped into predator mode. I sank into a bog of awkward, looking around and feeling really out of place. I couldn't imagine having anything to say to anyone in this entire building. If Jayla left me alone, I'd do about as well as a Simpson sister on the SATs—not Lisa and Maggie, the other Simpsons.

"Come on," she said resolutely. "I'm sobering up and people here are getting ugly. We need a drink." She grabbed my hand and adeptly navigated us through the throngs of glittery people, throwing air kisses out to those that she knew.

"Jay, are my boobs sticking out of this too much?" I tugged Jayla's shirt up over my non-cleavage as we eased up to the crowded bar.

"No way! You have to flaunt your best assets."

"You're right," I answered seriously. "But how is this shirt going to showcase my academic record and great personality?"

Jayla rolled her eyes at my joke and smiled at the shaggy-haired bartender who walked up and kissed her on the cheek.

" 'Allo, my lovely Jinxy!" he drawled in a thick Australian accent. "How's my favorite lass, eh? Who's this 'ere?"

I realized that he was waiting for me to answer, but before I could stutter out something that would have probably been mortifying anyway, Jayla cut in. "This is Domino, she's prelaw at Oxford and she's summering with me. Isn't she such a fox?"

The bartender's bright blue eyes looked me up and down appreciatively, and I blushed under his hunky gaze. Everyone in this city was so beautiful.

"Domino, you're quite a bird!" He winked and Jayla giggled into his neck and he turned suddenly and kissed her on the mouth. They exchanged heated eye contact and she mouthed something I thought looked like "Coatroom" but could have been "Go poo." He glanced back at the crowded bar and sighed heavily.

"Later, love. Gotta earn enough money to keep you 'appy!" He kissed her nose and started to walk away.

"Damien!" she called after him, and bit her lip coyly and nodded toward a bottle of some alcohol over the bar. He rolled his eyes in mock exasperation and gave her a knowing smirk before pouring us two huge cocktails. My stomach gurgled at the thought of another drink, but I took it anyway. It would at least be good to have something to hold so I wouldn't be standing with my hands at my sides like a soldier at attention all night. Jayla winked at her boy toy and then pranced away, me in tow.

Just as we sat down at a table, Chloe sauntered over carrying two drinks.

"Well, that didn't go well!" she snapped testily.

"What happened?" I asked. "You got drinks, right?"

Before she could even register how lame whatever I said was, a photographer came up and motioned for us all to get together. In two seconds, Jayla and Chloe were in perfect Paris Hilton, hands-on-hips-arched-back picture pose as I fumbled for a place to put my drink.

"And . . . one, two, three." He turned to show us the picture but Chloe said she looked like a velociraptor—whatever that meant—and made him take another. After getting her okay on that one, he thanked us and disappeared into the crowd.

"Who was that guy? Is that the paparazzi?" I thought the rich and famous hated photographers.

"Not really. He's from Jossip," Jayla said.

"It's gossip?" I could barely hear her over the *Can't keep her little model hands off me!* blaring from the speakers next to us.

"What?" she yelled back.

"Huh?"

"You wanna go smoke?" asked Chloe, interrupting my Three Stooges moment. Jayla nodded and motioned for me to come along.

"Oh, no thanks. I tried smoking when I was in middle school, because I thought that it would make me look cooler. But I really should have tried Accutane."

More silence and then they turned on their stilettos and walk away. I called out after them, "It was just a joke. I was already on Accutane in middle school. Kidding, again!"

I watched as they disappeared into the crowded darkness, then settled into my seat at the now empty table. I watched a pack of gorgeous blond girls try to dance while

145

simultaneously looking at themselves in the mirror *and* making eyes at a group of rich-looking guys in the corner. Although I doubt that these girls were really planning on meeting and talking to those guys. With all of the flashing lights, thudding bass, and people bumping into you, it seemed impossible to have a real conversation.

I realized that I had put my drink down at some point during my crowd scoping and hadn't really been paying attention to it. Not wanting to get roofied, I headed back to the bar. I had no idea what to order, as I was pretty sure Jayla Juice wasn't on any menu. I leaned into the bar, trying to act as natural as possible. A bartender who wasn't Jayla's Damien pointed to me and asked what I would be having. I totally panicked. "Um, just come back later. I'm still deciding," I said, my nervousness totally audible in my voice. I got a weird look from the bartender. There didn't seem to be a bar menu people were looking at, so I was completely unsure as to how I'd pick out a beverage. Why didn't they just have a keg here?

A guy pushed me a little as he slid up to the bar. He barked, "Long Island, please," at the bartender. So I yelled, "Yeah, same thing for me." I wondered if I should have specified shaken or stirred, but before I could add that, I was handed a glass of the most rancid concoction I'd ever tasted. Does anyone actually like this crap? My vile beverage in hand, I decided to hide in the bathroom for a while. I doubted there would be a line. I mean, at twelve dollars for a drink, who can even afford to fill their bladder up?

As I moved through the crowd of hips swaying to JT, I tried to steady my drink and keep it from spilling all over. Every bump and splash was a solid chunk of my allowance spilling onto my wrist. I thought about licking up the spills, just to get my money's worth, but if Jayla saw me doing that, she'd be so mortified that she'd never bring me out with her again.

I managed to make my way to the back staircase, and as I stepped down, I saw a few cameras flash. I turned to see long wavy blonde hair on the head of what looked like a twelve-year-old girl heading toward the VIP section. It had to be an Olsen twin.

I spun around to rush outside and tell the girls there had been an MK sighting. I was pumped to have an actual purpose besides being "Awkward Girl Who Makes Everyone Else Feel Cooler." But as I turned, I slammed myself into a pair of broad shoulders and sloshed my drink all over Jayla's shirt.

"Gahh!" I shrieked, and stamped my feet as I felt the alcohol seeping into the padding of my strapless bra. Before I could even take in the full embarrassment of the situation, someone was handing me a fistful of cocktail napkins and I was dabbing at my chest. I looked up to thank the napkin giver and melted at the sight of this guy—blond hair, green eyes, an easy smile, and perfect teeth. My jaw was practically unhinged it was open so wide. He was one of the hottest guys I'd ever seen not in an Abercrombie & Fitch ad. And he was standing right next to me! And he was looking at me! And he was talking to me!

"I'd help you out with that," he pointed to the stain on my chest. "But I usually like to buy a girl dinner first."

And he was funny! Oh my God, he was perfection incarnate. This could be love at first quip.

Twelve

Where the heck was Jayla when I needed her? What should I do now? I wished I had a secret earpiece that connected directly to her, like Ashton had on *Punk'd*. She'd make a hot director of my love life. But seriously, I needed to think like Jayla if I didn't want to completely drown in my own club scene ineptness. WWJD? I had no freaking idea. Maybe call him "dahhhling" and then lick her lips until he bought her a drink? For a second, I pictured myself doing that. He'd probably think I had gum disease.

While my brain was carefully considering my next move, my mouth fearlessly lunged forward into the deepest depths of awkwardness without ever looking back. "Yeah, and I normally like to French a little before sliding into second base like that." French? Second base? Was I in a fifth-grade game of spin the bottle? Could I be any more in high school?

"Second base?" he asked. I wanted to run and hide, but with all the roped-off VIP sections, it was like I was in a velvet prison with nowhere to go. Plus, with these mile-high heels, I'd probably just wind up falling down the stairs and breaking my neck. And there's nothing sexy about a full body cast.

"Ha! That's classic," Mr. Tall Blond and Helpful laughed, and not in a God-I-can't-wait-to-tell-my-friends-how-young-you-are kind of way. "I haven't heard that since high school."

Again, the mouth just started flapping without me knowing what was coming out. "Well, if leggings can come back, so can the bases, right?" I could not believe that I was having a real conversation with a hot guy in an awesome New York club. This was so *Sex and the City*, I wanted to pinch myself.

He nodded and smiled. A perfectly perfect smile. Not too perfect, like Nick Lachey dental-work-and-weekly-bleaching perfect. Jake Gyllenhaal perfect. And there were deep lines where his cheeks met his mouth that didn't make me think he was old, just that he was a guy who smiled a lot. I liked that. And through his perfectly perfect smile came, "Just as long as the Bloodhound Gang doesn't make a comeback, I'm down with the retro revival." I nodded, though I didn't follow. Was Bloodhound Gang one of those crump dancing groups? That was getting Wikipedia'd as soon as I got home.

"Let me buy you a replacement," he offered, grazing my elbow slightly as he gestured to the bar.

"Oh, no, that's okay. There's still some left." I shook the

glass, which only had a millimeter of melty ice left in it. Why did I say no? Jayla made it seem like getting a guy to buy you a drink was the ultimate goal. Well, not the ultimate, *ultimate* goal, but still something that I should not just *let* him, but *want* him to do. I made a mental note to start thinking before speaking.

"Unless you're planning on taking that straw and sucking down your shirt, there's none of that drink left. Come on." He put his hand on the small of my back, guiding me gently toward the bar. His hand was big and certain, sending a ripple of tingles up my back. I tried not to shudder, and let him move me forward, glad that he wouldn't be able to see my face as I blushed.

"A Jack and Coke, please, and . . ." He bent down, pretending to smell my skin, his nose almost rubbing my shoulder. I felt the pulsing tingles start again. "What's that? A Ketel One and tonic?" Okay, when I find out that this guy is famous—anyone this hot has to be famous—and relive this story for Rachel, I'm just going to say we went to second base at this point. I mean, his nose was like only inches away from my skin. Totally counted.

I giggled, and then tried to turn it into a deeper, more mature laugh but just ended up sounding like a dog before it throws up. Even though a Ketel One and tonic wasn't the fertilizer-and-soda special that I was drinking before, I said, "Exactly."

I hung back, letting him order for me and ask the bartender to add it to his tab. He passed me my drink and I thanked him, trying to sound casual and not like this was the first time a boy had ever bought me a drink in my entire life.

New drinks in hand, we made our way to an empty booth, positioning ourselves beside a gaggle of gorgeous girls. I eyed the girls and heard my heart thud as it sank. My blond Wentworth Miller was totally going to do a one-eighty and spend the rest of the night gawking at these Pussycat Doll rejects. Me and my sopping tube top would get ditched. But instead, he leaned in close—those lips not even an inch from touching my ear—and whispered, "You good here?" I could feel his voice more than hear it, wet and soft. With a slight turn of my head, I'd be kissing those lips.

Instead, in an effort to win the Awkward Olympics, I jerked back suddenly. "Who, me?" I pointed to myself with a thumb, drawing more attention to the wet spot on Jayla's tube top. "Yeah, I'm good. I mean I'm doing *well*. Good is an adjective and you need an adverb there. I mean, *one* would need an adverb there." I couldn't be more awkward if I started peeing myself right there.

Another so-sexy-it-has-to-be-illegal smile crossed his face. I wanted to take a picture of him, because I knew that with that grammar lesson, I wasn't going to be salivating at that smile in person for much longer. "An English major, I presume? At Penn, I was a twentieth-century lit guy." He was like the social Harry Potter—he could turn any of my blunders into legit conversations. Pure magic!

I nodded.

For the record, I had not just lied to him. That was simply avoiding the truth. Telling him that I was a barely eighteen-year-old high schooler would go over like a "yo' mama" joke at an orphanage. And I had thought about being an English major in college, maybe. I mean, I hadn't thought about *not* being an English major, okay? And I did read. Well, when I wasn't watching reality television. Whatever, I wrote a lot and I was signed up for AP English next year. That counted. Plus, I was never going to see this guy again. Lying to him totally didn't count. It's not like I was cheating on the SATs or anything.

I took a big sip of my drink. The effect of the Jayla Juices was tapering off, and as awky as I was acting now, I knew I'd be a hundred times more odd if I allowed myself to sober up and fully overanalyze the situation in progress.

"You let me know when you're done with that." He pointed to my glass, his finger touching my hand clenched around the tumbler. I'm surprised I didn't drop it, adding to the baby pool of mixed drink that was congregating in my cleave. "And we'll find a place to get you a Caipirinha."

"What's that?" Again with the mouth flapping before the brain can think. A Caipiriniaian or whatever was probably something that a club-going twenty-two-year-old would know about. I might as well have asked what Bud Lite was.

"Oh, it's this awesome drink they make in Brazil. I was there last year. I saved all of my vacation and lumped it together at the end of the year with the week of Christmas. After three weeks down there, I almost didn't come back."

I sat there, paralyzed by his hotness and charm as he gushed about his rain-forest hikes and all-night parties in a tone of enthusiastic appreciation that up until now I'd only heard guys use to describe boobs.

"Have you ever been to South America?"

It took me a second to snap out of my gaga-eyed daze to answer, "Well, no. But I did go to Central America."

"Really? Where did you go? I bet you have wild stories."

"I was in Costa Rica with my—" The truth was that I went to Costa Rica with my family when I was twelve. And the story about me popping a braces bracket on a corncob probably was not the kind of wild tale he was looking for. "—best friend last year, and yeah, totally wild time."

And while I thought the goal of tonight was to wear shoes so uncomfortable that I couldn't even concentrate on the emotional pain of the Brian breakup, I still couldn't help but compare my man of the moment with Bridgefield's resident fart-lighting expert. This new manfriend was so interesting. With Brian, if it didn't have to do with either how lame studying was or how awesome having a girl to make out with all the time was, we probably never spoke about it.

"So, what do you do?"

What do I do? What does that mean? "Like for fun?" I asked, confused. I couldn't tell him that I mostly just sat around in sweats, snacking and writing in a diary.

"No, like for work."

Shit. Cold terror flooded through me. I'd rather tell him about the sweatpants-and-cashew-chicken evenings, because I really couldn't tell him that I was a high school intern. "I work in marketing at a media-buying company in Midtown. It's called MediaInc, you've probably heard of it. There are flat screens in the elevator." I smiled. That sounded very believable, despite being a half lie.

He raised his eyebrows. "MediaInc? No way!"

I nodded. "Yeah, since graduation. *College* graduation, that is."

Who knew he'd be this impressed? It must be the plasmas in the elevator. Boys love technology. I was about to start telling him about the telephone system—which was, like, from 2038 it was so advanced—but he interrupted.

"I work there, too! I can't believe I've never seen you around."

My face went slack. "What?" I could hear my stomach drop to the floor and splatter. "You work there? At MediaInc? Like, really work there? Full-time?"

"Yep, full-time. Benefits, 401K. All of it. That's so funny that I've never seen you."

As the nerves kicked in, so did my sweat glands, and I could feel the skin on my face was now shiny and moist.

"Uh-huh, hilarious." Panic. Panic.

"So, the marketing department, eh? That means that you must work with Derek Dorfman? I'm in meetings with that guy all day long."

"You know Derek?" I gulped at my drink. Even though it was mostly water at this point, I hoped that maybe whatever vodka was in there would knock me out or make me puke or do something to get me out of this situation. Spontaneous death would work, too. I could feel my entire body flush and perspire. I was a sweaty liar trapped in my own deceit.

In the midst of my panic attack, my purse started vibrating. Rachel was probably calling in a fluster. I didn't think she'd even been in the apartment without me. I could imagine her phone call with the police.

"She's gone missing. There are no takeout containers and the TV is off. I'm really scared."

Thank God. This was a painless, not death-inducing, way to get out of the situation before my working-girl cover was totally blown. "Oh, sorry, I've got to take this," I told him, pointing to my flashing phone. "Nice meeting you."

I turned to dash away but he caught my hand. "Actually, we didn't meet. I'm Colin Christensen, associate sales supervisor."

"Emma Freeman . . ." He waited expectantly for my title. "Junior, um . . . media . . . coordinator."

"I'm impressed. You've obviously worked hard since you left college. Where did you go, by the way?"

What was this, Twenty Questions? I wanted to just run and leave him hanging, but it's impossible to not respond to a guy this foxy. I drew inspiration from my bag. "Brown." At least I didn't say "Clutch."

"Well, I guess I'll be seeing you around the office, right?" he chirped.

I smiled up at him and nodded, then turned as gracefully as I could in Jayla's foot smushers and wobbled away as fast as my strappy feet could carry me.

Great, I didn't even have a real job yet and I'd already committed career suicide.

I flipped open my phone to call Rachel to tell her that she could call off the search dogs, but instead saw four missed calls from Jayla. I dialed her as fast as I could, hoping that she hadn't left me there alone.

"Whurdafuckarlyou?"

Definitely Jayla's voice, but I could barely understand what she was saying.

"Jay? Jayla? Hold on, I can't understand you. I'm going to step outside so I can hear." I pushed through the mob of beautiful people, and when I lugged the club door open, I saw her standing on the street corner trying to hail a cab. She was a wreck—mascara tears rolling down her face, dress straps by her elbows, and one shoe in each hand. If she'd just had some nipple showing, I'd have mistaken her for Tara Reid.

How could she have gone from the fabulous Jayla to this makes-Paula-Abdul-look-emotionally-stable pile of weeping

155

couture and drippy makeup since she took off not even half an hour ago?

I rushed up to her, threw one arm around her in a hug, and held my other out to hail a cab as if I were a pro.

"Jinxy, what's wrong?"

"I fucking haythis!" Her words were slurred, but understandable.

"Hate what?"

"This shit." She motioned around the street corner. "Goinnoutto club evey nigh'. Getting fuckin' left behind by Chloe the sec she meets a boy. Explaining to my father how I spent three hundred fuckin' dollars in one night. I'm fuckin' sick of it."

The word "fuck" hadn't been used this much since *The Sopranos* went off the air.

"Okay, we don't have to do it ever again," I said in my mom voice, rubbing her back. Of course, that was pretty meaningless coming from me, as I would never go out to a place like that without Jayla leading the way.

"Well, what else is there to do in this stupid town?"

Wait, *she* was asking *me* what there was to do in this town? I mean, it's New York City! It's the concrete glam capital of the world. There are entire books, entire *long* books, written about what to do here—where to eat, where to shop, what to see. It's the background for every fabulous story there ever was. There's so much more to this city than using Daddy's Visa and getting ditched by friends. But how come I couldn't think of one goddamned thing to do?

A cab finally stopped in front of us and I flopped Jayla in one side and limped my high heels over to the other side and climbed in.

"We could catch some Broadway shows?" I offered lamely. Even I knew this was a wretched idea. She shot me a look that said that she'd rather move off this island if the only thing to do in this city was watch the little guy from *Queer Eye* prance around in *Rent*. And with that, she passed out, leaving me to figure out how to drag her up to the apartment on my own.

Thirteen

The next morning, after a night of dry-mouthed, nervous, restless sleep, I kicked Rachel's door open and barged into her room.

"Holy shit!" she shrieked, tearing off her "Princess" eye mask. "What the hell is it? You scared the crap out of me, Emma."

I was totally giddy—I couldn't even get my thoughts out in full sentences.

"I gotta talk!" I squealed and jumped into her bed. "Last night! Vodka! Hot guy! Coworker! High heels!" The story came tumbling out in fragments and spurts as Rachel wiped the sleep from her eyes and tried to keep up.

Rachel took a few secs to prop herself up in bed. "So wait," she interjected, trying to connect the dots. "You went out with Jayla and had plums and then you met some old guy who used to be your boss?"

"No, Rachel, goddamn it, keep up." I pulled myself together a little and started from the top. "The club was called Plumm and he's not my boss, he *knows* my boss. And he's so hot, I can't even stand it. He's a walking streak of foxiness! And now I'm freaking out because what if I see him at work? He's going to know that I'm not a junior media whatever and that I'm not twenty-two and I'll be completely screwed."

Rachel's clouds of confusion lifted.

"Ohhh! Okay, I get it," she said after a pause, and finally started to get excited. "And you exchanged numbers?"

"Uh, well, no, actually, we didn't." I hadn't realized that until now. I'd dashed off so fast, I might've left a glass slipper behind.

"Really? He didn't ask for it?"

I shook my head, my excitement melting into heartbreak mush.

"Oh, well then, you don't have anything to worry about. It doesn't even sound like he liked you that much." Rachel grinned at me as if she were being helpful and hadn't just muttered one of the worst sentences I'd ever heard.

I glared at her and sighed sharply, "Thank you, Rachel. That's precisely what I wanted to hear."

"No, Em. I don't mean it in a bad way," she protested.

Sometimes even best friends need a punch in the mouth. I held back, but just barely.

I needed real advice and some positive energy and I wasn't getting either in Rachel's bed. "I'm going to talk to

Jayla," I said gravely, and got up to leave. "Someone who actually interacts with real, live men, not lame computer profiles."

"Oh jeez." Rachel rolled her eyes. But as soon as I left the room, I heard her shuffling after me into Jayla's room, which, for once, she was actually in. She must have gotten up in the middle of the night. The mascara drips were wiped off and she'd changed out of the dress that I'd put her to bed in. As much as I wanted to be a friend to Jayla, my fingers were crossed that she'd never want to talk about her meltdown last night. And, from her "You met a boy? Tell me more!" I guessed that she felt the same way or maybe had just blacked out the last half hour of our evening.

Rachel and I flopped down on her gold duvet and I poured out the story of meeting my future boyfriend and then totally crapping everything up with the lies about graduating college and working in the real world. After I finished, I took a deep breath and waited for Jayla's verdict, hoping that it would somehow involve finding him immediately and then making out.

"Hmm." Jayla considered the situation, tapping her BeDazzled iPhone against her chin—yes, she slept with it—and weighed my options. "Well, obviously, you can't tell him the truth."

"Really?" I was a little surprised. It just felt like telling the truth would be the right thing to do. "I kind of think I should. I mean, I feel a little guilty about lying to this guy."

"Ha!" Jayla laughed, throwing her head back. "You feel guilty? Emma, do you have any idea how much men lie to us? Any idea? Let me tell you a little story. In the fall, Chlo set me up with this kid, Carter."

"Wait," I interrupted. "The guy you didn't want to see last night? The Shrek-in-Burberry one?"

"Yes," she sighed regretfully. "The fat donkey one. So he and I go out, we hit it off, and everything was going really, really well. We met each other's friends, he called me his girlfriend. I even met his parents!"

"*You* had a real boyfriend?" Rachel asked incredulously. Even though we'd only known her for like three and a half weeks, it was obvious to us that this girl was a wild child in every sense. Imagining her with one person was impossible— even for brunch, this girl traveled in packs.

"He was a good kisser and he was rich, nothing more than that," she huffed indignantly, but I sensed that she had really liked this guy. "Anyway, we were together for two months or so and he just stopped calling. For no reason. I e-mailed him and he's like, 'Sorry I haven't called. I should have told you sooner, but I'm bipolar.' "

Rachel and I gasped in unison and Jayla went on.

"Oh, that's not even the worst part. So I wait a few days to clear my head, I cry a ton, I do all this research on manic depression and I decided that, you know what? I liked him enough, we could work it out. I, Jayla Louise St. Clare, had enough happiness and stability in my life to support the two of us." I almost choked. After her breakdown last night, I'd say she was about as stable as a rocking chair on a balance beam. She continued, "I called him and told him that I was there for him and was willing to see it through. And do you know what he said to me? Do you?"

We shook our heads, wide-eyed.

" 'Oh Jayla, you're so funny. I was just kidding. I'm not bipolar. I'm just an asshole!' "

"What?" Rachel shrieked. "So he was lying about a serious mental disorder to get out of a relationship?"

Jayla nodded.

"Jayla, that's awful, I'm sorry." I suddenly felt really ashamed of my selfishness. Why was I forcing her to talk about boys when she was clearly still getting over this jerk-lips? "Did you end up running into him last night? Is that what happened?"

"Uh, we . . . I, no. No, I didn't see Carter." She fiddled with her Juicy Couture pillow and I had a sneaking suspicion she was lying, but Jayla sort of scared me and I didn't want to call her out on it.

"I can't believe your middle name is Louise," squealed Rachel, laughing and mercifully changing the subject before Jayla switched back into meltdown mode.

"Shut up!" Jayla laughed back. "It's a family name, okay? Anyway, the point is, girls lie about little things but guys lie big. *Big.* So don't even worry about this Colin thing."

After that horror story, Jayla's point did make a little more sense. But just because *one* guy lied to Jayla didn't mean that I had to seek revenge on *this* guy.

"So I really shouldn't tell him the truth?" I checked.

The girls both shook their heads.

"You'll look crazy," Jayla reasoned. "Don't tell him unless you have to, and then you just laugh and say you were kidding and he was too drunk to get the joke or something like that."

"Yeah," Rachel chimed in. "And I seriously doubt you'll see him again anyway."

Again, Rachel had the knack for zeroing in on exactly what I didn't want to hear. But what if I *didn't see him again*?

I could feel my face turning into a sourpuss just thinking about it. Thankfully, Jayla came to my rescue.

"You'd be surprised. Manhattan is a pretty small town when it comes down to it. I run into exes all the time. So you need to look fabulous all the time. You really need to kick it up a notch."

Looking fabulous *all the time*? Even with Jayla's extreme makeover last night, I was still a few clicks away from truly fabulous. "Done up every day? That's just so not me. Plus, I don't have any fabulous clothes," I whined. "I wear the same nasty black pants to work every day. I look like a waiter."

"Well, sister," Jayla said, throwing back the covers and prancing out of bed and into her closet. "You have a credit card that isn't going to max itself out, now is it?" She poked her head out of the walk-in and through a bright smile shouted, "Shopping trip!"

We were out the door a half hour later, Jayla and Rachel not letting the fact that my credit card was parent-sponsored be an excuse to keep me from spending mad money. By the end of the day, I had four new bags of clothes and we all had our New York aliases written in gold hanging from our necks. After explaining to Jayla that not everyone's parents get the idea of retail therapy, we concocted a pretty solid-sounding story to tell my parents about needing to put a ton of money on their card because my hair clogged the shower drain and caused a major emergency plumbing situation in the apartment that needed fixing. I felt bad about the lie. I mean, they were footing the entire bill for my summer in Manhattan, the least I could do was not drain their retirement savings.

• • •

Monday, I got up a half hour early to primp and put on the perfect oh-just-happened-to-run-into-you-in-the-high-tech-elevator-looking-fabulous outfit.

As soon as I set foot on the sidewalk, paranoia took over. What if Colin was on the train? Or right across the street from me?

I realized that since I didn't know where Colin lived, he could be walking right behind me the entire way to work. There were so many people on the street, I couldn't possibly inspect them all without looking like a total psychopath.

I held my breath as I walked through the MediaInc lobby and hugged the walls like a rat, nervously scuttling into an elevator. I couldn't even enjoy the televator today. All I could do was imagine the possible conversation starters I could use if I ran into him.

"*Oh, hi, you probably don't recognize me when I'm not dripping in spilled cocktail, but I'm that girl from the other night . . . the one you talked to for a while . . . well, maybe like only forty-five minutes, but that's kind of a while . . . and I thought you were flirting. . . . My best friend said you probably weren't, but . . . anyway, I'd be interested in jamming my tongue in your mouth. You know, making out.*"

Holy shit. This was going to be a nightmare. And way worse than the one I had about taking the PSATs naked.

I thought that once I was safely in my cubicle, protected by the gray pseudo-walls, I could relax. But sitting there, I realized that I was basically a sitting duck, totally immobile should Colin saunter past.

"Yo, Emmerino!"

I gasped loudly as Derek waddled his Dockers and

shirtsleeves over to my cube. I was jumpier than a virgin at a prison rodeo. This was going to be a very long day.

"Why are you all hunched over like that? You look like you're sad."

I realized I was slunk halfway down in my chair and had scooted all the files on my desk around my face like a fort.

"I'm not sad," I said quickly, scanning the office behind him like a CIA agent worried she'd been followed.

"Are you sure you're not sad about not having a boyfriend?"

Derek was like instant worst day ever. You could just insert him into any day of your life and boom, automatically, it's the worst day you've ever had.

"No, Derek, I'm not." I couldn't hide the frustration in my voice.

"Why, you *finally* got yourself a boyfriend?" He said "finally" as if I'd been single for fifty years and had seven cats and a facial deformity.

"What? Well, no." Why did I humor him with answers to his asinine questions? Tomorrow, I was just going to pretend that I went deaf overnight.

"Oh, well, don't worry about it. I was single for several years before I got married. So if you ever want to talk to me about your issues trusting men—"

I cut him off. "Derek, no. I don't have issues trusting men and I don't want to talk. Okay?"

He put his hands up like I was the one with the social problems in this equation. "Whoa-ho! Did someone wake up on the wrong side of the bed, or do you have PMS?" I tried to knock him dead with my thoughts, but he just kept right on. "Don't answer that, okay? Anyway, Nora's out sick today, so you get to help alphabetize the client fiscal report files from last year. Score!" He pumped his fists in the air and did what I could only assume was a touchdown dance but he looked more like Mick Jagger with two sprained ankles.

I feigned enthusiasm and followed Derek to a conference room with twenty-five boxes of files to be sorted.

The next six hours passed uneventfully, me tucked safely away from possible Colin sightings. And while this should have made me happy, I began to wonder which would be worse—constant office run-ins or never seeing him again? Those green eyes were meant to be seen again.

Sitting in the conference room alone with my Dymo label maker, I called it like it was. "This summer sucks!" I said out loud. Here I was, trapped in this god-awful job while the weather was warm and beautiful, and the one hot guy I'd met was totally out of my league . . . or on his way to becoming Derek Dorfman himself and I had just vodka tonic–ed myself into thinking he was cool. I tried to picture Colin ten years from now, with a little less hair and some fat wife named Peg. I laughed out loud and thought that anyone as hot as Colin would surely stay that way forever. But then again, look at Britney Spears. This could be his peak—his MTV Music Award performance in a gold thong and glitter. Now, that was a visual. A strangely erotic one.

"It has been way too long since I've hooked up," I confessed again to my label maker. Going from making out with Brian every day to nada for the past few weeks was affecting me big-time. "Sparkles and man-thongs should not be turning me on."

I shuffled the files in my lap and suddenly all I could think about was Colin.

I sat there, gaga-eyed, totally stalled in my alphabetizing for fifteen minutes before deciding to get some fresh air.

And by "fresh air" I meant "chocolate."

I had pretty much given up on seeing Colin and I was bummed that I'd wasted my cutest outfit on Monday. I could possibly wear it again later in the week, but I'd already spilled raspberry vinaigrette on my dress at lunch, and let's be honest, "dry clean only" means "dry clean never" in my world. The dress wasn't going to see the light of day again until I got back to B-field and Mama Freeman threw down the $7.50 to have it professionally cleaned.

I headed to my cubicle, grabbed a fistful of change from my wallet, and trudged over to the elevators for a trip to the vending machine, hoping chocolate would fulfill my need for male attention, excitement, and intellectual stimulation all at once. I knew it was a lot to ask from the Mars Candy Corporation, but dammit, it was worth a shot.

As I stood in front of the machine, pondering my junk food selection, I could hear someone walking up behind me. Not wanting to force a fellow three o'clock snacker to wait for his or her fix, I quickly decided and punched in the numbers for my lard-maker of choice.

"Well, hello, Miss Freeman," an easy voice said behind me.

"Wha?" I spun around, caught off guard. Colin! What was he doing on this floor? I turned four shades of purple, none of which went with my yellow dress. "Oh, I, um, hi! Hi, Mr. Christensen—I mean Colin—how are you?"

"Well"—he leaned in like we were sharing a secret— "I'm really glad we met Saturday. Cool people are hard to find around this place." I caught a whiff of his cologne—he smelled like pure, uncut man—and my knees almost gave out. Just then my king-sized peanut M&M's bounced out of the candy machine. Why couldn't he have seen me buying veggie chips or something? I should have pretended they were for someone else. As I bent down to pick up my four hundred candy-coated calories, he pulled out a pen and paper.

"Look, some friends and I are having a barbecue at my loft this weekend, you should come. Here's the address. Eightish."

I managed to stutter out that I'd be there. But I think I also muttered something about bringing enough moisty-naps for everyone. God, I'm such a waste of A cups. We both headed over to the elevators.

"Going up?" he asked as he pressed the up button for himself.

I think I would have combusted from the pressure of my crush if I had to ride in an elevator with him. "Um, no. I'm going down. Some people take cigarette breaks outside, I take chocolate breaks," I said, holding up my bag of M&M's.

"That's totally my kind of break," he said. As he pushed the down button for me, an elevator going up binged open. He hopped in and gave me a wink. A wink that was effortless and cute and flirty. Definitely flirty. So much for Rachel's theory about him not being into me. A party invite and a wink? One more into-me thing and he'd practically be asking me to marry him. I held his stare until the doors closed in front of his chiseled face.

As soon as I was sure his 'vator was gone, I pushed the up button. I flew back to my desk to text Rach about the encounter. As I was thumb-typing, Derek came around the corner.

"Emma, here's a question for you. How come you wear the same thing every day?" I looked down at my brand-spanking-new dress and then back up at him, not saying a word. "I feel like most women pay more attention to how they look. Just a thought. You better get back to those files, okay, missy?"

I watched his fat ass lumber off back to his office. Sweet shit, I hated that man. I hit Send on my text to Rachel and then—just as I was told to—lumbered my own smaller butt back to the conference room for more filing.

Fourteen

"What?" Jayla said with pure disgust as she popped out from behind the fridge door with her Diet Coke.

Why was she acting like I'd just announced that I was going to camp out to be first in line for the new Taylor Hicks album? "What's wrong? I just said I'm going to the barbecue tonight. That one that I've been sweating about all effing week! With Colin, the Humbert Humbert to my Lolita." I was joking, but I still felt way guilty about lying to him.

"Nuh-uh," Jayla said, shuffling for more stuff in the fridge. "That's not what you just said. You said that you're going to the barbecue with Jake."

"Oh yeah. I invited Jake. What's the big whoop?" Had I just said "whoop"? I was turning into my mother. Someone needed to kill me before I started wearing reading glasses as jewelry.

Jayla backed out of the fridge and slammed some food down on the counter. "But don't you like Colin? He's the one you described as a Chad Michael Murray look-alike?" I nodded. He was so Chad Michael Murray, except for not an obvious asshole.

"Well then, what the hell are you doing bringing Jake?" she asked, dumping some lettuce into a bowl. She spoke with that don't-be-such-an-imbecile tone my math teacher had whenever I forgot that the quadratic formula was all over 2a. "He's going to be a ginormous cockblock."

Inviting Jacob was part of my strategy for getting Colin. I leaned on the counter and explained my logic: "I invited him because he'll help me blend in. He actually is twenty-three and has a job as a junior something or other. Hanging with him is going to make me seem older."

Jayla had finished preparing our snack of lettuce and spray butter and we moved into the common area. "Hanging with him is going to make you seem like you have a boyfriend."

I immediately lost my appetite. "Crap, Jay. He's my cousin!" The memories of his bacne from our family Fourth of July bash a few years ago were enough to make me barf up my lunch.

"But Colin's not going to know that." She stuffed down a calorie-less mouthful. "Showing up with another guy, crustacean cousin or not, is bad form, Em."

Shit. She was right. My mind raced. I seriously couldn't

face the barbecue alone. There was no way. And I couldn't *un*invite my cousin. Suddenly and tragically, my adult plans were collapsing in on themselves.

"Well, what am I going to do?" I sputtered. "I can't find thirty-four Leonard Street by myself. I can only do numbered streets alone—TriBeCa is like a labyrinth."

Jayla's eyes widened, which, combined with her already enhancing liner, made her blue eyes look like Hope diamonds. Choking on a spray-buttered bite, she said, "Thirty-four Leonard? That's where the barbecue is?"

I fished around in the clutch borrowed from Jayla for the piece of paper Colin had given me on Monday. I uncrumpled it and flattened it on the coffee table.

"Yeah, Thirty-four Leonard. That's it."

"I'll come," she volunteered suddenly. "If I'm there, it won't look like you're dating Jacob. Just like a group of friends are coming to a party together. It'll be better for you."

Wow. That was fast and extremely nice of her.

"Really?" I asked hesitantly, but was already flooding with relief. "You're going to ditch your plans with Chloe tonight?" Though I wasn't sure I should really point out her other options. I really wanted her to come and be sure no one thought I was couplized with my own cousin. Gross.

With a transfatlessly greased smile she answered, "For you? Of course."

This totally wasn't very Jayla of her to be putting my social special needs before her own Saturday night plans. Maybe I'd judged her too quickly—just because she was a social butterfly didn't mean she couldn't also be a really good friend when she needed to, right? Whatever, I didn't care if she was only in it for the free veggie burgers, I was just psyched not to be doomed to lurk around the party as a to-tal untouchable.

"This still look good?" Rachel interrupted before I could start blubbering with gratitude and promising to do Jayla's laundry for the next month. Rachel waltzed out of her room wearing the same mini-and-cowl-neck outfit that she'd worn on her JDate two weeks earlier. "I've got another one tonight." She twirled for us to take in the ensemble.

I cooed like a third-grade class when their teacher got flowers delivered. "Another date with a bird! A plane! No, it's SuperJew!"

"Uh, *no*. He was like a hundred years ago." He was like barely two weeks ago, actually. I wanted to roll my eyes but kept them under control. "This is some guy who's interning at Goldman this summer." She paused expectantly for us to ooh and ahh at what a catch he was.

"It still looks cute, but you can't," Jayla said firmly.

"What?" Rachel and I said in sync, throwing puzzled looks at each other before turning to Jayla.

"I mean, a D&G skirt is always going to look cute. But you just can't wear that outfit again. It's been tainted."

This elicited another tag-team response of confused scrunched faces.

"Rachel, didn't you have an awful first date the last time you wore that outfit?"

"Well," she said defensively, crossing her arms and avoiding eye contact, "I wouldn't call it *awful*."

"You said that he took you to an Indian buffet and made you split the bill." Jayla sprayed some faux butter on her fingertip and licked it off as Rachel stuck her chin out indignantly.

"Maybe."

Jayla rolled her eyes. "Honey, a date that won't throw down the six ninety-five to pay for your food poisoning? That's bad."

I nodded reluctantly. Even Brian paid for me on our first dinner date.

"And so," Jayla continued, "that outfit's been on one bad date. It's tainted. Jinxed. You need to wear something fresh or there's no hope that tonight's going to go any better."

"Tonight *has* to go better," Rachel whined. "We're going to Union Square Cafe. I looked up the menu online and my summer stipend from Sirlie won't even cover the bread basket there."

Jayla sighed in mock exasperation. "Well, lucky for you, that's what fabulous, generous, almost-too-hot-to-look-at roommates are for! I am sure my black hole of a closet has something guaranteed to get you through dinner and"—she licked the last of the butter off her finger suggestively—"*way* past dessert!"

"Jayla!" Rachel laughed, blushing slightly. "Come on, I don't want to look like a ho!"

"Who you callin' a ho?" Jayla said in her sassiest Lil' Kim voice. "Are you trying to tell me that I look like some hoochie-ass when I go out?"

"No, no, no." Rachel realized her foot-in-mouth gaffe and tried to backpedal. "I just mean that, you know. Well, I'm not trying to dress like I'm easy or anything."

"Being easy isn't an outfit, it's a state of mind." Jayla got up and headed toward her room, motioning for us to follow. "Now come on, follow me into my office."

We dutifully shuffled into the master bedroom to sift through a closet of jinx-free ensembles.

If I bought into Jayla's outfit karma theory, I'd have to buy a new outfit for every single day of work. A day in that cubicle was way worse than paying for my own tandoori chicken. And Derek had either never heard of this contaminated-outfit theory or genuinely loved every second at work, because that dude had worn the same karmically polluted Dockers every single day since I started.

I lounged on Jayla's bed and watched Rachel try on outfit after outfit.

"Well, what kind of look are you going for here?" Jayla asked, studying her closet and glancing back at Rachel. We'd already been through three rejects.

"Uh, I don't know. Pretty?" Rachel looked at me for help but I just shrugged. I usually just shoot for the "No, my bra is in *no way* padded" look.

Jayla sighed and rolled her eyes. "No. No! Pretty isn't a look—it's what you naturally are, Rachel."

She blushed a little at the compliment. "Okay, then how about 'supersophisto Manhattan socialite girl'?"

Clearly, Rachel wasn't even inventing a persona, she was just describing Jayla. Clever.

Jayla immediately brightened. "I know *exactly* the outfit!" She rifled through the turquoise section of her closet until she found a silky Ella Moss dress with white piping and a plunging neckline.

"This is perfecto," Jayla announced, handing it to Rachel and then turning to her armoire and rifling through her accessories. "It'll bring out your eyes and your boobs, but it's long enough so that you won't look tacky. And with this heat, it won't get you all swampy and gross."

"Jam Master Jay has done it again!" I said, totally

impressed. She was like a younger, slightly less hot, not-consta-pregnant version of Heidi Klum.

Under an hour later, all three of us sauntered out of our lobby wearing our new gold alias-name necklaces. Jayla and I turned to head off to our evening of barbecue and boys, while Rachel blew us kisses and sashayed across Union Square in the borrowed Ella dress, borrowed Gustto bag, and borrowed Marc Jacobs slingbacks to meet the guy who could be buying her a Tiffany's ring in a few years. We waved back and headed down into the subway.

"I cannot believe we're taking the subway," Jayla said, clopping down the stairs and sneering at the entire station.

I knew my bank account balance and had to draw the line on charging things on my parental credit card somewhere.

"I just spent about a million and a half dollars of my parents' money on this dress." I struck a little model pose, displaying the overpriced but too-perfect-to-pass-up pink and green number from Intermix. I was trying to be as nonchalant as I could about the money situation—Jayla had absolutely no concept of my world and I didn't want to come off too poor. "I can't ask them to borrow any more money. I'm living the budget life—well, the budget-fabulous life—the rest of the summer, okay?"

"Fine. Fine. Fine." She crossed her arms and scowled. "But I am not touching anything down here."

A short subway ride later, we hit Canal Street. It might sound like a quaint little part of town, full of waterways and Venetian architecture, but all it was full of was the smell of sewers and garbage. The stifling heat of the subway gave way to the choking aroma of the Chinatown fish markets wafting into the subway station, and we held our noses as we climbed up the stairs and onto the street.

Canal was busy, stinky, and packed to the gills with all sorts of designer knockoffs. I thought I was going to have to shoot Jayla with a tranquilizer dart to keep her from freaking.

"Sweet Christ. Is this hell?" she said, glaring at the fake Pradas and Louis Vuittons as I pulled out my STREET-WISE map.

"No," I answered. Although this probably *was* Jayla's version of hell. "Only a few more blocks west and we'll be at the corner where I said I'd meet Jacob." I took her by the arm and started tugging her down the street.

"Wait, after that odyssey"—she pointed down to the 6 train—"we still have to walk? This feels more like 'budget boot camp' than 'budget-fabulous.'"

"Come on, you drama mama. If you'd just stop bitching, we can get out of Fish Town and into civilized society, okay?" I had to drag her like a stubborn puppy the next few blocks. I prayed we were walking in the right direction. I had a feeling that dealing with a Jayla-style meltdown was not going to leave me with enough energy to woo Colin.

I saw Jake waiting for us at the corner of Church and Canal and breathed a sigh of relief that I had steered us the right way.

"Yo!" he greeted me. And then he saw Little Miss Stiletto limping behind me. "Oh, hiya, Jayla. I didn't know you'd be coming. I mean, it's fine that you are. No, I mean it's *great* that you're here, way better than fine. So, this should be fun hanging out with you. Well, not just the two of us. Emma too. The three of us hanging out, all night, together. Fun." He sighed sharply. "So, um, never mind all that. I just meant 'Hi, Jayla.' "

God, I hope I didn't sound that spazzy when I talked to Colin. But I had a feeling it ran in the family.

Jayla didn't seem to notice his nervous yapping, or actually notice Jake at all. She pressed on in her Manolo marathon. Jake and I followed behind her royal queen of complaints, actually hustling a bit to keep up. Even though her heels could probably be used as ice picks come winter, she was totally outpacing us in our flip-flops. With all the rushing, I didn't have much time to take in TriBeCa—not like there was much to take in. The neighborhood mostly seemed like a weird mix of swanky lofts and stores that exclusively sold futons.

Finally, at the door to 34 Leonard, Jayla rang the buzzer and sighed, "Thank God that death march is over. Cab's on me on the way home."

A staticky sound came from the speaker and we pushed our way through the fingerprinted glass door and walked into the small lobby. Jake pressed the elevator up button and the doors opened immediately. We piled into the tiny cabin—it felt like we were in a shoebox on a pulley. I tried my hardest to will my pits to stop sweating as we rode up.

"Actually," Jayla added to her previous rant, smoothing her dress and running her fingers through her perfectly straightened hair, "cabs are on me for the rest of the summer. Never again." She was still grumbling about why the MTA should put sanitizing gel in each subway car as a tall, sunburned guy with red hair and a white V-neck T-shirt opened the door. He looked like a candy cane.

Jayla, Jake, and Mr. Minty looked at me expectantly.

"Oh! Uh, hi, I'm Emma. Freeman. Emma Freeman," I sputtered nervously, turning red enough to match the guy in the doorway. "Colin Christensen invited me."

"Oh, solid," he said with a stoner head nod. He took a sip of his beer and meandered back into the party, motioning vaguely toward the bar.

We stood in the doorway, surveying the scene. Exposed-brick wall to exposed-brick wall, the place was packed with beautiful young people. And even though everyone was obviously older than I was and, even more obviously, way cooler, I still felt a lot more comfortable at this party than at Plumm last week. It kind of reminded me of the few times I got invited to the A-List Only parties back home. So maybe I could dial down the awkward a notch or two when I talked to Colin tonight. Maybe.

"Yo, I'll grab us some beers," Jake volunteered.

"See if they have any chardonnay, would you?" Jayla demanded.

"I'm sorry." Jake cupped his hand to his ear. "Did you say Bud Lite or just Bud? Talk into my good ear this time."

"Neither, chardon—" Jayla started to yell. But her face changed when she got the joke. "Fine." Her mouth broke into an unwilling smile. "Bud Lite."

Jake waited expectantly, hand on hip.

"Please," she added.

He turned to head out on his beer hunt.

I called after him, "Bud Lite for me too." But he shot me his "But you're a minor" look. "Fine, nothing," I muttered. "I'm not thirsty anyway."

I glanced around the room and tried not to be bothered

179

by the girls looking me up and down. I knew my dress was cute, but in a room full of older, cooler hipster chicks who could actually go into a vintage store and not come out looking like Captain Jack Sparrow, I could've been wearing a garbage bag and felt less conspicuous. One scrawny American Apparel–draped girl whispered something to her equally Kirsten Dunst–y friend and pointed at Jayla's Manolo heels. Jayla glared icily at them and turned to me anxiously.

"Do I look okay?" she said nervously, tugging at her dress and looking at me intently for an honest answer.

"Jayla, please. You look amazing! You always do." She nodded tensely, throwing her shoulders back and thrusting forward her perfect cleavage. It wasn't like her to ask. I couldn't imagine her as one of those "Am I fat? Am I pretty?" sort of girls. When Jayla looked great, believe me, she knew. But she just chewed her lip and furrowed her brow, scanning the crowd. After a smelly subway ride and the choice between Skunk Beer 1 or Skunk Beer 2, I was worried she was just looking for an exit so she could ditch me.

I took her hand. "Let's go find my future summer boyfriend, okay?" I tried to lead her through the crowd, but no one would move out of my way. I had to get a little pushy, nudging through the sea of sideswept bangs. I was trying my hardest not to spill anyone's drinks, but I totally got some sneers from a group of girls who all had nose rings and cartilage pierces. "Should I ask where Colin is?" I shouted above the Mark Ronson remix playing.

Jayla looked at me like she'd seen the ghost of Christmas Moron. "No way. And try not to be so obvious that you're looking for him. Pretend that you're having a good time at a fun party and that he just happens to be here," she said.

I stopped my forward march and turned to look at her. Now I was totally confused. This wasn't some random field kegger that I heard about on a flier or something. "But I don't just happen to be here. I mean, he invited me." I'd look crazy if I came to his party and didn't say hi or anything.

She rolled her eyes at how not-boy-savvy I was.

"Fine." I crossed my arms. "I'll stop looking for him. Let's just stand here and look like we're having a good time. Now you fake laugh so that if he sees us, he'll think I'm funny."

Jayla threw her head back and laughed as directed. "That's my girl," she ventrilo-muttered through her flawless smile. "Let's check out the roof deck."

Jayla grabbed my arm and started leading me through the crowd. The dangly-earringed and skinny-jeaned folks of course easily parted for Jayla, and we made our way up the stairwell to the roof.

The outside party was a lot less crowded than the indoor soiree—just a bunch of people sitting on patio furniture, looking very New York casual.

I spotted Colin immediately. He was manning the grill and looking impossibly fine in his "Backyard Gourmet" apron. I spent a solid fifteen seconds staring at his butt. It would have gone on longer, but at second sixteen I was interrupted.

"Hey, you came!" Colin walked over to me, spatula and tongs in hand. Should I hug him hello? Were we at that point? I didn't know, so I just stood still, arms at my side like an ROTC cadet at attention. Ugh. Why was I being such an awkwardbot about this? He gave me a huge hug, ignoring my stiffness. Just feeling his manly warm chest against my (nonwomanly, flat) body sent tingles up and down my spine. Of course, instead of just letting a hug be a hug, I had to lean in more. But by then the window for normal-length hugs was over and I pretty much looked like I had a peg leg and was leaning on him for support. Real sexy! He pulled away, but his arms were still on my sides.

"You have to try my burgers. They're the best in the five boroughs, I've been told." I nodded and we headed back to the grill. He lobbed a burger onto a toasted bun. Why was he so supercasual and not totally awky around me like I was around him? Was that just an adult thing or maybe he just wasn't nervous because he didn't *like* like me. Wait, *like* like? Why was I perma-stuck in middle school when I was trying to be an adult?

"Ketchup? Mustard? What do you feel like, Emma?" Hearing him say my name made me tingle all over again.

"The more the merrier, chef."

Did I really just say that?

"Ha-ha. That's the kind of girl I like." He loaded up my burger with a little bit of everything. I didn't know what I was salivating over—him or the food. It had to be him. I swear, he was making relish look sexy.

My cell started to vibrate and I frantically fished around to get to it before "Canned Heat" started blaring. Too late. A polyphonic *"you know this boo-gie is for reeeeal"* echoed out of my—fine, *Jayla's*—bag.

"Love that movie," he said, arranging my tomatoes. "I'd do the whole dance, but I don't know if I can trust you yet.

182

If word of my sweet moves gets around the office, my stock will plummet."

He eyed me in mock suspicion. How could someone this smoking hot be flirting with me? And how could I not think of a comeback?

Finally, I found my phone. As I went to silence it I saw that it was Jayla calling. I was wondering where she'd gone off to. It wasn't even that crowded up on the roof. Could she seriously not just walk across the party to find me?

"Give me one second, I've got to get this."

"Okay, fine. But don't pull that ring-and-run thing you did last weekend," he joked, his green eyes bright through his smile-crinkled eyes.

God, the last thing I wanted to do was walk anywhere but right onto his lap, but if Jayla was calling me while at the same party, it must be kind of important. I walked toward the other side of the roof, where a group of drunk girls in Nicole Richie–esque headscarves were dancing.

"Jayla?" I said, flipping open the phone. "Where are you?"

"In the bathroom," she hissed in a low, frantic whisper. "Oh my God! You're never going to believe this."

"What's wrong?"

"You know fake-bipolar Carter? That little limp-dick is here."

I gasped, envisioning an unexpected run-in with Brian. I got that sinking-stomach feeling. I really couldn't think of anything worse.

"And I think he's with his new girlfriend."

Oh, that was worse.

"His new so-plain-she-can't-even-be-considered-ugly girlfriend."

"Oh, Jayla. Oh, babe, I'm so sorry!"

"Emma, what do I do?" she squeaked, and I could tell she was about to ruin her Dior mascara. But I was silent and useless on my end.

"I wish this had happened just a little further down the road," she said, and sniffled. "I'm so not ready now. In a few months or whatever, I wouldn't care if we ran into each other while I was standing on line to have my copy of *It's Called a Breakup Because It's Broken* autographed. Or even if he saw me at the pharmacy asking the clerk if they had any extra-strength Monistat in the back. But now"—her voice broke into high-pitched whimpers—"I just look stupid and overglossed and not fabulous. I feel like the wound is so raw, you know?"

"Oh God, I'm so sorry. Do you just want to go? You sneak out and I'll meet you downstairs in a few."

I silently cursed myself—and yes, I'll admit it, poor Jayla, too—the moment the words hit the air. Leave? I'd just gotten here! Colin would think I was a total bitchy snob if I left now. I thought guiltily about the "chicks before dicks" mantra and how sweet it was of Jayla to come with me in the first place. The least I could do was save her from the unimaginable hell of running into her ex with his new tramp girlfriend. If I were in her shoes, I'd totally drag Rachel or Kyle out of a party. But still, I hoped she wouldn't take me up on the offer.

"Whoa, whoa, whoa!" she protested, steadying her voice. "I'm wallowing in *self*-pity now. I'm not deep enough into this woe-is-me puddle to soak the whole world with me. You go and flirt your flip-flops off with the Burger King. I'll figure this out myself." I heard her click End on the call and closed my phone.

I was being a bad friend, I knew it. But I still shut my phone and trotted back over to Colin, who was holding my burger and one for himself.

"Perfect timing," he said as he handed me my paper plate. "Shall we retire to the dining room, Ms. Freeman?"

Bad friend, huh? Chicks before what now? All I could see was a perfect smile shining at me.

I followed him to a set of plastic patio furniture. Between bites of beef, we picked up right where we left off last Saturday night, minus the blaring Rihanna. He was funny and cool and not afraid to be a dork. Well, anyone that foxy couldn't really be a dork, but it was cute that he tried.

"You're right. This totally is the best burger I've had in New York," I said a few bites in.

"Stop, I'm blushing." I think he really was. "But you just graduated, right? You haven't really been here that long?"

I opened my mouth to say that no, I wouldn't be graduating until next year—then I realized he meant from *college*, not Bridgefield High. Or any other High for that matter. Now was so not the time to come clean. Soon, though. But this was going way too well for me to ruin with messy details like me being eighteen, living with my parents, and looking forward to my senior year of high school.

"No, just a few weeks, I guess." I tried to flash a sexy smile, but instantly wondered if I had lettuce in my teeth and quickly changed to a closed-mouth grin that looked more like I'd just eaten a rat than come from Brite Smile.

"So you probably haven't had anyone else's burgers."

I was going to tell him that my Chinese delivery friend didn't deliver burgers and I couldn't really betray him by ordering some other ethnicity's cuisine after we'd invested so much emotionally—but I stopped myself. Even Rachel thought my relationship with the delivery guy was weird. Impressing Colin with that story would be like trying to sell Eau de Bacon at the Chanel fragrance counter. So I just shrugged and giggled.

"Well, then I'll need to show you around town. How about we put my grilling skills up against some of the big dogs? I'll take you to one of New York's supposed 'best burger joints' and you can see how I stack up."

He did those supertrite air quotes around "best burger joints," but I was willing to overlook that. I was blinded by a bigger issue, one I'd read about in magazines, seen in chick flicks, but never thought really existed. I'd always thought this was just the Loch Ness Monster of girly folklore. But Colin was proving this myth true. He had just asked me on a date—a real live, not over-the-computer, not even school-dance, date, without me making out with him or considering him my boyfriend first.

With surprisingly un-Emma-like coolness, I looked him right in the eye and said, "Yeah, I'd like that. It'll be like our own burger throwdown."

I managed to get the entire sentence out before feeling my face turn red and having to look away. This was progress.

"All right." And he said it with a happily surprised tone. As if any woman could ever say no to those dimples. "So, Tuesday night work for you? You, me, and the Corner Bistro?"

I didn't want to tell him that I was free every night from now until Thanksgiving. I twirled my hair nervously and through a mouthful of burger said, "Sounds great."

I felt his eyes move down to my chest.

"So, new topic. I'm intrigued. What's Domino?"

"Oh." I grabbed at my necklace. "It's just this Manhattan alias-name thing I have with my friends. Like, what we're supposed to say to guys in clubs or whatever."

I froze when I realized the total idiocy of what I'd just said.

"So, you lie to guys you meet in clubs?" He was giving me what I thought was a jokey flirty look, but I could feel guilt pulsing through my body.

"*No!*" I yelled, and he jumped. "I mean, no. No, I do not." I smiled nervously and fingered the necklace. "It's just a joke thing. Not really lying."

Cool, calm, collected Emma had melted into hot, sweaty, nervous Emma. I was spitting the words out fast and defensive. "I'm Domino Frost. My best friend is Bitsy Onassis. And our roommate is Jinx." That reminded me, what the hell had happened to Jayla? I should go find her. No, I *should* tell Colin the truth. Before I could even make a decision about alerting Colin to my near-jailbait status, Jacob came bounding over to our al fresco alcove, his shaggy hair poufy with humidity and stress.

"Em, I'm taking Jayla home," he said in a panic. "She's on a speedboat to Drunk Disaster Island."

I glanced nervously at Colin, who was obviously confused at who this sweaty, jittery starfish boy was.

"I'll come. You'll need help," I said, grateful to escape before I said too much more about lying and boys and clubs and cheap necklaces.

I got up to bolt, which seemed to be my signature with Colin.

"I'm sorry," I said in a low voice as I turned away from an antsy Jake. "He's not a guy."

Colin looked curiously over my shoulder at Jake, "Uh . . . he's not?"

"Oh! No! I mean, he *is* a guy—he's just not, like, *my* guy or anything. He's a cousin. My cousin. And, like, I'd never date my cousin. At least, not a first cousin." Help! I've fallen into a downward spiral of awkward blathering and I can't get up.

"I mean"—I sighed with exasperation—"you know what I mean, right? Anyway, my roommate Jayla is kind of, um, sick, so we need to take her home."

He laughed and put his hand on my knee, warm and heavy. "Yeah, I gotcha. No worries, my friend Pete is always drinking himself into a coma."

I wondered if I should explain that Jayla wasn't just drunk, she was choking on ex misery, but whatever—I'd probably just end up making another horrendous incest reference. Ugh.

"Thanks," I said, relieved. "This sucks, I was having a really good time."

"Me too," he said, looking deep into my eyes. For a second I thought we were going to kiss, but my douche cousin hollered for me to hurry up. Jayla was right. Jake was a total cockblock.

I stood up to leave and wiped the bun crumbs off my dress. I stepped gingerly around the patio furniture, trying not to get my flip-flop caught in the hardwood deck as I walked away.

"Wait," he said, touching my arm. "We're still on for Tuesday, right?"

Tuesday, Wednesday, Sunday through Friday—I was all his. But casual, Emma! WWJD—what would Jayla do?

I shrugged slightly, picturing my roommate, the Queen of Nonchalant, tepidly accepting a date with Prince William or Josh Duhamel.

"Sure."

I lingered for a few seconds that felt like an eternity, forcing myself to look him in the eye. I managed to pull off a saucy smirk and even a wink which didn't feel too facial-ticky and then fled in the direction Jake was pulling me.

Fifteen

The fragile bubble of strength Jayla had mustered to stalk out of the barbecue burst as soon as the cab door shut.

"Oh my God!" she wailed as Jake threw his arm nervously around her. "Why-y-y-y is he with that girl-l-l-l?"

Jake and I fumbled awkwardly to comfort her, caught off guard at her sudden vulnerability. I did the only thing I could do. I made really bad jokes.

"Wow, Jay, you're so right. Carter is a total Shrek look-alike. But, like, troll-ier." I giggled halfheartedly. "You're way better off without him."

She looked up suddenly, wide-eyed with new rage. "You didn't even see him, Emma. And he didn't look like a troll.

He looked hot, hotter than usual. And," she said, her voice quavering again, "I am *not* better off without him. I loved him. And he was supposed to love me. We were meant to be together."

I shrugged helplessly as Jake patted her hair. I had a feeling he wasn't too upset about being wedged against her in her hour of need, even if she was puffy-eyed and manic. He slung his arm around her slender shoulders and she leaned instinctively into his chest, clinging slightly to his faded Guns N' Roses T-shirt. I totally saw him take a whiff of her hair.

"Wait," he said. "Who was this guy? An ex or something?"

"Not *an ex*," I explained. "*The* ex. They were bf/gf and then he just stopped calling and blamed it on an imaginary mental illness."

Uck, I was disgusted even saying it out loud. Was this what I had to look forward to when I got older—a world full of totally psychotic guys who did nothing but vomit up lies to perfectly normal girls?

"No, Em, seriously," he huffed, not at all believing the tale of feigned psychosis. "What happened between them?"

The cab lurched around a corner, heaving us to the left. Normally I'd call out "Jell-O!" and try to squish whoever was sitting next to me, but somehow that didn't seem appropriate. I opened my mouth to launch into an anti-man diatribe, but Jayla cut in. "He introduced me to his parents. I mean, who does that? Who does that to a fling?"

"An ass clown, that's who," Jake growled.

"He was the first guy who actually seemed to take me seriously. He didn't treat me like just some rich bitch maxing out her daddy's credit card, doing nothing with her life.

We'd talk about art and go to gallery openings and he'd say, 'This is Miss Jayla St. Clare. She's the hottest young artist in the city.' Why would he say that?"

As Jake opened his mouth to answer, the cab careened up to our building and screeched to a stop. I tried to wedge my hand into my purse, pinned against me from Jayla's dead weight, but Jake had already handed the driver a twenty. Even if he allegedly looked like something from a tide pool, he was at least a gentleman. I climbed out as Jake helped Jayla from the backseat. As soon as she was out of the cab, she folded herself back into Jake's arms, paper doll–style, expecting him to carry her up to the apartment. I could see there was no way that was happening alone—surprisingly, hours of playing Nintendo Wii hadn't left Jake with the burliest of physiques. I grabbed one of Jayla's arms and draped it around my shoulder, wishing that she hadn't worn such wobbly shoes.

"Jayla, those heels were made for walking, okay? So get them moving. We can't really carry you."

The girl was tiny, but total dead weight can be hard to maneuver in ninety-eight-degree heat. Even with that goading, she didn't really help us out much. Looking like some sort of six-legged, three-headed, crying, sweating monster, we hobbled into the lobby.

"Hi," I grunted at the white-haired doorman. His eyes went wide with panic, not used to seeing the mistress of Apartment 30B in such condition.

He scuttled over to us as fast as his seventy-year-old legs would take him. "What's happened to Miss St. Clare? Should I call a doctor?"

"Oof, no," I puffed, readjusting her feeble body so that I

could nudge her along with my hip. "She's okay, just had a bad day, that's all."

I saw him eye the brass luggage trolley, but then probably realized he'd get fired for heaving a tenant onto it like a battered old Samsonite.

"Bad day? To be quite honest, I'm used to seeing the young miss after a pint too many, but not anything like this."

A pint? As in, of beer? I smirked to myself at the thought of Jayla St. Princess consuming a pint of anything that wasn't nonfat yogurt.

He shuffled ahead of us and held the elevator doors.

"Yeah," I huffed, Jake and I practically dragging her toward the elevator as she started crying all over again. My back was starting to hurt. "Nothing a good mud mask can't cure. Thanks for your help!"

He waved unsurely, hobbled back to his desk, and craned his neck to watch Jayla as the doors closed behind us. A few minutes later we'd made it back to the apartment and into Jayla's room, its limp, miserable occupant in tow.

"Okay, can we start at the beginning here?" I panted as Jake gently laid Jayla down on her gold satin bedspread and sat beside her. I was confused and wanted answers. "What exactly happened the other night at Plumm when you melted? You saw Shrek Carter there, too, didn't you?"

I was hoping she'd forget that Jake was there and spill. She gave Jake a glance, clearly embarrassed that the poor guy was going to witness the most secret of girl activities— becoming "the crazy girl." But like drunken binges at Taco Bell, once you break the seal you can't stop. And her dramatic exit from the barbecue definitely counted as breaking the seal.

"Yes," she said miserably, sitting up and hugging a "No Shirt, No Shoes, No Juicy" pillow to her chest. I sat down on the foot of her bed. I knew this confession was going to be a biggie. Jake pushed up his glasses nervously and shoved his hands into his pockets, not knowing where to look or what to do. Poor guy, he was a Level Ten awkward even in the best of situations. His circuits must have been about to blow.

Jayla took a deep breath and started talking. "Okay, what happened at Plumm was that Chloe and I went outside to smoke, and he comes walking up looking"—her eyes glassed over as her mind pulled her back into the memory—"amazing in this black Burberry shirt. Once I got a whiff of his cologne, it was all over. I couldn't even help myself. Chloe actually had to physically grab at me to try and hold me back, but I wriggled loose and stumbled up to him. It's sort of blurry, but I think I just started gushing about how good it was to see him and how good he looked and then I noticed that he was with some girl, some ugly skank who I knew I recognized from somewhere. And then the girl came up to us, looked me up and down—as if she even could judge me, she was wearing freaking Banana Republic—and then swept him away inside and I was left outside, like a locked-out puppy. Like a dog, Emma, like a *dog*! I mean, it's one thing to get dumped, I can handle that—I really can." Her voice broke as she choked back tears. "But to have him leave me for her? It was like a knife through my heart. At least rebound with a model, a rocket scientist, a goddamn Bollywood actress!" She started sobbing, curling slightly into a fetal ball, her whole body shaking with her wailing convulsions. But suddenly she pulled herself somewhat together and sat up again, looking at me gravely.

"Then," she continued guiltily, "when you said you were going to Thirty-four Leonard today, I totally knew that Carter would be there. His best friend lives in that building." Her eyes darted back and forth between us and then down in psycho stalking shame. "And when I saw him there, he was with that same skankface. And I realized where I recognized her from. She was his coworker, the one he said was so lame and everyone at the office would call her Deadfish behind her back because she was personalityless and had bad breath. So I went up to them and I'm all, 'Oh! I know you, you're Deadfi—you're Heidi! I'm Jayla.' And she gave me this horrible look and said the nastiest thing ever!"

Jake and I waited as Jayla blew her nose.

"She said, 'Carter, who is this? A Hilary Duff drag queen?'" And with that humiliating insult, Jayla wailed afresh and buried her head in the pillows and bawled.

"Oh, that vicious slimy bitch." I scootched up from my spot on the bed to console her. "God, who is soulless enough to say something like that?" I asked as I finger-brushed her blond hair in what I thought was an act of comfort, but might have been more like molestation.

"What's bad about that? You do kind of look like Hilary Duff," Jake said brightly, before adding quickly, "I mean, she's superhot."

"Oh please!" Jayla hissed at him. I actually almost laughed when I looked over at him. He looked re-donk sitting on her pink tuffet of a makeup stool. "He knows that I'm sensitive about looking like that wannabe-punk Goody Two-shoes! Which means he probably told her that. God, I can just picture them in her lame apartment, in Williamsburg or someplace so sickeningly pretentious, lying in bed and laughing at reruns of *Material Girls* on HBO.

God, I wish he were dead. And by dead, I really mean, comes back to me!" She dissolved into moans and wails all over again.

"Well, if he's dead, then how can he come—" Jake mused, but I caught his eye and shook my head. Now was not a time for logic. Desperate for something to contribute, Jake tried again.

"You know, in my opinion, you look way more like," he started, and I realized with horror what he was about to say and I lunged for his face but the words made it out anyway, "Haylie Duff than her sister."

Three blocks away, people probably heard Jayla's blood-curdling scream. She shrieked us right out of her room, yelling for us to get out and hollering incoherently about horse faces and nepotism.

As the door slammed in our faces, I realized we were all in for a long night. I turned to my cousin and he was shaking like a wet Chihuahua from his first glimpse into the wild world of girl post-breakup craziness.

"I need a drink," Jake said, and rummaged through the fridge for a beer.

"Me too," I said, plopping down on my fave sofa cushion and flipping on the TV just in time to catch the last ten minutes of *Law & Order: SVU*.

"Emma," he scolded, "I'm serious about you not drinking. You're only eighteen and you're my cousin."

I threw him a steely gaze. "It'd be an awful shame if Jayla just happened to find out about those World of Warcraft tournaments you so enjoy, now wouldn't it Jacob? I would hate to just let it slip out, right now, when you're doing such a good job of being her knight in shining armor."

He gritted his teeth in defeat and huffed, "Fine. *One* drink."

As he passed me a beer we heard muffled crashes from Jayla's room and Jake shifted uneasily.

"Maybe I should go in there. I don't think she should be alone right now."

I started to protest but before I could stop him he grabbed a box of Kleenex and was marching headlong into Hurricane Jayla. I lay back down on the couch and tried to get absorbed in watching Detective Stabler collar the serial pedophile. But I was still digesting the insanity that was this night and couldn't pay attention.

Maybe being front-row center for Jayla's atomic meltdown was a sign from God showing me just how bad boyfriends and girlfriends can turn out. I mean, sure, I'd had crushes that didn't work out, suffered a broken heart, and definitely shed some tears, but nothing like what I'd just watched. Maybe Jayla was just weaker than I was. I felt a twinge of guilt for even thinking something like that about Jayla, who'd been nothing but supportive and helpful to me in my breakup/boyquest mission. Of course she wasn't weaker than I was. I guess I'd just never had someone lie to me like that.

The second the word "lie" floated into my head, I instantly thought about Colin and felt another stab of guilt. Lying about your age all the way through dating someone was way worse than a lie about a feigned mental illness to end a relationship. I shook my head, trying to knock out thoughts of me being an awful liar. But then, I shouldn't have been worrying about it anyway. I wasn't even in a relationship with Colin . . . yet. But that could hopefully change.

I mean, was it just me or had the night—aside from Jayla's quarter-life crisis—been a total success? What if he actually liked me?

The muffled wails and bumps from Jayla's room finally stopped, and I felt justified devoting the rest of the night to just lying there enjoying the butterflies in my tummy and envisioning a first kiss with Colin over and over and over again. I wondered if he would put his hand on my face or just kind of lean in for one of those cute first kisses that are supercasual, like in *Good Will Hunting*. Ah! This was too much to take. I got up and shuffled through the fridge, looking for something to sublimate my desire and restlessness, when the front door swung open and Rachel pranced in, sighing dreamily.

"I'm in love, Emma."

I jumped up and flapped my hands excitedly. "Me too!" I squealed, and Rachel rushed over to the sofa and we giggled and fought over who should tell their story first.

"Okay, okay. You go," she said. Rachel twisted her head in the direction of Jayla's room, wrinkling her nose at the closed door—Jayla usually left it open so we could paw through her closet in case of a fashion emergency while she was out being a party monster. "Wait, is Jayla actually home? It's Saturday night."

"Sweet cracker sandwich, woman. You don't even want to know!" But Rachel was just as fascinated/obsessed with Jayla as I was, and she totally did want to know. So I started the roller-coaster ride of a tale, kind of glossing over the Colin flirtfest so I could save it for when she really wanted to gush about it later. For now, I focused on the Jayla St. Clare firestorm. "Okay, I could kind of tell she was acting weird, but didn't really get why until the way end. It turns out that that Carter douche showed up, which she for sure saw coming, and the next thing I know, she's completely out of control. I practically had to carry all hundred and twenty pounds of her out of the party." The back of my neck, where Jayla had rested her arm and then pretty much swung from, was still sore. I moved my hand there to massage it.

"Hold up." Rachel shimmied herself around on the cushion so she was now sitting tall on her knees. "I'm still stuck on the part when I saw you guys go into the subway. How did you con her into that?" Her eyebrows were raised in sincere shock. "Did you tell her that every cab was carrying bird flu or something?"

I laughed. Jayla would probably rather take her chances with a tropical disease than spend time amongst the mass transit masses.

"It was *not* easy. I had to play the 'I'm poor' card." I cringed at the residual embarrassment of explaining my below-the-poverty-line budget to her. "And even then she almost burst into flames when these kids started break-dancing on the platform."

"That's classic!" Rachel howled. "God, I wish I'd seen it!"

"Yeah, well, maybe just that part. The Mount St. Clare explosion was ugly. Be glad you weren't at Colin's party."

Suddenly her face lit up. "Omigod, woman. How come you're not telling me about Colin? What happened with him?"

"I was a total awky-fest, no surprise." I could see Rachel try to feign shock at this, but my best friend well knew the kind of blathering, stuttering mess I turned into at the first sign of boy interest. "But he was great about it. He just made it so easy. And we're going out on a date on Tuesday." I smiled like I'd actually accomplished something and not just let it happen to me.

"So Colin asked you out?" she said excitedly. "Like in person? Not over a computer? That. Is. In. *Sane!*" She enunciated every syllable and nodded for effect. "I didn't know people actually did that. I mean, I'd heard of it, like on TV and stuff, but I thought it was like Pop Rocks and soda mixing in your stomach making you explode. Everyone talks about it, but, like, it just doesn't really happen."

"I know! Maybe it's, like, a grown-up thing." I said this based only on tonight's experience and *Grey's Anatomy*.

Rachel laughed. "Okay, you can't call Colin a grown-up if you're going to be making out with him."

"Rachel! God!" I covered my eyes with embarrassment. I hadn't even thought past the first kiss. Considering I could barely get a coherent sentence out when I was around him, the idea that I could actually seriously kiss him for longer than four seconds without exploding was pretty much out of the question.

"Hey, where did Jake go after Glitters McMeltdown detonated? Is he still here?" she asked, pointing to the size-twelve Converse in the middle of the floor.

"Jake? Yeah, he's . . ." Where was he? Could he still be in Jayla's room? "He's in Jayla's room or something. Anyway, tell me about your date!"

We both forgot Jacob at the mention of the word "date." Apparently, this was lucky date number thirteen and she had met her Jewish Prince Charming.

"He was perfect, Em! A rising sophomore at NYU, business major. His father owns a candy distribution company.

So, think of all the Nutrageouses we could score! Just think about that! Perf, perf, perfect," she sighed, completely content.

"So, do you think you're going to see him again?" I realized that I wasn't just faking excited and secretly hoping that she'd spend the rest of the summer home and couchbound with me. Who knew having a summer crush of my own would make me a better friend?

"Hello!" Rachel gave me the same incredulous look she did that time I came home from the mall carrying a pair of Keds, claiming that if Mischa Barton was wearing them, they were so the next big thing. "That's the best part. He already reserved me for Friday night. He said, 'I know that a girl like you has got to be booked early.' Well, something like that, but it didn't make me sound like a call girl. It was romantic."

We both sighed again, in unison, blissed out over our boys. I hadn't been this excited over a guy since . . . well, I couldn't really remember, actually. Brian and I were so middling, never bad or great, just kind of in between and a little boring. Suddenly a wave of fatigue hit me, the mental and physical calamities of the day towing my exhausted mind under. It was barely after midnight but I decided to go to bed. It had been an exhausting week and an even more draining evening. I hoped that Jayla wasn't planning on making breakdowns a weekly event. I didn't have the energy.

Rachel scampered into her room to start on her Friday date outfit *already*, and I poked around the kitchen looking for a bedtime snack. With a high-protein treat in hand— peanut butter Oreos have protein, right?—I made my way toward my bedroom, stumbling over Jake's Converse along the way. Where *was* he? I thought briefly about going to find him and see if he was all right with the Emo St. Clare, but he never seemed to mind being around her, so I continued to tuck myself into bed. Jayla was so messed up, she'd probably mistaken him for a pair of her shoes and shut him up in the closet. I started to giggle at the thought of my starfish cousin wedged among Jayla's Marc Jacobs pumps, but fatigue took over and it was lights out.

The next morning, Rachel woke me up to give a mini fashion show of possible date outfits.

"Rachel," I grumbled, pulling the covers over my head. "It's ten a.m. almost a full week before your date. Don't you think you're jumping the gun here?"

"Emma, I'd expect you of all people to understand what a hot, rich Jewish man means to me. This is no laughing matter. I could be his Charlotte and he could be my Trey."

"First of all, they got divorced because he couldn't get it up." I yawned, pushing my body pillow out of the way. "And secondly, they were Episcopalian."

I pulled back my blanket, slipped into my flip-flops, and got out of bed. We shuffled into the kitchen to see what cereals were still fresh enough to pass for edible, just in time to see Jake tiptoe out of Jayla's room.

"Oh my God!" Rachel exclaimed, almost falling over in her peep-toe pumps. "Am I hallucinating?" Rachel closed her eyes and felt around the kitchen like a blind girl. Funny, but totally didn't make sense.

"You're not, like, just now leaving?" I asked him. Maybe Jayla really had trapped him in the closet. "I mean, you didn't spend the night with her or anything?" Ew! For some reason, images of R. Kelly flashed through my mind and my skin crawled. Something felt so not right here.

Jake just shrugged and smiled. Ew, ew, ew! It was super-gross to picture Jake and his starfish face making out with anyone, let alone Jayla. One more time—*ew!* But like a blubbery workout scene in a reality weight-loss show, I couldn't get enough.

"No way you're getting away without spilling all of the details. We're going to find out either from you or her, so you might as well tell," I bullied, my revulsion being beat out by curiosity.

"There's nothing to tell." He raised his hands and shrugged, trying to look innocent. But I knew by his super-messed-up bed head and how he was being weirdly calm, that something was up. Status quo for this guy was what most would consider an awkward frenzy.

"So that's how it's going to be? We share like twenty-five percent of the same DNA, Jake. Does that mean nothing to you?" I stood with my hands on my hips, scowling at him from the kitchen.

"Really, there's nothing to tell."

I eyed him carefully as he pulled on his Chucks, examining his clothes for lipstick stains or signs that a post-melt-down socialite had tried to tear them off. I couldn't detect any evidence of pawing or petting—dammit! Why hadn't I paid more attention during that *CSI: Miami* marathon?

"Right, just your average cousin sleeping over in your impossibly hot roommate's bed. Nothing to tell at all, I'm sure." I tried to sound jokey indignant, but I was actually for-real indignant. My cousin, *my* roommate. Didn't I deserve a little info?

"Exactly. Nothing to tell." He smirked at us as he came

into the kitchen, pinched a peach from our fruit bowl, and then headed to the front door for his exit.

"Jacob Lewis Freeman!" I growled, stomping my foot.

"No dice, Emma," he said, pulling open our door and heading out. "And my middle name is Patrick, by the way."

He waved goodbye and left, taking with him any chance of getting some good gossip until Jayla woke up. And it could be dinnertime before that happened.

I hated him for not spilling the details. Was he seriously related to me?

Rachel and I stared at each other, fists clenched in frustration, trying to figure out what the hell had happened between those two last night.

Maybe Jayla cried so much that her eyes almost swelled shut and somehow mistook Jake for Carter or something . . . but even without sight, Jayla would know the difference between Burberry and Old Navy.

Or maybe Jake had been so weirded out by Jayla's mania that he actually killed her and then stayed up all night building a Jayla robot substitute.

Or Jayla let it slip that she thought my cousin looked like a starfish and he in turn called her a lobster and they had a giant crustacean battle until five a.m.

My mind was spinning, but thankfully, before anything major short-circuited, Jayla appeared in her doorway, a drowsy smile across her mascara-stained face.

"Good morning!" she cheeped with a coy grin. Even I knew coy when I saw it.

"Tell us everything! Immediately!" Rachel demanded.

"Oh, nothing happened," she scoffed, and she brushed past us to the coffeemaker, smelling faintly of Jake's Axe body spray. That stuff was douchiness in a bottle and this whole thing was totally suspicious. When had Jayla, Little Miss TMI, flipped into get-asked-but-still-don't-tell gear?

"Lies!" Rachel squealed, and demanded more details, but Jayla was still aloof.

"Seriously, we just talked." Jayla sounded matter-of-fact . . . until she sighed like a girl reading *Tiger Beat* at summer camp. "We talked all night. He was so sweet. He really listened to me and I listened to him. I don't know, we just really clicked."

Clicked? What in God's name did those two have in common? They both lived in New York, check. They both seemed to be mammals (but only one of them looked like it), check. Beyond that, I had no idea what it was exactly that "clicked."

"So, do you, like, *like* him or something?" I stammered. This was too weird. My nose-picking, headgeared cousin and Glitters St. Fabulous. Barf.

"No! I mean, I don't think so."

I could tell that Jayla was equally confused by the events of the previous night. But her philosophy on life was "If it feels good, do it," and I had a feeling that things were not over between her and Jake.

Total barf.

Sixteen

Monday passed uneventfully in the Colin department, meaning I didn't see him, which was a blessing and a curse. I so wanted to see him. But if he just happened to wander around the corner during a Derek disaster moment, the bluff about me being a twenty-two-year-old junior marketing whatever would totally be called.

And thank God he didn't see me that day. Derek must have been well rested over the weekend, because he was full throttle Monday morning.

He galloped his gut over to my cube first thing in the morning. *"So I took a big chance at the high school dance with a missy who was ready to play. It wasn't me she was foolin' 'cause she knew what was she was doin' when she told me how to walk this way."* And then he did the mime walk-down-the-stairs trick behind my cube wall as he shrieked out the chorus.

"Good one, Derek. You really look like you're going downstairs." I choked on my own bile saying that and trying to sound sincere.

"Learned that trick back in Nam!" He perched his face over my half-wall and stared around my cube for a while.

I had to be on film for some bizarre hidden camera show, I just had to be.

When I could still feel his lurking presence after a full minute had passed, I asked, "Yes, Derek? Did you want something?" while continuing to type a comment onto Rachel's Facebook wall.

"No, just thought I'd hang out today and watch you work because I'm going to have to write an eval of this internship and I want to be sure I'm accurate."

At that, I had to turn my head and actually look him in the eye to be sure he was serious. "So you're going to Big Brother me all day?"

"Yeah, think of me as the big brother you never had!" And then he joke punched me on the arm, like what he probably thought an older brother did to a kid sister, but from a boss, it bordered on harassment. Plus, how could he not get the *1984* reference or at least think of the reality TV show? God, he was denser than a black hole. And how dorky was I that I just referenced the concentrated mass of a black hole in a diss?

Anyway, adding to the wretchedness that was the day's hours in the office was my obsession over tomorrow's date with Colin, which was now only thirty-five hours away. I couldn't stop checking my cell for missed calls or texts whenever Derek wasn't totally breathing down my neck. Colin had said Tuesday, right? As in, the day after Monday, which was today. Surely he wouldn't wait to make plans till the day of our burger date. He was an adult and they made plans in advance, right? Or was I being crazy? Or maybe I should be the one to call him and set up the deets for tomorrow? I mean, he did ask me, so maybe it was my turn to reciprocate. I kept my cell propped open on my desk, positioned next to my monitor so I could look like I was working but still see any sign of life from Colin the second it came through.

In the middle of this tailspin of paranoia and angst, Derek rolled back up to my cube.

"Em-tastic, let me ask you a hypothetical question," he said, and then looked down at a Scantron sheet of paper, which I'm assuming was the summer intern eval form. "Let's just say I asked you to rate your meeting presence on a scale of one to five. Three being average, one being unacceptable, and five being superior. What would you give yourself? Again, this is not anything real, just 'hypothetical.' " And when he said "hypothetical," he used air quotes.

"You've never taken me to a meeting, so my meeting presence isn't 'hypothetical' "—finger quotes—"it's non-existent."

Derek's face lit up like I'd just explained where babies came from. "You're right! I'll call HR and see what bubble I should fill out for nonexistent." And with that, he slithered back into his office and I went back to my mental state of pandemonium.

By lunchtime I was officially frantic over my empty inbox. So I called my boy expert.

"Jayla!" I hissed into the phone from inside the supply closet. "I need your help!" I bent to sit down on some reams of copy paper and knocked over two boxes of highlighters.

"Oh sure, I'm just getting a wax. So if I yelp suddenly, it's not you. Go ahead."

As I picked up the dozens of fluorescent markers that were rolling around the closet floor, I filled her in. "First of all, Derek is re-dic today. He's pretty much shadowing me. I'm literally hiding in a supply closet to get away from him." She laughed and I uncapped one of the fallen highlighters and started giving myself a hot-pink manicure. "But the real ish is that I haven't heard from Colin yet about our D-A-T-E tomorrow and I am fuh-reaking. Do you think he somehow hacked into the company payroll and realized I'm only eighteen?" I asked, offering the only valid reason I could think of for his lack of communication.

"Are you high on Sharpies? You're not getting paid, so you're not on the payroll," Jay said logically, trying to keep her voice steady as she was defuzzed. "Secondly, he's at work. The stockbroker guys I see don't even come up for air until happy hour, so he's probably just busy."

I sighed deeply and put down the highlighter. "Right, busy!" Why did I immediately jump on the first train to CrazyTown instead of thinking about something as rational as that? Hello, Emma, not everyone at this company is as bored as you are!

"You're the best. Thanks, Jay."

"No worries. Every girl's the same way when it comes to predate stressing. Just distract yourself, buy stuff on eBay or something."

As I pressed End Call I felt loads better. She was right. Colin was probably just swamped and I needed to focus on something else. But eBay? Well, even though we did just go over the fact that I was getting paid nada all summer, I really did need a new purse and I was in love with Jayla's Kooba bag that I'd been borrowing. I wondered how much it cost. Maybe it was time to get one of my own.

I slipped out of the supply closet, bringing a box of paper clips to mask the fact that I was in there for a pseudo-therapy session. When I got back to my desk, Derek was mercifully nowhere in sight. I prayed that he was up in HR, turning in his evaluation so he could go back to ignoring me seven hours a day. I jiggered my mouse, the *Infinity on High* screen saver melting as my monitor came back to life. I quickly refreshed my Gmail and sighed as no new messages loaded. I logged onto eBay, ready to follow my life coach's advice to shop till it didn't hurt anymore. I searched for the Kooba bag and even a used one was four hundred dollars. Insane! I pictured my dad's head popping off after getting that credit card bill and decided to stalk bands on Buzznet.com all day instead. Maybe I'd discover *the* new screamo band and go back to Bridgefield and say I'd seen them in some tiny New York club.

By 5:01 all I'd done was leave comments on all Kyle's Facebook pics and check my phone a thousand times for texts. Sulky and anxious, I trudged to the subway.

Standing on the platform, I wished that I'd bought a *People* or something from the newspaper shack outside the office. The train was taking forever and I had nothing to do but read the ads for Lavalife online dating as I waited, which really only reminded me of my supposed real-life date the next day. I pulled my cell out to check if Colin had sent any word yet, but I had no service in the sweaty depths of the station. I slammed my useless Sanyo back into my bag, and something moving on the tracks in front of me caught my eye. I looked down and my stomach lurched up into my esophagus. There was a huge rat, and I really mean huge, like the size of a full-grown Olsen, staring back at me. Before I could even yelp, the rodent scampered away at the sound of the oncoming train.

My lips were still curled into a grossed-out sneer as I boarded the train.

"Smile, beautiful," a creepy guy in worker overalls said, motioning to a seat next to him. I turned my sneer into a grimace, making a point not to smile at him.

Of course the only seat on the entire subway was next to Icky McCreeps, so I stood and held on to a pole, probably contracting every New Yorker's summer cold and HPV strain. The doors connecting my subway car to the one in front opened and two middle schoolers—one tall and gangly, the other gangly and tall—walked through holding a Costco box of Peanut M&M's.

"Ladies and gentleman," the tall and gangly one started in a complete monotone, "my friend and I are here selling candy to help raise money for our basketball team."

The gangly and tall one continued in his buddy's same dead monotone, "So please, buy some candy for only one dollar. This will keep us out of two places: the poorhouse and your house." The combination of the lifeless delivery and the fact that almost everyone in the car had on earphones led to a painful silence after the joke.

I took pity on the kids. "Hey, I'll buy some candy," I said, fishing through my purse for my wallet. The two boys hustled over and opened their box to display their candy-coated wares. I opened my wallet to find that I had not a single bill in the holder. I unzipped the change purse and dumped the coins into my palm.

Counting them out, I said, "Seventy, seventy-five, eighty. Oh wow. Sorry, it doesn't look like I have a dollar. Would you take eighty cents for a pack? I'll throw in this stamp." I don't know where the stamp had come from or why it was even in my wallet, but it had to be old. It was a thirty-nine-cent one.

The tall and gangly fellow broke his deadpan and yelled, "Shit, lady. This ain't *Let's Make a Deal*. It's a fund-raiser."

The whole packed car was now staring at the drama. Even those whose music was too loud to take notice of the boys initially could somehow hear and were fully paying attention.

"Yeah, keep your pennies and Monopoly money, bitch. We'll find someone with real cash," added the gangly and tall one as the duo turned to head into the next car.

I had to stay in the car, totally shocked and embarrassed, for two more stops before I finally stepped out into Union Square. I pushed my way through a mass of sweaty and irritable commuters to make it to the stairs. Crap, what was I doing in this overcrowded city? My job sucked big-time, I had less money than people who begged on the street, my BFF was always too boy crazy to hang, no real social life to speak of, no boyfriend to go back to, a summer crush who had dropped off the face of the planet. And then, as I ascended onto Fourteenth Street, rousing me from my quagmire of self-doubt, I felt it. My phone, vibrating as it found a signal to tell me I had a message. Quickly I pulled the phone from my purse and flipped it open and saw a text! From Colin!

On 4 2sday burgers? 7ish? What's your addy, I'll pick you up. No eat n run this time missy!

Swoon! Even his texts were sexy. I managed to wait until I got home, said quick hi's to Rachel and Jayla, and locked myself in my room to respond. Holding off for ten minutes was grueling. I texted, *4sure, I'll bring my eating A game 14th and Broadway SE corner.*

Immediately after hitting Send, I pulled my journal out of my nightstand and flopped on my bed to document my completely unnecessary freak over Colin not messaging me earlier. I figured this entry would be something cute for us to laugh about when I read it to him on our honeymoon or something. Not even a first date and I was practically tasting the passed appetizers at our wedding? Apparently, Rachel wasn't the only boy psycho in the apartment. I stopped myself from thinking of names for our grandkids by switching gears and scribbling down the entire Derek intern evaluation exchange from this morning. He was such an ass. Even though now I was normally fed up to the point of tears around him, I knew that this definitely would be something I'd laugh about later . . . and not imaginary-honeymoon-when-I'm-thirty later. I'd probably start thinking The Dorf's dickness was funny in the middle of August when I stopped working for him.

I placed my journal back into the drawer and got ready for bed. Of course, I was so revved for the big date with the future Mr. Freeman that relaxing wasn't easy. But finally I managed to fall asleep. And thank God, I wouldn't want to have red-rimmed, puffy eyes for my big night.

I don't know how I made it through work on Tuesday, but I did. The minutes inched by even more slowly than normal, which I didn't think would be possible considering how painful a normal workday was for me.

As I was logging off my computer and readying to jet home to primp for the date, Derek waddled up.

"Oh, don't leave yet. I need help putting a video onto my MySpace profile."

I checked my watch: 4:57. Why now? I would have been happy—no, maybe even thrilled—to do this at any point during the eight previous hours when I was chained to my desk, bored out of my freaking mind. But now I needed to run home and prep for Colin. I had my shower, hair straightening, makeup, and outfit change planned out perfectly if I left the office at five. Any later and I'd have a wet head or only half a dress on.

"Um, Derek, can we do it tomorrow? I really need to go," I begged.

"But Em, you're going to love this video. I put eyes and a nose on my chin and covered my face and then had my wife film me upside down lip-synching to 'You Can Call Me Al.' It's comedy genius, if I do say so myself." He huffed on his fingernails and buffed them on his shirt. "And I need this on YouTube, too. I think this is going to be the biggest thing to hit the Internet since the Ooga-Chaga Baby!"

I realized that Derek just wasn't going to take no and standing around trying to get out of it was just going to eat into my make-me-look-like-Giselle time.

"Whatever. It will only take a minute. Let's do it," I

conceded, deciding to skip my shower and just give my hair a once-over with the flat iron. I did shower that morning, so it wouldn't be too bad.

What should have taken about a twenty-second upload wound up taking close to an hour because Derek couldn't remember the password to his MySpace account.

"Try 'DerekTheConquerer'? 'DorfusAurelius'? 'Napoleon Dorfaparte'? How about 'DubyaDorf'?"

After trying several combinations of leaders and dictators, even including some plays on Hitler, Derek finally remembered his password. It was "MySpacePassword." I would have hit him over the head with the keyboard if I didn't think it would make me even later.

With the world's lamest video now up for the World Wide Web to mock, I bolted out of the office and home to get ready. Thank God, Rachel and Jayla were already there and on duty for outfit, makeup, and hair patrol.

"Are you nervous?" asked Rachel, getting a contact high from my excitement.

I was beyond nervous, but in a good way. After several final panty line checks, mascara touch-ups, and last-minute hair fluffs, Jayla and Rachel declared me date ready.

You know this boo-gie is for reeeaaaaaaal.

I flipped my phone open, my heart racing like I just stepped out of a spin class.

"Hey, it's Colin. I'm downstairs, are you ready? Take all the time you need."

Wait, you mean he wasn't just pulling up to my house before prom and leaning on the horn until I stumbled out with curlers still in my hair?

"No, I'm all set. Be right down," I said coolly into my

phone. I hit End and yelped, "Do another panty line check, Rach. Something has to need fixing before I go."

"You're beautiful, babe." She tossed me a Juicy Tube. "Just gloss and go."

Once I was balmed up and officially ready, the girls wished me good luck and I promised to text from the bathroom with updates. I tried my hardest not to pit out the tank Jayla had lent me on my way down in the elevator, but as soon as I stepped outside, my nerves totally dissipated. Colin was way too cute to even think about anything but his hotness. He was leaning against the taxi, staring down the street in a way that made him look like James Dean, only not a gross smoker. Gorgeous.

"Well, well!" he said with that perfectly perfect smile. "You look fantastic."

A compliment? That I didn't have to ask for? Oh God, how was I going to make it through this night without begging him to marry me?

I smiled and pretended like I got compliments from model-level-gorgeous men all the time. "Thanks, you can borrow this outfit any time you want."

He laughed and opened the cab door for me.

When we sat down to dinner, I tried to steer the conversation away from work, Derek, or employment in general. The upside was that I was so busy trying not to get busted for being a total liar that I pretty much forgot to be awkward. We chatted about our families and sports—he was in Germany for the last World Cup and I confessed my deep, obsessive love for David Beckham. The conversation flowed like a well-written romantic comedy.

"You know, I wouldn't peg you for a Rachael Ray fan," he said, finishing off his cheeseburger.

"I love her! I think she's so cute and spunky. She's like the Kelly Ripa of food."

"Eh, she's not my style. I don't think she's cute at all."

"Really? Okay then, who is your style?" I asked flirtatiously.

"Ooh, let's see." He sipped his beer in mock concentration. "I like 'em about five five, green eyes, brown hair, ambitious, from upstate."

"Uh-huh," I smiled.

"Obsessed with Posh and Becks, unfamiliar with Brazilian cocktails, and able to make quick and healthy meals in thirty minutes. So, pretty extraordinary."

I blushed with pleasure as he asked for the check.

"How about you?" he asked, handing the waitress a twenty-dollar bill before I could even reach for my wallet. Normally, I hated this part of a date—the paying. Brian and I usually split it, unless it was a special occasion where he was expected to take me out. He said that going fifty-fifty was only fair because technically we'd be making the same amount over summer lifeguarding. How romantic.

"My type? I like girls like that, too."

He laughed and leaned his calf against mine under the table. Houston, we have contact!

"Ready?" he said in a low, sexy voice.

"Oh yes," I cooed back. Awkward Emma Who Makes Normal Situations Unbearable, where did you go? When did Sex Kitten Domino arrive?

We walked out onto the busy street and I shivered slightly even though it was at least eighty-five degrees.

"You're such a faker," he said, putting his hunkalicious arm around my shoulder and—omigod!—rubbing my arm. I thought my knees were going to give out.

"Huh?" What was I faking? Well, I mean, I knew what I was really faking. But what did he think I was faking?

"You can't be cold." I relaxed, realizing I wasn't getting busted. He leaned forward and whispered the way he had at Plumm, "You just want me to put my arm around you."

I blushed again—probably setting a world record for number of blushes in one date—and managed to peep out a response.

"Hmm, no, that doesn't sound like something I'd do."

He leaned in impossibly closer, turning me toward him, wrapping both his wonderful arms around me. We were so close that our noses grazed each other.

"Oh no? I think you're a tricky little lady, Miss Freeman. I bet there are all sorts of secrets hiding behind those green eyes."

For a split second the panic rushed back. I thought maybe he'd peeked at my driver's license when I was in the bathroom. But as I searched his face for clues that the jig might be up, our eyes locked. I felt a hand wander down to the small of my back and pull me even closer to him.

His eyes were closing and his face was moving toward mine and oh! A kiss! A soft, slow, warm, fantastic kiss! The kind where you start out holding your breath, thinking maybe this is just a smooch thing, but then you exhale and melt into each other and before you know it, you're full on making out.

We stood there for a blissful eternity, his hand on my cheek and my body pressed against his, letting the lights and the buzz of New York City fade into the balmy night.

After forever, we pulled away and he put me in a cab. I was too smiley to even return his "Good night."

• • •

I was dying to tell the roommates about my evening out of an urban fairy tale, but they were asleep by the time I floated back into the apartment. So I told the story to the next best thing, my journal, and then fell into a happy sleep.

In the a.m., I got myself office ready and then flitted over to Rachel's room to give her a date recap. I did a running slide onto her bed and started from the cab pick-up as she diffused her hair with one hand and attempted to put on bronzer with the other.

"Rach, I might seriously be asking you to be my maid of honor soon. Last night went so well," I singsonged.

She shot me a look of distress and stopped me. "I so want to hear about it, but they're letting me sit in on a phone interview with Lily Allen. And because she's like an ocean away, they scheduled it for the butt crack of dawn." She put the blow dryer down and grabbed my wrist to look at my watch. "Shit, I'm already late." I was bummed and gave her puppy dog eyes. "So sorry, Em. I promise I'll listen tonight." She grabbed her bag and nearly knocked me down as she flew out the door. Before slamming the door closed, she paused for a second to turn and say, "Really, I can't wait to hear. Tonight, okay?"

And even though I was absolutely dying to tell my date story to someone that wasn't made out of loose-leaf paper, there was no way I was going to wake up Princess Jay at eight-fifteen. So I lumbered out the door and over to MediaInc.

Even before I'd finished my morning iced coffee, Derek was up in my cube, announcing that he had a "Big Summer

Project" for me to work on. I seriously considered quitting. Hello! I had more important things to think about. Things like lips and hands and beefy arms and basically anything but Excel spreadsheets and pencils and stuff. This "project of infinite opportunity," as Derek called it, was to find out everyone's birthday and put it into a spreadsheet. Yep, that's it. Oh, wait, I forgot, and then to put it on a master calendar. It was totally going into the journal when I got home that night.

"Whoa! Derek, are you sure you want to leave that critical task to a lowly intern?" I said with mock seriousness that, of course, he didn't get.

"Em," he said soberly, and leaned his khaki-clad butt onto my desk, prompting me to wonder whether I had Purell in my bag, "Derek Dorfman doesn't take very many things seriously." Including business-casual fashion. "But birthdays is one of them!"

If only Brian had cheated on me months earlier. Then I might have gotten off my ass and applied for a cool television internship or something. I could be a PA for *The Hills* right now. But no, I was stuck on birthday patrol.

I assumed the project would take me ten minutes tops, but only a few people actually responded to the "When's your birthday" mass e-mail. And the responses that pinged their way into my inbox weren't pretty.

What is Derek going to do with this information? Embarrass me like he did Debbie Hannigan with an "I just got lei-d" themed party? I'm not volunteering myself for that.

Tell him I'm a leap year baby.

So he can "buy" me another keyboard wrist rest from the supply closet? Please let him know that I already have enough supplies this year.

When is he going to be out of the office on vacation? Tell him my birthday's then.

I ended up trotting around office to office, cubicle to cubicle, begging people for their birth date info, all the while dodging and weaving and trying to avoid Colin. This lame project was undeniably intern work and I couldn't let him see me.

It was a total pain in my ass, but at least now I had hard proof that I wasn't the only one who hated Derek. I was wondering how everyone else here had dealt with his bucketful of obnoxious for so long. It turns out they were just doing their best to plug their ears to his nails-on-chalkboard personality, too.

After I'd made my rounds and collected just about everyone's birthday—poor Debbie Hannigan refused to share her birthday, still scarred from last year—I stared at my color-coded birthday grid and sat back to daydream about my next run-in with Colin:

"Oh, hi! I didn't expect to see you here. I was just licking and pursing my lips for a reason completely unrelated to you."

"Lunch at Cité? Of course. Let me just run and grab my purse. Oh, no need for the purse because you're paying? Okay, then let's go. And make it Cipriani instead."

"You were watching an episode of Grey's *last night and the perfect curves and Crest smile of Izzie Stevens reminded you of me? You're too sweet, Colin dear."*

I should mention that in all of those above situations, I'd be wearing a button-down shirt, unbuttoned one button too sexy for work, revealing the lace of my purple bra; a tight leather skirt; and killer heels. I should also mention that I don't own a lace bra or leather skirt. But maybe my silver flip-flops and Old Navy polo buttoned all the way up would look the same to him? Whatever, a plan is a plan, realistic or not.

I was startled out of my office operator fantasy by a husky man's voice. "Hey, Emma. Whatcha up to?"

I looked up into two aqua eyes, reflecting the blue from his shirt. Is it possible to be caught off guard by someone when you're thinking about them?

"Colin! Oh, hey. I wasn't expecting . . . I mean, what am I doing? I've just been making out with Microsoft Excel all day." What? What just came out of my mouth? That was not coy or sexy or lace-boob revealing. Totally not part of my plan.

He chuckled awkwardly and headed into Derek's office to discuss whatever it was that people who actually have real jobs talk about. I slumped down in my chair, positive that I had just canceled out our hot post-date smooch with one lame computer joke.

After a few self-loathing seconds, I decided to take some action. If Colin walked past my desk to go into Derek's office, he was definitely going to pass me again on his way out. I glossed my lips and unbuttoned my shirt, nowhere near the point of sexy, but at least I didn't look like Mr. Garrison. I streamed in some jazz on my Media Player because listening to jazz was probably something a twenty-two-year-old would do. My legs were crossed in a way that showed a fair amount of thigh. My eyes were on Derek's door, stalking Colin like paparazzi outside celebrity rehab. After half an hour the door finally opened and out boomed Derek with the crush of my daydreams following behind.

"The homers make the game that much more interesting. That's why I don't care if they use steroids," Derek bellowed so loudly that a deaf person in China could hear him.

He and Colin walked past my desk, not glancing at me or my strategically exposed thigh.

He totally ignored me? God, that terrible Excel one-liner really had tanked this would-be summer fling. Why couldn't I have just said something normal? Or, even worse, could Derek have mentioned that he had an intern working for him and Colin put it all together? I spent the entire afternoon alternating between hating myself and my lame one-liner and despising Derek and his fat mouth.

That evening, I shuffled into the apartment wanting nothing more than some leftover takeout, a remote control, and some QT with my journal. I was shocked to see my couch real estate already occupied by Jacob, who was fully concentrated on the iBook in his lap.

"Did we have plans for tonight, Jake?" I tried to keep the irritation out of my voice as I kicked off my heels and limped toward the fridge for some mu shu. He could've at least sent me a text reminding me. "I totally forgot."

I heaved open the fridge door and poked my head in, rummaging through the various takeout boxes that no one ever bothered to throw away.

"No. I just came over because Jayla called."

"What? Ow!" The combination of Jayla calling Jake and

the smell of my leftovers-turned-petri-dish was so shocking, I banged my head on the fridge roof.

"Hey, Em!" Jayla yelled from her room. "Yeah, I think I have some sort of virus on my computer and I thought that Jake would know how to fix it."

I refolded the corners of my carton of takeout closed and placed it back in the fridge. Something was fishy here . . . and it wasn't just the five-day-old sushi. "Don't Macs, like, never get viruses or something?"

I craned my neck to peer into Jayla's room to see if I could catch her eye—she might be able to pull off the coy and innocent routine from the other room, but one look at her face and the jig would be up. Her door was half shut and all I could see was a pile of dresses scattered on her bed, and glimpses of her running back and forth trying on clothes.

"Yeah, they're pretty solid. I'm not really sure what's going on here," Jake said, clueless that my roommate was in a sartorial frenzy ten feet away.

Yeah, I didn't know what was going on here either. I jammed a spoon into a jar of peanut butter I'd fished out of our candy-stuffed cupboard. Why would Jayla ever want to hang out with my dorkus cousin? *I* didn't even want to tonight and I was, like, genetically obligated.

"I've been looking for the glitches she's talking about, but I'm not finding any." He went back to full concentration on the laptop.

"Well, if you can't fix it, no worries." Jayla smiled from the doorway of her room, modeling a bright green bandeau dress from American Apparel, the kind that can be worn twenty different ways or something. Wide-eyed and slightly slack-jawed, Jake's attention was no longer on the computer. "Maybe it healed itself or something."

"Jay, it's an Apple, not the Terminator. It can't just heal itself," I snarked, now pawing through the fridge for the jar of raspberry jelly I knew I'd seen last weekend. I mean, whatever, if she wanted to date someone like Jake, I guess I could understand that—she'd had enough bad boys and even worse luck. A safe, normal guy like him would have its appeal. But couldn't she go for someone *like* him—not him exactly? I'm related to him, so isn't that kind of like her dating me?

"Whatever. Since nothing's wrong, then maybe we . . ." She moved her eye contact from Jake up to me. "I mean, we *all* can grab dinner or something."

It totally felt like I was intruding on some weird, mismatched date. Like post–nose job Ashlee settling for one of the Yin Yang Twins. Though, my only other option was rancid Chinese or condiments on a spoon. "Sure. Should we wait for Rach?"

"Oh, she's on another one of her computer dates," Jayla informed me as she stuffed her clutch with two AmExes and about ten different lip glosses.

I couldn't help but be a little irritated that Rachel hadn't e-mailed me herself with a full dating update or even just a recap of how the Lilly Allen interview went. But I tried to pretend like I didn't care. "Oh wow. With that guy from the weekend that she's in love with? We're going to have to break out some celebratory Manischewitz when she gets back." I looked over at my killjoy cuz on the couch, who was giving me a dorky parental look. "Or maybe just some Kosher-for-Passover Martinelli's." I rolled my eyes at him to let him know that I was just saying that because of his pseudo-parental presence.

"No. Not him. She's with some other guy. I told her to

diversify her dating portfolio. I mean, she can't stick all of her Hanukkah candles in one menorah, right?"

Jake and I nodded in agreement.

I couldn't decide which of my roommates was surprising me more—Princess Jayla crushing on Jake Starfish-face or Little Miss Only-Kissed-Three-Boys Rachel becoming the dating queen of Lower Manhattan.

"Okay!" Jayla sang as she pranced toward the door in a pair of adorable tan heels I was sure I'd just seen on Jessica Alba in *Us Weekly*. "You guys ready?"

"Yeah," I said, and reached for my purse and then realized I was still in work clothes. I felt like such a prep school tool in my collared work shirts. Usually when I came home, I tore my work gear off so fast I was in my undies by the time I got across the living room. Rachel always said it looked like I melted or something, just a trail of empty clothes where Emma used to be. "Wait, I want to change real quick." I scuttled into my room and rifled through my closet to see what was clean and cute enough to put on. I didn't have a shot in hell of looking as foxy as Jayla, but I hoped that "non-grubby and discernibly female" was attainable.

"Ahhhh! I'm coming! I'm hurrying!" I hollered from the depths of my closet. I could hear Jayla's heels click-clacking around on the hardwood, probably impatient. She got so fussy when she was kept waiting, but I guess that's what happens when you grow up with an entire staff anticipating your every need at all four of your houses. I paused so I could hear whatever mildly bitchy response she had as I clutched a flowy, if kind of wrinkled, turquoise tunic in one hand and pair of black, also pretty wrinkled, leggings in the other. But instead of "Hurry your pretty ass up, Domino!" I heard, "So I learned this new pose in yoga, wanna see?"

And then a small, stifled gasp from my cousin. Envisioning the Kama Sutra coming to life in my common room, I poked my head quickly out the door. Jayla was in some wonky lunge pose, with one of her legs somehow hooked over the back of her shoulder, and she'd arranged her dress just right so that she was showing a ton of leg but nothing X-rated.

"Jayla!" I snapped instinctively.

Startled, she jumped and toppled over with an awkward thud, her dangly gold earrings clanging on the ground. Jake rushed over to help her as she fumbled to keep her lady parts covered.

"Ow! My elbow!" she whined, rubbing it and grimacing.

He looked at her totally not injured arm as she batted her eyelashes, the perfect damsel in Downward-Facing Dog distress. I rolled my eyes and closed the door to change.

I pulled on my outfit, touched up my melted makeup, fluffed my hair, and slowly opened my door, sure to make plenty of noise doing so just in case those two were playing doctor.

Thankfully, Jayla had been lured away from contortionist flirting by her iPhone and was furiously responding to texts as Jake flipped idly through the issue of *Nylon* magazine on the coffee table.

"Ready!" I announced, and we all quickly headed out.

We decided on Republic, right across Union Square. Over a steaming bowl of udon, I told them about my run-in and then walk-by with Colin.

"So, what do you think? Did I totally dork him away with that Excel make-out joke? Or what if it's because Derek blew my cover and told Colin I'm only an intern?"

"Em, you would know if he found out about you being a

high schooler. Trust me. He was most likely just trying to be discreet. What you two are starting up is probably against the rules," Jake said, fumbling for a mouthful of pad thai with his chopsticks.

"I'm eighteen! I mean, despite whatever he thinks, I *am* eighteen. Totally not against any rules!" I could hear my voice get shrill with defense.

As Jake set down his chopsticks and picked up a fork, Jayla cut into the convo. "He was talking about company policy, Em. Not the law. Hooking up with someone at work, intern or not, probably isn't a first-class ticket to a promotion. Haven't you seen *Love Actually*?"

"Yeah, most companies tell you not to piss in your own pool," sensei Jake added oh-so-eloquently.

Jayla rolled her eyes and laughed, "Ew, you're gross! Now shut up and pass the edamame."

I was too perturbed by this news to focus on the flirt-freak-fest taking place in front of me. I mean, Colin was risking his rep by dating me? I hadn't even thought about that. And he didn't even know just how much he was risking. I'm no workplace gossip expert, but I'd assume his dating an intern would be about as hot a topic as when The Hombres decided to bring those eighth graders to junior prom. I made a mental to-do for tomorrow—come clean to Colin. I had to. If I fessed up now, things could still totally work out. Who knew, maybe he'd like me more because I was so mature and honest, totally not what he'd expect from someone who had Cute Is What We Aim For under "Favorite Music" on their MySpace page? Oh no—my MySpace page! If Colin saw it, I was completely screwed. I had to change my profile picture to a snapshot of my dog and set my profile to private. Ugh, this was getting to be a huge fiasco. My mind raced thinking of all the other ways I could be found out, and then I stopped and resolved again, stronger this time, to tell Colin the truth.

I sat through the rest of dinner pretty quiet, stressing about MySpace, Facebook, and God knows what other Google hits were out there, just waiting to expose me as a fraud and an intern and a teenager before I could be the adult I was faking to be and tell Colin myself. Thankfully, Jayla and Jake were so consumed with their newfound "we have so much in common" moments that my silence went completely unnoticed. But even through my panicked haze, I could hear how odd the conversation had gotten.

"So wait," Jake said, pushing back his glasses excitedly. "You're telling me that you, Jayla St. Clare, can shoot an M16?"

"What's an M—" I started to ask.

"Yeah!" she squealed, unconsciously turning her chair away from me to face him. "Before my dad got into real estate, he was a Green Beret, so he'd always take me shooting out in the woods and stuff. I've shot a 16, an M60, AT4, and I can set up a Claymore mine."

"Oh my God!" Jake threw his hands in the air in amazement. "I totally did ROTC in college!"

"Shut up!"

"Seriously! I was going to go into aviation, but"—he tapped his glasses—"bad vision. No one wants the guy who can't see steering the Black Hawk."

Jayla dissolved into laughter as I tried to picture Princess Jayla tromping around the wilderness. The fiercest jungle I could picture her in was the Fourth of July sale at

Bloomingdale's. They then moved on to their mutual love of X-Men. Jayla said she wished on a daily basis that she were Magneto, while Jake told her all about Element, the mutant he'd invented, who could control earth, wind, water, and fire.

Jayla was digging these confessions of a dorkus? Well, there went my World of Warcraft blackmail. I was going to have to dig up some other dirt on him if I ever wanted to drink in his presence again.

"So does that mean Element could control the water inside someone's body?" Jayla mused, chewing thoughtfully on her chopstick as I tried not to ralph at this nerd-a-thon. "Because if it does, you'd totally be more powerful than Magneto."

After debating this point for a torturous fifteen minutes and even calling each other "Ellie" and "Mags," I had to make a move and asked for the check. And then immediately demanded that we leave already.

I guess it shouldn't weird me out so much that she and Jake were hitting it off. Rachel was meeting tons of guys, I had the Colin thing (or at least up until this afternoon I did), why shouldn't Jayla find someone she liked? But still, what could she *possibly* find so compelling about my cousin? She'd kissed half the Abercrombie catalog. I let her walk home in dreamy silence as I mentally rehearsed how to tell Colin that I was practically jailbait.

Seventeen

As soon as I sat down at my desk the next morning, still dewy with my a.m. commute sweat layer, Derek bellowed for me. I picked up a pad and pen and trudged over to his office, bracing myself for another excruciatingly boring Excel assignment.

Derek was reclining back with his feet up on his desk and his arms folded behind his head. The pose was kind of pinup girl–esque, but more a display of male-pattern baldness and midlife weight gain than of coy sexiness. "Hey, Em-a-licious, did I ever tell you about how I used to play football in college?"

Crap. Not another back-when-I-was-young-and-knee-injury-free story. "No, Derek. You haven't ever mentioned college football."

"That's because I never played college football! It was a joke." He unfolded his arms to shoot finger guns at me. "See? I'm a jokester! I told you back when you started, Emmarooni, that you always had to be on your toes with The Dorf or he'll get you good, like I just did."

I rolled my eyes and turned around. As much as I wanted to inform him that pointing his fat fingers at me after saying something that wasn't true made him a liar with a hand tic, not a jokester, I knew that would just lead to more Dorf time, and really, all I wanted was a quiet day of Googling myself and my loved ones.

So I shuffled back to my desk, threw my pad and pen down, and quickly busied myself with possibilities of how to break the news of my teenage wasteland citizenship to Colin. I drafted a few completely terrible e-mails.

Dear Colin,
I have some news to break to you. I'm not old enough to buy liquor, but I can buy cigarettes. Still want to be my summer boyfriend? Please keep in mind that cloves are making a comeback.

Hmm. No, too subtle.

Dear Colin,
Ever wanted a second chance to win Prom King? Well, have I got an opportunity for you!

Too game show–like. This wasn't *Who Wants to Get Arrested for Statutory Rape?*

Dear Colin,
Technically, this isn't pedophilia, but I bet (hope) it's the closest you've ever been.

Gah, I was realizing that e-mail was totally not the way to go about it. And who knew if he was even really still into me? After our evening of French fries and French kissing, had there been any real signs that he was? Not really. Maybe he was one of those guys who just liked the chase and once they got the prize, the thrill was over for them. I feel like there totally was a *Sex and the City* episode about that species of man. Actually, I think the entire series was about that species. I e-mailed Rachel my theory, hoping she'd say I was off the confession hook.

Her response:

Kissing hasn't been "the prize" since spin the bottle. At this point, a date that ends in just a kiss is a consolation prize, if anything. Even I know that. And honestly, do you really want him to be over you? Tell him the truth.

She was totally right, especially about the not-wanting-him-to-be-over-me part. I needed to kiss him again, to see his head tilt and lean in, to taste his lips, salty from French fries. What if he didn't buy the "age is just a number—a connection is a connection" spiel? Would I never see him again? I couldn't tell him and risk missing out on kissing skills like his.

But even if I didn't tell him about my age, what if he really was over me? Not because he'd won the grand prize of kissing me, but just because he'd met another girl. He very well could have gone out when we split ways on Tuesday night and met a girl who knew what the national drink of Brazil was and didn't run away every time her cell rang. Or he could have just gotten bored with me. From what I gather from *One Tree Hill*, a week is the standard life span of a relationship. Or maybe he decided against dating someone from work. He did seem like a guy who was pretty serious about his career.

I could hear my inbox ping with a new message, thankfully interrupting my pyschogirl inner monologue. Hopefully, Rachel had taken pity on my corporate hostage situation and sent a funny link and this wasn't just an e-mail from IT alerting me that my inbox was too full.

While the message was not from CurlyRach91, my inbox held something even better than a link to www.settle forbrian.com. It was an e-mail from CChristensen@media inc.com. The subject line read "Saturday, Miss Freeman?" Birds chirped and fat black women sang "Hallelujah" in the background as I clicked his message open.

> Emma,
> The weather is here, wish you were beautiful. No, wait—other way around. The weather is beautiful, wish you were here. Ah, that's better. What do you say to some Saturday afternoon hanging?
> —CC

I clapped my hand over my mouth and squealed as quietly as possible. Weekend hanging? Cheesy jokes? He so wasn't over me. My fingers twitched to write back immediately. But I knew I should stay cool—wait at least an hour before writing back.

But playing about as hard to get as mono, I only managed to wait eleven seconds before replying.

CC,
As long as you promise no more burgers, you're on for the hanging. Three burgers in one week is too much of a great thing.
—Emma

I sat totally still, my eyes on my inbox, waiting for a reply message. And within five seconds, I got a response.

Ha ha. No burgers, you got it. I'll call you on Saturday around noon.

More low-volume screeching and twittery foot stomping. But I didn't even have a moment to soak in the delicious fantasy forming in my head. Derek dropped a stack of papers on my desk, a sonic boom echoing through the office.

"I need one hundred copies of this. Double sided, stapled, and collated. And step on it, missy."

Step on it? I'm not a freaking cab in a car chase, I thought to myself. Or maybe I said it out loud, because Derek turned around.

"What, Emma?"

I just shrugged my shoulders innocently and beamed the biggest smile I could muster as I headed to the copy room. Forty-five mind-numbingly boring minutes later, I returned to my desk with a redwood forest's worth of paper. Just as I'd finished stapling the ninety-eighth packet, Derek sauntered over to my cube.

"Oopsie-daisy! Typo on page four, just found it. I'm

going to need you to go ahead and copy and collate this packet instead." He kerplunked a new pile of paper on my desk. "Hope you didn't get too far."

I restrained myself from strangling him—I figured that a juvie prison stay was not the kind of unique extracurricular activity a college admissions officer would be looking for. I silently slipped the 980 stapled pages into my recycling bin, then made my way back to the copy room to kill some more of the rainforest. When the packets were finally finished and typo free, I sank back in my chair and began my countdown of the remaining 270 minutes in the day.

At minute 245, my work phone rang.

"Em, I need you in here." It was Derek, sounding serious. "Bring some paper, it's important."

I immediately thought that he'd been monitoring my Internet time and I was going to get the smackdown for doing nothing but surfing Bluefly.com all morning. A nervous sweat broke out on my brow and my mind went into overdrive thinking about all of the ridiculous and in-no-way-justifiable-as-work-related websites that I visited on a daily—no, wait, hourly—basis. I hastily composed an "I was on eBay looking for a kidney for my terminally ill puppy" excuse and walked into his office, trying not to look as panic-stricken as I was.

"Yes?" I chirped, sounding as innocent as I could.

"Can you come here please and watch this?" He motioned to his monitor, his brow furrowed. Was it surveillance of me in the supply closet that day? Okay, my official story was that I didn't mean to take those four spiral notebooks, they just ended up in my purse.

But instead I was faced by something far more horrifying: I moved around to his side of the desk to get a view of his computer screen and was confronted with . . . home videos of his kid playing hockey.

"Look at this. What do you think of his form?" He chewed his lip pensively and waited for my expert evaluation.

This was unreal. I was on an emotional roller coaster and Derek was going to derail me.

"Uh, I don't know. He looks . . . good. Good, um, hitting skills." I was a soccer chick. I didn't know the first thing about hockey.

"Yeah, Wyatt's slap shot is strong but he's lousy at defense. Here, check this out." He fast-forwarded through the rest of Wyatt's—seriously, that was the worst name I'd ever heard—shooting drills and I saw with a sinking dread that the video was thirty-seven minutes long.

"I mean, do you think he's got what it takes to be the next Crosby?" Derek stared at me intently as I fumbled for an answer.

"Well," I said slowly, "that depends. Is he good at stand-up? There can only be *one* Bill Cosby, right?"

Derek laughed—I wasn't really sure why—and slapped me on the back. "Oh, Emma, that sense of humor of yours! Man, I'm writing that one down," he chuckled. "But seriously, sit on down here and tell me how you think he stacks up against Sid the Kid, because I gotta tell ya, Wyatt is freaking unstoppable in his Junior League games. Just last week that Anderson brat, James or whatever his name is, tried to hip check him and *bam!* Wyatt just went in for the—"

"Derek," I cut in, trying and failing to keep the exasperation out of my voice, "I really don't know anything about hockey. I don't even know who Sid Kid is. And I've got kind of a lot of work, so . . ."

I made a move to leave, but no such luck.

"You don't know who Sidney Crosby is? Do you live under a rock? He's going to be the next Gretzky." I tried to feign recognition but it was too late. I thought that maybe my total hockey ignorance could get me out of home video hell, but I was wrong, wrong, wrong. Instead I got an even more in-depth lecture on Wyatt's skating skills and an exhaustive biography on this Canadian hockey prodigy, Crosby. By the time he was done, I was actually glad to get back to my desk and stare blankly at my computer screen. At least then I didn't have to pretend to look interested.

That evening, I trudged through my apartment door, wondering how I could be so tired from a day spent entirely sitting down. Rachel was in the kitchen cutting up an apple.

"Question," I said exhaustedly, flopping my bag on the ground, too tired to care if anything got smashed. "How many times does a person have to sing the *banana fanna fo fanna* song before it's considered fighting words?"

Rachel laughed, spreading peanut butter on her apple slices.

"Because after the third time Derek passed my cube singing it, I honestly thought about tripping him. And have you ever heard of this hockey player, Sidney some-thinerother?"

"Ooh!" squealed Jayla from her room, busy re-BeDazzling her iPhone. "I love him! He was always so sweet to me."

Rachel and I just rolled our eyes and smiled—was there anyone famous that girl didn't know?

"Em, your Derek stories are seriously hilarious. You should write a book or something," Rachel said as she headed toward the couch to eat and watch *Friends* reruns.

A book? That would be awesome. Like, *The Derek Diaries* or something.

"You think? Well, I have been writing most of them down. I feel like if I don't, they'll slowly poison me to death. He has to be the worst boss in the history of the universe and I feel like it's my duty to catalog all of this douchiness. Like a time capsule of idiocy or something."

Rachel stopped in mid–apple bite and turned to me, her head cocked with curiosity.

"Em, I didn't know that. Can I read what you've written? I'm sure you could turn them into something ridiculously hilarious."

I felt my face flush with embarrassment at the thought of showing someone my journal. Not because I was a bad writer—which I probably was—but because I just wrote in my journal to get my thoughts down, not for it ever to be read. What if I showed the journal to Rachel this once and then from forever on, instead of just writing to write, I'd be writing thinking it was meant to be read? That would just change something in a weird way. Like, instead of writing for myself, I'd be writing for someone else.

"Um, yeah. Maybe I'll show it to you. Not now, though. Let me polish the stories a little bit more." I stole one of her peanut butter slices and changed the subject. "I feel like I haven't seen you in forever. How have things been going on the JDate front?"

She clicked off the TV just when Ross and Rachel were about to get back together for the seventh time and slumped into the couch cushion.

She turned to me with a pained look. "Things are a mess. Remember the future love of my life from Saturday night?" Dramatic sigh. "He never called, which I totally don't get. Is it possible for me to have an amazing let's-be-together-forever-and-name-our-kids-Jordan-and-Seth time on a date and the guy to not even want to spend another three hours with me?"

Mute and clueless Emma strikes again. I sat there making an empathetic face.

She went on, "So, whatever. I had that other date with another guy last night. And it was every shade of awful."

"Was it really? Worse than going halvsies on the Indian buffet?"

Her tone turned solemn. "He picked me up at the apartment and then made me take the subway uptown with him."

"Rach, that's not so bad. Don't let too much of Jayla rub off on you."

"No, that wasn't the bad part. I didn't have my Metrocard with me because I was just carrying a clutch and didn't think we'd be commuting to dinner. And I was totally willing to buy one. But he was like, 'No, use mine. It's unlimited. You just have to wait eighteen minutes for it to be valid again.' And, like, he really wouldn't hear of me buying my own. So we stood there for eighteen minutes in the rain forest of humidity that is the subway, him on one side of the turnstiles and me on the other. Obviously, I offered to pay for the cab home."

"Wow. Okay, yes, that is worse than Indian food, my friend. That's like something out of a budget sitcom or something."

"Tell me about it, total CW nightmare," she said through a mouthful of peanut-buttered apple. "How are things with you and your geriatric lover?"

240

"Twenty-three is so not geriatric! And things are going—" I was about to gush about dinner and the kiss on Tuesday and then the flirty e-mails today, but I realized that I couldn't be too enthused about the Colin situation in front of her. Rachel's entire summer quest was a boyfriend and here I'd just stumbled into a relationship like Adam Sandler at the end of every single one of his movies. "—okay. We're hanging on Saturday. So, I guess that'll be fun." I cut it off there, not wanting to rub in my happiness too much, and flipped the TV back on.

That night, I couldn't sleep. I was still really stressed about keeping my juvie status a secret from Colin. And that stress was only adding to my typical nightly restlessness, dreading the impending eight hours in cubicleville the following day.

I lay in bed staring at the digital clock with my mind wandering, replaying the day. And despite all the Colin happenings, what I kept coming back to was what Rachel said about my Derek stories.

You should write a book or something.

I mean, come on. Me? Write a book? I'm a kid! Kids don't write books! Well, except for that home-schooled one who wrote those dragon books that sold a billion copies. I guess if it worked for him, maybe I could give it a shot. At least then I'd have something worthwhile come out of this summer. It was becoming pretty clear that this MediaInc thing was never going to materialize into a real resume dazzler.

And those stories definitely were book worthy. And I did have a lot of stuff written down already. If my roommates liked them so much, other people would at least get a laugh out of them. And, like, everyone gets book deals these days, right? And oh, what sweet, glorious revenge to out Derek as the crapbag he was! And make a few dollars doing it? Nothing wrong with that. As it stood now, the only way I was going to make money off this summer at all was if I sold all of my pilfered Dr. Grip pens on eBay. So yeah, why not write a book about being an assistant for a crazy executive? And then genius hit me harder than a paparazzi-car-chase accident: *The Devil Wears Dockers*. My job totally *was* like working for a poorly dressed, potbellied, male Anna Wintour . . . well, you know, minus the fame, fortune, and free designer gear.

Eighteen

"Ladies," I announced grandiosely over Cinnamon Toast Crunch the following morning, "I, Emma Freeman, am taking time out of my busy schedule of lying to men and Googling Brandon Routh to write a book."

I puffed out my chest and smiled proudly and looked at them expectantly for a response. They both perked up—well, "perk" might be a bit strong, more like "made eye contact with me," but that's about as perky as they get before nine a.m.

"Really?" Rachel chirped, milk dribbling down her chin. "About your boss?"

"Yes ma'am. I figure that I should turn my brave story

into money and fame, like Fantasia Barrino or one of those kidnapped reporters."

"Good for you," Jayla said earnestly, putting down the latest issue of *Paper* magazine and giving me a small round of applause, Rachel dutifully following suit. "I wish I had gotten a jump on painting when I was your age. But Jake says that the best way for me to make up for lost time is to start working at a gallery ASAP."

Rachel and I exchanged WTF glances.

"Oh, you guys," Jayla laughed dismissively. "We're just friends! Jesus Christ, first Chloe and now you two."

Wait—Chloe knew about Jake?

"What does she say about Jake?" I pried. "Has she met him?"

"Oh God, no no no no. She's just like, 'Jay, he wants you, obvie!'"

"Jayla," Rachel said in a kindergarten teacher voice, "he does want you."

"He does not!" she shrieked.

"Ew, yeah, he does not!" I said, scowling into my cinnamilk.

"I mean, he doesn't just want your body," Rachel clarified. "I think he really likes you."

"No he doesn't!" I snapped before Jayla could answer, and they were both taken aback at my outburst of venom. Even though I really loved Jayla, I couldn't picture her sticking with a guy for more than a holiday weekend. She'd make Jake fall in love with her, they'd be happy for about five minutes, then she'd run into Josh Hartnett at some club opening and she'd forget my cousin's name. And besides, I'd probably have to see them make out and that's just gross.

Rachel threw a stern look my way and put her hands on her hips.

"What is your problem, Emma? They like each other, so what?"

I expected Jayla to come back with something sassy and defensive, too, but she just sat there looking hurt. God, what a bad friend I was. What did I want, the whole world to be single? I should be happy for them, whether or not I had Colin or Brian or Justin Timberlake or anyone else. And they were pretty much adults and could do whatever they wanted. Me bitching about it was only going to make Jayla feel crappy and probably ultimately unite them against me. I collected myself from my mini-episode. "Rachel's right," I said sheepishly. "He does totally like you, I mean, why wouldn't he? Go forth and have lots of fun."

Jayla laughed. "Well, thanks for the blessing, Mom, but there's nothing going on. He's just a friend. Guys don't like me, remember?"

I wrinkled my nose. Guys don't like Jayla? Was she crazy? She practically gave boys whiplash when she walked down the street!

"I'm like a diamond paperweight," she said with a weary sigh. "I'm pretty to look at and show off, but you don't really have a use for me. You just keep me around to tell people you have it."

Was this seriously what she thought? I mean, yes, she was eye-poppingly gorgeous and boys were definitely into that, but once you had a conversation with her, it was obvious that she was more than just a pretty face.

"That's not true, Jayla," I said. "You had some bad luck with Carter but that had nothing to do with you, okay? He was a psycho and a liar and a troll fatty. I mean, what sane person lies like that?"

"You mean besides you?" Rachel sniggered.

Ouch.

I stammered that I was going to tell Colin the truth . . . eventually.

Probably.

Not.

"I mean, I will tell him. I just need to figure out exactly how, you know?"

The girls looked at me skeptically.

"Who are you trying to fool?" Rachel said, getting up from the table and heading to the sink. "You haven't told him because you don't want to, and you're not going to tell him, because you're never going to want to. Plain. And. Simple."

I got up from the table and dumped my bowl in the sink. Then I leaned up on the counter and glowered at Rachel for her malicious—well, I guess just really true—verbal attack.

"No, I know what she means," Jayla said, coming to my defense. "It's not just what you say, it's how you say it. You could spin this a whole bunch of different ways, so you really need to plan it out exactly. Like last summer, when I hooked up with my friend Patrick—he's this really awesome artist from Brooklyn—I thought I was kissing his twin brother, Steve. So I could have been like, 'Pat, last night, I totally thought you were Steve, so please don't get mad when you see me flirting with your brother tomorrow.' But that would have been terribly mean. So instead I said, 'I know you'll never like me the way I like you, so if I ever kiss Steve it's only because he reminds me of you.' I mean, that was a *total* lie—I *in no way* actually like him—but whatever, it worked."

I nodded gratefully even though I really had no idea what the point of her story was.

"Yeah, well, whatever you say or whatever story you concoct, you need to do it soon, Emma," Rachel scolded. I hated it when she lectured me, especially about boys. Like, wasn't this the girl who just said she'd never been on a real date like three seconds ago? Uck, it was like when Dr. Phil told people to get in shape when he was about the size of a mobile home.

How in the hell did our conversation go down this road? I changed the subject and asked Jayla why she was up so early. She looked at the clock on the microwave and shook her head in disbelief that anyone could be up at an ungodly hour like eight-thirty a.m.

"Off to apply at galleries," she said, drinking the last of her Naked Juice smoothie and stuffing her resume into a Birkin bag. "I figure I've got a leg up on the competition be-cause I'll work for free."

"Well, good luck." I wearily put on my sensible-and-not-at-all-sassy work heels and headed for the door. "Anyone would be crazy not to hire you. If only to see you strut around in the newest Marc Jacobs shoes before anyone else has them."

Jayla giggled and almost shot carrot juice out her nose. I chuckled all the way to the elevator, happy to have such nice friends to wake up to. Coming home to them was the best part of my MediaInc summer. And if the best part of your job is leaving it, that says a lot.

I stepped onto the street and was hit by a wall of

ninety-degree air. I tapped on my iPod and played my "Good Morning!" playlist. A little Natasha Beddingfield always helped me face another day.

I spent most of my workday half-assing my already half-assed daily duties so I could devote my time to Googling literary agents and reading sample novel proposals online.

By lunch I had decided to write a thinly veiled narrative of my own life that focused on a horrible boss named, um, Eric Orfman, who spent his days torturing a girl named, um, Jemma. Okay, so it needed some work and a thicker veil, but I really felt good about the idea. I wolfed my turkey roll up at my desk and headed to Barnes & Noble to get some books on successful proposal writing during lunch.

"Thirty bucks for this huge book on lit agents, can you believe it?" I complained that night to Rachel over Easy Mac and *America's Next Top Model*. "But it lists, like, everyone in the book world."

"Wow, so you're really serious about writing a book?" Rachel said, awed at my motivation.

"Yeah, I am. But I mean, it's like how serious do I have to be? If Paris Hilton can write a book, I totally think that I can do it." I took a cheesy bite. "I figure I'll get started on writing this week and then send what I have out to all of these agents"—I tapped my tome—"en masse. On the company postage dime, obvie."

"Obvie," she agreed. "I mean, what good is working in an office if you can't steal supplies, postage or otherwise?" She curled her legs under her and spooned in another bite of cheesy sauce.

I had already plotted the lie I was going to use to con the mail guy into sending out the random envelopes with my apartment listed as the return address. I'd just say it was such important business that the client needed my home address so they could reach me 24/7. God, I was good.

"The weirdest part is that today I didn't even mind the stupid shit Derek did to me anymore. It was like I almost wanted him to or something. He did his typical asinine crap and I just smiled because I knew it was more material to write about." I shoveled in one last mac 'n' cheese bite and, aside from a thin coating of cheese mix, my bowl was clean. I looked over at Rachel's bowl and she was done, too. In under five minutes, Rachel and I had just polished off a family-sized pack of Velveeta Shells. Impressive and disgusting all at the same time.

"Did he do anything today?" Rachel asked, licking at her bowl of cheese resin.

"Of course. He burst into my cube and asked me to sort and collate these packets. He's all 'Let's move the needle on this and use some teambuildingmotivationorganization.' Like, what the heck does that even mean? So I walk after him and say, 'Uh, I put those packets on your desk an hour ago,' and do you know what he says? 'Ha-ha, I know that. I was just trying to sound productive. The CEO was around the corner.' I mean, really."

Rachel laughed so hard, she splattered cheese spit everywhere. "This book is going to be awesome. I'm totally going to have a friend on the *New York Times* bestseller list!"

For a few seconds I pictured my face on huge posters around Barnes & Noble and everyone calling me the younger, hotter J. K. Rowling! Eh, or even if I just made a few people laugh at Derek, that would be worth all of the times he's made me want to cry.

I didn't have real plans that night, so I kept Rachel and

Jayla company as they prepped for their evenings out with gentlemen callers, reliving more of Derek's idiocy.

"So today when he arrived to work, he comes straight to me and says, 'Man, I can't believe what good time I made getting here, my Eclipse was pushin' seventy-five at least! Is there some sort of Jew or Asian holiday today? Because there was no traffic on the Tappan Zee, it was like no one else was going to work.' As if Japanese national holiday observance could be measured in the bridges and tunnels of the New York metropolitan area."

"He cannot possibly be for real," Jayla laughed, shaking her head as she gave herself a final once-over in the mirror.

"Oh, he's real, all right. As real as Keira Knightley's eating disorder."

When my Saturdate with Colin rolled around, I was too amped on *The Devil Wears Dockers* to keep it to myself.

"I could totally be the next, um . . ." I groped for a respectable well-known author as the waitress handed us our menus, "Dan Brown. Except for I'd be unraveling the mysteries of middle management and not of Christian dogma." Colin was shaking his head at me. "Come on, Colin, you know The Dorf. He's so ridiculous. Someone has to put it on paper."

Colin laughed and shook his head. "Yeah, but you do realize he'll fire you once the book comes out, right? I mean, are you really ready to risk your job over this?"

Ah yes, the job lie.

I fumbled for an answer. "Uh, well, yeah. I think I could make a crapton of money and become superfamous. I kind of hate my job anyway."

"Really? You have a lot of responsibility, probably. Do you even interact that much with Derek?"

Oh boy. Time to change the subject in a major way.

"Ha, you're right. Maybe I'll just scrap the idea or write about my roommates instead. So, tell me about your week." I took a deep breath to quell the blush of panic I could feel spreading across my chest. Dammit! Why did I always walk into these stupid conversations where I could so get caught in my Lie o' the Century?

I tuned out most of what he was saying and just nodded along. I couldn't care less if MediaInc burned to the ground that very instant, and I could barely stand to hear Colin go on and on about it. Did I really have that much in common with this guy? I mean, did I really like him or just the idea of him?

Just then he put his hand on my bare knee under the table and a ripple of excitement went through me.

No, I totally liked him, the idea of him, the touch of him, the sight of him! Him. I really liked him.

After lunch we walked around the East Village and came across an indie movie theater playing some foreign film.

"Oh, I just read a great review of this. Come on, wanna see it?" He nodded his head toward the theater.

"You mean like now? Just walk in? We didn't even plan to see a movie today."

"But we didn't have plans to do anything else. Let's just go."

Why was I being such a prude? This was an unplanned movie, not an unplanned pregnancy.

I giggled and took his hand as he bought two tickets.

Just another chapter in my city girl summer. Strappy shoe wearing. Colleague kissing. Spontaneous afternoon movie seeing. Woo-hoo, Emma!

In total middle school flashback style, we made out through ninety-four percent of the movie. It started with our pinkies touching, and by the time the opening credits finished rolling, our lips had gotten reacquainted.

"Should we go back to my place?" he whispered hotly in my ear when the movie was over, and slid his hand dangerously high on my inner thigh. Panic! I really liked him, and yes, he was everything I'd ever collage-pasted into my dream boy book, but whoa. His place? If he'd been some guy my age, he probably wouldn't have expected more than a make-out session. But older guys expect a home run, right? In *Sex and the City* it seemed like after forty-five seconds of knowing a guy, it was almost expected. I never really understood how you could just go out, meet someone, and then feel that comfortable with them. Maybe I'd get it when I was older, but I really didn't think so.

"Er," I stalled, searching through my list of excuses for needing to peace out. "I have a . . . dinner . . . to go to." We were barely three hours out of lunch. I wasn't even hungry for an afternoon snack.

He sighed heavily and rested his head against my shoulder. "I think you might be the Antichrist, Emma Freeman." He chuckled and shifted again in his seat. I had to get out of there or I was going to freak right out.

"Ooh, ha-ha! That's me. Harbinger of evil."

I gave him a quick peck and slid my cheek against his. He shuddered at my touch—which I loved. As we walked slowly out of the theater, his arm around my shoulder, I caught an old couple smiling at us as they sat in the back row, waiting for the crowd to clear out. The lady grinned at me as her husband patted her hand. I saw her mouth, "What a cute couple!" And the man nodded. I smiled back and looked up at Colin, who was saying something about having melted Raisinettes on his shoe. He was so adorable. I guess we did look like a real couple. A real grown-up, happy couple. My stomach sank suddenly. We looked like a couple—not like a nice, wonderful guy and a horrible, lying, vile teenager conning him into moderately priced lunches and midafternoon movies.

"So did you like the movie?" Colin asked as we stepped into the damp heat of the late afternoon.

"Oh yeah, those opening credits? Brilliant. And the music when the closing credits rolled? Also amazing."

He laughed and I heard my text message alert go off.

"Ooh, one sec." I fished into my bag as Colin joked about one of my many suitors blowing my phone up. And when I saw who was texting, my heart stopped. It was a text from Brian. Well, it came up as a text from "Do Not Answer This," which is what I'd changed Brian's name to in my cell.

Hows NY?

Blood rushed to my head and I snapped my phone shut before Colin could see it. Brian! WTF did he want? We hadn't spoken since we broke up and *now* he's texting me? This probably meant Skylar Dichter had dumped him. I glanced up at Colin, looking so perfect in his sunglasses and started crafting vicious Brian replies in my head.

Superfun! I'm dating someone hot and new and not you.

Who is this? I don't have ur # in my phone anymore, jerkhead.

Great. Hows life with you, Mr. Dichter?

"Just my friend wanting to move our dinner date up," I said to Colin, forcing myself to forget the Brian text and promising myself to just ignore it.

"Are you really married or something? Or are you just that popular?" He smiled and backed away a bit to step into the street and hail me a cab. With his muscled arm stretched out and his perfect posterior, he looked so yummy. He could have been a model.

"A little bit of both," I said coyly, and pulled his face in for a big long goodbye kiss. "See you soon." And I jumped into the cab that had pulled over and sped away.

By the middle of the week, I'd kind of brainstormed out my entire proposal, but hadn't done much actual writing aside from what I'd originally done in my journal. I kept telling myself that I just needed one more great Derek anecdote to add in, something really insane and improbable. It was starting to look like I might have to just make something up, but since all my fiction skills were being used on Colin, I was running dry.

"Here we go, yo. Here we go, yo. So what, so what's the scenario?"

Speak of the devil.

"Good morning, Derek."

"Come on, Emma, don't tell me you don't recognize that song!" he said, caffeinated on life.

I shrugged.

"Um . . . Tupac?"

"Pffff! No! That's a classic, it's . . . um, A Clan Called— no no, it's Grand Master—nope, maybe . . ."

Leaning over the cube wall, he drummed his hands loudly on the flimsy gray partition, not caring that with every slap he was wrinkling my magazine cutouts of Daniel Radcliffe. I rolled my eyes and sighed.

"Look, it doesn't matter, that song probably was out when I was like five or something," I huffed. I was pretty much through trying to be nice to him. He had worn me down to a nub of nasty quips.

"Yeah, you're right. So, I've got something big for you, Em. Real, real big!"

If this was a new spreadsheet of the department's half-birthdays, I was going to scream.

"You, missy, are coming with me to our regional advertising trade show!"

He paused expectantly, his face frozen in a manic grin, apparently so I could gasp with excitement and throw my arms around him in gratitude, like I'd finally been given the birthday pony I'd requested ten years ago.

I just nodded mutely.

He deflated instantly. "I'm serious, Emma, this is a huge deal for us. We need people who represent the company well and can handle some solo networking with our main clients. You've done a great job all summer and I'd like to give you a shot."

"Really?" I was actually kind of surprised. Maybe this was the chance I'd been waiting for to do something beyond removing staples and counting sugar packets. I perked up slightly and began to feel a tad less bitter. Maybe this would be my chance to score that awesome college letter of rec.

In the taxi ride to the trade show across town, Derek regaled me with tales of his first two marriages, weekend gardening projects, and his most recent bout with gallstones. Manhattan had never felt so wide. The taxi was sweltering. Instead of blowing out cold air, the AC vent just blew the filthy dust around the floor mats and onto my last clean business-appropriate outfit. Derek was clearly feeling the heat, his pit sweat seeping into bigger and bigger wet stains as he talked in agonizing detail about the minutiae of his life.

When we pulled up to the Javits Center, he was midway through his college rush experience and I was at the edge of my sanity. Derek paid, we hopped out of the cab, and he immediately started sweating from his face. It was a gross sight, but if I were in ninety-degree weather in long sleeves, I'd probably have the face sweats twice as bad. We pushed our way through the revolving front doors and into some hardcore AC. Derek raised his arms slightly to let his pits dry out. As I averted my eyes from his now completely exposed puddles of sweat, I looked around the convention hall. Paunchy balding middle-aged men milled around as equally past-their-prime women sipped coffee and casually inspected each other's laminated badges. Barely anybody was talking and absolutely no one was smiling. There were rows and rows of exhibitor booths with different companies' informational pamphlets and promotional pens. Sensible shoes and boxy Ann Taylor suits that would've made Jayla's eyes bleed were in abundance. Basically, everything looked so grim and boring, a funeral procession would have given this place more zip.

"Okay, Em, you can take this box and just start setting it up on our table here. From now on, you and you alone are in charge of its contents," he said, tapping a box on the table in MediaInc's dinky display booth. "Are you ready?" He looked eagerly at it and hovered dramatically over the lid. "You can open it."

He said it with such seriousness that I imagined it full of PIN codes to the company's accounts in the Caymans. I pried it eagerly open and found . . .

"Water bottles?"

"Yep! They've got our logo on it!" Derek puffed up with pride and grinned, looking like he'd just done something really impressive but creepy, like won a competitive eating championship. "You hand them out as people walk by, okay?"

"Wait, you brought me here to hand out water bottles? This was the big huge responsibility?"

I rubbed my temples and tried to imagine calm blue oceans, puppies, Adam Brody shirtless—anything not to totally flip out. Not because I cared at this point what Derek thought of me, but I really didn't want to storm out and have to shell out fifteen bucks for a cab back home. Though on the bright side, I had found the last book proposal story I was looking for. I guess that meant that as soon as I got home, I should really start typing. I bit back the foulest words I could think of and spent the rest of the day hydrating boring shoulder-padded businesspeople.

By the end of the week, I'd hoped that *The Devil Wears Dockers* would be speeding toward New York's top—and not-so-top—literary agents, ready to be celebrated and praised. But in reality, I'd barely even gotten through cleaning up the initial Derek interview story to a point where I wasn't embarrassed to share it.

Still, even with it far from complete, daydreams about

fabulous book parties and movie option offers were creeping in on my Colin fantasy time.

Rachel came home straight from work on Thursday and caught me tapping my way through transcribing a journal entry into my laptop. "You're really doing the book thing? Not that I doubted you or anything, but, like, it's just really unbelievable!" She kicked the door closed behind her with her foot and slammed down a bag of takeout food.

"Yeah, I can't believe I'm giving it a try either. But the writing is taking forever." I could smell something tasty all the way from the couch. "What did you get us for dinner?"

"Excuse me! *Us?*" She mocked shock, then smiled. "Actually, there's plenty here and you know I'll eat everything if you don't stop me." She held up a plastic fork and a tub of red bliss mashed potatoes. And I did the only thing I could do—I hurried over and dug in.

As we settled down with our food, Rachel rekindled the book convo. "Yeah, I guess writing a book is a long process. And doesn't it take, like, a really long time to get a response from agents?" Rachel asked through a mouthful of biscuit.

"I don't know," I said, picking at the Trader Joe's rotisserie chicken between us and realizing that my summer in New York was only weeks away from wrapping. "I hope not."

I really wanted something awesome to happen with this book idea fast. I mean, how long did this kind of stuff really take? Was I going to have to wait until I was in college or something?

Nineteen

I spent most of my time at work the next day trying to mentally write out the proposal and avoiding Derek. Both of which were nearly impossible.

"*I know what Bo don't know. Touch them up and go uh-oh.*" Derek gangstarolled up to my cube and shoved a pen in my face, presumably as a microphone. "Show me what you got, girl."

"Derek, I don't know," I started to say, snaking my neck around so that I wouldn't be speaking into his Bic mike.

"You're supposed to go, '*Ch-ch-ch-chang chang!*' " Derek demonstrated. "Now you say '*Murderer*' after everything I say, okay?"

"No, no, Derek. I can't. I really need to get some work done so I can finally wrap up this birthday grid, okay?"

The Dorf threw his arms up in surrender and walked away humming what must have been the rest of whatever nineties rap song he was butchering. I looked down and realized that I'd dug my nails into my palms, leaving half crescents of suppressed aggression. Derek's presence was more intolerable than Lindsay Lohan's singing "career." The last three weeks of my internship stretched in front of me—an eternity of Excel, collation, and outdated rap lyrics. But, I comforted myself, I felt the same sense of endless awfulness every night when that two-hour block of *Everybody Loves Raymond* came on TBS, and I made it through that somehow. I'd pull through these last weeks as well.

Walking into the apartment that night, I saw Rachel sitting on the couch, of course perched next to her laptop, searching for Inter-dates.

"How's it going?" Rachel asked, not looking up, her eyes still on a Semitic stallion's profile.

And I don't know what got to me—the stress of lying to Colin, the idea that my awesome book idea was never ever going to get written, the fact that I'd barely seen my best friend all summer because she was so into boys she'd forgotten that this was *our* summer, or maybe just plain being away from home for too long—but I lost it. Completely.

"How am I doing? How am I doing?" I screeched, and Rachel finally looked up from her virtual love life. "Oh, great. Just great. It was great when I got to work at nine this morning and immediately started the miserable 480-minute countdown until I could leave. That was a great time! And then spending at least 240 of those minutes hiding from Colin and then the other 240 minutes hating myself for tricking such a beautiful boy. That made me feel great! And then coming home here to find that my book hasn't written itself yet, also great news!" Cue the heaving sobs. The anger and dejection and tears and snot poured out of me. I kept talking, but even I couldn't understand what I was saying. I was crying so hard that speaking real words hurt.

"You know, Em," Rach said, moving toward me for a hug, "I could tell you that Babe Ruth held the record for most home runs in a season but he also held one for most strikeouts, too. And that big winners all have their big loser moments. But let's be honest, that Babe Ruth thing is probably just some made-up Internet fact. And even if it is true, it's not going to make you feel better. But you know what *will* make you feel better?" She paused and I snotted on my cuff. "Chunky Monkey!"

She got up and walked me back to the couch, depositing me like a sickly child, then dashed over to the kitchen, fished spoons out of the drawer, and plucked a carton from the freezer. When she returned, I was on the couch and my crying had simmered into snot-sucking sniffles.

"Em, just to show you how much I love you, boy or no boy, book or no book, sucky internship and all, I'm going to let you have that first bite."

She pointed to a fudge chunk sticking out. Even though we'd stopped wearing our best friend necklaces in fifth grade, she was still so the "Be Fri" to my "st ends."

I dug into the pint and she listened as I went on about the book. "It's a really good idea for a book, I think. But writing a book is really hard. I just don't know how to do it and those how-to books aren't really that helpful. I've gotten so little done so far."

To that Rachel jumped in. "Oh, I'd love to read the

parts that you do have written. My boss has been letting me do some editing, so I could offer a pseudo-professional opinion—maybe it'll motivate you."

I nodded limply to the idea as "Canned Heat" rang from my bag. I cracked my first smile of the day. It's pretty impossible to be mopey with Jamiroquai playing. I looked at the caller ID and my smile grew into a grin. It's *very* impossible to be mopey with a summer crush calling.

"Hello," I answered in my least snotty voice.

"Hi there. I've been doing some thinking."

Rachel snuck off to her room when she heard it was Colin.

"Uh-huh," I prodded.

"And you do that crazy dash thing every time I see you. And it started out kind of cute, but now I'm getting a little tired of it. So I have a plan. I was going to invite you over to my place to watch a movie tonight, but then I figured you'd bolt halfway through and leave me stuck watching the last hour of some Sandra Bullock DVD all by my lonesome. So instead, I'm thinking that I'm going to invite myself over to your place to watch a movie. That way, there's nowhere for you to dash off to. What do you say?"

Honestly, before this phone call, I don't think I knew what it meant for a heart to be "aflutter." But now I totally did and mine totally was.

"I say that I would never make you watch a Sandra Bullock movie," I answered.

"And?"

And? Come over? Now? Ahh! I was puffy and snotty and ice creamy. Then I remembered the secret weapon Jayla had introduced me to—the tube of Preparation H—and de-

262

cided that my desire to see Colin outweighed the possible trauma he might suffer seeing me post-meltdown.

"And that sounds perfect." I did my best imitation of cool girl casual. "Come on over anytime."

"On my way," he replied.

I clicked my cell phone closed and sighed deeply. A little snuggle session was just what I needed to get my mind off my failing author aspirations. I hopped in the shower and washed the mascara and tear tributaries off my face. Back in my room, I stood in front of my closet, leaving a puddle on the hardwood floor. I wanted to look casual and bedtimey, but not sloppy. A beater and velours seemed to be the answer.

Outfit selected, I stepped out of my room to dry my hair and ran into Jayla.

"Whoa. I didn't know K. Fed was in the house." She must have come home while I was picking out my apparently white-thug ensemble. Thank God. This was my first casual not-datey date with Colin and I needed to feel cute.

"Really? The beater is trashed out? I thought it was kind of hot." Jayla shook her head in fashion contempt.

The phone rang as I turned to my room to find an outfit that made me look less like a wannabe gangster. I could hear Jayla pick it up, and from my closet, I heard her say the last four words I wanted to hear just then, "Sure, send him up."

Wet hair? No makeup? Stay-at-home-husband attire? So not ready.

I ran out into the living room. "Oh my God! Colin's here already? Since when has the MTA moved at the speed of light?"

"Chill out, lady. It's just Jake," she said. "I invited him over." I breathed a sigh of relief as she fluffed her hair in the hallway mirror. "We're going to watch season one of *Grey's*." She gave her boobs a final hoist in her dress before opening the door for Jake's arrival.

I guess that they were kind of becoming an item and I should get used to it, but still, those two together made about as much sense as body glitter on a straight man.

In walked Jacob with an armful of cheap street flowers. "Beauties for you three beauties," he said in a cheesy playboy voice as he handed the flowers to Jayla. Her lips curled in disgust at the sight of carnations, and she held the bouquet with only her fingertips, as if it were a bunch of poison ivy.

"Oh, Jake you . . . shouldn't have." Jayla thrust the flowers at me to deal with.

Then, ever the good hostess, Jayla perked herself up from the minor flora fiasco. "Make yourself comfortable on the couch, Jake. You have a ton to catch up on if you're going to be my *Grey's*-watching buddy this fall." She dashed into her room to find the boxed set.

"*Grey's*? You came all the way down here from Hell's Kitchen to watch old episodes of whiny chick TV?" I asked. As far as I knew, he still hadn't made a move. This was getting a little too pathetic and Duckie-like for comfort.

"Well, I, you know, should catch up on it, because you know . . . ," Jake stammered nonsensically.

"Come on, Jake. Just say it, man. You like her, right?"

His stammering stopped. So did his eye contact. "What? Pfffftttt, no."

"Oh, give me a break. Well, if you do like her, I'd say

264

make a move. And soon. Otherwise you're going to TiVo your way into 'just friends.' Ask her to Nobu and make this official. She would never say no to that."

He nodded. I rolled my eyes at the fact that he needed love advice from a high schooler and then bolted back to my room to complete the cute but comfy clothes quest for Colin's arrival.

I had just finished drying my hair and was wrapping the cord around the dryer when the phone rang announcing Colin. I ran over to the door and did the Jayla boob hoist in the hallway mirror. Except for with me, there wasn't much to hoist, and even if there were, my shirt was so high necked, my boobs would have to be growing out of my throat to show cleavage. I pulled the incredibly short shorts I was wearing down a little bit so they would cover the line where my butt met my thighs, took a deep breath, and opened the door just in time to see Colin walk out of the elevator and turn the wrong way.

"Yo, Christensen, over here." I waved and attempted to position myself sexily in the doorway without looking like I was trying to scratch my back on the frame.

"Hey, Emma." He came in for a hug and kissed me on the cheek. "You got an itch on your back or something?"

"What? No, I mean, kind of yeah. It's gone now, though." I had about as much sexy in me as Clay Aiken's lazy eye.

We tiptoed past Jake and Jayla in the living room. They were sitting on opposite sides of the couch, eyes glued to the flat screen. There was a full-screen shot of Ellen Pompeo walking out of the hospital alone. She looked skinny as hell and had on her trademarked just-sucked-a-lemon scowl. I couldn't tell what episode it was because I'm pretty sure that shot is in every single one. I tried to mouth "Nobu" to Jake as Colin and I slipped past the TV and into my room.

Colin sat down on my bed and pulled a DVD out of his bag. "If you like *Napoleon Dynamite*, you're totally going to love this. *Little Miss Sunshine*. It's awesome."

Even though he sounded a little like the recording on Moviefone, I didn't care. It was so cute that he tried to find something that I would actually like instead of just bringing over a horrible alien apocalypse film . . . not like I'm talking from ten and a half months of experience with Bad Boyfriend Brian or anything.

"Awesome." I took the disc from the case. "I hope it's okay if we watch it on my laptop. Those two are hogging the big screen," I said as I set up my computer on my chest of drawers and pressed Play.

Colin had already lay down in my bed. I was so unsure of where to put myself in relation to him. I mean, I definitely wanted to cuddle, but I wasn't his girlfriend or anything, so I didn't want to seem too comfortable. I decided to strategically position myself parallel to him, with several inches of room between us, but close enough that he could put an arm around me if he wanted to. And as soon as the credits started, he snaked his hand under my neck and closed the gap between us. His touch felt so good and right. The anxiety from my meltdown seeped out of me and all I could think of was him. I made myself comfortable in the crook of his arm and looked up to smile at him. His face was already moving toward mine, tilted in perfect kissing position.

The kiss melted me, sweetly gentle. I kissed back and the kiss kind of never ended. There were a few points where we took breaks and fake-watched the movie, but it pretty much was a make-out-a-thon. By the end of the movie, his arm was around me like a blanket and I had curled myself into his body. This is how I wanted to stay for the next three weeks I was in New York. No, actually, I wanted the three weeks to be a loop of the last two hours on repeat. Colin and me smooching up a storm. No internship. No stupid book idea. No roommates. No city.

Twenty

"Welly, well, well!" I whistled as Jayla scurried around the apartment in her favorite Ella Moss dress. "What are you all dressed up for, Ms. Fancy?"

"Date! Jake! Late! Ahhh! Shoes?"

Rachel extracted Jayla's favorite Manolos from under the sofa and tossed them over to her. I plunked down next to Rachel to observe the frenzy fest.

"I'm sorry, I just hallucinated," I said. "I thought you said you were going on a date with Jake. My starfish cousin Jake." Had my cousin finally grown a pair and followed my advice? Surely not. "Did you ask him out?"

"Puh-lease!" she stopped mid-dash. "I don't ask guys

out. It sends them all the wrong signals. I am a prize to be won, not some desperate freak who begs men to like her. Women should never show the first signs of interest. Ever."

I think Jayla alone set the feminist movement back about fifty years.

"But enough yapping, girls. He's coming, like, any second, and I still haven't had time to put on my fake lashes."

"Jay, come on," Rachel laughed. "He's seen you bawling and covered in snot, you don't need to pretend it's Halloween. I think he already likes you."

"But they're Shu Uemera. I paid like a hundred dollars for the set and they will make me look flirty and glam," Jayla said with a dramatic wave of her slender arms, clearly copying some makeup counter woman. She then dashed into her bathroom.

"Lady, if one of those falls off into your forty-dollar lobster tempura, you will look"—Rachel mimed her same jazzy-hand flit—"ridiculous and transsexual."

"Where are you guys going?" I asked, still in shock that my Geek Machine 5000 cousin had actually managed to ask her out.

"He's taking me to Nobu." I heard her curse the eyelash adhesive at the bathroom sink. "He said it's his favorite restaurant, and it's totally mine, too. I mean, what are the odds?"

Rachel and I exchanged knowing smiles and suppressed giggles.

The phone rang and Jayla ran from the bathroom and lunged to reach it.

"Yeah, send him up." Jayla flushed with—could it be?—nerves. I didn't think that Jayla St. Clare got nervous.

"I think I need a drink," she huffed.

"No!" we shouted in unison.

"You need to stop meeting and seducing men when you're drunk. That's starting out on so the wrong path," Rachel preached. She was going to be a pretty good mom one day.

I had never seen Jayla so anxious, not even before the Carter barbecue.

"Fine!" she sighed. "But I gotta open this door, I feel like I'm suffocating!"

She flung the front door open the same second Jake appeared, his fist poised to knock. I could have run over and squeezed his cheeks, he looked so cute in his button-down shirt with his messy hair all combed and parted to the side.

"Oh, Jay! I, uh . . . ," he stammered.

"Yeah, me. Just . . . you know, door!" she fumbled. They were like two robots set to "Awkward," a cacophony of fumbles and half thoughts.

"You . . . nice," he managed.

"Dinner. Dress," Jayla offered incoherently before Rachel mercifully stepped in and suggested they go downstairs and get a cab. The instant the door latched behind the Awky Twins, Rachel and I burst into laughter.

"Beep bop boop!" Rachel said robotically, jerking around the apartment doing her best impression of Jake and Jayla. "Jayla equals pretty. Cannot compute hotness. Overload! Overload!"

"Doot doot doot! De Niro's sushi. Place. Equals love," I responded in monotone.

I was too focused on my robot dance to dodge Rachel's hand as she slapped me on my arm.

"Ow! What the hell?"

"Colin was over here last night, wasn't he? I just remembered that! You are such a shitbird for not telling me every single detail." She collapsed on the couch and got suddenly serious. "So, what happened?"

"I know, I know," I said, covering my face and blushing. For the first time in my life, I kind of didn't want to tell Rachel the details. Like, I could tell her about him being a good kisser and whatever, but that just wouldn't capture it. There was just something so right about Colin, like maybe it was that he was mature. Or maybe it was that he just wasn't Brian. I don't know. But it was almost like talking about it would taint it or make it less real or something. So I changed the subject and I told Rachel that maybe I would let her look at the stuff that I had written for *The Devil Wears Dockers*.

"I'd really love to. I'm totally into this editing thing at work. It's like it just came naturally to me. And I really like doing it." I could tell she was a little embarrassed about bragging, but I'm sure it was totally true. Rachel always was a pretty hard worker and got decent grades. She was probably kicking ass at her internship while I was just working for an ass.

"Well then, I'd totally be into hearing your ideas for sprucing it up when the proposal's done," I said.

"For sure. But hey, why don't you try making it into an article before you tackle a whole book instead? Maybe I could get this to be one of our home page updates or something. I could pitch it to Jamie." She was bubbling up with excitement. And I had to admit, as I let it process, it really was a good idea. An article seemed so much more doable than a book.

"Really? She'd listen to one of your ideas?" That'd be a first for The Dorf. Unless I rapped my suggestions. *Well, my name is Emma and I'm here to say, I ain't going to collate no more today. That's right, boss, I'm talking to you. And I need some cash for this busted job, too.*

"Yeah. Jamie is really awesome." Again, Rachel's voice turned serious. "You know, it's weird. I came to this city wanting boys, boys, boys and totally not even caring if I ended up getting fired from Sirlie or whatever. But being around all women all the time, well . . . they never talk about boys. Never. They talk about art, and traveling, and weirdo French movies that I've never seen. And they seem really happy. I kind of understand the whole 'girl-only school' thing. I just get so much done when I'm not worried about my lip gloss and how my boobs look."

For the record, Rach's boobs always looked fan-freaking-tastic. Still, what she said made me think about my total uselessness at work. Had I not been spending so much time totally obsessing about Colin, maybe I could've come up with a way to learn something this summer. And I mean something more relevant than discovering how much more awesome the vending machine's honey wheat pretzels were than the plain salted kind.

I sat on the couch for a while, thinking. Getting something published on Sirlie.com would be awesome, not to mention a boost for my college apps, which could make up for the internship being such a dud. Eventually I said good night and made excuses about being tired. But once I was in my bedroom with the door closed, I devoted the rest of the evening to getting at least one of my Derek stories ready for Rachel to submit to Sirlie. But even writing a short article wasn't easy. I wrote and deleted and rewrote for nearly three hours, not getting much further than page one. I tapped away on my keyboard until I heard the front door unlock and Jayla entering the apartment. I saved and then clicked my laptop closed and rushed out to the living room.

"Omigod, spill, spill, spill!" Rachel was squealing and jumping around Jayla when I came out of my room. We dragged her over to the couch and flopped ourselves down.

Jayla had a dreamy smile on her face. "Okay, so we get to Nobu and he was a total gentleman—opening the door for me, paying for the cab. All that. And then he walks up to the hostess and is like, 'Table for two.' And she asks if he has a reservation and he says that he *doesn't*! Can you believe that? He thought we could get into Nobu without reservations." Considering I don't think he'd even heard of the place before I mentioned it, I totally could believe it. But I kept quiet. "So I was like, 'Jake, I thought this was your favorite place. How could you not know to get reservations?' And then he confessed that he'd never been and just said that he liked it because you told him I did."

I gave a guilty shrug.

"Anyway, so we just walked around SoHo until we found the cutest little sushi place. And, you know, it was kind of better being somewhere quiet with him. And, like, people I knew weren't coming up to me every five seconds, so I could give our conversation all my attention. And he was just so cute the whole night. Anyway, here's where the story gets interesting." Rach and I leaned in. "Interesting" in Jayla terms can mean anything from making out with a B-list celebrity to, well, making out with an A-list celebrity.

"So, I excused myself to go to the bathroom and then on my way out, I stopped in the hall outside the bathroom and was fishing for my lip gloss in my purse and a man walks up to me and says, 'I'm sorry, I know you're here with someone but I can't take my eyes off you.' And do you know who that man was?"

"Carter?" Rachel guessed. Jayla curled her lips in horror at the mention of his name. I quickly yelled "Adrien Grenier?" to get her mind off Carter and whatever Jayla meltdown he was about to induce.

"Been there. But still, better!" Jayla shrieked, clapping her hands. "Adam Brody!"

Rachel and I screamed. How have I gone through this entire summer without seeing even one D-list celeb and Jayla can't leave the apartment without seeing someone drool-inducingly hot?

"You are kidding me!" I wailed. "Please, please tell me you left with him or at least got his number or made out in the handicapped stall! Or somewhere. Please, Jayla!"

Jay furrowed her brow and shrugged her shoulders, bewildered by her own actions and my complete lack of family loyalty. "No. I didn't. I mean, I have loved and lusted over that sex god since, like, back when *The OC* was on. I knew that girls would give kidneys to be in my place. And let me tell you, ladies, he is beyond hot in person. But I don't know. I could see Jake sitting at the table and he had this cute little smile on his face and just seemed so happy. And I realized that I was really happy whenever I was with him, which is even weirder. So I said, 'Sorry, but I'm here with my boyfriend,' and went back to the table."

"Boyfriend?" Rachel yelped, wide-eyed with disbelief that anyone could remember a husband of fifty years let alone a night-long relationship in front of such total gorgeousness. After one date can you really call a guy your boyfriend? Didn't you need to have the going-steady talk or at least a first kiss before you got that label?

"I mean, if I'd give up a night with Seth Cohen for Jake, then he has to be my bf, right? What better test is there than that?"

We shook our heads in total confusion and awe. I wondered if Jake knew of his elevated status from geeky tagalong to full-fledged boyfriend.

"Who knew that a lowly crustacean would catch Jayla St. Clare?" I laughed, and Jayla pretended not to remember calling Jake a starfish.

"Hmm. That doesn't sound like something I'd say." She suppressed a smile in mock seriousness and I hit her with a pillow. "You guys, the kiss was perfection!" She took a moment to sigh to herself. "Wow. Emma, if those kissing skills run in your family, your Colin is one lucky dude."

I was trying to be supportive and cool with the Jayla/Jake developments, but family kissing references might be where I drew the line. Total gagfest.

The next day, Colin picked me up and we went to a really cute little street fair on Bleecker Street. There were tables and tables of supercheap jewelry—of which I fully took advantage and left with some chunky bangles—all kinds of food vendors, and kiosks with I ♥ New York gear. Colin and I walked through the fair hand in hand. It was such a nice way to spend a summer afternoon. It almost felt like I was a grown-up.

After passing the last table of crafts, we went to sit in Washington Square Park and gorged ourselves on gyros and chocolate-dipped bananas. Once we'd washed the tzatziki and chocolate off our fingers with our water bottle leftovers, I rested my head on his shoulder. I felt like I was in a "diamonds are forever" commercial.

"What do you want to be when you grow up?" I asked, and realized how stupid that sounded as soon as the words hit the air. "I, uh, I mean, what *did* you want to be. You know, when you were a kid and stuff." Why was I so worried about Derek spilling the beans about me being in high school when I was so clearly going to slip up and turn myself in?

He chuckled. "I know what you mean." He put a hand on my knee. "Well, I really thought I was going to be a pro soccer player."

"Really? You were going to be the next Beckham?" I eyed him closely. "Hmm, yes, you're definitely hot enough."

He pulled me in for a brief kiss and squeezed my thigh. "Well, thank you for the blatant yet flattering lies. I tore my meniscus at the very beginning of senior year and haven't really played since. I tried, though, and ended up taking thirty-five aspirin a day because my knee hurt so badly. Anyway, when my dad found out, he made me stop altogether." He muttered a curse softly and scowled into the distance.

"Do you get along with your dad?" I asked cautiously, not wanting to get into a *Dr. Phil* special if he would rather not talk about it.

"I don't know, kind of. I was really messed up about the soccer thing for a long time. He was the one who had pushed me to do it for so many years. He was my coach all the way through middle school, and then in high school never missed a game. Soccer was our thing. You know— what we talked about and related everything to. Then it was just like, 'Okay, I say you're done, son.' And it was hard. I mean, hard with him and just plain hard. Soccer had been my life and all of my friends were soccer players and all of my free time was soccer."

I didn't know what to say, so I just stroked his hair. Again, I found myself comparing Colin to Brian, even though I knew what I had with each of them was so different. But in all of the time I spent with Brian, he'd never opened up to me like Colin just had. It just made whatever was going on with Colin seem so much more important and real.

"Anyway," he said dismissively, "so I just moved here after school. That's the good thing about Manhattan. You can just kind of disappear into the city and find yourself. People can be totally different from who they used to be."

I swallowed and nodded. Eventually I was going to have to tell this guy the truth, right? Maybe now was the perfect time. As fear and foreboding began to creep into my mind, I decided that it was far too nice a day to spoil with such unpleasantness.

We walked slowly, hand in hand, back to my apartment,

where we found Jayla all dolled up in a gorgeous little cocktail dress, her hands covered in what looked like flour. But judging by her wide-eyed panic, well, it could have been something far more potent.

"Who in the *hell* let me think that cooking for Jake was a good idea?" she shrieked, fumbling around in the utensil drawer for something we probably didn't have. "This is Phillip Lim. Dry cleaning is never going to get this burnt disaster smell out."

Smoke swirled around the kitchen and something was bubbling over on the stove. There was an explosion sound in the microwave and brown goop oozed out the bottom of the door.

Colin waved a hand in front of his face to clear the smoke. "So, what are you cooking?" he asked dubiously.

"Cooking? I'm not cooking anything." She was yelling over the sound of a beeping timer. "You mean, what am I burning? I'm burning that." She pointed to an open Tyler Florence cookbook without looking up from the drawer.

"Shiitake mushrooms in phyllo dough purses?" Colin asked. I was hacking on the smoke.

"That's just the appetizer," she said breathlessly. "Tequila-glazed chicken with a lime reduction sauce for the main course. Crap! Emma, do we have a zester?"

Colin and I exchanged worried glances and he bit back a laugh.

A zester? Didn't she realize that nothing more than takeout eating and Easy Mac nuking went on in this kitchen? "Did it come with the George Foreman? If not, I'm going to say no."

"Oh my God, this is a fucking mess!" she sighed with exasperation, and sank miserably to the kitchen floor. "I hate cooking and I have no idea what made me suggest it. That's it, I'm calling Tiny Thai."

She sat in her slump for a bit longer. Colin stepped over her to the still-beeping timer and turned it off. "That was driving me crazy," he mumbled, and then started to turn off the oven and made some moves to clean up the rest of the gourmet explosion.

"Jay, get up. I'm not letting my boyf . . ." I trailed off, not sure if I could really call him my boyfriend yet. "Colin. I'm not letting Colin clean up after you."

"Fine," she groaned dramatically, and pulled herself up off the floor, little chunks of pastry flour stuck to the butt of her dress. We all worked together to scrape the oven clean and wipe up the splattered counters. As Jayla tossed the last of the burned chicken and soggy dough balls into the trash, she speed-dialed for takeout, ordering fifty dollars' worth of upscale Thai food.

"Do not blow my cover!" she warned us sternly just after she hung up. Colin crossed his heart and swore to secrecy.

"Okay, thanks for your help, you guys. Do I still look okay?" She looked like she'd been through a culinary minefield.

"Um, you might want to change . . . and shower again," I said, trying not to insult.

Jayla dashed into her beauty parlor of a room and reprepared herself as we waited for the delivery guy. She was date ready by the time Jake arrived—thankfully *after* the delivery guy did—and she made me hide the empty takeout containers in my bedroom trash can. I heard her say, "Oh, this recipe? Ha, just something I learned at culinary school last summer," as I closed the door to my room to let them be alone.

"So," Colin said mischievously as he tugged at my belt, "whatcha feel like doing?"

"Hmmm. We could . . . read the Bible?" I joked, knowing full well what was on his mind.

"Uh-huh." He smiled and pulled me down so I was sitting on the bed next to him.

"Or we could have a milk-drinking contest." I pretended not to notice his mouth moving toward my ear.

"Keep talking," he whispered as he nibbled my ear. The ear nibbles and cheek pecks quickly turned into real kisses that went on forever . . . in-a-good-way forever, not a-long-day-at-work forever. Finally, with all of the courage that I could summon, I asked him to sleep over. In all my time with Brian, we'd only had one real sleepover, and that was at his prom. And like a million other people were in the hotel room with us, so it barely counted. Even though it made me totally poor, living without parents definitely had its benefits!

The next morning, I woke up to Colin standing over me, holding a brown paper bag. I smiled at his bed head fauxhawk. It was pretty cute on him. And then I realized that I probably had a freaky punk hairdo going on, too. I tried to casually finger-comb my hair into something remotely normal.

"Oh, good. You're up, sleepy. I just ran out for bagels. I got five—I figured Rachel, Jake, and Jayla would want some, too," he said, and then headed out of my room and into the kitchen to set the spread out on the counter.

I followed behind him, doing the still-half-asleep zombie walk. "Wait. Jake's still here?"

"Well, yeah."

I could be so clueless sometimes. If we were all adults, why *wouldn't* he still be there? Colin laughed and patted me on the head as Rachel came shuffling drowsily out of her room. Her morning hairdo made Medusa look like a Pantene commercial.

The lovebirds didn't emerge from Jayla's bedroom until after Colin left. The second Jake was out the door, Jayla pulled Rachel and me into her room. Honestly, I wasn't sure I wanted to hear the details. Jayla's graphic retellings of evenings with boys already made me a little uncomfortable, but knowing that the boy was related to me would definitely make it more cringe inducing.

"Oh. My. God!" she exclaimed, hugging her Juicy pillow. "Jake Freeman is a make-out machine!"

"Sweet Jesus," I sighed.

I could feel myself turning purple. Jayla started reliving the night for us, beginning at the second Jake walked in the door. I could tell she was about to get into the graphic details of the evening, and I totally was not ready to hear any of it.

"Jeez, I drank a lot of OJ this morning. I've got to pee." It was a flimsy excuse, but I really wanted to get out of there for the most heated parts of Jayla's evening recounting. "But don't stop. Keep going with the story. I'll catch up when I get back." Rachel tried to yank me back in the room, but I bolted way too fast.

After what I thought was an ample amount of time to relive one night of hard-core spit swapping, I peeked back in. Jayla and Rachel were still in storytelling mode.

"I don't even want to know," I interrupted from the

doorway. "Can we just eat the bagels Colin got us and never speak about my cousin's sexpertise ever again, okay?"

Rachel laughed and rolled her eyes, "Okay, okay. Hey, will you get me a poppy seed? With some capers and nookie—" Her eyes opened wide at the shock of her own gaffe. "Omigod, I meant *nova*, Em! Nova!"

Twenty-one

There was no way around it, the summer was winding down. Jayla and Jake were already making beach house plans for Labor Day, which was two whole weeks away. Meanwhile, I was spending my last moments in the city duping, dating, and stressing over Colin.

"Emma, you should probably fess up to this, okay? If he likes you, then he really likes you," Rachel said seriously over Sunday evening sushi.

"So not right, Rach," Jayla interrupted. "You're going to be leaving in a week, and realistically, you two probably won't keep in touch. Just enjoy it and let it be a summer thing."

The thought of Colin and me parting ways, never to be together again, made me sick enough to hurl up my miso.

"But this isn't just a summer thing," I whined. "I mean, it will be if I don't tell him the truth, you know? But maybe if I do, we'll work past it."

Rachel nodded as Jayla's head shook.

"Look, you've got to keep the lie going." Jayla was firm. "Just tell him that you got hired by a rival company in the city or something, then figure out the rest later." She motioned for me to pass the edamame, which I did.

That didn't sound like much of a plan. I poked at my seaweed salad and felt the knot in my stomach cinch a little tighter. The more I thought about ending things with Colin, the more ill I felt. Later that night, long after my sushi had digested, I still felt really crappy about things. I lay in my bed and ran my Colin options over and over. I decided that Jayla was probably right. I'd tell Colin that I was leaving MediaInc—which was completely true—and that this week would be my last. Also completely true.

Even with the decision set, I woke up in the a.m. still sick with remorse about heaping more lies onto my already ginormous lie pile. My workday of collating and coffee making was even more unbearable than usual because I couldn't even look forward to going home at five. Instead, I was going out to dinner with sweet Colin to tell him a big fat hairy pimple-covered lie.

We met at the restaurant—because Colin didn't want people at work to know that he was dating someone in the office—and I immediately broke the fake news.

"So, I'm starting at Media Corp next week. It was such a good offer, I couldn't refuse." I finished my fat fib and shoved a piece of bread in my mouth so I couldn't yell "Psych!" and ruin weeks of my carefully crafted cover.

"Oh, babe, really? Leaving MediaInc? I didn't even know that you were applying other places," he said. He frowned for a second, and for an instant I hoped that he'd see through my disgusting lies and smack some sense into me. But almost as soon as his scowl formed, it dissolved, breaking into a smile. "Hey, that means I can squire you around town without worrying that we're going to ruin both our careers. Things could certainly be worse."

He leaned across the table to kiss me, but I turned away, too full of guilt and afraid one smooch would infect him with my liar's disease.

"Um, you know, I don't really feel that well," I lied, and grabbed for my purse.

"What is this, another Freeman dine 'n' dash? I thought we'd moved past this," he only half joked. But I knew I had to get the hell out of there before something unpleasant came out of me, whether it be the truth or my lunch.

"I'll call you tomorrow," I said lamely, and ran out of the restaurant, maneuvering through tables of diners that were probably a whole lot less dysfunctional than I was. Finally outside, I took a deep breath, hoping that some fresh air would help the situation. But the humid ninety-something-degree lungful just made me feel even more like retching. Too nauseous to take the subway, I hailed a cab and jumped in.

"Why am I doing this? How did I get here?" I wondered aloud to the stinky leather seats. The driver was too busy yelling into his earpiece to notice my backseat meltdown. I rubbed my temples and decided for the millionth time that no, I could not come clean. I was almost done in New York. I could do this. I had to.

• • •

"Hey, Emmarooni! What's cooking?" Tuesday morning Derek was lunging into my cube and was just too god-damned perky for nine a.m.

I looked up from Seventeen.com and scowled at him silently, too tired from yet another sleepless, guilt-ridden night.

"Great news, Em Dawg. I have an end-of-the-summer project for you. I can't believe that I forgot about this all summer. Thank God I remembered before you left." He plopped his Rolodex down onto my cube counter. "I'm going to need you to enter all of these contacts into my Outlook electronic address book."

I fingered through the plastic-encased contact information. "There are at least a thousand business cards in this thing!"

He either ignored or didn't register the desperation in my voice as a mercy plea. "I know! This is a great way for you to get familiar with names in the industry. Think of how much you're going to learn in this last week." He shot me his finger-guns special and disappeared into his office to manage his fantasy football team.

I mentally replayed his last few sentences. *The industry.* Wasn't *the* industry showbiz? This was just *an* industry. And a sucky, boring industry probably filled with sucky, boring people. And after weeks of working there, I didn't even know a single thing about this industry. I flipped through the Rolodex. A card for a dog groomer. A handwritten number labeled "gutter cleaning." And one for his proctologist. Gross. Yep, it looked like I was going to be doing a lot of industry insider learning with this project.

At 9:07 I realized that I'd been at work a whole seven minutes and hadn't checked my personal e-mail. That might be a summer record. I logged into Gmail and there was a blank e-mail from Rachel. All it had was a subject line that read "Check out Sirlie.com NOW! ! ! !"

I clicked over to Sirlie and I couldn't believe it. An article entitled "The Devil Wears Dockers" was up online! My name was in print! Well, on a computer screen. But that was still really awesome. I quickly speed-read my work.

The Devil Wears Dockers
by Emma Freeman

I'm an unpaid intern, so low on the corporate totem poll that I'm practically underground. And that's fine, really, I signed up for it. But what I didn't know was that I had signed up for a summer in a warped version of *The Devil Wears Prada*. Except in this version, my Anna Wintour is a khaki-clad, over-the-hill manchild, and aside from one swiped bottle of Wite-Out, I got no swag.

Just to give you a taste of this Devil in Kirkland Signature, here's one of our conversations:

"Emma, have you been crying?" he bellowed loudly enough for the entire floor to hear.

"No, Eric. I haven't been crying."

"Really, Em? 'Cause you look sad. And I just thought that it might be not being able to lose that little bit of weight you've put on since working here." He leaned over, his huge gut cascading over the khaki fabric of his pants. "Because, you know, it's so stylish to be stick thin these days and all. I could understand why you'd be upset." And then he did the point-to-his-eyes-and-then-my-eyes move, which brought his creep factor up to an 11 out of 10. "I'm watching you, kid."

A variation of this conversation has kicked off every single morning of this summer. If it's not about me growing an office ass, it's about me looking hungover, or looking like I don't have enough makeup on, or being sad about not having a boyfriend. Really, the list is as long as the summer. And even though these a.m. conversations are so regular, he still always catches me off guard. Mostly because he kind of creeps up behind me, surprisingly stealthy for an obese man, and drums on my cube wall so that the entire shanty structure quakes and at least four of my pinned-up pictures of Pete Wentz come fluttering down.

I was so excited, my eye darted back and forth reading the article, especially my byline, again and again. After scrolling through for the fourth time, I reached for my cell and went to the supply closet to call Rachel where no one would hear me.

She picked up immediately. I didn't even let her say hello.

"So awesome, Rach! Thank you soooooo much. This has totally made the entire awful internship worth it. I'm a star . . . a chic feminist website star!"

"Yay! I'm so glad you're happy! For a second I thought you'd be mad that I took it off your computer, but you're such a perfectionist, you would never have sent anything to me." It was only then that I realized that I hadn't actually sent her the piece. And normally I would be pissed that she was snooping, but I was way too excited to get into a bitch match over something so small as a little prying. "And what you wrote was so good, we really didn't have to edit it much. People here are really digging it, too. Jamie says that in the hour you've been up, you've already gotten twice the hits that an article normally gets. And it's going to be up until Friday." I was practically glowing in the dark closet I was so pumped. It wasn't a book deal. But it was pretty cool.

"Holy crap. I really *am* a feminist star! Think any lesbians are going to hit on me now?" I joked.

"How many times do I have to tell you? *Fem-in-ists!* Not lesbians!"

"Rach, I'm kidding! Of course I know the difference. Okay, I've got to go, Derek has me working on this totally lame end-of-summer project." And then, all of a sudden, reality sank in hard. "Rach, oh my God! Derek! He could see this. What would happen to me?" While the whole idea of the book was to kind of seek revenge on the King of the Doofs, I was in such a dreamland when I was thinking about the fame and fortune of a book that I had barely thought about his reaction. Plus, the book wouldn't have come out while I was actually still working for him. There would have been way more distance from MediaInc. But this was so in his face while *I* was still in his face! My skin started to get hot from panic.

"Honestly, do you really care about his feelings?" Rachel asked. "He's never cared about yours."

"It's not just that," I responded. "What if he fires me and tells Golf Gal! Eileen who tells my mom? She'd hit the roof."

Rachel was completely calm on her side of the phone. "Let's get real here. Derek isn't exactly the target demographic for a sassy feminist site. He's probably never even heard of Sirlie, let alone checks it on a regular basis. He's never going to see this."

Just as I let Rachel talk me out of a nervous breakdown, a whole other rush of panic crashed over me.

"Oh my God. Oh my *God*, Rachel! *What. About. Colin?*" I hissed frantically into the phone, choking on my own words. Colin was another thing that I hadn't worried about when the writing idea was just an idea, not a relationship-shattering reality.

Again, Rach assured me that Colin likely wasn't a regular on Sirlie and would never see it. "But maybe this is a sign that you should tell him, Emma. I really can't see lying to someone you care about like that," she mothered me. "But seriously, don't forget to be happy about this. Getting published on Sirlie is a huge first step, okay? I'll see you tonight and we can celebrate your writing debut."

I hung up the phone and headed back to my cube, deflated and worried. What would I do if Derek or Colin saw the article? Maybe I could hack into MediaInc's Internet server and cut out the service for the next week. By the time it got up and running again, my piece would be buried deep in the Sirlie archives and Derek and Colin would be none the wiser . . . and by "wiser" I mean hurt, embarrassed, and betrayed. True, Derek was a total jerkass and kind of deserved this Internet shaming. But if this did somehow trickle down to my mother, I'd probably be in my mid-thirties by the time I was ungrounded.

As bad as that scenario was, it was *nothing* compared to the supersized fiasco that would ensue if Colin found himself face to face with my masterpiece. Rather than entertain thoughts of the disaster, I did what any smart girl would do, I went to the vending machine and stocked up. If anything was going to get me through today, it was going to be a caffeine-laced sugar rush.

When I walked in the door that night, Rachel had set up a little celebration station for me with two cupcakes, confetti, and a noisemaker that she was blowing so loudly, I was surprised our neighbors weren't evacuating for a fire drill.

"Congratulations!" she yelled, and jumped over to me for a hug. She pulled me over to the kitchen counter and shoved a chocolate-frosted cupcake at me. "Here, let's celebrate!"

After a day of Diet Coke and candy bars, the last thing I needed was a cupcake. But me saying no to baked goods happens about as often as a successful celeb rehab. Of course I dug in, but I still was not really in a celebratory mood. I just couldn't stop thinking of Colin and how much damage I'd done, even if he didn't find out through Sirlie. The truth was bound to come out at some point, and he'd just be in so much pain. Not to mention pissed.

"And the best thing about this is that it's all expensed by Sirlie." Rachel was estatic and totally wasn't picking up on my bummed-out vibes. "My boss is all about treating our writers to a little fun. I tried to get us some champagne, but totally got carded. It was so embarrassing because I tried to do the 'Oh no, I must have forgotten my ID, but I swear I'm twenty-one' thing and then the alcohol guy was like, 'Okay, what year were you born in?' and I just totally panicked and said, 'Um, 1971.' " She started laughing at how ridiculous that was and I couldn't help giggling, too. "That would make me like 107 years old or something! Anyway, I put the bottle back and jetted out of there as fast as I freaking could."

"This cupcake is the best thing I've put in my mouth ever." I could feel the frosting all over my face, but I didn't really care. I kept eating. "Even if Colin sees the article and totally blows up and hates me, I think this cupcake is even better than being with him. It might just make up for it."

Rachel was pretty intensely into her cupcake, too. "Definitely better than any JDate I've been on."

I heard my cell ring in my bag and went over to get it. "It's probably Kyle!" Rachel screamed. "I told him all about the article and to call you right after work." She started singing "For She's a Jolly Good Fellow" loudly enough for Kyle to hear on the other side.

But when I flipped open my phone, Colin's name was on the caller ID.

"Hello?" I answered, plugging a finger in my ear to drown out Rachel's off-key homage to my success.

"Hey, it's me," Colin replied. "What's going on? Are you walking by a cat in heat?"

I mouthed "It's Colin" to Rachel and she quickly shut up.

"Ha, no. That's just Rach. She's making a big deal about celebrating my . . ." And I just stopped and gulped, trapped.

"Your new job, right?" he filled in my pause. I breathed a sigh of not-quite-relief—because I was still totally on edge—but maybe of less stress. "That's why I'm calling, too. I want to take you out to dinner on Friday to celebrate your move to the competitor. And I promise, I won't pump you for company secrets or anything."

I agreed to the Friday date and hung up faster than I normally would. Maybe my next Sirlie article would be called "Beauty and the Bitch" and it would be a story about a perfectly lovely boy who falls for a girl who he thinks is just your average twentysomething but turns out to be an awful lying teenaged bitch.

I was starting to think I didn't deserve my name in computer-screen print. Aren't journalists bound by some sort of oath of truth? Or was that Pinocchio?

I spent the next three days procrastinating through the Rolodex "project" and crossing my fingers that neither Derek nor Colin had any sudden urges to research modern feminism.

By Friday I had only made it to the "B's" of Derek's business cards, but finally, finally, *finally*, the Internship from Hell was over! I decided to spend my last day looking through everyone in Bridgefield's Facebook pictures from the past two months and packing up my personal belongings and some office supply mementos. The remaining unentered twenty-four letters in the Rolodex would have to wait for the next soul unfortunate enough to be dubbed The Dorf's intern.

Surprisingly though, I was ambivalent about the internship ending—completely filled with joy at no longer having to meter out creamer into Derek's coffee, but also brimming with dread about leaving my connection to my . . . boyfriend? That was a talk we still hadn't had. I guess when you're older, you don't need to have the going-steady convo. Things just kind of happen.

Colin had made reservations at Supper to celebrate the alleged new job. I'd told him that I would just meet him at the restaurant because I'd be oh-so-busy cleaning out my cube and "tying up loose ends," whatever that's supposed to mean. Basically, I wanted to avoid blowing my cover on my very last day. I was almost home free with the lie of the millennium. I spent the morning meandering around the office, looking over my shoulder for my perfectly perfect boy. By eleven-thirty I hadn't seen Colin and figured that if Derek pulled his typical Friday one p.m. dash and I followed close behind, I'd be in the clear. But then, at 11:46, things took a turn for the worse.

I was checking out my article on Sirlie one more time. After all, it was my last day to see my name on the home page and I wanted to make the most of it. Why not bask in my fleeting fame for one more page load, right?

As my forty-eighth refresh of the page loaded, I realized that I wasn't alone. Thinking it was Derek, I quickly alt-tabbed to another window, hiding the evidence of Internet exposure.

"Hey you," said a surprisingly warm voice behind me. I turned to make sure that Derek hadn't somehow morphed into a normal, nice, non-freak since I'd given him his coffee this morning. Instead of mutant Derek, Colin stood there with a good-luck bouquet of roses and a big smile. "I know you don't need luck or anything else to carry home, but hey," his voice dropped to a whisper, "no one said your boyfriend was the smartest guy." He winked at me as my heart skipped a beat with his mention of the b-word. *Boyfriend!* "Hey, what were you just looking at?" Shit, shit, shit. I was so distracted by my "boyfriend" being a genuine sweetheart that I forgot that I was lying scum.

"Oh, that old thing about being an intern?" I quickly

spun back around in my seat, trying to avoid eye contact. "Nothing. Just something I wrote a long time ago. Like, when I was an intern. A really *long* time ago. Even before the Internet existed, so I'm surprised it's up here. I was just randomly Googling myself and I found it."

And I would have kept babbling, probably telling Colin that I had coauthored the piece with a caveman it was so old, but Derek, never one to mind his own business, came out of his office and, in total doofus style, butted in.

"So, what are you two talking about?" he asked. Then, not waiting for a response, "I was thinking of having lunch at Smith and Wollensky. Christensen, you down?"

"Yeah, sure, Derek. Emma, do you—"

"Yep, make reservations. Two. Twelve-thirty."

Colin opened his mouth to ask why I wasn't coming to the power lunch, but Derek cut him off.

"Can you believe it's this gal's last day? Man, the summer just flew by. And hey, I've never seen an intern get flowers on her last day before."

Colin did a double take at the word "intern." I could almost hear the crash-and-splatter sound of my entire life tumbling down around me. The next thirty seconds unfolded in horrifying slow motion yet happened too fast for me to stop it. Before Colin had a chance to react, Derek pulled a plaque out of nowhere that said "World's Best Employee."

"I couldn't find one that said 'Best Intern Ever,' but you are the best *intern* I've ever had. Really, ever. I mean out of all my summer *interns*." Colin's face morphed from confused to angry to angrier with each mention of the word "intern." Derek labored on, sealing my fate as worst summer girlfriend ever. Wait, scratch that—worst *person* ever. "Usually I pick college kids, but you really impressed me, and not just for a high schooler."

The last words landed like an atomic bomb as Colin—my boyfriend—turned white and then red with fury.

"High school? *HIGH SCHOOL!*" Colin shrieked. He was beyond simple anger—he was enraged. He looked like a tick about to pop

This. Was. A. Nightmare. A nightmare wrapped in my worst fears and then battered and deep-fried in a vat of my own disgusting lies. Colin stalked off as tears welled up in my eyes. I couldn't even manage to stammer out an explanation. Probably because there really wasn't one.

And as the cherry on top of this calamity sundae, Derek placed the plaque on my monitor and turned to leave. Right before he got to his office door, he turned around and called back, "And Emmarooski, don't let that award go to your head, okay?"

Twenty-two

A solid half hour crying in the handicapped stall later, I emerged from the bathroom, puffy-eyed and not much more emotionally stable than when I entered. But as I was practically crawling back to my desk, I stopped being upset and started getting angry . . . with myself. *I shouldn't be allowed to cry now. I'm the one who created this situation.* It's like when I eat sushi on a Sunday and then am shocked that my tummy hurts on Monday morning. I know that Sunday fish can't be fresh, but I still eat it. I give myself that stomachache. Same thing here—I did this to myself. How many times over the past few weeks could I have prevented this explosion from ever happening?

At Plumm: "*No, I don't know what a Caipirinha is because I'm in high school. And high schoolers only know what keg beer and schwag is.*"

At the vending machine: "*Want a peanut M&M? They melt in your hand not in your . . . I'm in high school.*"

At a weekend breakfast: "*Hey, you know what would taste good with these bagels? A high school diploma. Do you have one of those? I don't . . . yet.*"

I could have said something at any point over the past month, but no, I didn't. Instead, I just let the lie simmer up to a boil, not expecting to get burned. And the worst part of this was that I did it to Colin. Colin, who had been nothing but sweet and . . .

"Em-money!"

I take that back. The *worst* part of it all was that Derek had witnessed the whole thing and now felt like he needed to get involved. He leaned himself against one of my half cubicle walls, letting the fiberboard cut into his stomach chub.

"Not that it's really any of my business, but now that I'm pretty much not your bossinator anymore, I've gotta ask. Was something going on between you and Christensen?" He stuck his two index fingers out and then squished his fingertips together making kissy sucking noises with his mouth. There was no possible way I could be more shocked, disgusted, or humiliated.

"No, Derek." I wanted to crawl under my desk and not come out until Derek and his perverted nosiness had left for the weekend, but Derek would probably crawl under my desk with me and assault me there, too.

"Listen, Em. I'm nearly forty, and I'm not talking dog

years, here. So I've been around the block a few too many times to think that Colin's little tantrum and your puffy eyes aren't related. And I doubt he flipped out when he found out you were an intern because he thought you had full dental." He glanced down at me with an almost paternal look. "So why don't you tell me what's wrong. It'll make you feel better."

I really did need to vent about it right now, and my best friends in the city were not accessible. Rachel wasn't answering her cell and Jayla—well, on the off chance that she wasn't on a conference call with Chloe reliving every gory detail of her most recent shack-up with Jake, she'd say something like "Just be grateful that you got more experience with guys this summer. Being with only one guy for so long can leave you kind of stale." Totally not the kind of advice I needed right now. But talking to Derek?

"Plus," Derek interrupted my thoughts, "this is going to add a nice twist to the recs I'm going to write you. Hey-yo!" He dribbled an imaginary basketball and shot, making a swish sound for added realism.

Yeah, talking to Derek would be a huge mistake.

"Derek, I'm fine. I'm just going to spend the rest of the day cleaning out my desk and packing up, okay?"

"Your call, Em. 'Kay, I'm heading out to lunch." And while I knew that he almost never came back to the office after lunch on Fridays, I still half expected him to come back and give me a proper send-off. That couldn't really be his big farewell for my summer of indentured servitude. But of course, he didn't return to give me a hug or a thank-you more meaningful than a plaque from the dollar store. Whatever.

I poked around in my cube for a while, cleaning up and

watching my in-box, hoping for an e-mail from Colin to pop up. I prayed for a subject line to the effect of "You say statutory rape, I say tomato," with an e-mail containing his apology for getting so worked up over a number as silly as age. We'd laugh about the whole fiasco over our candlelit dinner at Supper. "The grandkids are never going to believe our how-we-met story," he'd say, and then joke about carding me every time he poured more wine in my glass.

When I finally unspaced from my daydream of pitiful impossibility, I saw that it was 4:53. I shut off my computer and any chance of hearing from Colin. I made my rounds, saying my last goodbyes to the few people I'd met in the office—the guy who sat by the Xerox machine and helped with paper jams and the woman who had the candy bowl on her desk, with whom I became friendly for obvious reasons. Then I made my way to the elevator bank with my box of cleaned-up cubicle.

The elevator dumped me by the security gates and I swiped myself out of MediaInc for the last time. It reminded me of pushing through the thick metal doors on the last day of school. June could have been three years ago, it felt so distant.

As I was making my way across the lobby, struggling under the weight of my box, I heard *his* voice. "Emma!"

I considered dropping my box of pilfered Dr. Grips and bolting. Instead, I turned to face him. Before he could say a word, I started blubbering an apology.

"Colin, I'm so sorry. That first time in the club, I thought that—"

"That what? You'd never see me again? That you'd get away with all of this? That lying to me was a good idea?"

I searched for an answer, but had none.

"Look, Emma, I really liked you. And I might have still liked you if I'd known you were an intern. But I don't like liars."

Tears began to spill down my cheeks and I prayed for a fire drill. Or a natural disaster. One of those makeover shows where they swoop in, abduct you, and yell at you for wearing an improperly fitting bra on national TV. Anything but to hear Colin bitch me out, even though I totally deserved it.

"Colin, please. I swear I didn't mean to hurt you. I wanted to tell you, but . . ." I dissolved into sobs and his steely gaze softened slightly at the sight of this pathetic adolescent snotting and weeping in the middle of five p.m. lobby traffic. God, I was making such a scene.

"Em, you are good enough just being yourself. You don't need to lie or pretend, okay?" He sighed heavily. "And now, I'm . . . I guess I'm just . . . really hurt."

I looked at his frustrated green eyes and miserably wished that I'd never met him, that I'd never dragged him into the mess that is Emma Freeman: Eighteen-Year-Old Intern Liar.

"Look, can't we just start over?" I sniffled. "Can't we just pretend that we've never met and call a do-over?" I realized how young I sounded and hated myself for it. So I did what I always did during tense situations, made a nervous joke. "You know, like calling a T.O.?" I looked up at him, trying to smile through my tears.

"T.O.?" he asked, and his eyes narrowed on me, coldly. "This isn't fucking Little League."

I jumped when he cursed. I wasn't used to it. And it stung.

He looked into the distance bitterly. "T fucking O.

Unbelievable. What, Emma—you wanna settle this with a nice game of tetherball, huh? How about I just give you a detention for dating without a hall pass?" Now he was just being mean, and I teared up again and whimpered miserably.

"Colin, stop," I wailed, wishing I wasn't holding a box so I could cover my wet, red face with my hands. "Stop saying things just to hurt me!"

"You?" he shouted, making the security guard inch a little closer and reach for his flashlight. "*I'm* hurting *you*? Do you have any idea how hard it is to date people in this city?"

I shook my head slightly, bracing for another onslaught.

"Well, let me break it down for you, Emma. The last chick I dated turned out to be married and the one before her left me for someone else. Someone named Melissa. So here I was, stupid me, thinking I'd actually met someone normal. Someone who I could just stand still with. But oh no. You took me for the biggest ride of all." His face morphed into steely anger.

And with that horrifying, gut-wrenching statement, he stalked away. Now it was his turn to be the one who dashed and left me standing alone. I watched as he pushed through the revolving doors and turned toward Madison, never looking back.

I couldn't bawl in the office lobby all evening. I shuffled my sad self through the revolving door, maneuvering carefully to avoid getting the box smushed. The New York–evening heat almost felt good against my air-conditioning-chilled tears. I pushed through the foot traffic and made my way underground, barely able to see through the puddles that had replaced my eyes. I moved slowly, partly because I felt like a slimy slug, but mostly because my box of personal effects and less-personal pinched office supplies was pretty heavy. And Derek's commemorative plaque must have been made out of lead and Star Jones's lipo fat, it weighed so much. Getting through the turnstile involved a lot of shifting, repositioning, and side shimmying. I knew I was holding up the line of Friday commuters, eager to get back to their couches and frozen dinners, but what could I do?

"Lady, let's get a move on," an angry voice said from behind me.

I whipped my head around. "Listen, I've been yelled at enough today when I deserved it. I don't need any shit from your fat ass! I'm in high school!" As if admitting that to this rando meant anything now. I rolled my eyes and shoved through the turnstile, losing a packet of neon Post-its along the way.

"Crap!" I shrieked, kicking them toward a homeless man slumped by the trash can. "Goddamn Post-its!"

What was wrong with me? Just because I had ruined my life and Colin's summer didn't give me the right to kill every New Yorker's evening. Mercifully, I got a seat on the subway and could mope myself home in relative comfort.

I opened the door to the apartment, half closing my eyes because I didn't think I could stand seeing Jake and Jayla canoodling on the couch. I'd probably puke all over their age-appropriate relationship. But instead of the cuddle bunnies, just Rachel sat scanning through HBO On Demand for sex scenes from *Entourage*. She jumped up when I opened the door.

"Jay, she's back! Let's get started on our . . . Oh no, omigod, what's wrong with you, babe?" Rachel's bombastic voice melted into concern. Did I really look that bad?

303

Jayla galloped out of her room wearing an I ♥ NY shirt that she'd cut at the neck and sleeves so it almost looked cool. "Okay, I'm ready! Holy shit, Emma. Did you get hit by a cab or something?" I definitely looked that bad.

I set my office stuff down on the floor and kerplunked onto the couch. As painful as it was to relive it, I went through the day's events in so much horrifying detail that the story was pretty much told in real time. I winced as I verbatim acted out Colin's final diatribe. "I just want to melt into a greasy puddle of self-loathing and marinate for a few days, hating myself," I managed to squeak out before the hard-core tears started.

"Well, look at the bright side. At least you got to make out with someone who wasn't Brian. Being with the same person for—" Of course Jayla went there.

"Jay, she doesn't want to hear shit like that now," Rachel cut her off, mercifully. "I'm so sorry, hon. Are you just going to let this be or try and talk to him again?"

I collected myself a bit and looked at Rachel. "I don't know. I mean, I want to talk to him. But, like, what do I have to say to him? No way an apology alone is going to make this okay."

I wanted Rachel to come up with a plan, a way to explain away the summer of psycho to Colin. But instead she just nodded, agreeing that there was no way to mend what I'd done. My stomach knotted and I sank my head into Rachel's lap and began crying all over again.

"Well, you've heard me say it before, Em, I don't like crying in this apartment," Jayla said with levity in her voice. She bolted back into her room and out again. In her hands were two more hand-cut I ♥ NY T-shirts, which she threw to Rachel and me. Mine was cut into a belly-baring tank and Rachel's neckline was so low that there was barely any ♥ left.

"Put them on," Jayla demanded. "Since this is your last weekend in New York, I thought we'd do everything this town has to offer. You know, tourist-style. Like see a Broadway show and eat at one of those stack-'em-high delis and go to Chinatown and do whatever Asian stuff you're supposed to do down there."

"And see the Sears Tower?"

That made me smile, ending my afternoon-long sourpuss. I might be bad at boys but I had really lucked out in the friendship department. "That's still in Chicago, Rach."

"Whatever. Let's go do something fun now. It'll cheer you up."

I kind of wanted to stay in, wade in the aforementioned puddle of self-loathing, and try to will a text from Colin into my phone.

"Em, you are so not staying in tonight." It was like Rachel could read my mind.

"Uh, no way. Plus, *Law & Order* is a rerun. I checked. And we don't have any ice cream left. There's absolutely no reason for you to stay in," Jayla said, hands on hips. "So, get yourself into the T-shirt I so lovingly crafted for you and get ready to have fun."

I went into my room and pealed off my business-casual clothes. I threw my outfit on the floor and slipped on my homemade belly shirt and some jeans. Just as I was starting to feel less awful, I saw the *Little Miss Sunshine* DVD that Colin left the very first time he came over. Just days earlier that boy was in my room and everything was right with the world. My knees gave out and I sank to the floor, wailing into the sheepskin throw rug.

At the sound of my body thunking onto the floor, Jayla appeared in my doorway. "Oh, honey, no!" she said, rushing in and scooping me up, propping me against my full-length mirror. "Now think about this. Say things had worked out fine, he was cool with it, blah blah blah. Do you have any idea how miserable your senior year would be? He couldn't come to homecoming, prom, Sadie Hawkins, anything. And worse, you'd sit home every party, every weekend trip, just to call him and then obsess about whether or not he was cheating on you."

"No I w-w-w-ouldn't!"

"Yes you would! Remember my friend Chloe? I've known her since boarding school and our senior year she was dating this guy Jason who played for the Rangers. Her *entire life* revolved around talking to him or trying to fly out to see his games. Like, yeah, it was kind of cool, but looking back, she says she regrets that more than getting a perm in sixth grade. A *perm*, Emma!"

I laughed against my will and tried to picture the sophisto Chloe with poodle hair.

Jayla hugged me reassuringly and looked into my eyes. "Now, are you ready to have some fun now? Not a lot, just a little?"

I sighed with resignation. It didn't look like I was getting out of this easily. "All right, lady. Let's do it."

"Are you sure you're okay with me talking about this?" Jayla asked over a trough of Serendipity's frozen hot chocolate.

I shrugged back at her, not able to speak, my mouth so full of chocolate.

"I just don't want you to act all grossed out and leave like you did last time."

I swallowed. "Omigod, Jayla. He's my cousin! I knew him back when he wore holiday-colored rubber bands on his braces. It's just that I kind of don't want to hear sexy stuff about him."

"I do though!" Rachel butted in. "Spill it, spill it, spill it." She banged her spoon on the table and Jayla looked at me for clearance.

"Fine, I'll suppress all gag reflexes." I dug back into the goblet of chocolate we were sharing.

"All right, well, three words for you: lots of tongue!"

"Yeah?" Rachel egged her on. I had no idea how I managed to keep down the few bites of dessert.

"Like, I know it sounds gross. But it really makes him, like, the best person I've ever kissed."

"I've got to go to the bathroom," I said as I scooched my chair out.

"What, Em? I thought you said you were cool with this," Jayla said, hand poised so she could demo Jake's kissing abilities on it.

I never really said I was cool with this at all. But that's not why I was leaving the table. "Um, hello! I'm going to barf up my dessert because I want to be skinny, not because of Jay and Jake," I teased. But the sad truth was that I couldn't stop thinking about Colin. Gooey chocolate desserts are normally the Neosporin to my emotional wounds, but the Colin debacle was so traumatic that even dessert couldn't help me. What I needed was closure, a chance to offer an explanation or at least a real apology.

As soon as I was out of sight, I fished my cell out from

the gum wrapper depths of my purse. I waited through the five rings I knew were being screened and then his voice mail message. He sounded normal, warm, I could tell he was smiling just from listening; so different from the shrill shock of this afternoon and the deep anger in the lobby.

I took a breath at the sound of the voice-mail beep and then launched into my final plea. "Hi, it's me. Listen, I know I don't deserve to ask you for anything. But I'm leaving New York Monday morning and I really can't bear to end with you like this. Can't we just talk once before I go? Call or text if you feel like it, okay?"

I flipped my phone shut. There, at least I felt a little better making an attempt to end this like the adult I'd been pretending to be all summer. That was pretty much all I could do for now. I guess it was up to Colin now to decide how we were really going to leave things. I tried to forget about this drama and plastered on a happy face to head back to our table.

"Seriously, it's like so long," Jayla was saying to Rachel.

I rolled my eyes. "Please tell me you are not talking about anything having to do with Jake. Pretty please."

"No, Em. That's sick." Rachel was shaking her head. "Jay was just telling me about that line in Times Square where we can buy tickets for a Broadway show. I definitely want to go to one tomorrow."

"And as I was saying, the line is, like, ridiculously long. And by the time you get to the front, the only thing that's left is, like, *Tarzan the Musical*."

"That's cool, I'd see that," Rachel said, unaware that Jayla meant the show was awful.

True, at that point I may not have been at my best. But

mark my words, Emma Freeman will never know the kind of low it would take for me to willingly see *Tarzan the Musical*.

"Um, why don't we try to get student tickets to *Wicked* or *Avenue Q* or something else that's a lot less Phil Collins," I offered.

Jayla nodded eagerly.

"Okay, whatever." Rachel shrugged. "But that's tomorrow. What about the rest of tonight? We're done with this." She pointed to our spoon-scraped bowl.

"Okay, so I was thinking we could either go up to the top of the Empire State Building or go home and watch all of my *Sex and the City* DVDs and rest up for a day at Coney Island tomorrow." Coney Island? I remembered one time when she said that East Brooklyn was where store-brand douchebags go to die and she would rather spend three months in Guantanamo Bay than spend a day lying on a beach full of Guido trash. But the new, loved-up Jayla was in total tour-guide mode.

"I'll sleep when I'm in the suburbs. Let's do both!" Rachel cheered.

Twenty-three

The next morning, I woke up to the sound of Rachel's voice.

"Wakey, wakey! Rise and shine! Get out of bed, it's breakfast time! Are you up, Emma Freeman?" she boomed, and then bounded out of my room.

"Oh my God!" I yelled with sleepy contempt. "I am not one of your little campers, Wolfe. I'm the same size as you and I will beat you like I own you if you ever wake me up like that again."

I normally wasn't a morning person, but I was especially hurting today. I felt like I had an emotional hangover from all of yesterday's drama.

"Get up! We got you a New York breakfast," Jayla hollered from somewhere outside my room.

How could both of them be awake? I don't think that I'd seen either of them up before noon on a Saturday this entire summer. I shuffled out of my room, barely able to open my eyes. Jayla and Rachel were hustling about, already in beach gear and hot to go.

"How long have you little morning spazzes been up?"

"Like, since seven," Rachel said. We'd gone to bed at four a.m. the night before after watching two entire seasons of *Sex and the City*. How those two were up and bouncing around, I had no idea.

"Yeah. Sit, eat, then get ready, 'kay?" Jayla pointed to one of those huge deli cuts of New York cheesecake sitting on the kitchen counter. Half of the cake and almost all of the fruit topping had already been forked away.

"Thanks, ladies. But there's no way I'm going to eat that and then put on a bikini. I already have this"—I slapped my newly acquired four pounds of office butt—"from sitting down all day, every day this summer. I'm just going to get ready."

I shimmied into my swimsuit and packed a beach bag with a towel, sunscreen, and enough back issues of *Us Weekly* and *People* to keep me busy for a month.

The energy radiating off of those two must have been contagious, because suddenly I was pumped. I jumped from my bedroom doorway into the living room. "Ta-da! World's fastest getter readier is ready!"

With bikini bow ties sticking out the back of our tanks, we headed out of the apartment and into the subway station.

"Ms. Jayla St. Clare, I thought that you'd sworn off public transportation and all its germ-ridden horror," I said as I squeezed myself between Rachel and a sweaty man in a T-shirt with the sleeves cut off.

"Whatever. We're doing a New York tourist weekend and real tourists don't call their daddy's car service to chauffer them around. But"—she put her hands up—"I'm still definitely not going to touch anything." She lurched back as the train started moving, almost falling into a baby stroller.

A forty-five-minute ride through Brooklyn later, we stepped out into the blazing heat of Coney Island. The place was so packed, it felt like a mosh pit, only with fanny packs.

"Yowzah," Rachel said, looking at the mass of people milling around. "Looks like the rest of Manhattan had the same idea we did."

"Yeah," I agreed. "And all of Jersey, too."

I was expecting Coney Island to be like a mini Disney World, but it was more like Disney World's long-estranged, heroin-addicted second cousin. The ground was covered in a potpourri of cigarette butts and fast-food wrappers. The rides looked so rickety and not up to safety code that I assumed everyone on them had a suicide wish. And it seemed like there was a strict dress code for the beach involving at least seventy-five pounds of pure blubber, a highly defined T-shirt tan, and some variation of a mullet.

We finally managed to push our way through Nathan's-hot-dog-eating crowds. From the boardwalk, we scanned the towel-strewn beach for an open piece of sand and found nothing. Even with Rachel's nine a.m. wake-up call, we hadn't made it there early enough. Apparently, freakazoids were all morning people. We decided to walk around and see if there was anything else aside from overcrowded beaches and hairy men in tank tops that Coney Island had to offer.

In the mid-August heat, we strolled along a street lined

with water game booths and meat-on-a-stick vendors. Rachel's eyes widened at something she saw in the distance.

"Airbrushing! Let's all get matching T-shirts that say something sassy!"

Jayla and I shot her uncertain looks.

"Oh my God, you guys. Yesterday we wore I Heart NY shirts. There's nothing we could possibly put on these shirts that would be any lamer than that. Plus, what do we care what these people think of us?" She motioned to the swarms of sweaty people. "Most of them are probably too learning disabled to even read what we write anyway."

I looked around. She was right. "Okay, so what are we getting on the shirts?" I kind of wanted to suggest something like "Never leaving Manhattan again!" but thought that might get us knifed.

"Something really fun and New York. Like . . . New York Gals?" Rach suggested.

"It needs to be way more glamorous than that. Plus, only grandpas say 'gals,' " Jayla responded, rolling up her tank to try and get some color on her stomach.

" 'Sex and the Summer'? '30B Ladies'? 'New York 4-Eva'?" I listed off totally jacked ideas.

"I said glamorous, Em. We need something hot . . ." Jayla trailed off in thought.

I looked down at myself, sweat seeping through my tank top and feet muddied from a combo of perspiration and the short walk on the dusty street. I could even feel my cover-up and mascara melting off my face. "Ugh, well, right now I feel like a hot mess."

"That's it! 'Hot mess'!" Rach squealed, clapping her hands. "That's so what this summer was. So many boys. So much drama. So much fun. A total hot mess."

Rachel sounded just like the final scene of a chick flick, but she was so right. No two words could sum up this summer better than "hot mess."

"Done!" Jayla said, slapping her twenty bucks down on the counter.

As I hunted for my wallet in the black hole that was my bag, I felt my cell vibrating. Abandoning the wallet search, I found the phone and my heart jumped into my throat. I mouthed "It's Colin" to the girls and moved away from the airbrush booth crowd.

"Hello?" I asked, attempting to sound like I didn't know who was calling.

"It's me." His voice was so serious.

"Oh, hi there. Ummm . . ." I let it drift into an awkward pause that neither of us was quick to fill.

"You said you wanted to talk, Emma. So talk." His voice was still just as angry as it had been in the lobby the day before. And I was frozen. There was so much that I needed to say to him, but I couldn't squeeze anything out.

"I'd rather talk in person. What if you come over tomorrow and we can really talk?" My voice was squeaky with how nervous I'd suddenly become.

"I don't want to come over to your place ever again." I was taken aback by his harshness.

"Okay, then let's meet out, somewhere between our places," I offered.

"Fine, there's that place on Spring and Lafayette. Let's meet there tomorrow at eleven."

"Okay, that sounds good. We can get coffee or something and talk."

I was worried about how to end the conversation. *"Talk*

to you later"? *"Have a good day"*? *"No, you hang up first, silly"*? Nothing felt right. Apparently, Colin wasn't having the same struggle. "Bye, Emma." Click.

I found Jayla and Rachel back at the paint booth, Rachel already wearing her new hot-pink graffiti T-shirt and holding Jayla's tank top down while she slid hers over her head.

"How'd it go?" Rachel tossed me my shirt.

I bit my lip and put on my tee.

"That bad?"

"Yep," I said as my head popped out the neck hole. If I let myself think any more about how cold Colin had been, I probably would be shivering even in this boiling weather.

"Are you going to see him before you leave or anything?" Rachel asked, her eyes filled with worry.

"Yeah, tomorrow." I looked down at the ground, trying not to cry. "You know, I'd rather not talk about it now. Let's just focus on having some fun in this freakfest."

Jayla looked around and gave a dramatic sigh. "I think these T-shirts are all the fun we can squeeze out of this place. Let's get someone to take a pic and then get out of here and back to the motherland of Manhattan."

She tapped a somewhat normal-looking girl on the shoulder and gave her a minitutorial on how to point and shoot with her iPhone. The three of us wrapped our arms around each other and posed as the stranger clicked a shot. We wriggled out of each other's hold.

"I think I dripped a whole pint of sweat on you guys, sorry," Rachel apologized. I wiped off her sweat, telling her it was no biggie, and I felt my purse vibrate again. Thank God—Colin was calling back to apologize for being such a dickface. I opened the phone sans caller ID check.

"Baby, I'm so glad you—"

"EMMA MARIE FREEMAN!" my dad's voiced roared. "I just opened my credit card bill. Eleven hundred dollars?! This card was for emergencies only!"

"Daddy, I—"

"And just what in the hell is 'Anthropologie'? You spent three hundred dollars there alone!"

"Uh, it's kind of like the Learning Tree," I stammered. I'd totally forgotten about my spending sprees on my dad's dime and I'd kind of hoped the credit card company would, too. "You know, like for people who are interested in learning about New York culture."

I held my breath and prayed he'd buy that ridiculous lie. I thought I'd gotten away with it until I heard my mom in the background.

"Isn't Anthropologie where I bought you those hundred-and-fifty-dollar jeans for your birthday last year? I don't think you ever did wear them."

"So you used the emergency credit card on clothes?" my dad fumed. "Are you serious? We send you to New York this summer, pay your rent, give you a more than generous allowance, trust you to be out there on your own, and this is how you behave? Young lady, I expect to be paid back. And if that means you getting a job and working through Labor Day and having to miss our family trip to the Renaissance Festival, fine. No one's going to feel sorry for you."

A summer away from parents and you forgot what total Nazis they could sometimes be. Obviously I didn't care about missing the Renaissance Festival, but God, at least give me a chance to explain before launching into punishment central.

"Dad, I'm so sorry! I needed clothes for work and I've been really good with my budget here. I take the subway all the time." Saying it aloud made me realize how lame my summer financial strategy had been.

"Would you say you've saved over a thousand dollars on public transportation? I'd guess not. And what is all of that hullabaloo in the background?"

"We're at Coney Island."

"Oh, I see, a weekend vacation? Is this also going to pop up on my Visa bill?"

"No! Dad, Coney Island is in Brooklyn and it's totally ghetto. It's not a weekend trip."

"Emma, you have lost the privilege of calling people 'ghetto,' since you're currently in debt to your family."

And then he hung up on me. Is anything worse than your own father hanging up on you? Yes, knowing that he's probably going to charge you for the cell phone minutes you used while he yelled at you.

I put my phone away and buried my face in my hands. Things had gone from crappy to ultracrappy in under twenty-four hours.

"What's wrong?" Jayla asked, pulling the bottom of her "Hot Mess" shirt out so she could look at the airbrushed unicorn that she'd paid an extra five dollars for.

"Everything!" I moaned. "My dad's mad at me, Colin hates me, and I'm so sweaty that this stupid spray paint is staining my bathing suit."

"Yeah," Rachel mumbled. "We should've just gotten key chains."

"Look, I need to get out of here or I'm going to freak the heck out, okay? Can we just go home or something?"

"Fine by me," Rachel sighed, twirling her finger and scowling at the Guidos. "Let's get some hot dogs for the train ride home. Who knows how long it will take to get back to civilization?"

"Forty-five minutes on the subway or four minutes of whining to my dad until he agrees to send a car to pick us up," Jayla said, and winked at us as she pulled out her phone.

A few minutes and a lot of sweet-talking later, we were on our way back to Manhattan in leather-seated, air-conditioned luxury.

Twenty-four

"So, are we doing Broadway tonight or what?" Rachel asked. She had just stepped out of the bathroom and was footprinting water all over the apartment.

Even though this was our last weekend in New York and Rachel was so gung-ho on packing as much in as possible, I was beyond exhausted. The combo of Colin, Coney Island, and my dad had totally worn me down. "I don't know." I started my attempt to bail. "I feel like I have to prep for my talk with Colin tomorrow."

"What's there to prep for?"

"Hello! A ton of stuff," Jayla hollered from her room. "What do you want to say? How do you want to say it?

What's your theme? What are you going to wear? There's tons of prepping." She peaked out of her doorway and threw me a serious look. "So like, what do you want your theme to be?"

Theme? She was making this sound more like a costume party than an apology. "I don't know. How about 'I'm an asshole.' I hear it's *the* hot look for fall . . ."

Sensing my need for prep, Jayla came all the way out of her room, also sopping from a shower. "So okay, 'I'm sorry,' then what? 'I'm sorry, take me back'? 'I'm sorry, and you can't have me'? 'I'm sorry and I'm so upset I'm going to eat until I look like a postdivorce Jessica Simpson'?"

I bit my nails, totally unsure how to handle things, and waited for Jayla to tell me exactly what to do.

"Okay, I vote for 'I'm sorry, but you'll want me when I'm old enough,' " Jayla offered.

"What does that even mean?" Rachel asked from across the room.

"You know, like later he's going to regret that he dumped you for something as little as—"

"As lying about my age, education, and job?" I cut in.

"Yeah, like, so what? He's upset that you're not twenty-two? He wants you to be older? Let's show him what you'll look like when you're mature and twenty-two and then he'll know what he's missing."

The words coming out of Jayla's mouth made absolutely no sense to me, but Rachel was nodding from her side of the room.

"We'll need to start with the wardrobe." Jayla readjusted her towel and got up, heading back to her room and walk-in closet. She emerged with a pile of designer black. "Here, try all of this on." She tossed everything at me.

I slipped out of my "Hot Mess" tee and put on all of Jayla's gear. The dress was a black merino wool number, the shoes, while round-toed, were dangerously high, and patterned tights completed the ensemble.

"I don't know," I said as I tugged at the turtleneck.

"Are you kidding me? That's Dolce & Gabbana, honey. This is the outfit I bought for my great-aunt's funeral last February. Really, you're not going to get more sensible chic than this."

"Very sensible chic," Rachel parroted.

"And I'll give you a cute little chignon updo tomorrow and makeup. I'm thinking a dramatic look." Jayla nodded, agreeing to her own plan.

With my hair, clothes, makeup, and script for the next day's encounter set, Rachel moved the convo back to Camp New York.

"Okay, so seriously, are we doing Broadway or not?" Rachel whined.

"Uck"—Jayla rolled her eyes—"musicals are so . . . bourgeois. And now they're, like, where *American Idol* losers go to die."

"Jayla St. Clare, come on," Rachel huffed. "Have you ever even seen a musical?"

"Yes!" she said indignantly. "I saw *Into the Woods* in high school and it was terrible."

"Okay, that is not the same as Broadway," I laughed.

Jay rolled her eyes again, this time in defeat. "Fine, fine, fine."

As well-intentioned as Jayla's makeover for the Colin confrontation was, I needed more than just an ensemble and a tagline. I really just wanted some time to be alone with my thoughts. "You guys go. I don't feel up to it. Plus, Daddio has totally cut me off for the time being. I have no way to pay for the cab ride up there, let alone the tickets."

After several rounds of "Emma, are you sure . . . like really sure?" I convinced my two roomies that I wouldn't implode with nerves and self-pity if they left me alone for three hours. As the door slammed behind them, I nestled myself into the couch, relaxing comfortably into my nightly spot from my first weeks in the city.

"Oh, good. You still remember my butt imprint," I said out loud, patting the cushions and sinking in.

The next morning, I teetered on four inches of Christian Louboutin as I made my way out of the subway station on Spring Street. Barring a burlap sack or wetsuit, there was no other outfit in which I would have been less comfortable. I felt like a casserole baking inside the black wool, and the shoes had already blistered my feet on the walk from my apartment door to the elevator. Between the tight bun and the caked-on/sweated-off "dramatic look," my head looked like Dali had painted on a New Jersey facelift. And as a finishing touch, Jayla had let me borrow her very emo glasses, so I could barely see.

I wobbled into the restaurant at exactly eleven a.m. and up to Colin, who was talking to the hostess. Then, in a move that may have been too personal considering our frosty situation, I put my hand on his back and, as warmly as I could, alerted him to my presence. "I'm here."

"Emma, what are you doing?" came Colin's voice from behind me.

The Colin at the hostess stand turned around. I took off my glasses to see a fifty-year-old face staring back at me and whipped my head the other way to see the real Colin.

Feeling like a total moron, I folded up the glasses and shoved them in my purse, hoping that this wasn't a sign of how the rest of the Colin talk would go. I apologized to the older gentleman and then followed the real Colin as we were led to a booth. A waitress came immediately.

"Just coffee," Colin answered for the two of us. His idea of a talk was really just a talk, not the love reconnection over western omelets I had envisioned.

"So," I started, not sure where to take it from there.

"So," he said back to me, also not willing to be the first to delve into the real conversation.

Before I could even begin to figure out how to start, I was already wading in the middle of it. "Colin. I'm sorry. I am really, really sorry. I'm sorry that I deceived you. And I know that this sounds impossible, but it really wasn't intentional. I told you I was older at that club because you were just a stranger. And then when you became more than just a stranger, there was never a good way to fix it. And I know, any way I could've told you would have been better than how you found out. I know. I should have said something, but I didn't because I'm a coward and I'm selfish and I just wanted to keep seeing your face."

I realized that for the first time with him, I was being totally, 100 percent honest. I knew that at this point, honesty probably wouldn't be enough, but it was all I could do.

I pressed on in a steady and determined voice, "I wish I could undo the lies, but I can't. So, I'm sorry."

He nodded the whole time I spoke, stirring sugar into his coffee. He took a sip, leaving silence between us. When the mug was back on the table, he said, "Emma, I guess that's all I can ask of you, an apology. I wish it could all be undone, too, but it can't."

"Then can I ask you one more question?"

He sipped and nodded.

"Does it matter? So I'm in high school and so I'm eighteen, but we really connected. And even though you didn't know it, you connected with an eighteen-year-old high school almost-senior. If we got over the trust issues, could we make it work?"

He laughed. "Jesus Christ, Emma. You're eighteen! We're at totally different points in our life. I mean, I'm working here in New York and you're in high school in . . . you know, I don't even know where your high school is."

"Bridgefield," I answered, facilitating his rant on how not meant for each other we were.

"Upstate! You want long distance on top of all this bullshit? Come on. When I was in college, you were in middle school. I mean, do you even know who Nirvana is?"

"Of course I do." I looked down into my coffee, hoping he wouldn't push me for the facts on that one. He waited for more of an answer, definitely pushing. I lifted my chin in feigned confidence. "They did a commercial for Teen Spirit."

"Ugh," he sighed disappointedly. "Exactly my point. We're not on the same page at all." Why was nineties music the bane of my summer?

"Fine, whatever." I was actually getting a little bit pissed off. If he hadn't wanted to even entertain the idea of us getting back together, why the hell had he agreed to meet me? Pure humiliation? Spite? Screw that!

"So you and I don't work because I don't know enough about has-been rock bands, is that it? That makes a lot of sense. Maybe you can end your next relationship because your girlfriend never played Super Mario Brothers on the original Nintendo system. Sound good?" My head was starting to ache. Was it the mega-tight bun slowly ripping my hair out or the stress of my heart being crushed all over again?

"Em"—he reached across the table and grabbed my hand—"I'm not saying any of that to devalue the past month and a half. That did mean a lot to me, you know that."

I shook my head and blinked back tears. "It *did* mean a lot to you. Past tense."

He squeezed my hand. "It hurts me to see you upset, Emma. But realistically, where would this go? Am I even allowed to go to your prom? I mean, think of how ridiculous that is. You need to be with someone who really understands you, and honestly, I don't. I don't get who you are or where you are or any of that. This is how it is when you grow up. Things don't always turn out with kisses and sunshine and puppy dogs. It's not an episode of *Dawson's Creek*."

"You mean *One Tree Hill*, you decrepit old man." I meant it to sound harsh. He was being so superpatronizing, I wanted to strike back. But differentiating between angsty teen television shows was just plain ridiculous, and we both realized it. Giggles escaped our lips and loosened the knots in my chest.

It was then that I realized there was nothing else to say. As angry as I was when he'd said it, I knew that Colin was right about this never working out. Some things just aren't meant to be, and if you force them, they get ugly. Kind of like Britney being a mother.

So, with a big sigh, I gave up. I tried to buy his forgiveness by picking up the five-dollar coffee tab and we walked outside. On the street, we made vague promises about keeping in touch that I think we meant. But even High School McGee here isn't naive enough to believe we really would. I knew that the early fall e-mailing and MySpace messages would fade. And the only connection I'd have to him would be whatever popped up when I got bored enough working on my personal statement to Google him. I knew, in the deepest part of my crushed heart, it was over.

Twenty-five

On the ride home from the coffee date/breakup, I hung my head out the window like a cocker spaniel as the cab zoomed up Broadway. I didn't care that the taxi was going to put me another five bucks in the hole to my parents—I was going to be a chore workhorse for them until college to make up for the summer Visa bill anyway—or that my chic updo was going to end up looking like a frizzy cone.

When I got home, Jayla was helping Rachel stuff her belongings back into her body-sized rolling luggage.

"Did my clothes mate in the closet or something?" Rachel asked, not noticing me standing in the doorway. "I feel like there's so much more going back than when I arrived."

"Well, if you had stopped buying tacky-ass shoes at Strawberry all damn summer, you wouldn't need—" Jayla looked up from punching Rachel's tank top collection into the suitcase and saw me in all of my sweaty, windblown glory. "Emma! Whoa, your hair looks like . . ."

"I know, like I'm a unicorn. I don't care." I kicked off the Louboutins of torture and flopped onto Rachel's stripped bed to tell them my final Colin story ever. Jayla joined me on the bed and Rachel stayed sitting on her suitcase, trying to smush her belongings into fitting.

After I'd finished, Rachel came over to give me a hug. "I'm sorry, babe. I know you were hoping for more than just 'KIT.' "

"Yeah, I guess." I sat up and hugged her back. "But you know, I think it's okay the way it turned out. I mean, I would've had to tell him eventually and I guess any way it happened, it wouldn't have been less painful for me. Now I can go back home, focus on senior year and college apps, and not have to worry about faking out some long-distance boyfriend."

"Have you heard from Brian?" Rachel asked.

"Kinda. He texted me a while ago. But I'm really not even going to think about him when I get back to Bridge-field. And as awful as this whole Colin explosion turned out to be, at least I know that there are boys besides The Hombres."

"Um, excuse me? Colin taught you that?" Jayla looked jilted. "Come on, lady. You learned that from me. There are many, many, many boys aside from your high school Hombres. Many," she added one last time.

"Hey, Mrs. Monogamous. You're not allowed to talk like

that anymore," Rachel teased as she finally zipped the last two inches of her bag closed.

"Reminiscing is not cheating," came Jayla's retort. "Now go get packing, Em. We've got a busy night tonight." She bounced out of Rachel's room.

"Why?" I imagined another long ride out to Coney Island or someplace just as sleeveless and sweaty.

"Her dad is coming," Rachel explained as we heard Jayla fumbling with the vacuum in the living room. "He's taking us to dinner and taking stock of how Princess did on her own all summer."

"I'm freaking," Jayla yelled over the buzz of the Hoover.

I went out in the living room to witness the extraordinary once-in-a-lifetime spectacle of Jayla cleaning. I should have taken a picture, but instead I peeled off the wool bodysuit, dropped it on Jayla's bed, and helped clean the place.

"Where's he taking us?" I whispered to Rachel as I arranged the magazines on the coffee table in a neat fan. Tonight's meal would be my last act as New York Glamma Freeman—at least until next summer—and I was pretty sure that if Jayla picked the place, it was going to be memorable.

"Mr. Chow's!" she gushed back. "It's so nice, they don't even give you menus. They just bring food, Jay says."

I clapped my hands and let out an "Eek" of excitement. This was totally what I needed to counter my post-Colin numbness.

I spent the afternoon shoving my new Anthropologie wardrobe into my luggage and 409-ing every surface of the apartment with Rachel and Jayla until it sparkled and we were all high on cleaning chemicals.

"Ahhh! Yes!" Rachel yelped and fist-pumped from behind her laptop.

"You're so not backing out of dinner for a JDate," Jayla said, Windexing the hallway mirror one last time.

"Ugh. Boy crazy is *so* last-week-Rachel-Wolfe," she said. "I'm totally focused on my career now. Duh! And my big career gal news is that Jamie's letting me edit . . . drumroll, please, ladies."

Jayla and I were silent, confused, and drumroll-less.

"Fine. Whatever." Rachel threw up her hands in frustration. "Jamie wants Emma to be one of our regular contributors! You know, take their feminist message to where it really matters—young people. And how better than to give a young person a real voice on the site? So she wants a high school feminista blog thing from you. And I'm going to be allowed to freelance-edit it! Like your journal but with the possibility of Internet fame! Awesome, right, Em?"

"No way!" As I got up to hug my best friend-slash-editor, I wasn't really sure if the "No way" meant that I was pumped for this or "No way in hell." Putting myself out on the Internet like that? *So* not my usual style. But maxing out my dad's Visa, dating a twenty-three-year-old, not having a curfew, learning to walk in five-inch heels—what part of this summer *was* my usual style? I hadn't intended to roll out of New York a totally different person, but breaking the typical straight-As-and-sensible-shoes Emma Freeman mold was kind of liberating, even with the ups and downs. Maybe the summer wild streak could live on. I could be Bridgefield's own Carrie Bradshaw—blogging about my everyday happs—but with less boys and more college applications. Maybe Summer Emma could actually hang around all year long.

Jake showed up at our place around seven in an outfit I was certain Jayla had picked out.

"Oh, baby, you look great!" Jayla said, kissing him lightly on the mouth and getting some Dior gloss on him. She fussed with his Kenneth Cole button-down and made sure his cuff links were on properly.

"I've never even seen cuff links," he complained. "I had to have the guy at Bloomingdale's show me how to use them."

"Well, Daddy is going to love you!" she said, smoothing his emo bangs into a more presentable look. "Just don't bring up socialized health care or green-friendly industry, okay? They're sore subjects."

My cousin looked blankly at Jayla. "Um . . . those weren't high on my list of light dinner conversation, but all right."

At seven-thirty we headed down to the street to meet Mr. Alistair St. Clare. Waiting for us was a black stretch limo, and as soon as we hit the sidewalk, a tall, salt-and-pepper-haired man in a three-piece suit stepped out and into Jayla's waiting embrace.

"Daddy!" she squealed.

"My little girl!" he said. "Could it be that you've gotten more beautiful since the last time I saw you?"

Rachel, Jake, and I waited nervously for Jayla to introduce us. She started with Rachel and me, each of us offering our hands for a hearty shake and thanking him like crazy for letting us live in his apartment all summer.

"This is Jacob Patrick Freeman." She held her breath while her father, worth more than some countries, shook Jake's hand and looked at him closely.

"Jacob," he said slowly, "how is it that you know my daughter?"

"Umm . . . biblic—" I ground my heel in his foot to stop him from ruining dinner before we even got to the restaurant. The Freeman nervous babble was a family curse worse than Kennedy drinking. "I mean, we're dating, sir," Jake said with a sudden air of confidence.

Jayla blushed, turning away to hide her puppy-love smile. Mr. St. Clare furrowed his brow, as if deciding what to do with this information. "Well, you'd better treat her like the princess she is." Then he broke into a friendly grin. "And from what she's told me, you already do." He slapped Jake on the back as we all sighed with relief and headed upstairs to give Jayla's dad the grand tour.

"Button," he said to Jayla after examining the spotlessness of 30B. "You mean to tell me that not one of your utilities was shut off this summer?"

"Nope. Not one!"

"And those curtains? You hung them yourself?"

Jake coughed, hoping to get some brownie points for his handiwork, but Jayla was Daddy's Little Girl, full throttle.

"Yes, of course. And that wasn't even part of the deal. I went above and beyond just maintaining the apartment, I made it even better. Doesn't that mean that I'm responsible enough to go abroad with my full credit card privileges?" She gave her father her best Precious Moments eyes.

He chuckled softly. "St. Clare, you're going to be a

tough businesswoman one day." I smiled to myself at the thought of Jayla actually working. Her five-hour-a-week volunteer job would probably wear her out by next Friday. "Fine, Princess. Your credit card is your companion once again. And Emma and Rachel, because you clearly were responsible and courteous tenants, I would love to extend this apartment to you girls again next summer."

I cracked a huge smile at the news, and even though it wasn't even Labor Day yet, I was already getting pumped for next June. The three of us jumped up and down and couldn't help hugging him.

"All right, all right," he said after enough embarrassing embraces and kisses on the cheek, "Mr. Chow's is waiting!"

Dinner was an eight-hundred-dollar extravaganza of the finest food I had ever tasted. Jake and Mr. St. Clare were actually rather quiet for most of the meal, leaving the gabbing to the three of us until Mr. St. Clare asked, "So, Jacob, where do you see fuels going in the next few years?" We three were silenced at the other end of the table.

I waited to see what info Jake would regurgitate from CNN.com. But it seems that I gave my cousin too much credit to think that he actually read any form of news besides ColdPizza.com.

"Uh . . . ," he stalled, fiddling with his tempura, "into cars?" He sensed Mr. St. Clare was waiting for more. "And lighters?"

A little too late to avoid the conversation train wreck, Jayla jumped in.

"Daddy, Jake is a big football fan. He loves the Jets almost as much as you do."

"Really?" Her father brightened and the boys broke off into talk of stats and drafts and foul balls or whatever football entails.

By the time dessert arrived, Jayla's dad had offered Jake an open invitation to their cabin in Aspen. And then, full of champagne and truffles, we shuffled drowsily back into the limo and headed home.

After dropping Jake off, we pulled up to our building and Jayla scooted next to her dad to give him a goodbye hug. "Thank you, Daddy. I promise I'll make you proud of me again."

"Darling," he said, kissing her on the forehead, "you always do."

We climbed out of the limo and I'd never felt more glamorous. I'd only been in a limo once before, for Brian's prom, but it was so much cooler to not be wearing a pastel formal dress. I looked like I was in and out of limos all the time.

Upstairs in the apartment, I felt far less glamorous as Rachel and I finished packing the last of our things and took our "Panic! At the Disco" posters off the wall. Jayla iTuned up some old-school Destiny's Child and we busted our dance moves.

"Emma, can you handle this?" Jayla sang into her hairbrush. *"Rachel, can you handle this? I don't think you can handle this."*

We danced around to "Bootylicious," total middle-school-sleepover-style.

"I don't think ya ready for this Jayla, my body's too bootylicious for ya babbaaaay. I'm so Beyoncé!" She slapped her size 26 AG jeans.

"I call Kelly!" I yelled over the music.

"I cannot be Michelle!" Rachel whined as I bumped her with my hips. "She's all gospel now. Hello! I'm Jewish!"

We funked our way through the entire *Survivor* album until we collapsed on our bare mattresses.

The next morning, we had our final bagel breakfast and Jayla helped us drag our body-bag suitcases to the street corner.

Jayla pulled me in for a tight hug. "Domino! I'm going to miss you! Who am I going to gross out when I talk about getting hot and heavy with your cousin?"

"For as much as I love you, I want you to know that I pretty much hate you when you bring that crap up." I laughed and gave her another big hug.

"Bitsy, you know who to call when you want to relaunch your JDate profile."

"Are you kidding me, Jay? I'm going to iPhone your ear off, girl!" Rachel gave her a kiss on the cheek as I hailed a cab. I hated long goodbyes, and of course, we'd see Jayla again. I'd already secretly started planning New Year's Eve in the city. Hello, Times Square!

We heaved our stuff into the trunk and squeezed into the backseat. As the car started down Fourteenth Street, Rachel turned to me. "Ready?" she asked. I gave her my biggest grin and nodded. We both swiveled around to face the back window. "One, two, three!"

We peeled up our T-shirts to "flash" Jayla the "Hot Mess" tees we were wearing underneath.

She burst into laughter and, in true Jayla fashion, lifted her tank to reveal that she'd lost yet another La Perla bra.

"Ah, I'm gonna miss that girl," Rachel sighed.

"Don't worry," I said, patting her on the knee. "There are plenty of promiscuous girls you can get dating tips from back in Bridgefield. Maybe you could start hanging with Skylar Dichter."

I gave her an Indian burn on her arm and we giggled the rest of the way to Penn Station.

ACKNOWLEDGMENTS

Julie Kraut wants to say thank you to: Krista Marino—who makes dreams come true over the salad bar, Phil Frankel—a real-life superhero who came to the rescue, Ashley Messick, Julie Hochheiser, Kissy Hardeman, Kelcye Ball, Gabi Arnay, Emily Roumm, Jessie Zerendow, Vanessa Bayer, Ariana Jackson, Lauren Jaffe, Angela Carlino, Beverly Horowitz, Random House Children's Sales, Rosy and Tom Khosravi, Grandma and Grandpa, Mom, Dad, and Andy, and the glitter, glam, and talent that is the real-life Jayla, Ms. Shallon Lester.

•   •   •

Shallon Lester would like to thank her rabid cheering section, to whom she owes everything: Mama and Gigi, Dee Reynolds, the Goddess Temple of Orange County, Sam Paz, Dena Horton, Christine Huang, Ellen Chen, Dorit Barlevy, Jeff Clinard, Sarah Kloepfer, the Snip Snaps, and the hotness to my mess, Ms. Julie Kraut.

Dana Maxson

Julie Kraut hails from the not-so-mean streets of suburban Maryland. She now lives in New York City, where she shimmies her sensible pumps up the corporate ladder, and writes. This is her very first book.

Shallon Lester hails from Orange County, California, and was an editor at *FHM* magazine before writing *Hot Mess*. She currently lives in Manhattan, where she is a gossip writer for the *New York Daily News*. This is her first novel but certainly not her last.